A M

by I

'Don't fight what you're feeling,' he whispered roughly.

Meredith heard Rey's words as if through a fog, but her body obeyed him as he began to increase the teasing pressure of his mouth. She followed his lips and relaxed into the curve of his powerful body with a little shiver.

He devoured her mouth, tempting her until her mouth followed his, returning the arousing pressure. She could see the glitter grow in his narrow eyes, feel the grip of his lean hands as he pushed her hips against the sudden hardness of him. She gasped with embarrassment and then lost all sense of it as his mouth opened and pushed down hard against her parted lips, drowning her in passion.

It was like flying, she thought dazedly. He hesitated for an instant and her eyes opened, drowsy and curious. Her mouth was swollen, soft, tremulous. She looked at him with fascination, utterly helpless in his embrace.

'Why did you do that?' she asked huskily.

One dark eyebrow lifted. He didn't smile. 'Why did you let me?' he shot back.

The Millionaire's Pregnant Bride
by Dixie Browning

'I was afraid you'd changed your mind and skipped town.'

'I can still do that,' she told him. 'It's not too late to withdraw your offer.' So much for that old superstition about the bride and groom not seeing each other before the ceremony on the day of the wedding. Maybe it didn't count, since it wasn't that kind of a wedding.

'We had an agreement. I don't go back on my word.' He levelled a piercing stare at her and asked, 'do you?'

By then they were at the door. She thought fleetingly of what she had sacrificed for her mother. Her self-respect, for one thing. There was no real sacrifice involved in entering into a business arrangement, as long as both parties agreed in advance on the rules. For no real reason other than her woman's intuition, she trusted Will Bradford. He was the kind of man who looked you directly in the eye and spoke his mind, like it or not.

One who looked entirely too masculine, entirely too sexy, entirely too attractive…

Available in May 2003 from Silhouette Desire

A Man of Means
by Diana Palmer
(Texan Lovers)
and
The Millionaire's Pregnant Bride
by Dixie Browning
(The Millionaire's Club)

Cowboy's Special Woman
by Sara Orwig
and
For This Week I Thee Wed
by Cheryl St. John

Of Royal Blood
by Carolyn Zane
and
In Pursuit of a Princess
by Donna Clayton
(Royally Wed)

A Man of Means
DIANA PALMER

The Millionaire's Pregnant Bride
DIXIE BROWNING

SILHOUETTE®
DESIRE™

First published in Great Britain 2003
Silhouette Books, Eton House, 18-24 Paradise Road,
Richmond, Surrey TW9 1SR

The publisher acknowledges the copyright holders of the individual works as follows:

A Man of Means © Diana Palmer 2002
The Millionaire's Pregnant Bride © Harlequin Books S.A. 2002

Special thanks and acknowledgement are given to Dixie Browning for her contribution to The Millionaire's Club series.

ISBN 0 373 04864 5

51-0503

Printed and bound in Spain
by Litografia Rosés S.A., Barcelona

A MAN OF MEANS
by
Diana Palmer

For Cissy at Writerspace, Sara, Jill and Celeste, and all the wonderful readers, many of whom I was privileged to meet in Atlanta in 2001 at our author tea, who visit me online there at my website. Love you all. DP

One

Meredith Johns glanced around her worriedly at the out-of-control Halloween party-goers in their colorful costumes. Meredith was wearing an outfit left over from college days. She made a good salary at her job, but there was no money for little luxuries like Halloween costumes. She had to budget just to be able to pay the utility bill in the house she shared with her father.

The past few months had been traumatic, and the wear was telling on her. She needed to get out of the house, Jill, one of her colleagues, had said firmly—especially after her most agonizing experience at home. Meredith was reluctant. Her father was only just back at their house after three days. But Jill was insistent. So she'd put on the only costume she had, a bad choice in many ways, and walked the three blocks to her friend's downtown apartment. She grimaced at her surroundings. What an idiot she'd been to come to this wild party.

But it really had been a tumultuous week for Meredith

and she'd wanted to get her mind off her troubles. Her father's violent behavior at the house they shared was unnerving. They were both still grieving, but her father had taken the tragedy much harder. He felt responsible. That was why a scholarly, conservative college professor had suddenly retired from his job and turned into an alcoholic. Meredith had tried everything she could think of to get him into treatment, but he refused to go on his own accord and the treatment facilities which would have taken him wouldn't unless he went voluntarily. Only a violent episode that had landed him in jail had temporarily spared her of this saddening experience. But he was out three days later and he had a new bottle of whiskey. She still had to go home after the party. He'd warned her not to be late. Not that she ever was.

Her grey eyes were sad as she sipped her soft drink. She had no head for alcohol, and she was as out of place here as a cup of tea. Not only that, her costume was drawing unwanted attention from the men. So was her long blond hair. It had been a bad costume choice, but it was the only thing she had to wear on the spur of the moment. Going to a Halloween party in her street clothes would have made her stand out, too.

She moved away from a slightly tipsy colleague who wanted to show her around Jill's bedroom and unobtrusively put her glass on a table. She found Jill, pleaded a headache, thanked her for a "good" time and headed out the front door as fast as she could. Once on the sidewalk, she drew in a long, sweet breath of fresh air.

What a bunch of wild people! She coughed delicately, remembering the unmistakable smell of that smoke that had been thick enough to obstruct clear vision inside. She'd thought it would be fun to go to a party. She might even meet a man who would be willing to take her out and cope with her father. And cows might fly, she told herself. She hadn't been out on a date in months. She'd invited one prospective date to her home for supper. But after a good look at her father, who was mean when he drank, the prospective suitor took off. Her heart wasn't in it, anyway. Recently she'd given up trying to attract anyone. She had her hands full already. Her grief was still fresh, too.

An odd noise attracted her attention as she started back toward her own house. She felt self-conscious in her getup, and remembering the lewd remarks she'd drawn from a man who was normally very polite and gentlemanly, she was sorry she hadn't had a coat to wear. Her clothes were mostly old, because by the time she made the mortgage payment and took care of the bills, there wasn't much left over. Her father couldn't work and wouldn't get help, and she loved him too much to desert him. It was becoming a costly proposition.

She wrapped her arms around herself and hoped she was covering up enough skin to discourage stalkers. But her skirt was very short and tight, and she was wearing fishnet hose, very high heels, a low-cut blouse and a flaming pink feather boa. Her blond hair was loose around her shoulders and she was wearing enough makeup to do justice to a ballet recital. She winced, hoping she hadn't been noticed. She'd gone to the party as a burlesque dancer. Sadly she looked more like a professional hooker in her garb.

She rounded a corner and saw two shadowy figures bending over what looked like a man on the ground.

"Hey! What do you think you're doing there?!" she yelled, making as much noise as possible. Then she started running toward them and waving her arms, yelling threats as she went.

As she expected, the surprise of her aggressive presence shocked them into retreat. They jumped up and ran away, without even looking back. The best defense, she thought with faint amusement, was always a good offense. It was a calculated bluff, but she'd seen it work for women smaller in stature than she was.

She ran to the downed man and examined him the best she could in the dim glow of the streetlights.

Concussion, she thought, feeling his head and encountering a metallic smelling wetness. Blood. He'd been hit on the head by his assailants, and probably robbed as well. She felt around under the jacket he was wearing and her hand touched something small and square on his belt. She pulled it out.

"Aha," she said with a triumphant grin. A man dressed as well as he was could be expected to have a cell phone. She dialed 911 and gave the operator her location and the condition of her patient, staying on the line while the dispatcher got an ambulance en route.

While she waited for it, she sat down on the pavement beside the man and held his hand.

He groaned and tried to move.

"Don't do that," she said firmly. "You'll be okay. You mustn't move until the EMTs get here. I haven't got anything to treat you with."

"Head…hurts."

"I imagine it does. You've got a heck of a bump. Just lie still. Feel sick, sleepy…?"

"Sick," he managed weakly.

"Lie still." She lifted her head to listen for the ambulance, and sure enough, a siren sounded nearby. The hospital was less than two blocks from her home, maybe four from here. Lucky for this guy, whoever he was. Head injuries could be fatal.

"My…brothers," the man was whispering brokenly. "Hart…Ranch. Jacobsville, Texas."

"I'll make sure they're contacted," she promised.

He gripped her hand, hard, as he fought not to lose consciousness. "Don't…leave me," he ground out.

"I won't. I promise."

"Angel," he whispered. He took a long, shaky breath,

and went back into the oblivion he'd left so briefly. That wasn't a good sign.

The ambulance rounded the corner, and the headlights spilled out onto Meredith and her patient. She got to her feet as two EMTs, one male and one female, piled out the doors and rushed to the downed man.

"Head wound," she told them. "Pulse is slow, but steady. He's coherent, some nausea, his skin is cold and clammy. Blunt force trauma, probably mild concussion..."

"Don't I know you?" the female EMT asked. Her face brightened. "Got you! You're Johns!"

"That's me," Meredith said with a grin. "I must be famous!"

"Sorry, not you—your dad." She winced at the look on Meredith's face.

Meredith sighed. "Yes, he spends a lot of time on ambulances these days."

"What happened here?" the woman asked quickly, changing the subject. "Did you see anything?"

"I yelled and scared off two guys who were bending over him," she volunteered. "I don't know if they were the ones who hit him or not. What do you think?" she added as the woman gave him a professional once-over.

"Concussion, definitely," she agreed. "Nothing broken, but he's got a lump the size of the national debt here on his head. We'll transport him. Coming along?"

"I guess I should," Meredith said, waiting until they loaded him onto the gurney. He was still unconscious. "But I'm not exactly dressed for visiting a hospital."

The EMT gave her a speaking glance. "Should I ask why you're dressed like that? And does your boss know you're moonlighting?" she added wickedly.

"Jill Baxley had a Halloween party. She thought I should come."

The other woman's eyebrows levered up. "Jill's parties

are notorious for getting out of control. I've never even seen you take a drink.''

"My father drinks enough for both of us," came the reply. "I don't drink or use drugs, and I need my head examined for going to that party. I escaped early, which is how I found this guy."

"Lucky for him," the woman murmured as they loaded him into the back of the ambulance. "Judging by his condition, he could have died if he hadn't been found in time."

Meredith climbed up into the back and sat down on the bench while the driver got in under the wheel and the female EMT called the hospital emergency room for orders. It was going to be a long night, Meredith thought worriedly, and her father was going to be very upset when she got home. He and her mother had been really close, but her mother had been fond of going to parties and staying out until the early morning; sometimes with other men. Recent events had made him dwell on that behavior. Her father seemed to have transferred that old contempt to her. It made her uneasy to think of arriving home in the wee hours. Anything could happen. On the other hand, how could she leave this man? She was the only person who knew who to contact for him. She'd promised to stay with him. She couldn't let him down.

He was examined by the resident on duty in the emergency room, who diagnosed concussion. He'd been unconscious most of the way to the hospital, but he'd come out of it just once to look up at Meredith and smile, tightening his big hand around the fingers that were holding it.

His family had to be notified, and Meredith was coaxed into making the call to Jacobsville for the harassed and overworked emergency room staff.

She was given a phone and a telephone directory which also listed Jacobs County, of which Jacobsville was the county seat. She looked through it until she found a listing for Hart Ranch Properties, Inc. That had to be it.

She dialed the number and waited. A deep, drawling voice answered, "Hart Ranch."

"Uh, I'm calling for a Mr. Leo Hart," she said, having found his driver's license in the wallet his assailants hadn't had time to steal. "He's at Houston General..."

"What happened?" the voice asked impatiently. "Is he all right?"

"He was mugged. He has a concussion," she added. "He can't give the staff any medical information..."

"Who are you?"

"I'm Meredith Johns. I work..."

"Who found him?"

"I did, actually. I called the ambulance on his cell phone. He said to call his brothers and he told me where they were..."

"It's two o'clock in the morning!" the voice pointed out angrily.

"Yes, I am aware of that," she began. "It only happened a little while ago. I was walking down the street when I saw him on the sidewalk. He needs his family—"

"I'm his brother, Rey. I'll be there in thirty minutes."

"Sir, it's a long way to Houston from where you are. If you drive that fast...!" she said at once.

"We have an airplane. I'll get the pilot out of bed right now. Thanks." He added that last word as if it hurt him, and hung up.

Meredith went back to the waiting room. Ten minutes later, she was admitted to the room where the victim had been examined.

"He's conscious," the attending physician told her. "I'm going to admit him overnight, just to be sure. Any luck with his family?"

"His brother is on the way, in his own plane, apparently," she said. "I didn't get a thing out of him. Sorry."

"People get upset and they don't think," the resident said with a weary smile. "How about staying with him? We're understaffed because of that respiratory virus that's going around, and he shouldn't be alone."

"I'll stay," she said with a grin. "It's not as if I have a hectic social life."

The resident pursed his lips and smirked at her outfit.

"Halloween party," she said, grimacing. "And next time I get invited, I'll have a broken leg, I swear it!"

Forty-five minutes later, there was a problem. It was six feet tall, had black hair and dark eyes and it erupted into the hospital cubicle like an F-5 tornado, dressed in jeans and boots and a fringed rawhide jacket thrown carelessly over what looked like a beige silk shirt. The wide-brimmed hat slanted over those threatening eyes was a Stetson, one of the most expensive made, with its distinctive feathered logo pin on the hatband. He looked impressively rich, and excessively angry.

The man was livid when he saw his big brother, still drifting in and out of consciousness, on the examining table. He gave Meredith a scrutiny that could have peeled paint off old furniture, his eyes narrowing contemptuously on her costume.

"Well, that explains why you were on the street at two in the morning," he snarled angrily. "What happened? Did you feel guilty and call for help after you tried to roll him?" he added sarcastically.

"Look here," she began, rising.

"Save it." He turned to the big man on the table and laid a lean, strong hand on his brother's broad chest. "Leo. Leo, it's Rey! Can you hear me?" he asked in a tone that combined affection with concern.

The big man's eyes blinked and opened. He stared blankly up at the leaner man. "Rey?"

"What happened to you?" Rey Hart demanded gently.

Leo grinned wearily. "I was thinking about new forage grasses and wasn't paying attention to my surroundings," he murmured drowsily. "Something hit me in the head and I went down like a brick. Didn't see a thing." He winced and felt clumsily in his pockets. "Damn! My wallet's gone. So's my cell phone."

Meredith started to tell him that she had the phone and wallet in her purse for safekeeping, but before she could speak, Rey Hart gave her a furious, speaking glance and walked out of the cubicle like a man hunting a fight.

His brother drifted off again. Meredith stood beside him, wondering what to do. Five minutes later, Rey Hart walked back in accompanied by a tall man in a police uniform. He looked familiar, but Meredith couldn't quite place him. She knew she'd seen him before.

"That's her," Rey told the policeman, indicating Meredith. "I'll sign anything necessary as soon as I see that my brother's going to be okay. But get her out of here."

"Don't worry. I'll handle it," the policeman said quietly. He handcuffed Meredith with easy efficiency and pulled her out of the cubicle before she could protest.

"I'm being arrested?" she exclaimed, stunned. "But, why? I haven't done anything!"

"Yes, I know, I've heard it all before," the officer told her in a bored tone when she tried to explain what had happened. "Nobody's ever guilty. Honest to God, dressed like that, out on the streets alone after midnight, you were bound to be up to no good. What did you do with his cell phone and his wallet?"

"They're in my pocketbook," she began.

He confiscated it from her shoulder and propelled her out of the building. "You're going to be in a lot of trouble. You picked the wrong man to rob."

"See here, I didn't mug him! It was two men. I didn't see their faces, but they were bending over him as I came down the sidewalk."

"Soliciting is a felony," he pointed out.

"I wasn't soliciting anything! I'd just come from a Halloween party dressed as a burlesque dancer!" she raged, furious that she was being punished for having done someone a good turn. She read his name tag. "Officer Sanders, you have to believe me!"

He didn't say a word. He drew her with him, firmly but gently, and put her into the back seat of the police car.

"Wait," she told him before he could close the door. "You get my wallet out of my purse and look in it. Right now," she insisted.

He gave her an impatient look, but he did what she asked. He looked through the plastic inserts in her wallet and glanced at her with a changed expression. "I thought you looked familiar, Johns," he murmured, using her last name, as most people she knew at work did.

"I didn't mug Mr. Hart," she continued. "And I can prove where I was when he was being mugged." She gave him her friend Jill's address.

He gave in. He drove to Jill's apartment, went to the door, spoke to an obviously intoxicated and amused Jill, and came back to the squad car. He let Meredith out of the back of the squad car and took off the handcuffs. It was cool in the night air, and Meredith felt self-conscious and uncomfortable in her garb, even though the police officer knew the truth now.

"I'm really sorry," he told her with a grimace as he met her grey eyes. "I didn't recognize you. All I knew was what Mr. Hart told me, and he was too upset to think straight. You have to admit, you don't look very professional tonight."

"I do realize that. Mr. Hart cares about his brother, and he doesn't know what happened," she pointed out. "He walked in and saw his brother on the table and me dressed like this," she indicated her clothing, "and his brother said his wallet and cell phone were missing. He doesn't know me from a stump. You can't blame him for thinking the worst. But those two men who hit him would have gotten his wallet if I hadn't come along, and they're still on the loose."

"Can you show me where you found him?" he asked.

"Of course. It was just down the sidewalk, that way."

She led and he followed her, with his big wide-angle flashlight sweeping the sidewalk and the grass as they walked. She pointed to an area of flattened grass. He left her on the sidewalk and gave the area a thorough scrutiny, looking for clues. He found a candy wrapper and a cigarette butt.

"I don't guess you know if Mr. Hart smokes or likes candy?" he asked.

She shook her head. "Sorry. All he told me was his brothers' name and where they lived. I don't know anything more about him."

He stood up. "I'll ask his brother later. Wait here while I call for one of the technicians to bag this evidence," he told her.

"Okay," she said agreeably, drawing the feather boa closer. It was getting cold standing around briefly clad, waiting for crime scene investigators. "Somebody's going to love being turned out of bed to come look at a cigarette butt and a candy wrapper," she stated with helpless amusement.

"You'd be surprised at what excites those guys," he chuckled. "Catching crooks isn't exactly a chore to them. It's high drama."

"I hope they catch these two," she said firmly. "Nobody should have to be afraid to walk down the streets at night. Even after dark, dressed like this, alone," she added pointedly, indicating her clothes.

"Good point," he was fair enough to admit.

He called in his location and requested crime scene technicians. Meredith was ready to go home, but she couldn't leave until she'd given the policeman a statement for his report. She sat in his car, with the overhead lights on, writing out what she knew of the attack on Leo Hart. It didn't take long, because she didn't know much.

She handed it back to him. "Can I go home now?" she asked. "I live with my father and he's going to be upset because I'm coming home so late. I can walk. It's only about three blocks from here."

He frowned. "Your father is Alan Johns, isn't he?" he asked. His expression changed. "Do you want me to go with you?"

She didn't usually flinch at facing her irate parent. She was gutsy, and she could handle herself. But tonight, she'd been through a lot. "Would you?" she asked, uneasy because her fear was visible.

"No problem. Get in."

He drove her to her house and went to the door with her. The house was dark and there was no movement inside. She let out a sigh of relief. "It's okay. If he was awake, the lights would be on. Thanks, anyway," she said with a smile.

"If you need us, call," he said. "I'm afraid I'll be in touch again about this. Rey Hart already reminded me that his brother is our state attorney general. He's not going to let this case go until it's solved."

"I don't blame him. Those guys are a menace and they're probably still running around looking for easy targets to rob. Take care."

"You, too. And I'm sorry about the handcuffs," he added, with the first smile she'd seen on his lean face since her ordeal began.

She smiled back. "My fault, for wearing a costume like this on the streets," she admitted. "I won't do it again. Thanks for the ride."

Back at the hospital, Rey Hart sat by his brother's bedside until dawn, in the private room he'd obtained for him.

He was worried. Leo was the hardiest one of the lot, and the most cautious as a rule. He was the prankster, always playing jokes, cheering them up in bad times. Now, he lay still and quiet and Rey realized how much his sibling meant to him.

It infuriated him that that woman had thought nothing of robbing his brother while he was sick and weak and helpless. He wondered what she'd hit him with. She wasn't a big woman. Odd, that she'd been able to reach as high as Leo's head with some blunt object. He recalled with distaste the way she'd been dressed. He was no prude, but in his early twenties he'd had a fling with a woman he later found out was a private call girl. He'd been infatuated with her, and thought she loved him. When he learned her profession and that she'd recognized him at once and knew how wealthy he was, it had soured him on women. Like his married brothers had been, and Leo still was, he was wary of females. If he could find a man who could bake biscuits, he told himself, he'd never let even an old woman into the house ever again.

He recalled their latest acquisition with sorrow. He and Leo had found a retired pastry chef who'd moved in with them—the last of the Hart bachelors—to bake their beloved biscuits. She'd become ill and they'd rushed to the drugstore to get her prescriptions, along with candy and chocolates and a bundle of flowers. But her condition had worsened and she'd told them, sadly, that the job was just too much in her frail state of health. She had to quit. It was going to be hard to replace her. There weren't a lot of people who wanted to live on an isolated ranch and bake biscuits at all hours of the day and night. Even want ads with offers of a princely salary hadn't attracted anyone just yet. It was depressing; like having Leo lying there under white sheets, so still and quiet in that faded striped hospital gown.

Rey dozed for a few hours in the deep night, used to sleeping in all sorts of odd positions and places. Cattle ranchers could sleep in the saddle when they had to, he thought amusedly, especially when calving was underway or there was a storm or they were cutting out and branding calves and doing inventory of the various herds.

But he came awake quickly when Sanders, the police officer who'd arrested that woman last night, came into the room with a murmured apology.

"I'm just going off shift," Officer Sanders told Rey. "I thought I'd stop by and tell you that we've gone over the scene of the attack and we have some trace evidence. The detectives will start looking for other witnesses this morning. We'll get the people responsible for the attack on your brother."

Rey frowned. "Get 'them?'" he queried. "You've already got her. You arrested her!"

Officer Sanders averted his eyes. "Had to turn her loose," he said uneasily. "She had an alibi, which was confirmed. She gave me a statement and I took her home."

Rey stood up, unfolding his intimidating length, and glared at the officer. "You let her go," he said coldly. "Where's my brother's cell phone?" he added as an afterthought.

The policeman grimaced. "In her purse, along with his wallet," he said apologetically. "I forgot to ask her for them when I left. Tell you what, I'll swing by her house and get them on my way home…"

"I'll go with you," he said curtly. "I still think she's guilty. She's probably in cahoots with the guys who attacked Leo. And she could have paid someone to lie and give her an alibi."

"She's not that sort of woman," the policeman began.

Rey cut him off angrily. "I don't want to hear another word about her! Let's go," he said, grabbing his hat, with a last, worried glance at his sleeping brother. He wondered how the policeman could make such a statement about a woman he'd just met, but he didn't really care. He wanted her in jail.

He drove his rental car, with the off-duty policeman beside him, to Meredith's home, following the directions Officer Sanders gave him. It was in a run-down neighborhood, and the house was in poor condition. It only intensified Rey's suspicions about her. She was obviously poor. What better way to get money than to rob somebody?

He went to the door, accompanied by the policeman, and knocked. Hard.

He had to do it three times, each with more force and impatience, before someone answered the door.

Meredith Johns was disheveled and white-faced. She was clutching a bulky washcloth to her face and wearing a robe over the clothes she'd had on the night before.

"What do you want now?" she asked huskily, her voice slurred and jerky.

"Been drinking, have you?" Rey Hart asked in a blistering tone.

She flinched.

Officer Sanders knew what was going on. He read the situation immediately. He stepped past Rey, grim and silent, grimacing when he saw Meredith's face. He went by her and into the living room and began looking around.

"Hard night, I gather? It must be a continual risk, in your profession," Rey said insinuatingly, with a speaking glance at her dress in the opening of the old, worn robe. "Do your marks make a habit of beating you up?" he added with cold contempt.

She didn't answer him. It was hard to talk and her face hurt.

Officer Sanders had gone into the bedroom. He came back two minutes later with a tall, disheveled but oddly dignified-looking man in handcuffs. The man, who'd been quiet before, was now cursing furiously, accusing Meredith of everything from prostitution to murder in a voice that rose until he was yelling. Rey Hart looked at him with obvious surprise. His eyes went to Meredith Johns, who was stiff as a poker and wincing every time the man yelled at her. The policeman picked up the telephone and called for a squad car.

"Please, don't," Meredith pleaded, still clutching the ice-filled cloth to her face. "He's only just got out..."

"He isn't staying. This time, he's going to be in jail for longer than three days," the officer said firmly. "You get to the hospital and let one of the residents look at you, Miss Johns. How bad is it? Come on, show me," he demanded, moving closer.

Rey stood by, silent and confused, watching as Meredith winced and moved the bulky cloth away from her face. His breath was audible when he saw the swelling and the growing purple and violet discoloration around her eye, cheek and jaw.

"God Almighty," Rey said harshly. "What did he hit you with?"

"His fist," the policeman replied coldly. "And it isn't the first time. You have to face facts, Miss Johns," he told her. "He isn't the man he used to be. When he drinks, he doesn't know what he's doing. He'll kill you one night when he's like this, and he won't even remember doing it!"

"I won't press charges," she said miserably. "How can I? He's my father! He's the only family I have left in the world...."

The policeman looked at her with compassion. "You don't have to press charges," he told her. "I'll provide them myself. You'd better phone your boss and tell him you won't be in for a few weeks. He'll have kittens if you walk into the office looking like that."

"I suppose he would." Tears ran down her pale cheeks,

all the more eloquent for being silent. She looked at her raging, cursing father and sadness claimed her features. "He wasn't like this before, honest he wasn't," she told them. "He was a kind, loving, caring man."

"Not anymore," Officer Sanders replied grimly. "Get to the hospital and have your face seen about, Miss Johns. I'll take your father outside until the unit comes…"

"No," she groaned. "Please, spare us that! I can't bear to have the whole neighborhood watching, hearing him…like that, again!"

He hesitated. "Okay. I'll watch for them out the window. The unit can drop you by the hospital, since it's going there first…."

"I'll take her," Rey said at once, without wondering why he should do such an about-face. He didn't trust the woman, or even totally believe her story. But she did look so pitiful. He couldn't bear to leave her in that condition to get to the hospital. Besides, whatever her motives, she had gotten help for Leo. He could have died if he hadn't been cared for.

"But…" she began.

"If," he added coldly, "you change clothes first. I am *not* being seen in public with you in that rig!"

Two

Meredith wished she felt up to a fight. Her long blond hair was down in her face, her grey eyes were sparking fire. But she was sick to her stomach and bruised. She would rather have gone to bed if these stubborn men would just have let her alone. But her face could have broken or shattered bones. She knew that. She grimaced, hoping her insurance would cover a second "accident" in as many months.

When the unit arrived, Meredith turned away from the sight of her raging father being carried off and closed the door. Probably it wasn't surprising to the neighbors anymore, it happened so often. But she hated having everyone know.

"I'll get dressed," she said in a subdued tone.

Rey watched her go and then shoved his hands into his pockets and looked around the room. It was shabby. The only bright things in it were books—hundreds of them, in bookcases and boxes and stacked on tables and chairs. Odd, he thought. They were apparently short of cash, judging by the worn old furniture and bare floor. There was only a very small television and a portable stereo. He glanced at the CD case and was surprised to find classical music dominating the discs. What a peculiar family. Why have so many books and so little else? He wondered where the woman's mother was. Had she left the father, and was that why he drank? It would have explained a lot. He knew about missing parents, especially missing mothers—his had left the family while the five Hart boys were young, without a backward glance.

Minutes later, Meredith came back, and except for the bruised face, he might not have recognized her. She was wearing a beige sweater set, with a tweed coat over it. Her blond hair was in a neat bun and her face devoid of makeup. She wore flat-heeled shoes and carried a purse that looked new.

"Here's your brother's cell phone and his wallet," she said, handing it to him. "I forgot to give them to Officer Sanders."

He glared at them and put them in his pocket. He wondered if she'd have given them back at all if he hadn't come here. He didn't trust her, regardless of what the policeman had said. "Let's go," he said stiffly. "The car's outside."

She hesitated, but only for a minute. She wasn't going to be able to avoid a checkup. She knew the problems that negligence could cause. Even a relatively minor problem could become major.

Unexpectedly Rey opened the car door for her. She slid in, surprised to find herself in a new luxury car. She fastened her seat belt. His brother, Simon Hart, was state attorney general. Rey owned a ranch. She remembered how his injured brother, Leo, had been dressed last night, and her eyes went to Rey's expensive hat and boots and silk shirt. Of course, they were a wealthy family. Considering her state of dress—or undress—the night before, she could understand his misgivings about her character.

She sat wearily beside him, the ice-filled cloth still in her hand. She held it to the side of her face that was bruised and hoped that it would spare her some of the swelling. She didn't need a doctor to tell her that it was a bad blow. The pain was almost unbearable.

"I took a hit to the face a few years ago in a brawl," he volunteered in his deep, slow drawl. "It hurt like hell. I imagine your face does, too."

She swallowed, touched by the faint concern. Tears threatened, but she never cried now. It was a weakness she couldn't afford.

He glanced at her, puzzled. "Nothing to say?"

She managed to get her voice under control. "Thank you for taking me to the hospital," she said huskily.

"Do you usually dress like that when you go out at night?" he asked belatedly.

"I told you. There was…a Halloween party," she said. It hurt to talk. "It was the only costume I had."

"Do you like parties?" he asked sarcastically.

"My first one…in almost four years," she managed to say. "Please…hurts…to talk."

He glanced at her and then was quiet. He didn't like her. He didn't trust her. Why was he taking care of her? There was something unexpectedly vulnerable about her. But she had spirit.

He walked her into the emergency room. She filled out forms and was ushered back into a treatment cubicle while Rey sat in the waiting room between a squalling toddler and a man coughing his head off. He wasn't used to illness. He'd never seen much of it, and he didn't know how to cope with it. Accidents, sure, he was a good hand in an emergency, and there were plenty on a ranch. But he hated hospitals.

Meredith came back a good thirty minutes later with a prescription and a frown.

"What did he say?" he asked conversationally.

She shrugged. "He gave me something…for pain," she said, waving the prescription.

"They sent me to a plastic surgeon," he volunteered as they went through the automatic door.

She didn't speak.

"I had a shattered bone in my cheek that they couldn't repair," he persisted.

"I'm not…going…to any damned…plastic surgeon!"

His eyebrows arched. "Your face could be distorted."

"So what?" she muttered, wincing because it really did hurt to speak. "It's not…much of a face, anyway."

He scowled. She wasn't pretty, but her face had attractive features. Her nose was straight and elegant, she had high cheekbones. Her mouth was like a little bow, perfect. Her eyes, big and grey, fascinated him.

"You should go," he said.

She ignored him. "Can you…drive me by the pharmacy?"

"Sure."

She gave him directions and he waited while she had the prescription filled. He drove her back to her house and left her there reluctantly.

"I'll be at the hospital with Leo if you need anything," he said as if it pained him to say it.

"I don't need any help. Thanks," she added stiffly.

His eyebrows arched. "You remind me of me," he murmured, and a thin smile touched his lips—a kind one. "Proud as Lucifer."

"I get by. I really am…sorry about your brother. Will he be all right?" she asked at her door.

He nodded. "They want to keep him for two or three days. He'll want to thank you."

"No need. I would have done it for anyone."

He sighed. She was going to look bad for a long time, with her face in that condition. She'd been beaten and he

felt responsible, God knew why. He took a breath. "I'm
sorry I had you arrested," he said reluctantly.

She pursed her lips. "I'll bet...that hurt."

"What?"

"You don't apologize much, do you?" she asked, as if
she knew.

He scowled down at her, puzzled.

She turned away. "No sweat. I'll live. So long."

She went in and closed the door. Rey, who'd done without companionship for a number of years, suddenly felt
alone. He didn't like the feeling, so he shoved it out of his
mind and drove back to the hospital. He wouldn't see her
again, anyway.

Leo came back to himself with a vengeance late that
afternoon. He had Rey lever the head of his bed up and he
ate dinner with pure enjoyment.

"It's not bad," Leo murmured between mouthfuls. "But
I wish I had a biscuit."

"Me, too," Rey said on a sigh. "I guess we could buy
a restaurant, as a last resort," he added dejectedly. "One
that serves breakfast."

"Who was that woman who came in with me?" he asked
Rey.

"You remember her?" Rey was surprised.

"She looked like an angel," he mused, smiling. "Blond
and big-eyed and all heart. She held my hand and sat down
on the sidewalk in the cold and talked to me until the ambulance got there."

"You were unconscious."

"Not all the time. She even came in with me on the
ambulance," he said. "She kept telling me I was going to
be all right. I remember her voice." He smiled. "Her name
was Meredith."

Rey's heart jumped. He felt uneasy. Leo usually didn't

pay much attention to strange women. "Meredith Johns," he agreed.

"Is she married?" Leo asked at once.

Rey felt threatened; it irritated him. "I don't know," he said.

"Do you think you could find somebody who knows how to get in touch with her?" his brother persisted. "I want to thank her for saving me."

Rey got up from the chair where he'd been sitting and walked to the darkened window, peering out through the blinds while he played for time. "She lives near the place where you were attacked," he said finally, unable to lie.

"What does she do for a living?"

"I don't know," Rey said, feeling uncomfortable. He couldn't get her father's accusing remarks out of his mind. She'd said she was dressed up for a party, she'd even found someone to give her an alibi, but Rey didn't completely believe her. What if that whole defense was a lie? What if she was some sort of prostitute? He didn't want his brother getting mixed up with a woman like that. He didn't trust women, especially strange women. Then he remembered her poor, bruised face and he felt bad about his suspicions.

"I'll ask one of the nurses," Leo said abruptly.

"No need," Rey told him. He turned back around with his hands in his pockets. "If you're determined, I'll go get her in the morning and bring her in to see you."

"Why not tonight?"

Rey let out an impatient breath. "Her father roughed her up because she got home late last night. I took her to the emergency room this morning before I came back here."

Leo's eyes narrowed and went cold. "Her father beat her? And you took her back home to him?" he said angrily.

"He wasn't there. They took him off to jail," he said. His face hardened even more. "She'll have a hell of a bruise. They said she couldn't go back to work for a few weeks." He moved one shoulder restlessly. "Considering the way they live, I don't know how she'll manage," he added reluctantly. "They don't seem to have much. Apparently the old man doesn't work and she's the only one bringing home any money." He didn't volunteer his opinion of how she made it.

Leo leaned back against the pillows. His big frame was without its usual vibrance. His dark eyes were dull, and his lean face was drawn. His blond-streaked brown hair was unkempt, and looked odd in the back where they'd had to shave it to put stitches in. It was a reminder of how tricky head wounds were. Leo was very lucky not to have brain damage. Rey thought about the assailants and his eyes blazed.

"I'm going to phone Simon tonight," he told Leo. "I'm sure the local police will do all they can to catch the guys who waylaid you, but they'll work even harder if they get a call from the state attorney general."

"There you go again, pulling strings," Leo mused.

"It's for a good cause."

"Did you find my wallet and my cell phone?" Leo asked.

"The woman had them. They're in my pocket."

"Good. I didn't think she had anything to do with mugging me. Don't forget your promise to bring Meredith here in the morning," he said.

Now it was "Meredith." Rey didn't like the whole idea of having Leo around the woman, but he didn't have a legitimate reason for keeping her from Leo's side. It would sound even more suspicious if Rey started throwing out sarcastic remarks about her. Leo did love to pull his chain.

"Okay," he said reluctantly.

"Good man," Leo replied with a wan grin. "Nothing like family to look after you."

"Next time, watch your back instead of daydreaming about forage grasses," Rey said firmly. Then he leaned forward in the chair. "So, tell me what sort of grasses the Cattleman's Association is advocating."

Rey got a hotel room near the hospital, so that he could have a bath and get some rest. The night staff had the phone number, so they could call him immediately if he was needed.

He phoned Simon before he went to bed.

"Leo's been mugged?" Simon exclaimed. "And you didn't call me last night?"

That tone was still intimidating, even though Rey was thirty-one. Simon was the eldest of the five brothers, and the bossiest, next to Cag.

"I was too upset to phone anybody," Rey returned, "and too busy trying to handle…another problem that cropped up. He's all right. Honest. I didn't find out until the early hours of the morning, and it's been a long day. He was already out of danger before it occurred to me that I needed to let you know."

"All right," Simon said, sounding as if he was more relaxed. "Do they have a suspect?"

"No. I thought we did, but it turned out to be a dead end," he added, without going into details about Meredith Johns. "There were two of them, and they haven't been caught. It's a miracle he wasn't killed, and that they were stopped in time before they robbed him. You might give the local police chief a call. Just to let him know we're all interested in solving the case."

"You want me to use my influence for personal gain?" Simon drawled.

"Hell, yes, I do!" Rey shot back. "This is our brother, for God's sake! If a big, strong man like Leo can get mugged in a residential neighborhood, so can anybody else! It doesn't say a lot for the security in this area."

"No, it doesn't," Simon agreed. "I'll point that out to the police commissioner, first thing tomorrow. Then I'll run down to Jacobsville and get Cag and Corrigan and we'll be right up to see about Leo.''

Rey chuckled. It was the first bit of humor he'd felt so far. The five brothers rarely went so far as to gang up on people, but considering the size and reputation of them, they got results when they did. This was an emergency, anyway. They could have lost a brother. The perpetrators had to be caught.

"They should be home by now," Rey replied. "I couldn't phone them because they were showing those Japanese businessmen around the ranch and the town."

"I'll see how much luck they had. Japan is very careful about its import beef. The fact that we run organically raised cattle will certainly go in our favor," Simon said.

"Yes, it will. Get some sleep. And don't worry about Leo. He's fine. I'd never have left the hospital if I'd had one doubt about that."

"I'll stop worrying."

"Give my love to Tira and the boys," Rey added.

"I'll do that. See you tomorrow."

Rey hung up, thinking about Simon and his family. Tira was redheaded and gorgeous, and the boys favored both of them, although they had Simon's dark eyes and hair. Corrigan and Dorie had a boy and a girl. Cag and Tess had just a boy, but they were talking about how nice a daughter would be. Meanwhile, Rey and Leo enjoyed being uncles, but had no interest in joining the ranks of the married.

If it wasn't for those biscuits, Rey thought miserably. It was going to be expensive to have the local café make biscuits for them every day until they employed a new biscuit maker, but if they got desperate enough, and offered enough of an incentive, they could probably manage it.

Turning his attention elsewhere, Rey gave a thought to poor Leo with his stitches and his headache, and another to Meredith Johns's bruised face. Tomorrow, he'd have to deal with Leo's request to see her, and he wasn't looking forward to it. He wished he knew why.

Rey went to Meredith Johns's house the next morning after he'd had breakfast. It took her a minute or two to answer the door, and for an instant, he thought that perhaps she might not be in any condition to answer it. She'd been badly bruised.

But she opened the door and peered up at him bravely, even though she looked like a refugee from a bar brawl. Her left eye was swollen shut completely now.

"Leo wants to see you," he said easily, noticing how the top of her blond head only came to his shoulder. She wasn't tall. Even bruised, her face had a beautiful complexion. Her mouth was pretty. He shook himself mentally. "He wants to thank you for what you did. He remembers that you rode in on the ambulance with him. You didn't tell me that," he added with faint accusation.

"I wasn't thinking," she said. "I was worried about what would happen when I came home late."

"Have you heard any more about your father this morning?" he asked grimly.

"They're going to charge him with simple battery," she said heavily. "I can't afford a lawyer. He'll have a public defender and he'll probably have to stay in jail for a few weeks." She looked up at him. "It will be a godsend, you know, because he'll dry out completely."

He hated the compassion he felt. "Did your mother leave him?" he asked.

She averted her face. She couldn't bear to talk about it yet. "In a way," she said huskily. "Are you going to drive me?" she added, glancing at him over her shoulder. "The bus doesn't run for another thirty minutes."

"Sure," he agreed.

"Then I'll get my jacket and purse."

She went into another room and came back quickly, leading the way out the door. "Is he conscious now?"

"Very," he murmured dryly. "When I left him, he was telling a nurse what she could do with the wash basin, and how far."

She chuckled. "He didn't seem like that kind of man," she murmured. "I had him figured for a gentleman, not a renegade."

"We're all that kind of man," he replied.

"All?"

He led her to the car and put her into the passenger seat. "There are five of us. The other three are coming up this morning to have a talk with the police."

"I remember. You said that your brother was the attorney general."

"He is," he replied. "We tend to stick together."

Her eyes went to his hands on the steering wheel. He had nice hands, very lean and strong with neat, clean fingernails. He was a tough-looking man, like a cowboy.

"How's your face?" he asked unexpectedly.

She shrugged. "It still hurts. It will for a while, but I'll be fine."

"You should see that plastic surgeon."

"Why?" she asked heavily. "My insurance won't pay for cosmetic surgery, and there's not much chance that they can do any major repair on tiny shattered bones."

"You're not a doctor. Stop giving yourself medical advice."

She stared at him for a long moment and started to speak, then lost the opportunity when he pulled up in the hospital parking lot, cut off the engine, and got out.

Rey waited for her and led her up to the floor where his brother's room was located.

Leo wasn't alone. Three other men were with him, one big and dark and missing an arm, the other lean and light-eyed and handsome, and a third big one with black eyes and a threatening face towering over both the others.

"That's Cag," Rey indicated the black-eyed man. "Corrigan," he nodded toward the light-eyed man, "and that's Simon," he finished, smiling at the one-armed man. "This is Meredith Johns. She rescued Leo."

"Nice to see you and know who you are," Leo said, alert now and interested as his dark eyes swept over the neat woman just inside the door. "Miss Johns, I presume?"

She smiled self-consciously, because everybody was looking at her bruised face. "Yes," she said.

Simon Hart frowned when he got a good look at her. "What the hell happened to you?" he demanded.

"Her father," Rey said for her. "She got in late and he beat her up."

Leo looked suddenly as intimidating as the other three. "Where is he?" he asked.

"In jail," Meredith said heavily. "For several weeks, at least, and he'll have time to dry out."

"Good." Leo looked toward Simon. "Maybe you can find a way to get him into rehab before he gets out."

"I'll look into it," Simon said at once.

"And some counseling wouldn't come amiss," Rey put his two cents worth in.

"I'll see about that, too," Simon replied. "Nice to meet you, Miss Johns. We're all grateful for what you did for Leo."

"You're all very welcome," she replied. She clutched her purse, intimidated by the group of brothers.

"Come here," Leo said, holding out his hand. "They're big and they look tough, but they're really marshmallows. You don't have to feel threatened. I'll protect you."

"She doesn't need protecting from us!" Rey snapped.

The others gaped at him. It wasn't like Rey to act that way.

He cleared his throat. He didn't want them asking themselves embarrassing questions about his attitude. He shoved his hands into his pockets. "Sorry. I didn't sleep much last night," he explained.

Meredith went to stand beside Leo, who took one of her small, cold hands in his and looked up at her with interest.

"Have you seen a doctor?" he asked.

"Your brother took me to the emergency room yesterday," she said.

"Rey. His name's Reynard, but he's called Rey," Leo informed her.

She smiled. "You look much better today. Head hurt?"

"A bit, but my vision's clear and I'm not disoriented," he said, quoting the doctor. "I have a good prognosis."

"That's nice to hear. You were in pretty bad shape."

"I'd have been in a lot worse shape, but for you," Leo said. "I hear that you can't work out in public for a while, until your face heals," he added. "Can you cook?"

She blinked. "Of course," she said at once.

"Can you make bread?"

She frowned. "Bread?"

"More specifically, biscuits," he added, and had the oddest expression on his face.

She shifted her purse in the hand he wasn't holding. "Well, yes, those and rolls and loaf bread," she said, as if everybody could do it.

Leo shot a glance at Rey, who was just staring at him without daring to say a word. He knew what was coming, and he couldn't decide how he felt about it. He didn't want to think about it.

"How would you like a brief stay in Jacobsville, Texas, in a big sprawling ranch house where your only job would be to make biscuits every morning?" Leo asked with his best smile.

Rey and the other brothers were staring at her, waiting. She wondered why. And Rey was frowning, as if he didn't like the idea at all. Probably he still secretly thought she was a hooker. He couldn't seem to credit her with any sense of decency.

She thought about his attitude for a few seconds, and decided that it wouldn't be a bad idea to take the job, and show him that you really couldn't judge a book by its cover. It wouldn't hurt that arrogant cowboy to be taken down a step or two, and she was just the girl who could do it.

She smiled. It hurt her face, but what was a little pain for a good cause? She turned back to Leo. ''Mr. Hart, I think I'd like that job very much!''

Three

"**G**ood for you!" Leo exclaimed, animated and smiling. "You won't be sorry, Meredith. Honest."

She smiled back at him. He was nice, like a big brother. She liked him already. "I can do housekeeping, too," she told him. "I'll earn my keep."

"You'll go on salary, of course," he insisted. "It won't be a holiday."

"Nothing is a holiday with those two," Simon murmured dryly. "They aren't kidding about biscuits. They'll run you crazy baking them."

Rey and Leo gave their brother a disgusted look.

Meredith grinned. "I don't mind," she assured Simon. "I love to cook."

"It won't be that hard," Leo promised, with another speaking glance at Simon. "We just love biscuits. But we'll make you feel right at home. Anything you need, you can have—a new stove..." he added mischievously.

She thought about her father and her job, and her smile

faltered. "I have to wrap up a few loose ends first," she began.

"No problem," Leo assured her. "I can't get out of here for another day at least, or so that doctor said," he added with impatience.

"You'll stay until he lets you out," Rey said firmly. "Concussions are tricky. You know that."

Leo grimaced. "I guess so. I hate hospitals."

"I'm not too wild about them myself," Rey had to agree.

"It would be a very sad world without them," Meredith spoke up.

She seemed irritated, Rey thought, and wondered why. "I'll run you back home when you're ready," Rey told her. "We'll be in touch before we're ready to leave."

"All right." She held Leo's hand again and squeezed it gently, to the amusement of all the Harts except Rey. "You get better. I'll see you soon."

"Thanks again," Leo told her with genuine gratitude.

"It was nothing." She gave him another smile, tugged her hand free, and let Rey herd her out the door after a quick goodbye to the other brothers.

"I thought your brother was big until I saw all of you together. Goodness, you're all huge!" she exclaimed when they were outside in the parking lot. She gave him a long scrutiny. "And there doesn't seem to be an extra ounce of fat on any of you."

"We don't sit behind desks. We're ranchers, not office workers, and we work hard, right alongside our cowboys," he said. His dark eyes cut sideways. "Leo likes you."

She smiled. "I'm glad, because I like him, too."

That set him off and he tried not to let it show. He didn't want her to like Leo. He wished he knew why. He glanced at her as he wove skillfully through traffic toward her house. "Do you have family besides your father?" he asked.

"A cousin or two near Fort Worth," she said. She

glanced out the window, absently rubbing the ring finger of her left hand, trying not to choke up over the question. "What is Jacobsville like?" she asked to divert him from any further questions.

"It's small," he said easily. "There are a lot of ranches in the area. We have good pasture and soil, and we get enough rain to manage healthy crops." He grinned. "A lot of us are heavily into organic cattle raising. And with the industry under threat right now, we'll probably keep our financial heads above water when some other ranchers are going under."

"I like organic food," she said. "It may have a few more blemishes and bug bites, but if it doesn't kill bugs, it won't kill me," she added with a grin.

He chuckled. "Good point. Do you like animals?"

"I love them. I'd like to have a cat, but it's not possible. Dad's allergic to them." She sighed wearily, leaning her head back against the headrest. Her bruises were still giving her a lot of pain. Her hand went to them and she winced.

"You should see that plastic surgeon," he reminded her.

She shook her head. "Can't afford it. Even if I could, I don't want to go through weeks of surgery."

He hesitated and then he shrugged. "Have it your way."

"I'll heal." She touched her cheek again self-consciously. "I'm not sure going to work for you is a good idea. I mean, people might think the five of you beat me up!"

He laughed wholeheartedly. "Nobody who knows us would ever think that. Especially," he added, "if you can bake. Simon was right. I'm afraid we're famous locally for our addiction to biscuits."

Actually they were famous a lot further out than Jacobsville, but he didn't want to make her think they were loopy.

She took the words at face value. "I like to cook."

He glanced at her again, taking in her very conservative

way of dressing. "You don't look like the same woman I met just after Leo was assaulted."

"I almost never dress up," she confided. "And it really was a costume," she pointed out. "I wasn't lying. I don't make my living on the streets."

"How old are you?"

Her eyebrows arched. "Old enough."

"Are you over twenty-one?" he persisted.

"I'm twenty-three, almost twenty-four," she replied.

"And not married?"

"I've had responsibilities for the past few years," she said distantly, staring out the windshield. "My father has become the largest of them. I've been afraid to leave him alone."

"He's obviously dangerous when he drinks."

She hesitated, fingering her purse. "He seemed to lose himself in the bottle overnight. I thought I could handle him, control him, break the cycle. I couldn't even get help for him. My father doesn't think he has a drinking problem, so nobody would take him." She looked over at him. "I'm very grateful to your brother for his help. As I mentioned the night he was arrested, my father has only been like this for the past few months. It's not a long-standing problem. But I couldn't solve it alone."

"You're going to work for us," Rey said. "And it's not that much of a problem for Simon. He's good at his job."

"Is it a big ranch?" she asked unexpectedly.

"Enormous," he replied, "and one of five ranches we own as a family. Things get hectic during roundup, as you'll find out if you're still there next Spring."

"I won't be," she said with some certainty. "When I heal, I have to get back to my job."

"What do you do?" he asked curiously. "Is it house-cleaning or working as a cook in a restaurant?"

She almost bit her tongue at the demeaning comment. "You don't think I'm qualified to do anything else?"

He averted his eyes to the road. "I don't know you, Miss Johns," he commented carelessly. "But you seem pretty domestic to me."

She didn't feel well enough to retaliate. But one day, she promised herself, she was going to make him eat those condescending words.

"I've made beds and done light cleaning," she said, talking around her actual profession.

"Aren't you ambitious?" he persisted, with a faint frown. "Most women are, these days."

"That sounded bitter," she commented. "Did you get thrown over by an ambitious woman?"

"By a couple of them," he said curtly, and his expression became hard.

She hadn't thought of him that way. They'd been adversaries from the first contact. But it occurred to her as she gave him a quick, covert scrutiny, that he was a sensuous man. He wasn't handsome—except for Corrigan Hart, the rest of the brothers seemed cursed by a lack of conventional good looks.

But Rey had a lithe, graceful stride, and a strong face. He had good hands, clean and long-fingered. She liked the blackness of his straight hair, the high cheekbones, the long, thin, chiseled mouth. He was the sort of man who could have attracted women, except for his personality. The Harts didn't strike her as particularly gregarious or good mixers from her brief acquaintance with them. Leo was the one with the warmest personality. He made her feel at ease. The man beside her made her uncomfortable, insecure, nervous. She wasn't usually so strung-out by a man's proximity. Not that she'd had a lot to do with men in very recent years. Her father's overprotective, possessive nature had seen to that. He'd been so certain that she was going to end up like her mother.

She closed her eyes briefly, hating the memories.

"If you want to go and see your father before we leave for Jacobsville, I'll ask Simon to arrange it."

She stiffened. "I don't want to see him again until he's sober," she replied. "We both need time to get over what happened."

"Is your face the only place he hit you?" he asked unexpectedly.

"He got me in the back and the side, too, but those were only bruises. The doctor checked me over thoroughly." She sighed wearily. "I'm so tired," she murmured absently.

"I'm not surprised. You can get some rest. I'll phone you tomorrow, when we'll know more about Leo's condition and when he'll be released."

"Okay."

He stopped in front of her house and parked the car, walking to the door with her. He looked down at her while she fumbled the key into the lock. She was, in some ways, the most vulnerable woman he'd ever met. But there was steel in her makeup. He sensed that she wasn't like this usually, that she was fiery and independent and determined.

"This isn't the first time your father's laid into you, is it?" he asked suddenly.

She glanced at him, surprised. "No. But until this happened, it was more humiliating than painful." She frowned. "How did you know?"

He seemed concerned. "When I was in school, I had a couple of friends whose fathers got violent during binges. There's an…attitude, a posture, that people get when they've been beaten. I can't explain it, but I recognize it when I see it."

"Do you want to know what it is?" she asked with a world-weary smile. "It's a feeling of futility, of knowing that no matter what you do, you can't hold out physically against a man who's enraged and bent on hurting you. Because you know if you fight back, it will be even worse, maybe fatally worse. I don't like it," she added, her pale eyes beginning to glow, "and he's never getting the chance to do this again. He's my father. I love him, and I feel sorry for him. But I'm nobody's victim. Not even his."

He pushed his hands into his slacks' pockets and smiled at her. Her face was bright with color, and her eyes were alive, like peridots in sunlit water. He remembered her long blond hair around her shoulders and he wondered what she'd look like in pink silk. The thought shocked him and he scowled.

"Did I glue my nose on upside down?" she asked, raising her eyebrows.

He let out a short laugh. "No. I had a wild thought. Do you need an advance on your salary? I mean, is there anything you have to get for the trip that you can't afford?"

"I don't have a car," she began, and hated remembering why.

He glared. "I didn't say you were going to have to get to Jacobsville on your own. You'll go with Leo and me. Simon drove my car up from Jacobsville."

"Do I get to ride in the car, or have you got me earmarked for the trunk?" she returned.

He pursed his lips. Odd feelings were kindling inside him. "Keep that up and you'll be riding on the back bumper."

She wrinkled her nose. "Nice. Real nice. I can see you're going to be a great boss."

"If you don't burn the biscuits, I will be," he said.

"I'll stick close to your brother," she promised. "He'll protect me."

He didn't like that, but he wasn't going to let it show. "Leo's a tease," he said flatly. "Don't get your hopes up. He's not a marrying man. Neither am I," he added deliberately.

Her eyes widened. "Well, gee whiz, that's a major disappointment! And to think, I was only willing to take the job because of the marriage prospects!"

His face shuttered. "Sarcasm doesn't get you any points with me. I'm just making the position clear. We need a cook, not a prospective soul mate."

"Speak for yourself," she told him, turning back to her door. "I think Leo likes me already."

"I just told you…!"

She opened the door and looked back at him with pure irreverence. "Your brother can speak for himself. You don't own him, and you don't own me. I'll do what I please."

"Damn it…!"

"With charm like that, it's no surprise to me that you're still single," she said as she walked into the house.

"I can be charming when I've got a reason to be," he said icily. "But that's something you'll never know!"

"Lucky me!" ·

He started to speak, closed his lips tight, and walked back to his car.

She closed the door quickly and leaned back against it, almost shivering with anger. Of all the conceited, infuriating men she'd ever met, that one took the cake!

The next day, Rey phoned her midmorning to tell her that he and Leo would pick her up at one for the drive down to Jacobsville.

She had her suitcase packed and the house closed up when the big luxury car pulled into the driveway. It was a late-model car, and it looked odd, sitting in front of the shabby little house.

As she walked to the car, Meredith saw curtains fluttering and knew that the neighbors were getting an eyeful. They probably thought she was being carried off by the mob. That amused her and she smiled, glad that something diverted her mind from her father and her pain, and the misery of the past few months.

"We hadn't planned to ask you to help us move cattle,"

Rey drawled when he saw how she was dressed, in jeans and a striped shirt and boots.

"I haven't volunteered, either," she assured him. "But I didn't think you'd want me to do housework in a dress." She gave him a wry glance. "Those old black-and-white sitcoms weren't historically accurate, you know. I never saw a woman vacuum the carpet wearing a dress and high heels and pearls!"

"You can do housework in a suit for all I care, as long as you can bake me a pan of biscuits every morning," Rey said, taking the suitcase and putting it in the trunk.

"Good morning," Leo called from the open window of the front seat, grinning as Rey opened the back door and helped her inside.

"Good morning," she said brightly. "You look much better."

"I feel better, except for the headache." He gave her a long look. "You aren't in very good shape yourself. Face hurt?"

"Yes. I guess we're both like walking wounded, huh?" she asked with a grin as she leaned back into the warm leather seat.

"Maybe we should take a nurse with us," Rey muttered as he got in and started the car.

Meredith cleared her throat, but before she could speak, Leo turned to his brother. "I don't need nursing, thank you very much!" Leo said curtly.

"Neither do I!" Meredith agreed.

Rey glanced at them as he pulled out into the street. "I've seen accident victims who looked better than the two of you."

"Don't let him insult you, Meredith," Leo told her. "I'll tell you all about his weak spots so that you can deal with him."

She wouldn't have expected Rey to have any of those, but she was keeping her mouth shut and her options open for the time being. Her new boss looked formidable, and even Leo seemed curious about his lack of warmth.

"Are you all from Jacobsville originally?" Meredith changed the subject.

"No, we're from San Antonio," Leo said. "We inherited the Jacobsville property and it needed a lot of work, so we made it our headquarters. It's convenient to Houston and San Antonio, and frankly, it's isolated and gives us some privacy. We don't like cities as a rule."

"Neither do I," she said, recalling her grandmother's beautiful flower garden at the old place near Fort Worth. She smiled. "I wish Dad hadn't taken the job in Houston in the first place."

"What does he do?" Leo asked.

"He's retired," she said, not wanting to go into specifics. It hurt to talk about her family. Her father was a sore spot just now, anyway.

"Simon talked to the authorities," Rey interrupted. "They're going to make sure he gets counseling and he won't be released until he's kicked the alcohol habit." He glanced over the seat at her, his dark eyes intent. "They think it will be better if you don't have any contact with him for a few weeks, until he's through the worst of the withdrawal symptoms."

"I know about withdrawal," she replied, absently smoothing her hand over her jeans. "Bad habits are hard to break, even new ones."

"You two must read a lot," Rey replied. "I never saw so many books in one place as I did at your house. Even our library isn't that stuffed, and we all read."

"I love reading," she agreed. "We have a television, but neither of us had much time to watch it. Until recently," she added reluctantly, and winced at the thoughts that went through her mind. "I hope they get those men who mugged you, Mr. Hart," she told Leo fervently.

"Leo," he corrected. "It's really Leopold, but nobody

calls me that," he added with a grin. "We're pretty informal with our employees."

"Do you have a lot?" she asked curiously.

"A good many in Jacobsville," he replied. "Although we don't have a full-time vet, we do have several accountants, livestock managers, computer programmers, salesmen…you name it, we've got one. It's big business these days to run cattle. We even have a man who does nothing but keep up with legislation that may impact us."

"Do you have dogs and cats?" she asked.

"Always," Rey replied. "We have border collies that help us herd cattle, and we keep cats in the barn to help handle the rats."

"We had a cat in the house," Leo added, "but it was Cag and Tess's, and they took it with them when they moved into their new house. At least she won't have to cope with Herman," he told his brother, and laughed.

Rey smiled involuntarily. "You might not have wanted to work for us if we still had Herman."

"Who's Herman?" she wanted to know.

"He was Cag's albino python," he told her. "He weighed a hundred and ten pounds and lived in a cage in Cag's bedroom. He gave Herman up when he married Tess. He said it would be crazy to keep an animal that big and dangerous around their son. They're still over the moon about that little boy."

"Yes, but there are people who don't even consider things like that," Meredith murmured absently. "I remember a little girl who had to have plastic surgery because she was bitten in the face by her father's pet boa constrictor."

"Herman didn't bite, but Tess almost had a heart attack when she first came to work for us and found him in the washing machine."

"I can sympathize with her," Meredith said. "I haven't come across many snakes. I'm not sure I want to."

"We have rattlers and water moccasins around the

place," Rey told her. "You have to watch where you walk, but we've only had one person bitten in recent years. Snakes are always going to be a hazard in open country. You can't be careless."

"I'll remember."

"We've got a big garage apartment," Leo told her. "It's got picture windows and a whirlpool bath. Tess lived there until she and Cag married. I think you'll like it."

"I don't mind where I stay," she said easily. "I'm grateful to have a job at all. I really couldn't go to work in Houston looking like this. It would have been embarrassing for my boss."

"You won't have people staring at you on the ranch," Leo assured her. "And it won't take too long for those bruises to heal."

"I'll be fine, but you'll have to take it easy for a few days still, I'm sure they told you that," she returned at once. "No violent exertion. Concussion is tricky."

"I know that," Leo told her. "We had a man who was kicked in the head by a horse. He dropped dead three days later while he was walking into the corral. It was a hard lesson about head injuries. None of us ever forgot it."

She averted her eyes. She didn't like thinking about head injuries just now.

"I've got to stop for gas," Rey said as they reached the outskirts of the city and he pulled into a self-service gas station. "Anybody want something to drink?"

"Coffee for me," Leo said. "Meredith?"

"I'd like a small coffee, black, please."

"I'll go get it after I fill the tank," Rey said. He got out and started pumping gas.

Leo leaned his arm over the back seat and looked at Meredith openly, his dark eyes quiet and gently affectionate.

"You're still having a hard time with Rey, aren't you?" he asked her.

"He doesn't really like me," she confessed with a wry smile. "And I have to admit, he puts my back up, too. He seems to want to think the worst of me. He was convinced that I mugged you."

He chuckled. "You aren't tall enough to have knocked me out," he said. "But Rey doesn't like women much. He had a bad time of it with a young woman who turned out to be a call girl," he added, noticing absently how stunned Meredith seemed to be at that remark. "He had the ring bought, the honeymoon spot picked out, and then he found out the truth about her. It took him years to get over it. He was crushed."

"I guess so," she said heavily. "Good Lord, no wonder he thought the worst when he saw how I was dressed."

Leo frowned. "I just barely remember the rig you had on. What was it, some sort of costume?"

"I'd been to a wild Halloween party and had just escaped when I saw those men bending over you," she told him. "I ran at them waving my arms and yelling, and frightened them off."

"That was taking a hell of a chance!" he exploded.

She shrugged. "I've done it before," she said. "I learned it from my…from my brother's best friend," she amended, forcing the words out. It was much too soon to try to talk about her tragedy. "He taught karate in the military. He said that sometimes all it needed was a yell and the element of surprise to spook an attacker and make him run. It works."

"Not all the time," Leo said darkly, "and not for women. I'm all for equality, but most men are bigger and stronger than most women, and in hand-to-hand, you'd lose. You can't count on a man running, loud noise or not."

"Well, it worked for you," she amended, and smiled at him. "I'm glad, because I couldn't have wrestled those guys down."

He nodded. "See that you remember it," he told her. "Don't take chances. Get help."

"Some help those partygoers would have been," she scoffed. "Half of them were drunk, and the other half probably wouldn't have walked across the street to save a grandmother from a mugging!"

"Then why were you at a party with them?" he asked reasonably.

She picked at a fingernail. "A girl I know from work said I needed a night off and insisted that I come. I wore an old costume, the only one I had, and thought I'd enjoy myself. I don't do drugs or drink, and one of the men made a blatant pass at me." She wrapped her arms around her body in a defensive posture that betrayed her fear. "I was anxious to get away from the whole mess, luckily for you," she added with a grin.

"I don't like parties much, either," he said. "Getting drunk isn't my idea of a good time."

She glanced out the window. Rey had finished pumping gas and was inside the convenience store now. "Does he drink?" she asked.

"Very rarely. I've been known to, under provocation, but Rey's levelheaded and sober. He can be mean, and he's got the blackest temper of all of us, but he's a good man to have on your side when the chips are down."

"He doesn't like me," she repeated.

"He'll come around, give him time," Leo told her. "Meanwhile, you've got a job and a place to stay while your face heals. We all have hard times," he added gently. "But we get through them, even when we don't expect to. Give yourself time."

She smiled. "Thanks," she said huskily. "You really are a nice man."

"Nice, clean, sober, modest and incredibly handsome," he added with a wicked grin. "And I haven't even gotten to my best points yet!"

"Compared to your brothers," she began, "you—"

The door opened before she could hang herself, and Rey shoved a cup of coffee at her before he handed the second one to Leo.

"It's hot," he told them as he slid in and took the soft drink out of his jacket pocket and put it in the cup holder.

"Cold caffeine," Leo said, shuddering. "Why can't you drink coffee like a normal man?"

"I drink coffee at breakfast," Rey told him haughtily.

"So do I, but you don't have to have rules on when to drink it!"

Rey started the engine with a speaking glance.

"See that look?" Leo indicated it to Meredith. "When he looks like that, you've already lost whatever argument you're in the middle of. We call it 'the look.' I once saw him break up a fistfight with it."

"I don't plan to argue," Meredith promised.

Rey gave her "the look," and it lingered before his attention turned back to the windshield.

Meredith sat back against the leather seat and wondered suddenly if she wasn't making the biggest mistake of her life.

Four

The Hart Ranch was almost as Meredith had pictured it, with neat wooden fences concealing electrified fencing, improved pasture land and cattle everywhere. There were also pastures with horses, and there was a barn big enough to store a commercial jet. But she loved the house itself, with its graceful arches reminiscent of Spanish architecture, and the incredible number of small trees and shrubs around it. In the spring, it must be glorious. There were two ponds, a decorative one in the front of the house and a larger one behind the house in which a handful of ducks shivered in the November sun.

"Do you have goldfish in the pond?" she asked excitedly as Rey stopped the car in front of the house on an inlaid stone driveway.

"Goldfish and Koi," he answered, smiling reluctantly at her excitement. "We have a heater in the pond to keep them comfortable during the winter. There are water lilies in there, too, and a lotus plant."

"Does the other pond have goldfish, too, where the ducks are?" she wondered.

Leo chuckled. "The other one is because of the ducks. We had to net this pond to keep them out of it so we'd *have* some goldfish. The ducks were eating them."

"Oh, I see." She sighed. "It must be beautiful here in the spring," she said dreamily, noting the gazebo and the rose garden and stone seats and shrubs around the goldfish pond.

"It's beautiful to us year-round," Leo told her with lazy affection. "We all love flowers. We've got some more roses in a big flower garden around the back of the house, near a stand of pecan trees. Tess is taking courses in horticulture and she works with hybrids."

"I love roses," Meredith said softly. "If I had time, I'd live in a flower garden."

"I suppose cleaning rooms is time-consuming," Rey murmured sarcastically as he got out of the car and went in the front door of the house.

Leo glanced at her curiously while Rey was out of earshot. "You clean rooms?"

"I don't," she told him with a sharp grin. "But I'm living down to your brother's image of my assets."

Leo pursed his lips. "Now, that's interesting. You sound like a woman with secrets."

"More than you'd guess," she told him heavily. "But none that I'm ashamed of," she added quickly, just in case he got the wrong idea.

"Rey doesn't like you, does he?" he murmured, almost to himself. "I wonder why? It's not like him to pick on sick people."

"I'm not sick," she assured him. "I'm just battered, but I'll heal."

"Sure you will," Leo promised, smiling. "You'll be safe here. The only real chore you'll have is baking. By the time you're completely back on your feet, your father will be sober and in counseling, and your home life will have changed drastically.''

"I hope so," she said huskily.

He watched her eyes grow tragic and haunted. He frowned. "Meredith," he said slowly. "If you need to talk, ever, I can listen without making judgments.''

She met his clear dark eyes. "Thanks, Leo," she said with genuine gratitude. "But talking won't change a thing. It's a matter of learning to live with…things.''

"Now I'm intrigued.''

"Don't push," she said gently. "I'm not able to talk about my problems yet. They're too fresh. Too painful.''

"And more than just your father, or I'm a dirt farmer," he drawled.

She shrugged. "Perhaps.''

"Anyway, just take your time and let the world pass you by. You're going to love it here. I promise.''

"Am I?" She watched Rey come back out of the house with an elderly lady in tow, wringing her hands on her apron.

"That's Mrs. Lewis," Leo told her. "We talked her into coming back to bake biscuits for us, even though she'd retired, but now we're losing her to arthritis. She's going to show you the ropes. But not right now," he added quickly.

"No time like the present," Meredith disagreed with a smile. "Busy hands make busy minds.''

"I know how that works," Leo murmured drolly.

Rey opened the back door and helped Meredith out. "Mrs. Lewis, this is Meredith Johns, our new cook. Meredith, Annie Lewis. She's retiring. Again.'' He made it sound like a shooting offense.

"Oh, my, yes, I'm losing the use of my hands, I'm afraid," Mrs. Lewis said. "Glad to meet you, Miss Johns.''

"Glad to meet you, too, Mrs. Lewis," Meredith replied.

"I'll take your bag to your room, while Mrs. Lewis
shows you around the house," Rey added.

"She just got here," Leo protested.

"And there's no time like the present to show her the
house," Rey replied.

"That's just what she said," Leo sighed.

Rey glanced at Meredith, who gave him a wicked grin
and followed along behind Annie Lewis, who was making
a valiant effort not to ask about the terrible bruises on Meredith's face.

"It's a big, sprawling house, and it takes a lot of cleaning," Mrs. Lewis said as she led Meredith down the long
hall and opened doors to the very masculine bedrooms both
with dark, heavy Mediterranean furniture and earth tones
in the drapes and carpets. "The men aren't messy, thank
God, but they track in all that mud and dust and animal
fur! They had beige carpeting when I came here." She
glanced at Meredith with a shake of her head. "Red mud
just won't come *out* of beige carpet!"

"Or anything else," Meredith added on a soft laugh.

"They work hard, and they're away a lot. But the foreman lives in the bunkhouse with a couple of bachelor cowboys, and they'll look out for you."

"I don't know that I'll be here very long," Meredith
replied quietly. "They offered me the job so that I can have
time for these to heal." She touched her face, and looked
straight at the older woman, who was struggling not to ask
the question in her eyes.

"Nobody will hurt you here," Mrs. Lewis said firmly.

Meredith smiled gently. "My father got drunk and beat
me up, Mrs. Lewis," she explained matter-of-factly. "He's
a good and kind man, but we've had a terrible tragedy to
work through. He hasn't been able to cope with it except
by losing himself in a bottle, and now he's gone too far
and he's in jail." She sighed. "I tried so hard to help him.
But I couldn't."

Mrs. Lewis didn't say a word. She put her arms around Meredith and rocked her in them. The shock of it brought the tears that she'd held back for so long. She wept until her body shook with sobs.

Rey, looking for her, stopped dead in the doorway of his bedroom and met Mrs. Lewis's misty eyes over Meredith's bowed shoulders. It shocked him to see that feisty, strong woman collapsed in tears. It hurt him.

Mrs. Lewis made a gesture with her eyebrows and a severe look. Rey acknowledged it with a nod and a last glance at the younger woman as he walked back down the hall.

Supper was riotous. Meredith had made a huge pan of homemade biscuits and ferreted out all sorts of preserves to go with them. For an entrée, she made fajitas with lean beef and sliced vegetables, served with wild rice and a salad. Dessert was fresh fruit and fresh whipped cream, the only concession besides the biscuits that she made to fat calories. She'd also found some light margarine to set out.

"This is good," Rey commented as he glanced at her. "We usually have broiled or fried steak with lots of potatoes."

"Not bad once a week or so, but terrible for your cholesterol," she pointed out with a smile as she finished her salad. "Lean beef is okay for you, but not in massive doses."

"You sound like a dietician," Leo chuckled.

"Modern women have to keep up with health issues," she said evasively. "I'm responsible for your health while I'm working for you. I have to be food-conscious."

"That's fine," Rey told her flatly, "but don't put tofu and bean sprouts in front of me if you want to stay here."

Her eyebrows arched. "I hate tofu."

"Thank God," Leo sighed as he buttered another biscuit. "I got fed tofu salad the last time I went to Brewster's for supper,'' he added with absolute disgust. ''I ate the olives and the cheese and left the rest.''

''I can't say that I blame you,'' Meredith said, laughing because he looked so forlorn.

''Janie Brewster thinks tofu is good for him,'' Rey commented. ''But she thinks he needs therapy more. He doesn't like fish. She says that has some sort of connection to his fear of deep water.'' He glanced at his brother with wicked affection. ''She's a psychology major. She already has an associate degree from our local junior college.''

''She's twenty,'' Leo said with a twist of his lower lip. ''She knows everything.''

''She just got her associate degree this spring,'' Rey added.

''Good. Maybe she'll get a job in New York,'' Leo said darkly.

''Why New York?'' Meredith asked curiously.

''Well, it's about as far east as she can go and find her sort of work,'' Leo muttered. ''And she'd be out of my hair!''

Rey gave him a covert glance and finished his fajitas.

Meredith finished her own meal and got up to refill coffee cups. She had a feeling that Leo was more interested in the nebulous Brewster girl than he wanted to admit.

''We need groceries,'' she told them when she'd served dessert and they were eating it. ''Mrs. Lewis made me a list.''

''You can use one of the ranch trucks to drive to town,'' Leo suggested carelessly.

Her fingers toyed with her fork. ''I haven't driven in several months.''

''You don't drive?'' Rey exclaimed, shocked.

She couldn't meet his eyes. ''I take buses.'' Cars made her feel guilty.

''Why?''

She remembered a day she should have driven. The memories were horrible...

"Meredith, it's all right," Leo said gently, sensing something traumatic about her behavior. "I'll drive you. Okay?"

"You won't," Rey replied. "You're in worse shape than she is. Which brings up another point. You don't need to be walking around town like that," he told her.

She wasn't offended; it was a relief. She even smiled. "No, I don't guess I do. Will you do the shopping?" she asked him, her wide, soft eyes steady on his.

He felt wild little thrills shooting through his body at the impact. It had been years since he'd been so shaken by eye contact alone. He didn't move. He just stared at her, his dark eyes unblinking, curious. His body rippled with vague hunger.

Leo, watching the eye contact, tried not to grin. He cleared his throat, and Rey seemed to remember that he had a forkful of fruit halfway to his mouth. He took it the rest of the way and chewed it carefully before he spoke.

"I'll get the groceries," Rey volunteered. He glared at both of them, noting the shaved place where Leo had stitches near the back of his head. "Obviously I'm the only one here who can walk around without drawing curious stares from bystanders!"

Leo buttered another biscuit. "That sounds like sour grapes to me. If you want attention, try walking around without your pants."

"I didn't say I wanted attention," Rey returned hotly.

"Good thing." He glanced at Meredith with a mischievous smile. "He looks like hell without his pants," he said conversationally. "Hairiest legs of the bunch."

"That's debatable," Rey shot back. "Yours aren't much better."

"What a good thing you two aren't Scottish," Meredith said demurely.

It took a minute for them to get it, then Leo burst out

laughing, trying to picture his younger brother in a kilt. Rey lifted a corner of his thin mouth, but he wasn't in a smiling mood. It bothered him, that Meredith had been crying in Mrs. Lewis's arms, that she didn't drive, that she was so mysterious about her life. She was twenty-three, almost twenty-four. Most women by that age had been involved in a serious relationship, some more than one. Many had been married.

His heart skipped. Was that her secret? He remembered watching her rub her ring finger in the car. He glanced at it curiously. She didn't wear a ring, and there was no sign that she'd been wearing one there. She didn't act married. She hadn't talked about having a husband. She was single, apparently by choice. But had there been men in her past? He was still carrying scars from his one great love affair, from the deception he'd endured. Meredith had gone out walking to a party in a rig that made her look like a prostitute, and she'd been comfortable doing that. It wasn't something an innocent girl would have considered.

Knowing that, he looked at her in a different way, speculatively. She had a nice figure and she wasn't all flushing smiles like Janie Brewster when Leo was around. Meredith was oddly mature for her age, almost matronly. She seemed to be used to giving instructions, too. She was a puzzle that disturbed him. What if she was hiding something sordid in her past? He and Leo had taken her in on faith and pity, but now he wondered if they'd made a terrible mistake. If she were in league with the men who'd robbed Leo, they might have a dangerous situation developing. What if she'd planned the whole thing as a means to an end?

Basically Rey didn't trust her. He wasn't going to let down his guard, either, no matter if looking at her did raise his blood pressure. She wasn't going to know that she did. And he'd keep his eyes open, all the time, just in case.

The days turned to a week. Meredith's painful bruises faded slowly. She lost some of the brooding sadness that seemed to cling to her like the jeans she wore around the house when she was working. She found the slower, easier pace strange, and she missed the urgency of her daily routine. But as the days went by lazily, she realized that she hadn't really given herself time to think. She'd avoided it, ignored it, hoping that the past would vanish. Now she was face to face with it, forced to reflect on what had happened.

She sat beside the fishpond one sunny afternoon, between chores, and watched the goldfish under the surface of the dark water as they moved sluggishly. The water wasn't frozen, but it was cold. The pond heater only kept a small area heated, so the fish were limited in movement. She could imagine how it would be to sit here in the summer and watch them move around in their watery world, with flowers blooming all around.

She'd loved planting flowers. She missed her home, her bulbs and shrubs, the familiar things that she'd accumulated around her. Now it was all gone, sold without a second thought to make the memories bearable. It was too late, and she wished she'd been more sensible. There were things she should have kept. Mike's stupid baseball cap, the one he always wore on the rare occasions when he wasn't working, and when he went fishing. She missed her mother's collection of small silk Chinese boxes and her pretty evening gowns. She'd thrown all those things away. At the time, it had seemed reasonable to cut all the ties with the past. It didn't, now.

The sound of a truck pulling up to the front door caught her attention. Rey and Leo had been out of town for two days, attending another cattle convention, this time in Denver.

They climbed out of the cab of the big six-wheeled pickup truck and retrieved their suitcases from the back, waving as the ranch truck pulled right out again and took off down the road.

Meredith got up and went to join them.

"Want some coffee and pie?" she asked with a smile.

"That would really hit the spot," Leo said, returning the smile. "I hate commercial flights."

"You're the smart guy who said our jet needed to be overhauled," Rey reminded him.

"It did," Leo replied.

Rey was looking at Meredith openly. "The bruises are fading," he remarked. "You have more color, too."

"I've been getting out in the sunlight," she replied easily. "I like to watch the fish, even though they don't move much."

"We might put a big aquarium inside," Rey remarked, unaware of his brother's quick, curious glance. "I like fish myself."

"They've done studies," Meredith volunteered as they stood aside to let her enter the house first. "They say watching fish swim is calming. It helps relieve stress."

"God knows, we could use some of that," Leo chuckled. "Especially when cattle prices fall and feed prices go through the roof."

"Cattle raising must be a complex process," she remarked.

"Very complex," Rey said. He frowned as he watched her walk. "Hip sore?" he asked.

She laughed self-consciously. "Well, yes, it is. How did you know?"

"You've got a light limp on the right side. Barely noticeable."

She rubbed her hip self-consciously. "I fell on that side, the night Dad hit me," she told him. "The floor's pretty hard."

"There's a whirlpool bath in your bedroom," Rey reminded her. "It'll help the soreness."

"I discovered that," she said, grinning. "What a luxury! We only have a shower at home, and it's temperamental."

Rey gave her a long look. "When we've had time to

catch our breath, I'll see what I can find out about your father, if you'd like.''

Her face brightened. ''That would be nice.''

He smiled slowly, liking the way her pale eyes seemed to glow when she was pleased. She wasn't bad-looking at all, and her figure was just about perfect. He wondered how she could have remained single for so long, with her home-making skills, not to mention her sweet personality and that knockout body.

She was watching him with equal appreciation, and totally unaware of it. He had a lithe, powerful physique that made her think of rodeo. He walked with a unique sort of grace, and he didn't stoop or slouch, ever. She liked his eyes best of all. They were almost a liquid-brown, and they had black rims around the pupils. He was rugged and sensuous, and she looked at his wide thin mouth and wondered for the first time how it would feel to kiss it.

Her thoughts horrified her. She dragged her eyes away and excused herself in an absolute fluster to go make coffee.

Leo lifted both eyebrows and stared at his brother after she was out of earshot. ''Well, well,'' he murmured. ''You do seem to be making an impression on her.''

''Cut it out,'' Rey said testily.

''And vice versa,'' came the irritating reply.

Rey made a rough sound in his throat and stomped off down the hall to his room. He put down his suitcase, took off his suit and dress shirt and got into jeans and a checked long-sleeved work shirt. He glanced at himself in the mirror as he buttoned it, his eyes blank as he recalled the wild flush on Meredith's cheeks. It shouldn't please him. He didn't trust her. She could be trying to play them all for suckers. But he smiled, just the same.

Meredith had coffee and cherry pie in saucers on the table by the time the brothers were changed and walking into the kitchen.

"Coffee's fresh," she said.

"Aren't you having any?" Rey asked.

"I have to get the clothes into the dryer," she excused herself with a quick smile. "Yell if you need anything."

She was gone in a flash.

Rey stared broodingly at his pie and frowned. She didn't want to have coffee with them. Why?

"You make her nervous," Leo said, answering the unspoken question. "She knows you don't trust her."

Rey frowned as he nibbled at his pie and sipped coffee. "I don't know her," he replied. He gave his brother a speaking glance. "We've always done background checks on employees," he added firmly. "I don't think we should make an exception of her, even though she's temporary."

"Translated, that means you want to know more about her than you do," Leo drawled, grinning.

"Maybe I do," Rey confessed. "But she's in a position to do a lot of damage if she isn't what she seems. You could have been killed, or suffered brain damage," he added quietly. "If she's in cahoots with the guys who mugged you…" He let the sentence trail off meaningfully.

Leo grimaced. "I don't like poking into peoples' private business," he replied. "But you're right. It's risky not to check her out."

"I'll get the agency on it first thing tomorrow," Rey said. He took another bite of the pie. "She's a hell of a good cook," he murmured.

"Makes good coffee, too," Leo commented.

They looked at each other and grimaced. It was going to upset Meredith if she found out what they were up to. But it was too much of a gamble not to find out what they could about her background and character. On the other hand, Leo promised himself, he was going to intercept that background check before Rey had a chance to see it. If Meredith had secrets she was hiding for a good reason, he wasn't going to give her away to Rey.

It took several days for the private detective to get to the case and send a report to the Harts.

Rey was out of town at a one-day seminar on a new spreadsheet computer program the brothers were using for herd records when the report arrived. Leo carried the report into his office and closed the door while he read it.

When he finished, he let out a harsh breath. So that was Meredith's secret. No wonder her father drank. No wonder she was so reticent and quiet about her past. He smiled as he considered her true profession, and he was determined that Rey wasn't going to know about it until disclosure was inevitable. Rey was too prone to conclusion-jumping and rushing to judgment. It was about time he had a set down, and Meredith was just the woman to give it to him. Meanwhile, he'd let Rey work on hanging himself. Obviously Meredith was enjoying her anonymity, and considering the high-powered pressures of her daily job, it wasn't surprising that she found mundane housekeeping a nice change. It wouldn't hurt to let her enjoy the vacation from stress, without probing into her feelings. No doubt she still felt the grief, even after several months.

He touched the report with idle fingers, frowning as he recognized one of the names on it. Mike had been a Houston policeman. He was also a friend of Colter Banks, a Texas Ranger and cousin of the Harts, who worked out of the Houston ranger office. It really was a small world. He wanted to tell Meredith that he remembered Mike, but he didn't want to blow her cover. He also didn't want her to know that they'd been checking up on her.

He put the file into the filing cabinet, deliberately putting it under the wrong letter of the alphabet. If Rey asked, he'd just tell him that the agency was working on it but had other, more urgent cases to assign agents to first.

* * *

Meredith was alone in the house when Rey came in, late that night, from his business trip. Leo had gone to dinner at the Brewsters' house again, presumably at the invitation of Janie's father, to talk about a new breeding bull the Brewsters were trying to sell him.

She'd just started the dishwasher and was ready to turn the lights off in the kitchen when she heard Rey come in.

He paused in the kitchen doorway, a black Stetson slanted over one dark eye, wearing a grey vested suit that clung lovingly to the hard, muscular lines of his tall body. Meredith felt ragged by comparison in her jeans and red T-shirt, and barefoot. Her hair was disheveled because she'd been scrubbing the floor with a brush, and she wasn't wearing makeup. She hadn't expected to see either of the brothers before she went to bed.

Rey's dark eyes went to her pretty feet and he smiled. "You don't like shoes, do you?"

She grimaced. "No, and it's not good to go without them. No arch support." She studied his lean face. He had dark circles under his eyes. "Would you like some coffee and something to eat?"

"I would," he said heavily. "They gave me peanuts on the plane," he added with absolute disgust.

She chuckled. The sound was pleasant, and Rey was surprised at how it touched him to hear her laugh.

"I'll make you a nice thick low-fat ham sandwich with sauce."

"Thanks," he said, sliding a chair out so that he could straddle it. He tossed his hat into the chair beside him and ran a hand through his thick dark hair. "Make the coffee first, Meredith. I've got paperwork that has to be done tonight before the accountant comes to do the books in the morning."

"Can't it wait?" she asked gently. "You look worn to a frazzle. You need an early night."

His eyes searched hers intently. "I don't need mothering," he said, angered out of all proportion.

She flushed and turned away. She didn't apologize or say another word, but her hands shook as she filled the coffeepot and started it brewing.

Rey cursed himself silently for snapping at her. It was unkind, especially after she'd volunteered to feed him. She'd been working hard, too, he could see the spotless floor and the brush and bucket she'd been using on it. She must have done it on her hands and knees. It was a big kitchen, too. He wasn't the only one who was tired.

He got up from the chair and moved to stand just behind her. His lean hands caught her small waist and pulled her back against him. "I'm sorry," he said, his voice deep and husky with sudden emotion.

Her cold fingers came to rest on his and her whole body went rigid as a flash of white-hot pleasure shot through it. She caught her breath. He heard it. His own body tautened and the hands around her waist suddenly grew possessive, rough, insistent, as they pulled her tight against him.

He could hear her breathing change. He could feel the faint tremor of her hands over his. Impulsively he bent his head and his mouth touched the side of her neck.

Five

Meredith knew her knees were shaking. She hoped she wasn't going to fall on the floor at his feet with sheer excitement. It had been years since a man had made her feel such a rush of pleasure, and even then, it had been one-sided. She'd been crazy about a man who only saw her as a sort of unrelated sister. But even that wasn't as powerful as what she was feeling with Rey Hart.

His mouth became insistent as it moved slowly up her neck. He began to turn her, in the silence that was suddenly alive with passion. His hard lips traveled to the hollow of her throat, where a tiny pulse hammered, and then up to her chin. His teeth nibbled her chin, moving on to her lower lip. He tugged it away from the top one and tasted it with his tongue. All the while, his lean, strong hands were sliding up and down at her waist, smoothing her body completely against him.

His teeth nipped at her top lip with a sensual approach that made her breath shiver in her throat. He was experienced, far more so than she was. For all her professional capability, in this way she was a novice, and it showed.

He noticed her lack of sensual response with absent curiosity. She was attracted to him, that was obvious, but it was as if she didn't know what to do.

He guided her hands to his vest and flicked open buttons while his lips teased around hers. She fumbled and he laughed softly, his nose rubbing against hers as he moved her hands and unfastened the buttons on his vest and shirt with deft efficiency. He coaxed her hands inside, against thick hair and hard, warm muscle, while his mouth began to bite at hers, tempting her lips to part. She was stiff, trying not to respond, but her body was hungry.

"Like this," he whispered gently, teaching her mouth the lazy, sensual rhythm he wanted from it. "Taste my mouth, the way I'm tasting yours. Don't fight what you're feeling."

She heard the words as if through a fog. She didn't understand what he was saying, but her body obeyed him. She was in a sensual limbo, her hands flat against his chest, her head lifted, her eyes slitted and looking up into his as he began to increase the teasing pressure of his mouth. She followed his lips. She relaxed into the curve of his powerful body with a little shiver.

He devoured her mouth roughly, again and then again, tempting her until her mouth followed his, returning the arousing pressure. She could see the glitter grow in his narrow eyes, feel the grip of his lean hands as he pushed her hips against the sudden hardness of him. She gasped with embarrassment and then lost all sense of it as his mouth opened and pushed down hard against her parted lips, drowning her in passion.

It was like flying, she thought dazedly. He hesitated for an instant and her eyes opened, drowsy and curious. Her mouth was swollen, soft, tremulous. She looked at him with fascination, utterly helpless in his embrace. He felt an unfamiliar protectiveness toward her. It had been years since he'd kissed an innocent. Meredith's lack of experience was obvious. He was enjoying it.

"Yes," he murmured gruffly, and he bent again. His arms enfolded her, tender arms that no longer forced her into intimacy. His mouth was tender, too, exploring hers with slow mastery, careful not to overwhelm her.

She sighed into his hard mouth, relaxing against him. Her hands moved restlessly on his broad, bare chest, and contracted in the thick mat of hair that covered him.

He lifted his head, staring down into her wide eyes with somber delight. His hands smoothed hers deeper into his thick hair and hard muscle. He traced the edges of her short nails with his thumbs. His breath was jerky. He didn't like having her see that he was vulnerable. There were too many things he still didn't know about her, and he didn't trust her. She seemed innocent, but he couldn't forget the dress she'd been wearing and the accusations her father had made about her. He didn't dare trust her on such short acquaintance. On the other hand, his body was singing with pleasure from the long, hot contact with hers. He couldn't force himself to let her go. Not just yet.

"Why did you do that?" she asked huskily.

One dark eyebrow lifted. He didn't smile. "Why did you let me?" he shot back.

She felt uncomfortable. Despite the effort it took, she moved away from him. He let her go with no show of reluctance. He watched her struggle for composure while he refastened buttons with easy confidence, concealing the effect she had on him. He didn't even look ruffled.

"The coffee must be done by now," he pointed out when she seemed unable to move.

She turned stiffly and went to fill cups and put them, along with cream and sugar, on the table.

While he fixed his coffee, she made him two thick ham sandwiches with hands that slowly lost their tremor. She was devastated by a kiss that didn't seem to have disturbed him at all. She remembered the sudden hardness of his body, but she knew all about anatomy. A man couldn't help that reaction to anything feminine, it was part of his makeup. It wasn't even personal.

Somehow, it made things worse to know that. She felt his eyes on her back, and she knew he was measuring her up. She had no idea why he'd kissed her, but she didn't trust his motives. He didn't like her. She couldn't afford to let her guard down. Rey Hart would be hell on a woman who loved him. She knew that instinctively.

By the time she had the sandwiches made, her hands were steady again and she was able to put them on the table with a cool smile.

"I have to tidy up the living room..." she began.

He caught her hand as she started past him. "Sit down, Meredith," he said quietly.

She sat. He sipped coffee and studied her for a long moment. "I talked to Simon while I was away," he said. "Your father has been released from jail and placed in an alcohol treatment center. It's early days yet, but the prognosis is good. It helps that he hasn't been drinking that heavily for a long time."

She looked relieved and anxiously waited to hear what else Rey had to say about her father.

He continued. "The therapist wouldn't reveal any intimate details to Simon, you understand, but he was able to say that your father had been unable to deal with a family tragedy. Now that he's sober, he's extremely upset about what he did to you." He looked grim. "He doesn't remember doing it, Meredith."

She averted her eyes to her coffee cup. For something to do, she lifted it and took a sip of blistering black coffee, almost burning her lip. "That's common in cases of alcohol or drug abuse," she murmured absently.

He studied her over the rim of his coffee cup. "You

won't be allowed to communicate with him until he's through the treatment program, but he wanted you to know that he's desperately sorry for what he did."

She ground her teeth together. She knew that. Her father wasn't a bad man. Until he'd started abusing alcohol, he'd been one of the gentlest men alive. But, like all human beings, he had a breaking point which he reached when tragedy erupted into his life.

"He isn't a bad man," she said quietly. "Although I know it must have seemed like it."

"I've seen drunks before," Rey replied. "My brothers have gone on benders a time or two." He smiled faintly. "In fact, Leo holds the current record for damage at Shea's Bar, out on the Victoria road. He doesn't cut loose often, but when he does, people notice."

"He doesn't seem the sort of man who would do that," she remarked, surprised.

"We're all the sort of men who would do that, given the right provocation," he told her.

She smiled. "Do you get drunk and wreck bars?" she couldn't resist asking.

"I don't drink as a rule," he said simply. "A glass of wine rarely, nothing stronger. I don't like alcohol."

She smiled. "Neither do I."

He leaned back in his chair and studied her quietly. His hair was still faintly disheveled where her hands had caught in it when he was kissing her, and his lower lip was swollen from the pressure of her mouth. She knew she must look almost as bad. Her hand went unconsciously to her unruly hair.

"Take it down," he said abruptly.

"Wh...what?"

"Take your hair down," he said huskily. "I want to see it."

She'd just gotten her wild heart under control, and now

it was galloping all over again from that sultry tone, from the dark, intent caress of his eyes on her face.

"Listen, I work for you," she began with a tremor in her voice.

He got up from the chair and moved toward her with a lazy, almost arrogant stride. He drew her up in front of him and started pulling out hairpins. Her hair, unbound, fell in soft waves down her back, almost concealing one eye.

"It's hard to manage when it's down," she said self-consciously.

"I love long hair." He tangled his lean hands in it and coaxed her face up to his. He searched her eyes at point-blank range. "I've kissed girls years younger than you who knew even more than I do. Why are you still a novice?"

She swallowed hard. He was making her knees weak again. She couldn't quite get a whole breath of air into her lungs. Her hands rested on his chest lightly and she felt her heart choking her with its rapid beat as she stared into his narrowed, dark eyes.

"What?" she asked, barely having heard much less understood the question.

His hands were exploring the cool length of her hair with fascination. "You're not bad-looking, Meredith. Surely you've dated."

"Yes," she said, disconcerted. "But I'm old-fashioned."

Both eyebrows went up over a cynical smile. "That's a pitiful excuse in this day and age."

"Why?" she asked, her clear grey eyes staring up into his with no thought of subterfuge. "The whole reason for the women's movement is so that women can have the freedom to do as they please. I'm not promiscuous. Why should I need an excuse?"

He blinked. She made his question sound unreasonable. "I thought sexual liberation was the soul of the movement," he drawled.

"Being chaste is sexual liberation, in my book," she

replied. "You'd be amazed how many women in my graduating class practiced abstinence."

"In high school, I gather," he said absently, tracing the length of her hair with his hands.

She almost corrected him, but then, she really mustn't destroy the illusions he had about her as a domestic. "Yes. In high school."

He moved closer to her, his lean body a sensual provocation that made her breath catch. He laughed softly. "Care to test the hypothesis?" he murmured softly.

"I work for you," she repeated, playing for time.

"So?"

"So it's not wise to mix business…"

"…with pleasure?" He caught her waist and drew her close. "It's been a while since I found a woman so desirable," he whispered, bending to her mouth. "Experience bores me. You," he bit off against her soft lips, "are a challenge."

"Thank you, but I don't want to be," she whispered, trying to pull away.

He lifted his head and searched her eyes. "No curiosity about the great unknown?" he taunted.

"No desire to treat it as a sophisticated game," she corrected abruptly.

He hesitated, but only for an instant. His lean hands contracted and then released her. He went back to his chair and sat down. "Touché," he said with a curious glance. "All right, Meredith, I'll sit here and eat my sandwiches and we'll pretend that we're still strangers physically."

"Good idea," she approved. She reached down for her half-empty coffee cup and put it in the sink.

He was halfway through a sandwich when she excused herself and went to fluff up the pillows in the living room and put magazines and books back in their places. Leo had left things strewn about before he'd gone to the Brewsters'.

She was glad, because it gave her a valid reason not to sit next to Rey with her emotions in turmoil.

By the time she'd gone back to the kitchen, Rey had finished his sandwiches and coffee and was coming out the door.

"You're safe," he drawled. "I'm going to change and get to work in the study. Where's Leo?"

"Having supper at the Brewsters' house," she told him. "He said he'd be early."

"That means he'll be late," he mused. "Janie Brewster will have found twenty excuses to keep him talking to her father. She's one determined young lady, but Leo's equally determined. He doesn't want ties."

"Doesn't that sound familiar?" she murmured wickedly.

His eyes slid up and down her body in a silence that teemed with tension. "I never said I didn't want ties," he corrected. "I said I didn't want marriage. There's a difference."

"Don't look at me," she said carelessly. "I don't have time for relationships."

"Of course. All that cleaning must demand a lot of you," he said deliberately.

She flushed. He had no idea what her life was like on a daily basis, and she wanted very badly to tell him. But he was so almighty arrogant and condescending that he put her back up. She wasn't going to tell him a thing. He'd find out soon enough.

She put her hands on her hips and stared at him. "And what's wrong with being a housekeeper?" she demanded, going on the offensive. "Where would you and your brother be right now if there weren't women you could hire to bake and clean for you? I guess you'd have to get married then, or learn to cook, wouldn't you?"

He glared at her. "I could cook if I wanted to."

"You're the sort of man who makes a woman wish she

didn't have a culinary skill to her name,'' she said icily. ''You are so 'lord of the manor-ish', Mr. Hart!''

''It isn't a manor,'' he pointed out. ''They have those in England. We call this a ranch.''

She glared at him.

He grinned. ''You really do rise to the bait beautifully,'' he murmured, and something flashed in his dark eyes. ''The sandwiches were good,'' he added.

She looked surprised. ''Nothing but ham and a home-made sauce,'' she faltered.

''You do that a lot with food,'' he remarked gently. ''I like the way you experiment with dishes. I even like the way you garnish the plates. You make things look appetizing.''

She didn't realize that he'd even noticed. ''I learned that from a dietician,'' she said without thinking. ''If food is decorative, sometimes it makes up for bulk.''

He smiled quizzically. ''You can't decorate biscuits,'' he teased. ''But you make really good ones.''

''Thanks.'' She smiled back. ''I'll tidy up the kitchen if you're through.''

''I am. Don't stay up too late,'' he added and his eyes were suddenly bright with mischief. ''You need plenty of rest so that you can make biscuits for breakfast!''

''Okay. I'll get an early night.'' She laughed and went on past him to the kitchen.

He stared after her for several long seconds with an expression that he was glad she didn't see. He liked the taste of her. That hadn't been wise, kissing her that way. He was going to have to make sure it didn't happen again. He didn't need complications.

Nothing was the same between Meredith and Rey after that day. They were aware of each other. It wasn't blatant, but she could feel tingling in her spine when Rey was in a room. It was instinctive. Her eyes followed him like puppies, and she flushed wildly when he caught her at it and gave her that amused, wordily glance.

Leo noticed, too, and it worried him that Rey was encouraging Meredith. He knew Rey too well to think he'd had a change of heart toward his bachelor status.

"You're leading her on," Leo accused his brother one evening when they were alone in the study with the door closed. "Why?"

Rey gave him a surprised glance. "You make it sound like a crime to flirt with her."

"In your case, it is," his brother said flatly. "You're a rounder. She isn't."

Rey shrugged. "She's not exactly off limits," he told his brother. "Not at her age."

"And what do you have in mind? Seduction?" Leo persisted irritably. "She's already been damaged enough by what happened with her father. The bruises are barely healed, and the mental scars are still there. Don't play games with her."

"Aren't you self-righteous all of a sudden?" Rey shot back angrily. "You've been stringing Janie Brewster along for weeks, and we both know you don't have any intention in hell of getting serious about her. All you want is first chance at that damned seed bull they're thinking of selling! Does she know?" he added maliciously.

Leo's eyes began to glitter. "Janie is a child," he said furiously. "I pick at her, and not because of any damned bull. I'm certainly not hell-bent on seduction!"

"She's not a child," Rey countered. "You're leading her down a blind alley, when you know full well she's in love with you."

Leo looked shocked. "She's not in love with me! Maybe she's got a crush. That's all!"

"You don't see the way she looks at you, do you?" Rey replied solemnly.

Leo cleared his throat. "We're talking about Meredith," he said firmly.

Rey's eyes narrowed. "Meredith is an adult."

"And she works for us," Leo went on relentlessly. "I'm not going to stand by and let you make an amusement of her."

"Jealous?" his brother taunted.

Leo was very still. "Is that the draw?" he asked softly. "Are we competing for a woman again?"

Rey's eyes flashed. "I would never have known about Carlie if you hadn't started propositioning her in front of me. Do you think I can forget that?"

"I keep hoping you will someday. She would have taken you for the ride of your life," Leo said quietly. "You're my brother. I couldn't stand by and do nothing."

Rey turned away with a muttered curse. Leo was right; he had saved him from even worse heartache, but the memory was still raw enough to hurt.

"Don't try to take it out on Meredith," Leo told him firmly. "She's had enough tragedy. Let her do her job."

Rey glanced at him over his shoulder. "I would, if she'd remember why she's here," he said venomously. "It's not my fault that every time I turn around, she's drooling over me! A saint could be tempted by a woman whose eyes worship him like that. I'm only human!"

"Don't raise your voice," Leo cautioned.

"Why? Do you think she's standing outside the door eavesdropping?" Rey drawled sarcastically. "What if she did hear me? It's the truth. She wants me. A blind man could see it."

"That's no reason to take advantage of her. She's not like your usual women."

"No, she's not. She has no ambition, no intellect. Besides that, she's so inexperienced, it's unreal. I never thought kissing a woman could be boring, until she came along," Rey added coldly, trying not to let Leo see how attracted he was to their housekeeper. "She's so naive, it's nauseating."

Outside the door, Meredith stood poised like a statue with a cup of coffee in a saucer shaking in her hands. She'd come to offer it to Rey, and overheard words that had never been meant for her ears. She fought tears as she turned around and went quickly and silently back down the hall to the kitchen.

Hearts couldn't really break, she told herself firmly, as she dabbed at the tears with a paper towel. She was just feeling the aftereffects of her devastating experience at home. It wasn't as if she was really drooling over Rey Hart.

She felt like sinking through the floor when she realized that she did spend an inordinate amount of time staring at him. He was handsome, sensuous, attractive. She liked looking at him. And maybe she was infatuated, a little. That didn't give him the right to say such horrible things about her.

If she hadn't been listening, she'd never have known about them in the first place. She'd have gone right ahead, mooning over him and having him know it and be amused by it. Her pride felt tattered. She'd never been one to wear her heart on her sleeve, but Rey had kissed her as if he enjoyed it, and she'd built dreams on those kisses. She realized now how truly naive it had been. The first man who paid her any attention in years, and she fell head over heels for him. Seen in that context, perhaps it wasn't surprising after all. She'd heard Leo accuse him of being a rounder, and she had to admit that his experience ran rings around hers. Apparently he was accustomed to playing sensual games with women. That was all those devastating kisses that had brought her to her knees had meant to him—just a game. And she'd taken it seriously!

Well, she told herself firmly, he needn't worry that she'd throw herself at his feet again. From now on, she was going to be the perfect employee, polite and courteous and eager to please—but she'd never stare at him longingly again. Thank God she'd overheard what he said to Leo. It had spared her a terrible humiliation. A little hurt now was far better than being wrung out emotionally down the road because she'd been ignorant of the facts. Wasn't she herself always telling people that the truth, however brutal, was always best in the long run? It was time to take her own advice.

When Rey and Leo came in to breakfast the next morning, she put bacon and eggs and biscuits on the table with a cool, professional smile.

Rey was oddly subdued. He didn't give her the arrogant scrutiny that had become force of habit in recent days. In fact, he didn't look at her at all. Leo kept up a pleasant conversation about the day's chores. They were moving some sick cattle into a pasture near the house so the vet could examine them, and stock was being shifted into closer quarters as well, within easier reach of the hay barn.

"I thought you had those big round bales of hay?" Meredith asked curiously.

"We do," Leo agreed. "But we still bale it the old-fashioned way and stack it in the barn. You lose some of the round bales through weathering by sun and rain. The hay that's kept dry in the barn has less deterioration and better nutrition."

"But you feed more than hay?"

Leo chuckled. He buttered a second biscuit. "You are sharp. Yes, we have a man who mixes feeds for better nutrition. No animal proteins, either," he added. "We're reactionaries when it comes to ranching. No artificial hormones, no pesticides, nothing except natural methods of pest control and growth. We're marketing our beef under the Hart Ranch label, as well, certifying it organic. We've already got several chain supermarkets carrying our product, and we've just moved onto the Internet to extend our distribution.''

"That's amazing," Meredith said with genuine interest. "It's like having custom beef," she added, nodding.

"It is custom beef," Leo told her. "We're capitalizing on the move toward healthier beef. Quick profit methods are going to fail producers in the long run, especially with the current attitude toward hormones and antibiotics and animal-product proteins for feed. We think that once organic beef catches on, the market will justify the added expense.''

"Word of mouth will take you far, too," Meredith said. "Hospitals teach nutrition these days, not only to patients but to the community. Tailored beef will find a market among consumers with heart problems, who'll pay the extra cost for healthier cuts of meat grown organically.''

Rey was listening. He finished his biscuit and poured himself another cup of coffee from the carafe on the table. "J.D. Langley pioneered that organic approach locally," he remarked. "He and the Tremayne boys got into terrific fights with other producers at seminars for a while. Then we saw the disasters overseas and suddenly everybody else was jumping on the bandwagon.''

"They'll be glad they did, I think," Meredith said.

"Which reminds me," Leo said, eyeing her. "Mrs. Lewis said her larder hadn't been opened since you came here. So…what are you making these biscuits with?''

She gave them a wary glance. "Light olive oil," she said slowly.

Rey gaped at his biscuit as if it had suddenly sprouted hair. "Olive oil?!" he gasped.

"Listen," she said quickly, aware of horrified stares, "olive oil is so healthy that people who live on a Mediterranean diet have only a fraction of the vascular problems we have in abundance in this country. The fat content is still there, but it's a vegetable fat, and it's actually good for you. Until I told you, you didn't even know you'd given up great gobs of animal fat in those biscuits!''

The brothers looked at each other. "Well," Leo had to admit, "they taste just as good as the others did."

"That's true," Rey agreed reluctantly.

"And we're getting older," Leo continued. "We don't want clogged arteries giving us heart attacks and strokes."

"Or bypass surgery," Rey sighed.

"So I guess olive oil isn't so bad, after all," Leo concluded, with a grin at Meredith.

She grinned back. "Thank goodness. I had visions of being tarred and feathered," she confessed.

"I'm not giving up butter, though," Rey told her firmly, dipping his knife into the tub next to the biscuit basket. "Nothing tastes like real butter on a biscuit."

Meredith didn't look at him. She couldn't confess that what he was eating was not butter, but rather a light margarine that actually lowered cholesterol levels. She only smiled and poured herself another cup of coffee.

Leo and Rey had started moving bulls into the lower pasture, where new forage grasses were thriving even in autumn, when a mangy old longhorn bull suddenly jerked his head and hooked Leo in the shoulder.

Leo yelled and threw a kick at him, but the aggravating animal was already trotting nonchalantly into the new pasture without a backward glance.

"How bad is it?" Rey asked, leaving the cowboys to work the cattle alone while he looked at his brother's shoulder.

"Probably needs stitches," Leo said through his teeth. "Drive me to the house and let me change shirts, then you can take me to Lou Coltrain."

"Damned bull," Rey muttered as he put his brother into the ranch truck and took off home.

Meredith was sweeping off the back steps when they drove up. She gave Leo's bloodstained shirt a quick glance.

"Come on in here, let me have a look," she said gently.

Disconcerted, Leo let her remove the shirt from his shoulder and bathe the blood away with a clean cloth.

She probed around the edges of the cut and nodded. "You'll need stitches. Here. Hold this tight against the cut until you get to town."

"I need to change shirts," he began.

"You need to get to the doctor. Which one do you use?" she persisted, picking up the mobile phone she kept on the table.

"Dr. Lou Coltrain," he said.

"I'll phone and tell them you're on the way," she said firmly.

Rey gave her a curious glance, but he hustled Leo out the door and into the truck again.

When they got to the office, Dr. Lou Coltrain's nurse, Betty, came right out to meet them and guide them back into a cubicle.

Lou walked in, took a professional look at the cut, and grinned. "Stitches," she said. "How about a tetanus jab?"

Leo grimaced. "Well…"

She patted him on the shoulder that wasn't injured. "We'll have you fixed up and out of here in no time."

He sighed, glancing at his brother. "I hate shots."

Rey shrugged. "You'd hate tetanus more," he told Leo. "Besides," he added, "I hear she gives sugarless gum to the good patients."

Leo made a face at him.

When Leo was stitched up and given his tetanus shot, Rey drove him back to the house, where Meredith made him a cup of coffee and cut him a slice of cherry pie, making sure he had a cushion for his back in the straight chair at the table.

Rey glared at the special treatment his brother was getting. "Maybe I should get gored," he commented drolly.

Meredith stared at him, and she didn't smile. "You'd get a vinegar dressing and a cup of cold coffee," she said.

He glared at her, too. He felt as if he'd been put in the corner without supper. It wasn't a feeling he liked. He gave them both a hard look and went back out the door, smoldering with bad temper.

Six

___

"**I** shouldn't have said that," Meredith said wryly when Rey was gone. "I set him off again."

"It won't hurt him to have one woman who doesn't fall all over herself when he's around," Leo told her flatly. "Sometimes too much success can ruin a good man."

She toyed with her coffee cup. "Women like him, I guess," she said.

He gave her a quick glance that she didn't see before he started on his pie. "He's had girlfriends since he was in grammar school. But there was only one serious one. She turned out to be a real loser," he added quietly. "She soured him on women."

She sipped coffee. "You can't judge an entire sex by one woman," she pointed out.

"Well, we had our mother as an example, too," he continued. "She left Dad with five young boys and never looked back. We haven't been overawed with sterling examples of womanhood, although Simon and Corrigan and Cag have made good marriages in spite of that.''

She smiled absently as she looked at him. ''I had a brother of my own,'' she said without thinking.

''Yes, I know,'' Leo replied, surprising her into silence. ''His name was Michael Johns. He worked for Houston PD.''

Her gasp was audible. ''How…do you know about him?''

''Remember Colter Banks?''

''Yes. Colter was Mike's best friend.''

''Well, Colter's our second cousin,'' he told her. ''I knew Mike, too. I'm sorry.''

She clenched one fist in her lap and tried not to give way to tears. ''Do the others…know?''

''No, they don't,'' he replied. ''They weren't that close to Colter, and they never met Mike. I haven't told them, and I'm not planning to.''

She searched his dark eyes. ''What else do you know about me, Leo?'' she asked, because of the way he was watching her.

He shrugged. ''Everything.''

She let out a long breath. ''And you haven't shared it with Rey.''

''You wouldn't want me to,'' he murmured dryly. ''He's having too much fun being condescending. When the time comes, he's got a few shocks coming, hasn't he?''

She laughed softly. ''I hadn't meant to be cloak-and-daggerish. It's just that it still hurts too much to talk about,'' she said honestly.

''Colter told me the circumstances. It wasn't your fault,'' he replied. ''Or your father's. I gather that he drinks because he feels responsible?''

She nodded. ''We both dined out on 'what-if' just after it happened,'' she confessed. ''I know that it probably wouldn't have made any difference, but you can't help wondering.''

''It doesn't do any good to torment yourself over things that are history,'' Leo said gently.

''I don't do it intentionally,'' she murmured.

''The first step was getting your father into treatment,'' he said. ''Getting you out of your rut was the second. You don't have any memories to contend with here. I've noticed the difference in you just in the past week.'' He smiled. ''You're changing already.''

''I suppose so.'' She smiled back. ''I've never even been on a ranch before. I could love it here. It's such a change of pace.''

''When you're back to normal, we've got plenty of opportunity around here for your sort of job,'' he pointed out.

She chuckled. ''Don't rush me. It's far too soon to think about leaving Houston.'' She didn't add that she didn't want to be that close to Rey, considering his opinion of her at the moment. ''I've only been down here a week.''

''Okay. I'll let it drop, for now.'' He leaned back in his chair and winced, favoring the arm he'd had stitched. ''Damned bull,'' he muttered.

''Did they give you something for the pain?''

''No, and I didn't ask for anything. I have over-the-counter painkillers if it gets really bad. So far, it hasn't.''

''You know, of course, that statistically farm and ranch work have the highest ratio of accidents,'' she said.

''Any job can be dangerous,'' he said easily.

She pursed her lips and lifted her coffee cup to them. ''Your brother's a walking job hazard,'' she said thoughtfully.

''Oh? In what way, exactly?'' he asked.

She wouldn't have touched that line with a pole. She laughed. ''He's abrasive. I don't think he wants me here.''

''I've noticed his attitude. I hope you haven't let it get to you?''

"I haven't. Anyway, he'll mellow one of these days," she said.

"He could use some mellowing. He's a disillusioned man."

She smoothed the lip of the cup. "Did he love her very much?"

He knew she was talking about Carlie. He sighed. "He thought he did. His pride suffered more than his heart." He hesitated. "I didn't help matters. I made a play for her deliberately, to show him what she was. That was a miscalculation. A bad one. He's never forgiven me for it. Now, if I pay any attention to a woman, he tries to compete with me…"

She noticed the way his voice trailed off, and she averted her eyes. "I get the picture," she said.

"It's not like that, not with you," he began.

She forced a smile. "He's not interested in me," she said bluntly. "And just in case you're worried that I might be falling all over him, there's no danger of that, either. I was outside the door when he was talking to you. I wasn't eavesdropping, but he was speaking rather loudly. I heard what he said. I'd have to be certifiable to lose my heart over a man like that."

He grimaced as he read the faint pain that lingered in her eyes. "I wouldn't have had you hear what he said for the world," he said deeply.

She managed a smile. "It's just as well. It will keep me from taking him seriously. Besides, I'm not really down here looking for a soul mate."

"Just as well, because Rey isn't any woman's idea of the perfect partner, not the way he is right now. I love him dearly, but I can afford to. It's another story for any woman who loses her heart to him." He studied her warily. "Just don't let him play you for a fool."

"I wouldn't dream of it," she said. "Even if I got the chance."

He nodded. He finished his pie and coffee and got to his feet. "I'd better change and get back to work. Thanks for running interference, by the way. You're a cool head in an emergency," he remarked with a smile.

"I've had lots of practice," she said modestly and grinned. "But try to stay away from horned things for a while."

"Especially my brother, the minor devil," he said, tongue-in-cheek, and grinned back when she got the reference and started laughing.

After Leo went back to work, Meredith went out to gather eggs. It seemed very straightforward. You walked into the henhouse, reached in the nest, and pulled out a dozen or so big brown eggs, some still warm from the chicken's feathered body.

But that wasn't what happened. She paused just inside the henhouse to let her eyes adjust to the reduced light, and when she moved toward the row of straw-laced nests, she saw something wrapped around one nest that wasn't feathered. It had scales and a flickering long tongue. It peered at her through the darkness and tightened its coils around its prey, three big brown eggs.

Meredith, a city girl with very little experience of scaly things, did something predictable. She screamed, threw the basket in the general direction of the snake, and left skid marks getting out of the fenced lot.

Annie Lewis, who was doing the laundry, came to the back door as fast as her arthritis would allow, to see what all the commotion was about.

"There's a…big black and white *snnnnnakkkkkke*…in there!" Meredith screamed, shaking all over from the close encounter.

"After the eggs, I reckon," Annie said with a sigh. She wiped her hands on her apron. "Let me get a stick and I'll deal with it."

"You can't go in there alone with the horrible thing and try to kill it! It must be five feet long!"

"It's a king snake, not a rattler," Annie said gently, recognizing the description. "And I'm not planning to kill it. I'm going to get it on a stick and put in the barn. It can eat its fill of rats and poisonous snakes and do some good out there."

"You aren't going to kill it?" Meredith exclaimed, horrified.

"It's a king snake, dear," came the gentle reply. "We don't like to kill them. They're very useful. They eat rattlesnakes, you know."

"I didn't know." Meredith shivered again. "I've never seen a snake except in a zoo, and it was a python."

"You'll see lots of them out here in the country. Just remember that if one rattles at you, it means business and it will strike. Rattlesnakes are venomous."

Meredith looked around as if she expected to be mobbed just at the mention of them.

"You can finish the washing," Annie said, trying not to grin. "I'll take care of the snake."

"Please be careful!"

"I will. After all, you get used to things like…"

Rey drove up and stopped the truck just short of the two women, exiting it with his usual graceful speed.

"What's going on?" he asked as he pulled a box of assorted bovine medicines out of the boot of the truck.

"There's a snake in the henhouse!" Meredith exclaimed.

He stopped with the supplies in his arms and stared at her curiously. "So?" he asked.

"I'm just going to move it for her, Rey," Mrs. Lewis said with a grin. "It sounds like a king snake. I thought I'd put him in the barn."

"I'll get him for you." He put the box on the hood of the truck. "Scared of snakes, are you?" he scoffed.

"I'd never seen one until a few minutes ago," she said

huffily, and flushed. He was looking at her as if she were a child.

"There's a first time for everything," he said, and his eyes made a very explicit remark as they lingered on her breasts.

She gave him a glare hot enough to fry bacon, which he ignored. He walked right into the chicken lot and, then, into the henhouse.

Barely a minute later, he came back out with the snake coiled around one arm, its neck gently held in his other hand.

"Would you look at this, it's Bandit!" he exclaimed, showing it to a fascinated Mrs. Lewis. "See the scar on his back where he got caught in the corn sheller that time?"

"So it is!" she said. "Hello, old fella!" She actually petted the vile thing under the chin.

"How can you touch that thing?!" Meredith groaned. "It's a snake!"

Mrs. Lewis glanced at Rey. "Reckon we should tell her that he used to live in the house?"

"Probably not," Rey suggested, aware of her white face. "I'll just stick him up in the loft. Come on, Bandit, I'll put you in a safe place."

Meredith was holding both chill-bump laden arms with her hands and shivering.

"There, there," Annie said gently. "He wouldn't bite you unless you provoked him. He's very gentle."

"If you say so."

"I do. Now you go back in there and get the eggs. Don't let Rey see how frightened you are. Trust me, he'll take advantage of it. You'll find rubber snakes in the refrigerator, the blender, the washer..."

"No!" Meredith exclaimed, horrified.

"Just grit your teeth and go back in the henhouse," Annie suggested. "Quick, before he comes back out."

Meredith took a quick breath and gave Annie a miserable glance, but she did as she was told.

Her skin crawled when she had to pick up the basket and gather the eggs, especially the ones the snake had been curled around. Now, every time she went to the henhouse, she'd be shivering with apprehension.

You've looked at gunshot wounds, accident victims, every sort of horror known to human eyes, she told herself firmly. The snake wasn't even lacerated! So get it done and move on.

She did, walking back out into the sunlight with a full basket of eggs and a forced look of composure on her soft face.

Rey was waiting for her, leaning against the bumper of the truck with his arms crossed and his hat pulled low over his eyes.

She didn't dare look at him for long. In that indolent pose, his lean, muscular body was shown to its very best advantage. It made her tingle to think how it had felt to be held against every inch of that formidable frame, to be kissed by that long, hard mouth.

"You get thrown, you get right back on the horse," he said with approval. "I'm proud of you, Meredith. It would be hard for even a ranch-born girl to go back into a henhouse where a snake had been lurking."

She took a slow breath. "We don't face things by running away from them, I guess," she agreed.

His eyes narrowed under the wide brim of the hat. "What are you running away from, Meredith? What is your father running away from?"

She clutched the basket to her chest. "That's nothing that you need to concern yourself with," she said with quiet dignity.

"You work for me," he replied.

"Not for long," she pointed out. "In another week or so, I'll be a memory."

"Will you?" He lurched away from the bumper and went to stand just in front of her, a tall and sensual threat. His fingers touched her soft mouth lightly. "Those bruises still look pretty fresh," he pointed out. "And you did ask for a month's leave, or so you said. Did you?"

She grimaced. "Well, yes, but I don't have to stay here all that time."

"I think you do," he returned. He bent and drew his mouth slowly over hers, a whisper of a contact that made her breath catch. He smiled with faint arrogance as he stood up again. "Anything could happen," he drawled. "You might like ranch life."

"I don't like snakes already."

"That was a fluke. They're generally hibernating by November, but it's been unseasonably warm. Spring is generally when you have to watch where you put your hands. But you don't need to worry. I'll protect you from snakes. And other perils."

"Who'll protect me from you?" she asked huskily.

He raised any eyebrow. "Why would you need protection?" he asked. "You're well over the age of consent."

"I've lived a very sheltered life," she said flatly.

He pursed his lips as he studied her, examining the statement. "Maybe it's time you walked out of the cocoon."

"I'm not in the market for an affair."

"Neither am I." He smiled slowly. "But if you worked at it, you might change my mind."

"I don't think so," she said. Her eyes were cool as they met his. "I wouldn't want you to think I was 'drooling' over you," she added deliberately.

His face changed. He knew immediately that she'd overheard what he'd said to Leo. He was sorry, because it wasn't true. He'd been desperate to throw Leo off the track. He didn't want his brother to know how attracted he was to her.

"Eavesdroppers never hear anything good about themselves, don't they say?" he asked quietly.

"Never," she agreed. "Now, if you'll excuse me, I'll go wash the eggs."

"I said something else that you'll remember with sordid ease," he murmured as she started past him. He caught her by the shoulder and tugged her close, bending to drag his mouth roughly across hers. "But I didn't mean that, either," he whispered against her parted lips. "Your innocence makes my head spin. I lay awake at night thinking of all sorts of delicious ways to relieve you of it."

"You'd be lucky!" she exclaimed, shocked.

He laughed softly as he let her go. "So would you," he drawled. "I've been called 'sensual hell' in bed, and I can assure you it wasn't meant to be a derogatory remark."

"Rey Hart!" she burst out.

"But why take anyone else's word for it?" he teased. "I'll be glad to let you see for yourself, anytime you like."

"If you think…I have never…of all the…!"

"Yes, it does tend to make women flustered when I mention what a great lover I am," he said with a wicked grin.

She couldn't get one coherent sentence out. She stomped her foot hard, turned around, and stormed into the kitchen, almost knocking herself down with the door in the process. It didn't help that Rey stood out there laughing like a predator.

If she expected Rey to be apologetic about what he'd said, she was doomed to disappointment. He watched her with narrow, assessing eyes as she went about her household duties. He didn't harass her, or monopolize her. He just watched. The scrutiny made her so nervous that she fumbled constantly. Her heart ran wild at the attention from those dark, steady eyes.

"Why don't you want to do something else besides keep house?" Rey asked her one evening when she was putting supper on the table. Leo, as usual, was late getting in. Rey had volunteered to set the table while she fixed Mexican corn bread and chili.

"Keeping house has less stress than most outside jobs," she said, not looking at him.

"It pays lousy wages," he continued, "and you could get into a lot of trouble in some households, with men who'd see you as fair game."

"Do you see me that way?" she asked, wide-eyed.

He glowered at her. "No, I don't. The point is, some other man might. It isn't a safe career. In a profession, there are more laws to protect you."

"Most professional people have degrees and such. Besides, I'm too old."

"You're never too old to go back to school," he replied.

She shrugged. "Besides, I like cooking and cleaning."

He eyed her curiously. "You're very good at handling injured people," he said suddenly. "And you're remarkably calm in an emergency."

"It's good practice for when I have kids," she said.

He drew in a short breath. "You like being mysterious, don't you?"

"While it lasts, it's fun," she agreed.

His eyes narrowed. "What dark secrets are you keeping, Meredith?" he asked quietly.

"None that should bother you, even if you found them out," she assured him. She smiled at him from the stove. "Meanwhile, you're getting fresh biscuits every day."

"Yes, we are," he had to agree. "And you're a good cook. But I don't like mysteries."

She pursed her lips and gave him a teasing glance over her shoulder. "Too bad."

He put the last place setting on the table and sat down at his place, just staring at her, without speaking. "You know," he said after a minute, frowning, "there's something familiar about your last name. I can't quite place it, but I know I've heard it somewhere.''

That wasn't good, she thought. He might remember Leo talking about her brother. She didn't want to have to face the past, not just yet, when she was still broken and bruised and uncomfortable. When she was back on her feet and well again, there would be time to come to grips with it once and for all—as her poor father was already doing.

''Think so?'' she asked with forced nonchalance.

He shrugged. ''Well, it may come back to me one day.''

Fortunately Leo came in and stopped his train of thought. Meredith put supper on the table and sat down to eat it with the brothers.

The next morning, Rey came out to the kitchen with a bright silver metal gun case. He set it down beside the counter, out of the way, before he started eating his breakfast.

''Going hunting?'' Meredith asked impishly.

He gave her a wary glance. ''Skeet shooting,'' he corrected. ''The season's over, but I practice year-round.''

''He won two medals at the World championships in San Antonio, this year,'' Leo told her with a grin. ''He's an 'A' class shooter.''

''Which gauge?'' she asked without thinking.

Rey's face became suspicious. ''All of them. What do you know about shotguns?''

''I used to skeet-shoot,'' she volunteered. ''My brother taught me how to handle a shotgun, and then he got me into competition shooting. I wasn't able to keep it up after I grad…after high school,'' she improvised quickly. She didn't dare tell him she gave it up after she finished college. That would be giving away far too much.

He watched her sip coffee. ''You can shoot, can you?'' he asked, looking as if he were humoring her. He didn't seem to believe what she claimed.

"Yes, I can," she said deliberately.

He smiled. "Like to come down to the range with me?" he asked. "I've got a nice little .28 gauge I can bring along for you."

By offering her his lowest caliber shotgun, he was assuming that she couldn't handle anything heavier.

"What's in the case?" she asked.

"My twelve gauge," he said.

She gave him a speaking glance. "I'll just shoot that, if you don't mind sharing it. Uh, it doesn't have a kick or anything…?" she added, and had to bite her tongue to keep from grinning at her innocent pose.

He cleared his throat. He didn't dare look at Leo. "No," he said carelessly. "Of course it doesn't have a kick."

In truth, it would kick worse than any other of the four gauges, but Rey was planning to call her bluff. She was putting on an act for his benefit. He was going to make her sorry she tried it.

"Then I'll be just fine with that gun," she said. "More apple butter?" She offered him an open jar and spoon.

"Thanks," he replied smugly, accepting the jar. He put it down and buttered another biscuit before he spooned the apple butter into it. "Don't mind if I do. Leo, want to come along?" he asked his brother.

Leo was also trying not to grin. "I think I will, this time," he told his brother. This was one shooting contest he wasn't about to miss. He knew that Mike Johns was a champion shooter. If he'd been the one who taught his sister, Meredith would shock Rey speechless when she got that shotgun in her arms. He was going along. He didn't want to miss the fun.

"The more the merrier, I always say," Rey chuckled.

"Funny thing, that's just what I was thinking," Leo replied, tongue-in-cheek.

Meredith didn't say another word. She finished her breakfast, waited until they finished theirs, and put the dishes in the dishwasher. Then she dressed in jeans, boots, and a long-sleeved flannel shirt with a down-filled vest and a bib cap, and went off to let Rey show her how to shoot a shotgun.

The target range was unusually busy for a lazy Friday afternoon in November. It was a cool day, with a nice nip in the air. Meredith felt good in the down vest. It was one she'd often worn when she went to the firing range with Mike in cold weather. Coats were cumbersome and often got in the way of a good, quick aim.

Rey and Leo stopped to pass the time of day with two elderly shooters, both of whom gave Meredith a warm welcome.

"This is Jack, and that's Billy Joe," Rey introduced the white-haired men, one of whom was tall and spare, the other overweight and short. The short one had walked briskly the short distance from the red pickup truck parked at the clubhouse, and he was out of breath already. "We all go to district, state and national shoots as a team from our club."

"But we get honorable mention, and Rey wins the medals," Billy Joe, the shorter man, chuckled, still trying to catch his breath. "We don't mind. We're just happy that somebody from our club breaks records!"

"Amen to that," Jack agreed, smiling.

"All right, let's get to shooting," Billy Joe said, turning back to his truck. "Stay where you are, Jack. I'll bring your gun, too!"

He turned back toward the truck, rushing and still breathless. Meredith frowned. His cheeks were unnaturally pink, and it wasn't that cold. His complexion was almost white. He was sweating. She knew the symptoms. She'd seen them all too often.

"You might go with him," Meredith said abruptly, interrupting Jack's banter with Rey.

"Excuse me?" Jack asked.

Just at that moment, Billy Joe stopped, stood very still for a minute, and then buckled and fell forward into a crumpled heap at the door of his truck.

Meredith took off at a dead run. "Somebody get me a cell phone!" she called as she ran.

Leo fumbled his out of the holder on his belt and passed it to her as she knelt beside Billy Joe.

"Get his feet elevated. Find something to cover him with," she shot at the other men. She was dialing while she spoke. She loosened the man's shirt, propping the phone against her ear—the worst way to hold it, but there was no other way at the moment—and felt down Billy Joe's chest for his diaphragm. "Get his wallet and read me his weight and age from his driver's license," she added with a sharp glance in Leo's direction.

Leo dug out the wallet and started calling out information, while Rey and Jack stood beside the fallen man and watched with silent concern.

"I want the resident on duty in the emergency room, stat," she said. "This is Meredith Johns. I have a patient, sixty years of age, one hundred and eighty pounds, who collapsed without warning. Early signs indicate a possible myocardial infarction. Pulse is thready," she murmured, checking the second hand of her watch as she took his pulse with her fingertips, "forty beats a minute, breathing shallow and labored, grey complexion, profuse sweating. I need EMTs en route, I am initiating cardiopulmonary resuscitation now."

There was a long pause, and a male voice came over the line. With her voice calm and steady, Meredith gave the information again, and then handed the phone to Leo as she bent over the elderly man and did the spaced compressions over his breastbone, followed by mouth-to-mouth breathing.

Rey was watching, spellbound at her proficiency, at the

easy and quite professional manner in which she'd taken charge of a life-or-death emergency. Within five minutes, the ambulance was screaming up the graveled road that led to the Jacobsville Gun Club, and Billy Joe was holding his own.

The EMTs listened to Meredith's terse summary of events as they called the same resident Meredith had been talking to.

"Doc says to give you a pat on the back," the female EMT grinned at Meredith as they loaded Billy Joe onto the ambulance. "You sure knew what to do."

"Yes," Rey agreed, finding his tongue at last. "You've obviously had first-aid training."

He probably meant it as praise, but it hit Meredith in the gut. She glared at him. "What I've had," she emphasized, "is five years of college. I have a master's degree in nursing science, and I'm a card-carrying nurse practitioner!"

Seven

Rey stared at his new cook as if she'd suddenly sprouted feathers on her head. His summation of her abilities was suddenly smoke. She was someone he didn't even know. She was a health care professional, not a flighty cook, and certainly not the sort of woman to streetwalk as a sideline.

She nodded solemnly. "I figured it would come as a shock," she told him. She turned her attention back to the EMTs. "Thanks for being so prompt. Think he'll be okay?"

The female EMT smiled. "I think so. His heartbeat's stronger, his breathing is regular, and he's regaining consciousness. Good job!"

She grinned. "You, too."

They waved and took off, lights flashing, but without turning on the sirens.

"Why aren't the sirens going?" Rey wanted to know. "He's not out of danger yet, surely?"

"They don't like to run the sirens unless they have to,"

Meredith told him. "Some people actually run off the road and wreck their cars because the sirens rattle them. They use the lights, but they only turn on the sirens if they hit heavy traffic and have to force their way through it. Those EMTs," she added with a smile, "they're the real heroes and heroines. They do the hardest job of all."

"You saved Billy Joe's life," Jack said huskily, shaking her hand hard. "He's the best friend I got. Thank you."

She smiled gently and returned the handshake. "It goes with the job description. Don't try to keep up with the ambulance," she cautioned when he went toward Billy Joe's truck, which still had the key in the ignition. The two men had come together.

"I'll be careful," the older man promised.

"Whew!" Leo let out the breath he'd almost been holding, and put up his cell phone. "You're one cool lady under fire, Meredith."

She smiled sadly. "I've had to be," she replied. She glanced at Rey, who looked cold and angry as it occurred to him, belatedly, that she'd played him for a fool. "I can see what you're thinking, but I didn't actually lie to you. You never asked me exactly what I did for a living. Of course, you thought you already knew," she added with faint sarcasm.

He didn't reply. He gave her a long, contemptuous look and turned away. "I've lost my taste for practice," he said quietly. "I want to go on to the hospital and see about Billy Joe."

"Me, too," Leo added. "Meredith…?"

"I'll go along," she said. "I'd like to meet that resident I spoke with. He's very good."

Rey glanced toward her. "You'll get along. He keeps secrets, too," he said bitterly, and got behind the wheel.

Leo made a face at Meredith, opening the third door of the big double cabbed truck so that she could sit in back.

He put the gun cases in the boot, in a locked area, and climbed in beside Rey.

The resident turned out to be a former mercenary named Micah Steele. He was married to a local girl, and he'd gone back to school to finish his course of study for his medical license.

"I couldn't very well carry a wife and child around the jungles with me," Micah told her with a grin. He was tall and big, and not at all bad-looking. She could picture him with a rifle in one arm. But now, in a white lab coat with a stethoscope thrown carelessly around his neck, he seemed equally at home.

"When's Callie due?" Leo asked.

"Any minute," he said, tongue-in-cheek. "Can't you see me shaking? I'm the soul of self-confidence around here, but one little pregnant woman makes me a basket case!"

"Callie's quite a girl," Rey agreed, smiling at the big man.

Micah gave him a look. "Yes, and isn't it lucky for me that you hardly ever went into her boss Kemp's office for legal advice, while she was still single?"

Rey pursed his lips. "Kemp eats scorpions for breakfast, I hear. I like my lawyers less caustic."

"Last I heard, the local bar association had you down as a contagious plague and was warning its members to avoid you at all costs," Micah replied wickedly.

"I never hit any local lawyers." Rey looked uncomfortable. "It was that Victoria lawyer, Matherson," he muttered. "And I didn't even hit him that hard. Hell, he's lucky I wasn't sober at the time! Otherwise, he'd have had twice the number of stitches!"

Meredith listened to the repartee with wide, fascinated eyes, but Rey wouldn't meet her eyes and Micah, too, cleared his throat and didn't pursue the subject.

"Matherson took a client who accused us of assault,"

Leo volunteered. "Cag had hit him, several times, after he got drunk and assaulted Tess, who's now Cag's wife. But the bounder swore that he was the injured party, that we falsely accused him and all took turns pounding him. He convinced a jury to award him damages. Not a lot of money," Leo added solemnly, "but the principle was what set Rey off. He was in a bad mood already and he had a few too many drinks at Shea's Bar, out on the Victoria road. To make a long story short," he added with a chuckle, "Matherson was having a quiet beer when Rey accused him of handling the ex-employee's case for spite because he lost an argument with us over Tess when he was handling her inheritance. Matherson took exception to Rey's remarks, and the two of them set about wrecking the pretty stained-glass window that used to overlook the parking lot."

"Used to?" Meredith fished, sensing something ominous.

"Yes, well, Matherson made a rather large hole in it when Rey helped him into the parking lot the hard way," Leo concluded.

Micah Steele looked as if it was killing him not to burst out laughing.

"He," Leo jerked his thumb toward Steele, "had to remove quite a number of glass particles from Matherson's rear end. *And* we got sued again, for that!"

"But the jury, after hearing Kemp's masterful summation of our grievances," Rey interrupted, "decided that Matherson was only entitled to the cost of the repair job on his butt. Shea had insurance that replaced the stained-glass window with one of comparable age and exclusivity." Rey smiled smugly. "And the judge said that if she'd been sitting on the first case, the rat Matherson was representing would have gotten a jail sentence."

Leo chuckled. "Only because Kemp put Tess on the stand and had her testify about what really happened the night Matherson's client took her on a date. The jury felt that Rey was justifiably incensed by the former verdict.'' He glanced at Meredith wryly.

"Yes, but I understand that Shea's two bouncers meet Rey at the door these days and won't let him in if he's not smiling,'' Micah contributed.

Rey shrugged. "I never get drunk anymore. I've learned to handle aggression in a nonphysical manner.''

The other two men actually walked down the hall. Meredith noticed their shoulders vibrating.

Rey took a step toward Meredith, half irritated by the character assassination job his brother and Micah Steele had just done on him, and even more put out by Meredith's unmasking.

"You knew I had no idea about your education,'' Rey accused Meredith. "Why didn't you say something at the outset, when Leo first went to the hospital?'' he demanded in a low, deep tone. "I may have jumped to conclusions, but you provided the springs, didn't you?''

She grimaced. "I guess so. But it was only a little jump from telling you about my job to talking about the reason Daddy started drinking. It's…still very fresh in my mind,'' she added huskily. "It's only been six months. The memories are—'' she swallowed and looked away "—bad.''

Unexpectedly he reached out and caught her fingers in his, tugging her closer. The hall was deserted. In the background there were muted bell-tones and announcements and the sound of lunch trays being distributed. "Tell me,'' he said gently.

She bit her lower lip hard and lifted her tormented eyes to his curious ones. "Not…yet,'' she whispered tightly. "One day, but…not yet. I can't.''

"Okay,'' he said after a minute. "But I'd like to know how you learned to shoot.''

"My brother, Mike, taught me,'' she said reluctantly, staring at his broad chest. She wanted to lay her head on

it and cry out her pain. There hadn't been anyone to hold
her, not when it happened, not afterward. Her father with-
drew into his own mind and started drinking to excess at
once. Her job was all that had kept Meredith sane. She
hadn't been able to let out her grief in any normal way.

Rey's mind was working overtime. He stared down at
her, still holding her fingers entwined tightly with his own,
and he frowned as bits and pieces of memory began fitting
themselves together.

"Mike. Mike Johns." His eyes narrowed. "Our cousin
Colter's best friend, and one of Leo's acquaintances. He
was killed…!"

She tried to tug her fingers away. He wouldn't let her.
He pulled her into his arms, holding her there even when
she struggled. But a few seconds of resistance were all she
had. She laid her flushed cheek against his broad chest and
let the tears flow.

Rey's arms contracted roughly. He smoothed his hand
over her nape, caressing, soothing. "There was a bank robbery in Houston," he recalled quietly. "Mike was a cop.
He was at the bank with your mother. It was Saturday. He
was off duty, but he had his service revolver under his
jacket." His arms tightened as her sobs grew painful to
hear. "He drew and fired automatically, and one of the
robbers sprayed fire from one of those damned little automatic rifles in his general direction. He and your mother
died instantly…"

Meredith's fingers dug into his wide back. He rocked her,
barely aware of curious glances from passersby.

"Both men were caught. You don't kill a cop and get
away with it in Texas," he added softly. "They were ar-
raigned and treated to a speedy trial just a month ago. You
and your father testified. That was when your father really
went off the deep end, wasn't it, when he had to see the
autopsy photos…"

Micah and Leo came back down the hall, frowning when

they saw the condition Meredith was in. Even as they watched, her eyes rolled back and she would have fallen to the floor except for Rey's strong arms lifting her.

Later, she wouldn't recall much except that she was hustled into a cubicle and revived. But when she started sobbing hysterically, they'd given her a shot of something that put her out like a light. She came to back at the ranch, in her own little garage apartment.

She opened her eyes, and there was Rey, sitting by the bed, still wearing the same jeans and shirt and boots he'd worn to the shooting range. Meredith was aware of the bedspread covering her up to her waist. Her boots were off, but she was also wearing the same clothes she'd started out in that morning.

"What time is it?" she asked in a husky, slightly disoriented tone.

"Five hours past the time you flaked out on me," he said, smiling gently. "Micah knocked you out. He thought some sleep might help." The smile faded into quiet concern. "You don't sleep much, do you, Meredith?" he asked surprisingly.

She sighed, brushed back her disheveled blond hair, and shook her head. "When I go to sleep, I have nightmares. I wake up in a cold sweat, and I see them, lying there on the floor, just the way they looked in those vivid crime scene photos." She closed her eyes and shivered. "People look so fragile like that, they look like big dolls, sprawled in pitiful disarray on the floor. Everybody stares at them…"

He brushed back her hair with a lean, gentle hand. "They got the guys who did it," he reminded her. "Including the trigger man. He'll serve life without any hope of parole. He'll pay for it."

Her pale eyes were tormented as they met his. "Yes, but it won't bring them back, will it?" she asked. "And do you know why they said they did it? For a bet. For a stupid bet, they killed two innocent people!"

"They also ruined their own lives," he reminded her, "and the lives of their own families."

She looked at him blankly, scowling.

"Don't you ever think about that?" he asked softly. "Criminals have families, too. Most of them have loving, decent parents who took care of them and disciplined them and blame themselves for what their children do. It must be pure hell, to have your child kill someone, and feel responsible for it."

"I haven't considered that," she admitted.

He continued. "When I was in high school, one of my best friends was arrested for murder. He killed the old man next door in the process of stealing his wallet. He wanted to buy his girl a diamond necklace she liked, and he didn't have any money. He figured the man was old and didn't need money anyway, so he might as well take it. He was sorry about it, but he never figured on killing the man or getting caught."

"Was he a good friend?" she asked.

He looked at their linked fingers. He nodded. "We were pals since grammar school. He wasn't quite as bright as some of the other boys, but he had a gentle nature. Or so we thought." He met her eyes. "His mom and dad always had a houseful of other peoples' kids. They were everybody's mom and dad. It shattered them when Joey went to prison. Even the children of the old man felt sorry for them."

"Funny," she mused. "I never even thought of how it would feel to have a child or a parent or a sibling who broke the law in some terrible way." She met his eyes. "I guess I'd feel guilty, too."

"Most kids are raised right. But some of them have a wild streak that nobody can tame, others have poor impulse control. Many are handicapped. Nobody goes to jail because he wants to."

"I never thought of you as a sensitive man," she blurted out, and then flushed at the insult.

His eyebrows lifted. "Who, me? I stop to pick worms out of the highway so my tires won't bruise their little bodies, and you think I'm insensitive?"

It took a minute for the words to make sense, and then she burst out laughing.

"That's better," he said. He smiled and squeezed her fingers. "You're going to be okay. You've had a lot of traumatic experiences just lately. No wonder you caved in."

"Lucky for you," she shot back.

"Me? Why?"

"Because if we'd unpacked those shotguns, I'd have destroyed your ego," she said with a smug smile. "At Mike's gun club, they used to call me 'dead-eye.'"

"Oh, they did, did they?" he challenged. "Well, we'll see about that when you step up to my gun range."

She studied his lean face. He wasn't handsome, but he had strong, stubborn features. He was familiar to her now, almost necessary. She thought about going back to Houston with real panic.

He touched her cheek where the bruises were a mixture of purple and yellow, much less vivid now. "He really knocked you around," he said, and his face hardened visibly. "I don't care if a man is drunk, there's no excuse for hitting a woman."

"Shades of primitive man," she chided with a smile.

"Women are the cradles of life," he said simply. "What sort of man tries to break a cradle?"

"You have a unique way of putting things."

"We had Spanish ancestors," he told her. "They were old-world men, conquerors, adventurers. One of them made his way to Texas and was given a huge tract of land under a Spanish land grant, for services to the crown of Spain."

He noticed a start of surprise on her face. "Do you know the legend of the Cid?"

"Yes!" she exclaimed. "He was a great Spanish hero. Cid is for the Arabic 'Sidi' which means Lord."

"Well, our ancestor wasn't El Cid," he said on a chuckle. "But he fought his way through hostile neighbors to claim his land, and he held it as long as he lived. Our family still holds it, through our late uncle, who left us this ranch."

"This is the original grant?" she exclaimed.

He nodded. "It isn't nearly as big as it was a couple of hundred years ago, but it's no weekend farm, either. Didn't you notice the antique silver service in the dining room?"

"Yes, I've been afraid to touch it. It looks very old."

He smiled. "It came from Madrid. It's over two hundred years old."

"An heirloom!" she breathed.

"Yes. Like the ranch itself." He tilted his head and studied her for a long time. "Now I understand. Your father wasn't violent until the killer's trial, was he?"

"No, he wasn't." She looked down at Rey's big, warm hand wrapped around her own. It made her feel safe. "He told Mike to drive Mama to the bank," she added reluctantly. "He had papers to grade. He couldn't spare the time, he said, and he snapped at her when she protested that Mike was spending his day off, carting her all over Houston." She glanced at him. "I was called in to work at a clinic my boss holds in the Hispanic community every Saturday. There's a regular nurse, but she was at home with a sick child. I went to stand in for her." Her eyes fell to his broad chest. "I could have asked someone to go in my place. I didn't. So he and I both have our guilt."

"Because you lived and they didn't," Rey said bluntly.

She gasped. "No, that's not true!"

"It is true." His black eyes held hers relentlessly. "The same thing happens to people who survive airplane crashes,

automobile wrecks, sinking ships. It's a normal, human reaction to surviving when other people don't. It's worse
when the victims include close relatives or friends.''

"Where did you learn that?'' she asked.

"From Janie Brewster,'' he said.

She frowned. "That name sounds familiar.''

"We've mentioned her to you. She's the daughter of a
neighboring cattleman,'' he related. "She got her associate
degree in psychology from our community college, and
now she's studying it in Houston,'' he added with a grin.
"She's almost twenty. They let her take college courses
while she was still in high school, so she's ahead.''

"Oh.''

"She's not hard on the eyes, either,'' he murmured,
avoiding her eyes. "She and her father live alone. Leo and
I have a standing dinner invitation, any time we care to
show up.''

She started to say "oh'' again, and realized how juvenile
she was behaving. She straightened her shoulders against
the pillow that was propping her up, and tugged at the hand
Rey still held. "Then if she can bake biscuits, you're saved
when I leave, aren't you?'' she asked coolly.

"Well, she can't exactly bake stuff,'' Rey had to admit.

"Why?''

"She has no sense of time. She sets the timer and it goes
off, and she never hears it. So the chicken bounces, the
heat-and-serve rolls usually come out black, and I won't
even mention what happens to vegetables she tries to cook
on *top* of the stove.'' He gave her a sad look. "She did try
to make us a pan of biscuits once.'' He actually shuddered.

"Not a successful try?'' she fished.

"We had to take the damned things home, or her father
would never have let us near the Salers heifers he was
offering for sale.'' He glanced at her. "Leo just bought us
a big Salers bull, and we needed purebred heifers to breed
to him. Purebred breeding stock brings a big price, espe-

cially if you show cattle and win ribbons.'' He shrugged. ''So we took the biscuits home.''

''Did you eat them?'' she persisted.

He shook his head and he shuddered again.

''Then what did you do with them?'' she asked, thinking he probably fed them to the cattle dogs or some livestock.

''Well, actually, we took them out to the skeet field and used them for clay pigeons,'' he confessed with a grin. ''They were the best damned targets we ever had, but we didn't dare say where we got them!''

She put her face in her hands and burst out laughing. ''Oh, the poor girl!'' she chuckled.

''Don't worry, we'd never tell her,'' he promised. ''But we did ask her for another pan of biscuits, without telling her why.'' He sighed. ''That woman has a ready-made profession as a target maker, and we haven't got the guts to tell her so. Hell of a shame!''

She brushed at her eyes with the hem of her blouse. Poor Janie. And she'd been jealous.

''What does she look like?'' she asked, curious.

''She comes up to my shoulder. She's got light brown hair, longer than yours, and her eyes are green. If she didn't know everything, and tell you so every time you saw her, she might get married one day.''

''You don't want to marry her?'' she teased. ''Not even for an inexhaustible supply of skeet targets?''

''I don't want to marry anybody,'' he said bluntly, and he looked her straight in the eye when he said it. ''I love my freedom.''

She sighed and smiled. ''So do I,'' she confessed. ''I don't think I could ever settle for diapers and dishes. Not with my background.''

''You were a science major, weren't you?'' he asked abruptly.

''Yes. Chemistry and biology, genetics—stuff like that. I made good grades, but it was hard work. Then I went right to work for my boss, straight out of college. I need to be two people, just to catch up. I run my legs off. The stress is pretty bad sometimes.''

"No wonder keeping house and baking biscuits seemed like a holiday to you,'' he said to himself.

"It's been fun,'' she agreed. "I love to cook. I do it a lot, at home. I used to when Mama was alive,'' she recalled. "She hated housework and cooking. I came home from work and did it all.''

"I've read about the sort of work you do,'' he commented, recalling articles he'd seen in the daily newspaper. "You're second only to a physician in authority. The only thing you can't do is write a prescription without his supervision.''

"That's true.'' She smiled.

He studied her slender body, her exquisite figure nicely outlined by the garments she was wearing. "All those years, nothing but textbooks and exams and, then, a hectic career. No men?'' he added, with a calculating stare.

"I dated,'' she replied. "I just couldn't afford to get serious about anybody. My father scraped and begged and borrowed to get the money to finance my nursing education,'' she told him. "Even Mike...contributed to it.'' She drew in a steadying breath and locked her fingers together on her lap. "It would have been so petty of me to throw all that up, just so I could go to parties and get drunk with the other students.''

"Surely there wasn't much of that, at a community college?''

She laughed. "You'd be surprised. There was all too much, for my taste. But I didn't live on campus. I lived at home and commuted.'' She met his searching gaze. "That party I was at, when Leo was attacked—the woman who gave it was a college classmate who works for a doctor in our practice. I knew she sort of had a reputation. I guess I should have realized how wild things would get, but I was so depressed that I let her pressure me into going to the party. It was a mistake."

"A lucky mistake, for my brother," Rey said gently. "He might have been killed, if you hadn't come along when you did." He scowled. "You said, you ran at the attackers, waving your arms."

She nodded. "Mike taught me about shock tactics," she said sadly. "I was afraid it wouldn't work, but I had no weapon, no other way of stopping them. So I took the risk."

"I'm grateful that you did." He shook his head slowly. "But it was an act of lunacy, Meredith. You could have been lying on the grass next to Leo."

"But I wasn't." She hunched her shoulders as if she felt a chill. "I think there might be a force behind every single chain of events," she said thoughtfully. "I don't believe in chaos," she elaborated. "The body is such a messy, beautiful miracle. A single cell has chemical processes that are so complex, so meticulously crafted, that I can't believe life is an accident. If it isn't accidental, it has to be planned." She shrugged. "That's simple logic. That's why I don't think God is a myth."

They were silent for a moment. "You're the most intriguing woman I've ever met," he murmured, and his dark eyes fell to her soft, full mouth.

"Surely not?" she asked demurely. "I don't have any secrets left."

"That's what you think," he said in a soft, low tone.

She looked up and he moved toward her, one hand catching the wooden headboard as he levered his hard mouth down against her soft one.

Her hands instinctively went to his chest, but its muscular warmth was fascinating. She'd never done anything really intimate with her infrequent dates, having been completely turned off by men with fast reputations. She preferred gentlemen to rounders. She knew that Rey had been a rounder. She wanted to draw away. She really did.

But Rey Hart was completely out of her experience. He wasn't aggressive and insistent, as one of Meredith's rare dates had been. He didn't rush at her. He didn't insist. He wasn't insulting with the speed of his advances. He simply bent and kissed her, slowly and gently, with nothing more intimate than his hard, tender lips touching hers. He nibbled her upper lip and lifted his mouth slowly.

"You're doing a surfboard imitation," he murmured. "There's no need. I'm too good a cattleman to rush my fences."

She was trying to understand the slow, sensuous speech when his lips came down on hers again and caressed her upper lip. Her hands pressed flat against his muscular chest. She liked the way he felt. She could feel the quick, strong pulse of his heart under her palms. She could feel the growing rise and fall of his breathing.

His teeth nibbled her lips again, tenderly, and she found her hands moving under his arms and around him. She wanted to be held close, tight. She wanted him to envelop her against him. She wanted something more than this torturous teasing of his mouth on hers.

She made a husky, high-pitched little cry into his mouth and her nails bit into the solid muscles of his back.

"What do you want?" he whispered just above her lips.

"Kiss me," she moaned huskily.

"Kisses are dangerous, didn't you know?" he murmured, smiling against her responsive mouth. "They can be very addictive."

She was following his lips mindlessly. Her body was on fire. She'd never felt such headlong desire. Belatedly she realized that his hands were at her rib cage. Whether by accident or design, they were moving slowly up and down, up and down, so that his long fingers just lightly brushed the underswell of her breasts. It was extremely provocative. It was arousing.

She caught her breath as they moved ever closer to entrapment, and her eyes locked into his.

"Don't you like it this way?" he asked at her lips, brushing his mouth against them.

"Like…it?" she murmured mindlessly. Her body was reaching up toward those tormenting hands. She was shivering with every pulsating motion of her body, trembling with new and exciting surges of pleasure.

He laughed softly, sensuously. "Never mind." He lifted a hand to her hair and tugged out the hairpins, so that her beautiful long hair fell down around her shoulders. He tugged aside the top she was wearing, so that her shoulder was bare. Then he bent to it with his mouth, and she felt the warm, moist press of his lips right in the hollow of her shoulder.

Her nails dug into him. She lifted toward his mouth with a hoarse moan as she felt the slow tracing of his tongue against skin that had never known a man's touch. She was on fire. She was going to go up in flames right here. She didn't want to think, see, hear anything. She only wanted Rey to keep on touching her, to keep on holding her, to never, never stop…!

Eight

Just when the world was spinning away in a warm, plea-surable oblivion, the sound of loud, urgent footsteps echoed down the hall and brought Rey upright.

He looked at her with narrow, blank eyes as the sound grew louder. He cursed under his breath and got to his feet, keeping his back to her as he moved to the window, gripped the curtains and stared out at the pasture beyond.

Meredith dragged the bedspread up under her arms, over her clothes, and tried to steady her breathing. When she remembered what she and Rey had been doing, she blushed.

The door, ajar, was pushed completely open, and Leo came in with a tray. On it were a china cup and saucer, with a silver coffeepot, a silver cream and sugar service and a napkin and spoon. On a china plate were some dainty little chicken salad sandwiches.

"I thought you might be hungry," Leo said with a gentle smile as he put the tray on her lap. It had legs, so it would stand alone over her lap. "Mrs. Lewis came over to fix supper, and I had her make you these."

"Thank you!" she exclaimed. "And thank Mrs. Lewis, too. I was just starting to feel empty!"

Rey made an odd sound and she reached for a tiny sandwich very quickly, not daring to glance at him after the enthusiastic and unwise remark she'd just made.

Leo turned his eyes toward his brother. "Something wrong with you?" he asked curiously.

"Stomach cramp," Rey said without turning. "I had chili and salsa for lunch. Heartburn's killing me!"

"You should go and take an antacid tablet," Leo advised. "And drink some milk."

"I guess I'd better." Rey took a long breath and turned around, feeling more normal, finally. He glanced at Meredith. "I'm glad you're okay."

"I'll be fine. Thanks for the conversation," she said, and wouldn't meet his eyes. But she smiled shyly.

He just looked at her. Suddenly his dark eyes began to burn. He studied her intently, as if something had just happened that shocked him.

"Are you all right?" she asked impulsively.

He took a slow breath. He was still staring at her, to his brother's covert amusement. With her hair around her shoulders like that, sitting up in bed, smiling at him, he felt as if his whole life had just shifted five degrees. She was uncommonly pretty with her hair down. She had a warm, kind heart. She'd put her life on the line for a total stranger. Why hadn't that occurred to him in Houston, when they first told him that she'd saved his brother from attackers?

"Leo probably owes you his life," Rey said carefully. "But it bothers me that you risked your own to save him."

"Wouldn't you have done that same thing, even for a total stranger?" she mused.

He hesitated. "Yes," he said after deliberating for a few seconds. "I suppose I would have."

"See? You have all sorts of potential as a prospective husband," she added with a wicked smile, which got wider when he reacted. "You're sexy, you're rich, you drive a nice car, and besides all that, you like animals." She began nodding her head. "Definite potential."

His high cheekbones flushed and he glared at her. "I don't want to get married."

"Don't worry about it," she said soothingly. "It's perfectly natural for a bachelor to resist matrimony. But you'll come around." She wiggled both eyebrows. "If you get me a ring, I'll let you see my collection of used chewing gum wrappers and bottle caps."

He was still glaring.

Leo chuckled. "I'd love to see your used chewing gum wrappers, Meredith," he said enthusiastically. "In fact, I may start collecting right now!"

Rey stared a hole through his brother while, inside him, something froze.

"I'll even consider marrying you," Leo added wickedly.

She laughed, not taking him seriously. "Sorry. It's Rey or nobody. My heart's set on him." She frowned. "Pity I couldn't trade you something for him," she murmured to Leo.

Rey was getting angrier by the second, and uncomfortable at the idea that Leo was trying to cut him out.

"Make me an offer," Leo told her. "But he can't cook, and he has a temper worse than a sunburned rattler. Besides that, you can't domesticate him. He wears his spurs to the dinner table."

"So do you!" Rey accused.

"I sit more daintily than you do," Leo said imperturbably.

Rey rammed his hands into the pockets of his jeans and glared at Meredith again. "You can't give people away."

"I'm not trying to give you away," Leo said calmly. "I

want to make a profit.'' He scowled suddenly and his eyes
widened as he looked at his brother's boots.

Meredith was staring at them, too. She pursed her lips
and exchanged a look with Leo.

Rey glared back at them belligerently. ''What?'' he demanded hotly.

Both Leo's eyebrows went up, along with both hands,
palms out. ''I didn't say a word!''

''Neither did I,'' Meredith assured him.

Rey looked from one to the other and finally looked
down. There, on one of his feet, was a dainty little foot
sock with a tassel on it, covering the steel toe of his brown
cowboy boot. He'd unknowingly picked it up under Meredith's bed while he was kissing her.

Rey jerked it off, cursed royally, shot a furious glance at
Meredith and his brother, who were trying valiantly not to
look at him, and stomped out.

Helpless laughter erupted from the two people left in
Meredith's room, and the sound of it infuriated Rey.

Leo was obviously ready to set up shop with their recently disclosed nurse, and Rey didn't like it. Leo was the
plague of housekeepers everywhere, but he was also easier
on the eyes than the other brothers, and he was charming.
Rey had never learned how to use charm. He always looked
uncomfortable when he smiled. Especially with women like
Meredith, who was painfully shy and naive. He wasn't used
to such women. But what made it so much worse was the
dropping sensation in his stomach that he'd experienced
when he'd stared at Meredith. He hadn't had anything like
that since Carlie, who made his pulse race almost as fast
as Meredith did when he kissed her.

He could still taste Meredith on his mouth. She didn't
know much, but she made up for her lack of knowledge
with enthusiasm and curiosity. He thought about carrying
the lessons much farther, about baring her to the waist. His
heart began to slam into his throat as he tried to imagine

what she looked like under her blouse. He already knew that the skin of her shoulder was warm and soft, like silk. He remembered her husky moan when he'd kissed her there, the way her fingers had bitten into his back like little sharp pegs.

He'd been away from women for a long time, but he still knew what to do with one, and his imagination was working overtime just now. Meredith had attracted him when she was just his cook. Now that he knew about the intelligent, capable woman underneath the flighty camouflage, he was fascinated with her. She was everything a man could wish for.

Not that she wanted him, oh, no. She'd made it plain. But that teasing speech about marriage had unnerved him. His freedom was like a religion. He didn't want to get married. Of course he didn't!

But it was natural to think of Meredith with children. He could picture her baking biscuits for him every morning and holding a child in her arms at night while they watched television. He could picture her playing catch with a little boy out in back, or picking wildflowers with a little girl at her skirts. She was kind and sweet. She'd make a wonderful mother.

There was her job, of course. He knew something about her profession, that it was supposed to be high pressure. She'd be called upon to make life and death decisions, to comfort the sick and grieving, to make herself involved in the daily lives of her patients so that she should counsel them on how to maintain good health. Besides all that, she had a college degree.

Rey was college educated, too, with a degree in management and a minor in marketing. He was the mind behind the business decisions, the coordinator of the labor pool, and the director of marketing for the brothers' cattle co-operative. He was good at what he did. He enjoyed conversations with other educated people, and he'd convinced himself that Meredith wouldn't know Degas from Dali, Domingo from Dwight Yoakum, Hemingway from Dr. Seuss. Now he knew better, and his respect for her increased.

She'd saved Billy Joe's life at the gun club. He recalled that she must have known what to do for Leo as well, when she'd found him after he was mugged. Leo really did owe her his life. She was competent, confident, and she wasn't hard on the eyes, either. She had wonderful qualities.

But he didn't want to marry her. He wasn't sure about Leo. His eyes narrowed as he recalled the way Leo conspired with her. Leo had known all about her already. Obviously they'd been talking together since her arrival at the ranch, because Leo hadn't been a bit surprised when she rushed over to manage Billy Joe's heart attack.

Why hadn't he noticed that? Leo had called for Meredith when he was in the hospital. He was obviously fond of her. Maybe he was interested in her romantically, too. He'd been interested in Tess, before Cag had walked off with her, but Tess hadn't realized it. Or if she had, she'd ignored it. Leo wasn't hard on the eyes, either, and when it came to charm, he had his share and Rey's as well.

As he walked down to the barn to talk to one of his men, Rey had a terrible premonition that Leo had been serious when he joked about being willing to marry Meredith. Would she be desperate enough, lonely enough, frightened enough, to marry Leo and give up her job and living with her father? Her father had beaten her badly. She might be looking for a way out of the torment, and there was Leo, successful and handsome and charming, just ready to take her in and protect her.

Rey felt himself choke on dread. He couldn't imagine living in a house with Meredith if she was married to his brother. He'd rather throw himself headfirst into a cement mixer!

But, then, Leo had been teasing. Leo was always teasing. Rey forced himself to breathe normally and at least give the appearance of someone who was relaxed. Sure, it was just a joke. He didn't have to worry about the competition. There wasn't any. He pulled his hat lower over his eyes and walked on down the aisle to the man who was doctoring a heifer.

Several days later, Meredith received a huge bouquet of assorted roses from Billy Joe, now out of the hospital and back on the shooting range. She put them in water in the kitchen, along with the card, which the brothers blatantly read.

"He'd marry you," Rey drawled with pure acid in his tone as he dragged out a chair and sat down to lunch. "He's been widowed twenty years."

Meredith gave Leo a mischievous glance and fiddled with putting biscuits in a linen-lined basket. "He's not bad-looking for a man his age, and it wouldn't hurt him to have a nurse under his roof." She glanced at Rey's eloquent back. "But can he cook?"

Rey sipped coffee noisily.

"And does he slurp his coffee?" she added without missing a beat.

"That was done deliberately, to show you that I don't give a damn about manners!" Rey growled.

"All right, just don't expect me to take you to any nice restaurants while we're courting," she said easily, setting the basket of biscuits on the table.

"Lady, you aren't taking me as far as the mailbox," he said curtly.

He looked ferocious. That black temper was already kindling. Meredith studied his bent head curiously. You never knew about men. She'd seen some very mild-mannered ones come to the emergency room with wives who'd been beaten within an inch of their lives. It didn't hurt to see how far a man would go when he got mad. Especially after her experience with her father.

"You'll have to learn to scrape the mud off those enormous boots, too," she went on in a conversational tone. "And not slurp your soup. Your hair could use a good trim…"

"Damn it!"

He shot to his feet, eyes blazing in a rigid face, with a dusky flush creeping along his high cheekbones with all the warning color of a poisonous reptile.

Meredith stood her ground, watching him clench those big fists at his side.

"Rey," Leo cautioned abruptly, and started to get to his feet.

Meredith went right up to Rey, looking him in the eyes, quiet, still—waiting.

Rey was breathing through his nostrils. His jaw was clenched with fury. But intelligence won easily over bad temper. His chin raised slowly. "You're testing me," he said out of the blue. "You want to know if I'll hit you."

"It's something a woman needs to know about a man," she said very quietly. "And she needs to find it out where she can get help if she needs it." She didn't look at Leo, but Rey knew that was what she meant. She smiled gently. "No, you don't hit," she said in a soft, quizzical tone. "You do have a temper, but it's not a physical one."

He was still breathing through his nose. "If you were a man, it might be," he told her bluntly.

"But I'm not a man," she replied.

Her eyes were almost glowing with feeling. He got lost in those soft, warm, grey eyes. He hated the way he felt when he was near her. He'd been fighting it ever since he carried her up to her garage apartment after she'd fainted at the hospital. He liked the feel of her in his arms. He liked kissing her. He liked the way she picked at him and teased him. No woman had ever done that before. As his older brothers had been before they married, he was taciturn and uncommunicative most of the time. His very attitude put most women off.

It didn't put Meredith off. She wasn't afraid of his temper, either. She made him into a different person. It wasn't something he could easily explain. He felt comfortable with her, even while she was stirring him to passion. He could imagine just sitting in front of the television with her and holding hands, late at night.

The image intimidated him. He sat back down, ignoring Meredith, and started putting butter and strawberry preserves on four biscuits.

Leo gave him a measuring look. "Don't eat all the biscuits."

"I'm only getting my share. She," he jerked his thumb towards Meredith, "didn't make but eight this morning. That's one for her, four for me, and three for you."

"And why do you get four?" Leo asked belligerently.

"Because she proposed to me," he said with pure smug arrogance, and a look that made Leo's teeth snap together.

"I did not," Meredith said haughtily, sitting down across from him. "I said I was thinking of you as a marriage prospect, not that I actually wanted to go through with a ceremony." She cleared her throat. "I'll have to see how you work out."

Rey smiled faintly. "That sounds interesting."

He didn't necessarily mean what it sounded like he meant. She mustn't jump to any conclusions here. But her cheeks were getting very rosy.

He noticed that. It was a devilish game they were playing, and he could do it better. He stared pointedly at her soft mouth as he put a cube of fresh pear into his mouth, slowly and deliberately.

She felt very uncomfortable in odd places when he did that. She ate her beef and gravy and tried to ignore him.

"I like having fresh fruit," Rey said with a slow smile.

He speared a grape with his fork and eased it slowly between his lips.

She moved restlessly in her chair. "It's healthy stuff."

"No wonder you were trying to get us to eat right," Leo said, trying to break the growing spell Rey was casting on her. "You teach nutrition, I suppose."

"In a way. I'm supposed to counsel patients on changing bad habits and making lifestyle changes when they're warranted," she explained. If only her hand didn't shake while she was holding the stupid fork. Rey saw it and knew why, and she hated that damned smug smile on his lean face!

He picked up a piece of perfectly cooked asparagus spear and slowly sucked it into his mouth, using his tongue meaningfully.

"I have to fix dessert," Meredith choked, jumping to her feet so quickly that she knocked her chair winding and had to right it.

"I saw that chair jump right out and trip you, Meredith," Rey commented dryly. "You ought to hit it with a stick."

"I ought to hit *you* with a stick instead!" she raged at him, flushed and flustered and out of patience.

"Me?" Both eyebrows arched. "What did I do?"

She pictured hitting him across the jaw with the biggest frying pan she had. It was very satisfying. Pity she couldn't do it for real.

She went to the cupboard and drew out the ingredients for an instant reduced fat pudding. She had some low-fat whipped cream in the freezer that she could top it with. Meanwhile, Rey would finish his meal and stop using fruits and vegetables to torment her with. She could have kicked him.

Behind her, Rey was talking comfortably to Leo about some new equipment they were ordering, and about routine chores that had to be completed before Thanksgiving this month and the Christmas holidays next month. Most of the ranch hands would have Thanksgiving, the day after, and that weekend free. Next month, they'd have Christmas Eve and Christmas Day free, along with four days before or after, depending on the schedule. Some of the men had families in far-flung locations and they had to travel a distance for the holidays. The Harts made a practice of giving the men time off to go home during the holiday season by staggering work schedules, so that there was an adequate crew here to work when days off were assigned.

Then they moved on, naturally, to a discussion about Thanksgiving dinner.

"You're going to stay until after Thanksgiving, aren't you?" Rey asked Meredith.

She had her back to them. "Yes, I'd like to," she said, because she'd already been planning special menus and light, noncaloric desserts for it. "Unless you're planning to go away for it," she added quickly.

"The family has a Christmas party, when we all get together. We sort of save Thanksgiving for just us, so the others can have the day with their wives and kids," Leo told her. "It's been sort of hit and miss since Mrs. Lewis has been plagued with arthritis. As you know, we got her to come back to work just briefly, but her hands won't hold out to make bread and do any scrubbing with them, despite medicine. She has her children up from Corpus Christi for the holidays and cooks for them. We sort of got leftovers."

She grimaced. "Well, I'll make sure you have a big Thanksgiving dinner this year," she said gently. "With all the trimmings. Including biscuits," she added when they both looked her way.

She finished whipping the pudding, and put it in bowls in the refrigerator to chill before she sat back down. "That will make us a nice dessert tonight," she commented. "I don't suppose you want it any sooner?"

They shook their heads. "I've got a meeting with our marketing staff in half an hour," Rey said, checking his multifunction watch.

"And I've got to go over the new equipment list with our mechanic and see if we've got everything ready to order," Leo added.

"How about a nice Greek salad for supper?" Meredith asked. "I make it with Feta cheese and black olives and eggs. I bought the ingredients yesterday at the store. Except for the eggs, of course. I'll get those out of the henhouse."

"Sounds nice," Leo said with a grin.

"Watch where you put your hands," Rey murmured without looking right at her. "I haven't seen my pet snake in the barn lately."

She gave him a cold look. "If I see him, I'll get him on a stick and put him right back in the barn," she said with pure bravado.

Rey glanced at her with dancing dark eyes. "I'd pay real money to see you do that," he chided.

So would I, she thought, but she didn't say it. She just smiled smugly.

The brothers finished their last swallows of coffee and went out the door still talking business.

Later, Meredith went out to the henhouse to gather the eggs, with her straw basket on her arm. Rey had unnerved her with his comment about the damned snake. Now she was sure it was in there, waiting for a gullible victim to frighten.

She took a deep breath and walked carefully into the dim confines of the henhouse. She bit her lower lip and approached the nest slowly. She stopped dead. There was actually a snake in there. He was wrapped around the eggs. He was licking his snaky lips.

She shivered with fear, but she wasn't going to let the stupid thing make her a laughingstock twice.

She saw a long, thick stick on the straw-covered floor. She put her basket down, still watching the snake, and picked up the stick.

"It's okay, old fellow," she said to the snake. "It's okay.

I'm just going to ease you out of the nest. Don't get mad, now. I won't hurt you. It's okay.''

While she was talking, softly, she eased the stick under its coils and very carefully lifted it. It was very still, not moving its head except to hiss. So far, so good. She had it up on the stick. It was heavy.

As she pulled it out of the nest, she noticed that it was really quite long. It really didn't look much like that black and white one Rey had put in the barn. This one had a pretty brown pattern on its back and had a white underbelly. But, then, it wasn't striking at her or anything, so she wasn't worried.

She held it far out in front of her and stepped carefully out of the henhouse into the bright light. As she did, the snake hung from the stick, looking rather bored by the whole thing.

She carried it through the yard and out toward the barn. One of the men was standing by a truck, watching her progress. His jaw fell. She wondered what was wrong with him. Maybe he'd never seen a woman carry a snake around before.

''Nice day,'' she called to him.

He didn't answer. She shrugged and kept walking.

The barn was empty, except for the bales of hay that were stacked neatly on the bottom and the loft of the huge structure. Over against one wall there was a corn crib with stacks and stacks of dried corn, and a machine that shelled them.

''Here we go, old fellow,'' she told the snake. She eased him over the wooden box and slid him down into the piles of unshelled corn.

He drew back in a threatening pose and hissed at her again.

Odd, the shape of his head, she thought, frowning as she studied him. It looked like an arrowhead. That other snake's head had been rounded.

Well, it might be some other species of king snake, she supposed. Weren't there several?

She walked back out of the barn into the daylight, whistling softly to herself as she started back to the henhouse. She was so proud of herself. She'd gotten the snake on the stick all by herself, without screaming once, and she'd carried him all the way to the barn and put him in the corn crib. She wasn't afraid of the snake anymore. As Rey had said, they were beneficial. It wasn't right to kill something just because you were afraid of it, she told herself.

The man who'd been standing by the truck was nowhere in sight, but the truck was still running and the driver's door was standing wide-open. She wondered where the driver had gone. He must have been in a hurry for some reason.

Meredith went back to the henhouse, put the stick down, picked up her basket and went to gather eggs. There were no more snakes, but there were plenty of eggs. She could boil several to go in her nice Greek salad. The spinach she'd bought to make it with was crisp and cold and almost blemishless. The brothers would love a salad if it had enough eggs and cheese and dressing.

She got the last egg into the basket and walked back out again, pausing to reach down and pet one of the big red hens who came right up to her and cocked its head curiously toward her face.

"Aren't you a pretty girl?" she said, smiling. She liked the way the chicken felt. Its feathers were very smooth and silky, and the chicken made the sweetest little noises when she petted it. She'd never been around farm creatures. She found that she enjoyed the chickens and the cattle dogs and the endless cats that hung around outside begging for handouts.

Two other hens came up to her, curious about the tall creature in jeans and tank top. She petted them, too, laughing as they crowded close. But then one started to peck the eggs, and she stood up again.

She turned back toward the house, her mind on the snake and her bravery. She'd have to remember to tell Rey and Leo about it…

"Meredith!"

The loud, urgent deep voice sent her spinning around. Rey was running toward her, bare-headed, with the cowhand who'd been next to the running pickup truck at his heels.

"Hi, Rey," she said hesitantly. "What's wrong?"

He stopped just in front of her. He caught her a little roughly by the arms and took the basket away from her, setting it aside, while he looked at every inch of her bare arms and hands. He was breathing rapidly. He seemed unnaturally pale and tight-lipped.

"It didn't bite you?" he demanded.

"What?"

"The snake! It didn't bite you?" he snapped.

"No, of course not," she stammered. "I just got it on a stick, like you did, and put it in the corn crib."

"Get my Winchester," Rey told the other man in a harsh tone. "Load it and bring it back here. Hurry!"

"I don't understand," Meredith said with noticeable confusion. "What's wrong with you? Why do you need a gun?"

"Oh, baby," he whispered hoarsely. He pulled her against him and bent to kiss her in view of the whole outfit, his mouth hard and rough against hers. "Baby!"

She had no idea what was wrong, but she loved the faint tremor in his hard arms as they crushed her against his body. And she loved the way he was kissing her, as if he couldn't get enough of her mouth. He'd called her "baby…"

She held on and moaned under the crush of his lips.

He drew back. "I'm sorry. It was such a shock. I was

scared out of my wits, I didn't even stop to grab my hat when Whit came into the office…!''

Her mouth was pleasantly swollen. She looked up at him dreamily and smiled.

"You don't have a clue, do you?" he asked huskily, searching her soft grey eyes.

"Mmm. About what?" she murmured, only half hearing him.

The other man came out with a rifle. He handed it to Rey. "Safety's on," the man advised.

"Thanks, Whit."

He moved back from Meredith. "I'll go kill it."

"Kill it?" Meredith exclaimed. "You can't! It will eat the rats, it's harmless…!''

"Sweetheart," he said very gently, "you were carrying a copperhead moccasin."

"Yes?" She stared at him blankly.

"It's one of the most poisonous snakes in Texas!"

She stood looking after him with her mouth open and her heartbeat choking her. She'd been carrying the damned thing on a stick, with it hissing at her. She felt the blood leave her head. Seconds later, she was lying on the hard ground. Fortunately she missed the basket of eggs on the way down.

Nine

"**Y**ou're making a habit of this lately," Rey murmured as he carried Meredith up the stairs to the garage apartment. "I never figured you for a fainter, Meredith," he added dryly.

He was still bare-headed, but he wasn't grim now. He was smiling.

"Of course I fainted! I picked up a poisonous snake!" she gasped, still in shock.

"Well, you've got guts, woman, I'll give you that," he said with a slow smile, shifting her a little closer. "Picked up a poisonous snake with a stick and carried it all the way to the barn, and it didn't bite you. Now I've heard everything."

"It did hiss a little," she recalled, shivering.

"It had eaten three eggs," he murmured. "Probably it was too busy digesting to care where it went at the time. Lucky for you."

She laid her cheek against his broad, strong shoulder and

held on tight. She had a sudden thought. "It didn't bite you?" she asked worriedly.

"It didn't get the chance. Didn't you hear the shot? I got it as it was crawling down from the corn bin onto the floor." He chuckled. "If I hadn't gotten it, though, Bandit would have. King snakes are natural enemies of any poisonous snake. They eat them. I hate to kill even a copperhead, but we can't have poisonous snakes around the livestock, or the men. Or, especially," he added with a warm glance at her, "in the henhouse. At the very least, a bite from one can put a man in the hospital."

She shivered, and her arms tightened around Rey's neck. "I was so proud of myself," she murmured. "I had no idea I was taking my life in my hands. It didn't look exactly like the other snake, but the patterns were sort of similar. I know about snake bites because I've helped treat them, but I don't know one snake from another unless I see pictures of them!" she added defensively.

"You'll learn." He kissed her forehead with breathless tenderness. "My brave girl," he whispered. "You'll never know how scared I was when Whit came running to tell me what you were doing."

It made soft little ripples of pleasure run through her body when he said that. He was being protective about her. She closed her eyes and drank in the warm nearness of him, the easy strength of his arms as he carried her. She felt safe as she'd never felt in her whole life. It was nice to lean on somebody strong, just for a little while.

He felt the vulnerability. He told himself that he wouldn't take advantage of it, but who was he kidding? She was soft and cuddly like this, and it was almost an involuntary action when his mouth slowly moved over hers as he reached her door.

The pressure was light, comforting. She sighed under the warmth and delight of it, and her lips parted, just the least little bit.

His whole body contracted with desire at that faint response. He looked down into her half-closed, misty eyes with growing hunger.

The look was as new as the tenderness. She couldn't tear her eyes away from that dark hunger in his. She forgot the snake, the scare, the people outside in the yard, everything. He bent back to her, and she met his mouth hungrily with her own, her arms clinging fiercely to his shoulders.

He groaned aloud. It was too soon, but he didn't care. He managed to open the door and close it behind them, making a beeline for the neatly made-up bed. He barely took time to put her down on the coverlet before his body slid against and over her own, his arms under her, taking his weight while his mouth made new, insistent demands on her innocence.

He lifted his head a torturous few seconds later, and his eyes blazed into her own. One lean hand slid deliberately under the hem of her tank top. At the same time, one long, powerful leg eased between both of hers and his hard mouth began to tease around the corners of hers.

"Danger will do it every time," he murmured deeply.

"Will...do what?" she asked, burning with new longings as his hand began to move up her rib cage toward the lacy little bra she was wearing under the top.

"This." His mouth opened on hers and became quickly insistent. While he kissed her, his fingers found the catch on her bra and flicked it open. She jumped when she felt his hand on flesh that had never known a man's touch before. He lifted his head and looked into her eyes. "I know. It's new territory," he said gently. His fingers stroked the delicate, warm flesh as lightly as a breeze. "Try to think of it as a rite of passage."

She felt strange new sensations. There was a tightening, a swelling, in her breasts as he touched them. She lifted involuntarily, and her eyes mirrored her surprise.

"Innocence is a rare, rare thing these days," he said at

her lips. "I respect it. And you'd better thank your lucky stars that I do," he added as his mouth bit hungrily at hers. "Because with an experienced woman, I'd lock the door and I wouldn't hesitate a minute."

She felt the words like the caress of his hands on her body. She moaned huskily under the demanding crush of his mouth. She felt his tongue tracing her lips, teasing under them, darting and touching and withdrawing. She felt his teeth, too, in a sensual caress that only intensified the new sensations he was teaching her to feel.

She felt her back arch again as he traced around the curves of her breast without ever touching the hard, taut nipple. She wanted him to touch it. Her body ached to have him touch it. She didn't understand why it should be such a violent, aching need...!

He laughed in a soft, sexy way against her lips. "Is this what you want?"

He caught the nipple between his thumb and forefinger and she lifted off the bed with a sharp cry. Heat spread over her, through her. Her short nails dug into his back fiercely and she gasped with pleasure.

"Baby," he groaned roughly, aroused by her unexpectedly ardent response. "Baby, you turn me on so hard...!"

The top was suddenly around her collarbone and his mouth—his mouth!—was right on her nipple, suckling her while his tongue tasted the hardness with a subtle caress that made her shiver. Her hands caught in the thick strands of his dark hair and held him to her body while he explored it with his mouth. She'd never imagined that she was capable of so much passion, and so unexpectedly swift. He could do anything to her, and she didn't have the willpower to stop him. Even a simple "no" was beyond her now. She wanted more. She wanted his eyes on her, his hands on her. She wanted his body closer.

As if he knew that, both lean hands smoothed up from her waist and onto her soft breasts. His fingers were rough from hard work, but their touch was pure heaven. She caressed his nape, moving rhythmically with each slow brush of his fingers, lost in pleasure.

He lifted his head to look at what he'd uncovered. She was beautiful, not too big or too small. She was just right. He loved the way her body moved when he touched it. He loved knowing how innocent she was. He'd never been with an innocent. Making love to one was a whole new experience, with levels of pleasure he'd never tasted. Her soft little moans excited him as much as those enthusiastic fingers caressing his back.

She felt his eyes and she opened hers, looking up at him. "Am I doing it right?" she whispered breathlessly.

His body tautened even more. "Yes," he whispered. "Just right."

He bent and drew his mouth gently over hers with a soft, cherishing pressure. He felt it open under his, felt her arms pulling at him. It wasn't a good idea to let this go any farther than it already had. While he was thinking it, he was moving slowly between her long legs until his body rested in the fork of hers. He eased down against her, letting her feel the slow burgeoning of his body against her belly.

She caught her breath.

He heard it, and lifted his head. His eyes were smoldering with desire, his body was rigid with it. He was getting little surges of insistent pleasure that ran the length of his spine. Her hips moved as if they were responding helplessly to the touch of him. She was making him ache like hell.

His hand moved to her hip and bit into the soft flesh, stilling the faint motion of her hips instantly while he rested on the elbow of his other arm. "Meredith," he said softly. "That will get you seduced. Right now."

She felt hot all over. Her mind seemed barely under her control. She searched his dark eyes with wonder. Her hands were against his shirt, right on the buttons. She felt him against the lower part of her body, and it felt right. It felt wonderful. She wanted to writhe under him and tempt him into intimacy.

His hand contracted and he gave her a wise, challenging stare as he read the look on her face. "Don't do it," he said huskily. "I'm years ahead of you in experience, but I can still lose my head. You don't want me to do that. Not really."

She pulled at a stabilizing breath. Her heart was still whacking around at the walls of her chest, as if she'd been running a race. "Are you sure I don't want you to do that? I mean, if you get pregnant, I'll marry you," she said breathlessly, and with deathbed humor. "Honest!"

He looked at her as if he couldn't believe his ears. The passion drained out of him, replaced by howling amusement. He started laughing. "Damn you, that wasn't fair!" he accused.

"Well, I like that! You're laughing, and here I've made you a solemn promise," she persisted, eyes twinkling.

"Hell!" He rolled away from her and sat up on the edge of the bed to run a lean hand through his disheveled hair. He glared down at her. "Now you've got fingerprints and lipstick and perfume all over me. The men will laugh themselves sick if I go to work smelling like a flower garden."

She tugged down her top and gave him an impish grin. "We could rush into my bathroom and shower it off, together," she offered wickedly.

He laughed again. He'd never laughed as much in his life as he did with her. Was this the way she'd been, before the tragedies of the past year that had marred her life? She'd said she didn't date much, but how in the world could men ignore a sweet, pretty little woman like that?

"I can't believe you spend your weekends watching television with your father," he murmured.

"I don't. I work."

He frowned. "On the weekends?"

She sat up, reaching under her blouse to refasten the bra

he'd unsnapped. She wondered why she didn't feel embarrassed. "Seven days a week, for the past six months," she said honestly. "Before that, six days a week, and I had to rest on Sunday. I usually work ten-hour days, sometimes longer if we have an emergency."

He didn't like that. "You don't have any free time, do you?"

She shook her head. "I've been dedicated to the job since I got out of college."

"And no men," he murmured with a speculative glance.

She grimaced. "Well, there was one I liked very much. We went out together for four months, and I was very nearly in love with him. But he never touched me. I thought he was building up to it, or something." She sighed. "Then I saw him, with another man." She shrugged. "He thought of me as a friend. I thought of him as a boyfriend. I sort of lost confidence in myself after that."

"It happens, in the modern world," he replied quietly.

"Before that, I had crushes on boys who never noticed me, except to ask me to help them with math or chemistry." She searched his eyes. "Of course, I didn't exactly look like this until last year."

"How did you look?" he asked curiously.

She got off the bed, went to get her purse, and took out a plastic insert. She pulled a photo from behind a credit card and handed it to him.

His eyes widened. "Good heavens!"

She winced. "I was sixty pounds overweight, and I couldn't lose it at all. I guess I tried every diet known to man. Then I took nutrition classes and learned how to get it off the sensible way. That's why I know so much about low-fat cooking."

He looked from the photo to her face and smiled. "You were pretty before, too," he said slowly. "You know, Meredith, it's not the outside that attracts people. It's what you are, how you treat other people, that makes friends of them.

You risked your life to save my brother, then you stayed with him until his family came. I wasn't very flattering to you when we first met, but I've had a lot of time to think about what you did. You're good people. Really good people.''

She flushed and cleared her throat. ''Thanks.'' She gave him a mischievous look. ''So, would you like to get married Friday, or is Monday better for you?'' she added with a grin.

He chuckled. ''Sorry, I have to wash my dogs.''

She sighed. ''Rejected again.''

He pursed his lips and let his eyes run over her slowly. ''You could lie back down and we could discuss it again.''

''Absolutely not. I only have so much willpower. You shouldn't throw yourself at women that way unless you're asking to be seduced. It's unfair.''

''You're not bad yourself, kid,'' he murmured with a warm smile. He got up. ''I've got to go back to work. Come here.''

She went to him. ''Changed your mind?'' she asked. ''I can get a ring today…''

He put a finger over her mouth. ''How do I smell?''

''Is that all you want?!'' she exclaimed. ''Good Lord, you got me all the way over here to *smell* you?''

He bent and kissed her hungrily, pulling her so close that she could feel him against every cell of her body. But before she could cling, he put her away. ''How do I smell?'' he persisted.

She sniffed him. ''You smell like aftershave.''

He bent and sniffed her, and frowned. ''You're not wearing perfume, are you?''

She shook her head. ''I'm allergic to most strong fragrances.''

''You smell like flowers.''

She smiled. ''Herbal shampoo. Flowers don't bother me. Well, real ones do sometimes, but not flowery scent. I can use scented shampoos and wear one or two colognes, but no perfumes. They're too strong."

"At least I don't smell womanly," he said with mocking relief. "I'd never live that down."

She cocked her head and stared up at him. "There goes the shower," she sighed.

He tapped her nose. "Now, cut that out." His fingers traced the fading bruises on her cheek and jaw and his eyes narrowed. "He'll never touch you again, I swear he won't," he said in a low, dangerous tone.

Her heart lifted at the look on his face. "Oh, my, aren't we getting possessive?" she teased.

He didn't smile. "Careful," he told her quietly. "I'm not teasing."

Her eyes widened with something like wonder.

"Hasn't anyone ever stood up for you?" he asked curiously.

"Just my brother. But he never had to protect me from Daddy. I know it looks really bad, but my father was the most gentle man on earth until we lost Mama and Mike. He goes crazy when he drinks, and he never remembers what he did." Her eyes fell to his chest. She toyed with his shirt buttons, wondering absently how it would feel to smooth her fingers over his bare chest. "I miss my brother terribly," she added simply.

"I'm sure you do. And your mother."

She grimaced. "She and I weren't really very close," she confessed. She searched his eyes. "You see, what Daddy yelled about her that night you were at the house was pretty much true. She was a very attractive woman, and she had lovers." She winced. "I hated knowing that. You can't imagine what it did to Daddy. She even bragged about them."

"She doesn't sound like much of a wife," he murmured.

"She didn't act like one, either. She did love to spend money, though. That's why she picked rich lovers." Her face clouded. "I was so ashamed of her. I guess she saw herself as a modern woman. I'm not. There's a big difference between sleeping with someone you truly love, and jumping into bed with anyone who has some money."

He nodded and touched her soft, swollen mouth. "She's soured you on men, hasn't she?"

"Sort of. Until you came along, at least," she admitted, without looking at him. She stared at his shirt button. "Bad temper and all, you've got some wonderful qualities."

He gave her a wry look. "I'll have to tell my brothers. They didn't know."

She chuckled. "Thanks for letting me come here to heal, anyway."

He felt uneasy. "That sounds like goodbye, Meredith."

She sighed. Her fingers stilled on his buttons. "I can't stay much longer," she said sadly. "Even though I'd like to. My boss is shorthanded as it is, and the woman filling in for me doesn't like leaving her kids in day care. She retired when she had the second one."

"Retired?"

"Yes. She said keeping two kids in day care ate up her whole paycheck." She lifted her eyes to his. "Since her husband got a raise, it was actually cheaper for her to stay home with the kids than it was to work. She loves it."

There was a strange look on his face. He rubbed his fingertips over her short fingernails absently. "Would you want to stay home with your kids?"

She stared up at him, transfixed. "Yes, I would. Those first few years are so important. If I could find any way to do it, I would, even if I had to sacrifice some little luxuries."

"That would be tricky. You're a highly trained professional."

"One of my friends was a highly trained doctor," she replied. "She gave up her job and stayed home with her little boy until he was in kindergarten. Even then, she arranged her schedule so that she'd be there when he got home in the afternoons."

He was frowning, and his fingers were still smoothing over hers. He wanted to ask if she thought she could get used to ranch life and snakes. He was afraid to say it. The act of commitment was still very new to him. He couldn't rush her.

He sighed, troubled. "What does your father do, by the way?" he asked suddenly.

"Oh, he teaches in the veterinary department of his college in Houston."

His hand stilled on hers. "He's a veterinarian?"

"He has a doctorate in veterinary medicine, yes. Why?"

Wheels were turning in his head. He stared at her thoughtfully. "Will he have a job to go back to, after all the trouble he's had with the law?"

"You're very perceptive," she said after a minute. "Actually, no, he won't. The college phoned before his last bender and told him not to come back. You can't blame them, either," she added sadly. "What would it do to the college's image, to have an alcoholic on staff with a dangerous temper?"

"Not much," he had to admit. "Did he drink before the shooting?"

"Never. Not even a beer," she replied. "But he's set records in the past six months. I couldn't get him near a treatment center. At least he's in one, now."

"Not only in it, but improving by the day," Rey said unexpectedly. "He'd like you to come see him. I can run you up there Sunday, if you'd like to go."

That was surprising. "You've spoken to him?" she asked.

He nodded. "I had Leo phone Colter. He has contacts who helped arrange it." He drew in a deep breath. "Your father seems pretty rational right now. Of course, he isn't drinking, either.'' His eyes darkened. ''I meant exactly what I said. He'll never touch you again in anger.''

''When he's sober, he never would. I can't believe…he really wants to see me?'' she asked haltingly.

He brushed his hand against her cheek. ''He loves you. I'm sure you love him, too. You don't throw people away because they make a mistake—even a bad one. You get help for them.''

''I tried.''

''Sure you did. But it's better this way. When he comes home, we'll decide where to go from there. For now, I'll drive you to Houston on Sunday to see him. Want to go?''

''Oh, yes,'' she said. Her expression was soft, wondering. ''You'd do that, for me?''

He smiled. ''Anything you want, kiddo,'' he murmured. ''It's the least I can do for the only woman who's ever proposed to me.''

She pursed her lips and gave him an impish look. ''We could lie down and talk about it.''

''No, we couldn't,'' he told her firmly, and chuckled as he removed her hands from his shirt. ''I have to get back to work. I was in the middle of a meeting when you did your snake charmer routine. I left twelve employees sitting in the boardroom with glasses of water and no ashtrays. At least six of them smoke, despite all the regulations. I expect they've attacked the other six with chairs by now, or vice versa. I've got to get back. Quick.''

''I'd love to go Sunday,'' she said.

''Fine. I'll run you up there Sunday afternoon. We can go to church first.''

Her eyebrows lifted. ''I'm Methodist.''

He grinned. ''So are we. It's a date.'' He opened the door. Before he went out it, he glanced back over his shoulder. ''And stay out of the henhouse for the rest of the day, will you?''

"Anything for my prospective fiancé," she said with a theatrical gesture of her arm.

He shook his head and walked out, still chuckling.

Later, she wondered what he'd meant, about making decisions when her father got out of rehab. She didn't dare think too hard about it. But it sounded very much as if he wanted to go on looking out for her.

She was a modern woman. She could look out for herself. But it was kind of nice to have a man act protective and possessive, especially one like Rey, who didn't seem the sort to do it habitually. She remembered the hunger in his lean body when he held her, when he kissed her. She remembered the strange tenderness he reserved for her. It was an adventure, just being around him. They'd known each other such a short time, really, but she felt as if she'd known him all her life. The thought of going back to Houston without him was suddenly frightening.

She did the routine things until Sunday, except that when she gathered eggs, she was overly cautious about going into the henhouse. She'd learned from Rey that snakes often traveled in pairs, so she was careful to look before she stepped anywhere that the ground was covered.

She'd become something of a legend among the Hart ranch hands already. They removed their hats when she walked by, and they spoke to her in respectful tones.

"It's really strange," she remarked at the dinner table on Saturday evening, glancing from Leo to Rey. "The men seem sort of in awe of me."

Rey chuckled and exchanged an amused look with his brother. "They are. None of them has ever picked up a copperhead on a stick."

"It let me," she reminded him.

"That's the awesome thing," Leo remarked. "You see, Meredith, copperheads have a nasty reputation for attacking without provocation. It's kind of mystic, what you did."

He pursed his lips and gave her a teasing glance over his buttered biscuit. "Any snake charmers in your family?"

"No, but Mike had a pet boa for a while, until it ate one of the neighbor's rabbits," she sighed.

"Yuccch!" Rey said, and shivered.

"It was an accident," Meredith insisted. "It escaped out the window and was gone for three weeks. We figured it was starving, because it hadn't been fed in so long. Besides that," she added, "the rabbit was vicious. It attacked everybody who opened the cage."

"Why did the neighbor keep rabbits?"

"He sold them for meat to a specialty grocery store."

Rey chuckled. "Maybe the boa was a reincarnated taste-tester," he mused.

Leo made a face. "I wouldn't eat a rabbit if I was starving. On the other hand, snake's not so bad. Remember when we were in Arizona on that hunting trip, camping out, and our guide caught that big, juicy rattler?"

"Sure do," Rey agreed, nodding. "Tasted just like chicken!"

Obviously that was a private joke, because the brothers looked at each other and burst out laughing.

"What became of the boa?" Leo asked, interested.

"Mike had just sold it to a breeder," she recalled sadly. "He was engaged to the sweetest, kindest girl I ever knew. It devastated her when he was killed. They had to sedate her for two days, and she couldn't even go to the funeral." She shook her head. "I felt as sorry for her as I did for Dad and me."

"What happened to her?" Leo asked.

She finished her coffee. "She became a missionary and went to South America with a group of them." She winced. "She had the worst luck…it was that plane that was mistaken for drug smugglers and shot down. I think she was one of the survivors, but she didn't come back to America with the others."

"Poor kid," Rey said.

"Colter was upset over the shooting for a long time, too," Leo recalled. "Just between you and me, he was sweet on Mike's girl, but too much a gentleman to do anything about it. He thought the sun rose and set on Mike."

"I never knew," Meredith said softly.

"Neither did Mike. Or the girl," Leo added with a smile. "Colter's a clam. He never talks."

"Is he still with the Texas Rangers?" Meredith asked.

Leo nodded. "Got promoted to lieutenant just recently. He's good at his job."

She pushed back from the table. "If you two are through, I'll just wash up. Rey's going to drive me up to see my dad tomorrow."

"What a sweet guy!" Leo exclaimed with a wide-eyed look at his brother.

"He's being nice to me, because I'm the only woman who ever proposed to him," Meredith volunteered with a wicked grin. "He feels guilty because he turned me down."

"Good. I'll marry you, Meredith," Leo volunteered at once. "You just name the time and place, and I'll buy a new suit…!"

"Shut the hell up!" Rey said curtly, and hit his brother with his Stetson.

Leo protected his shoulder. "Meredith, he's picking on me!" he wailed.

"Do you want biscuits for breakfast?" she asked Rey.

He stopped flogging his brother. "All right. But only for biscuits," Rey said. He got up and deliberately bent and kissed Meredith, right in front of Leo. "Don't stay up too late. Leo and I have to check the livestock in the barn."

"Okay. Wear a jacket," she said, smiling up at him.

He bent and brushed his mouth against hers one more time. "It's not cold."

"It is. Wear a jacket," she insisted.

He sighed and made a face, but he picked up his light-

weight denim jacket from the hat stand by the back door
as he went out.

Leo followed him, but with a new expression on his face.
He'd seen something he hadn't expected during that teasing
exchange. He wondered if Rey realized that he was in love
with that sweet little biscuit-making woman. And unless he
missed his guess, it was mutual.

Ten

___

The next morning, Meredith sat next to Rey in church and felt his hand holding hers almost all the way through the service. She felt different with him than she'd ever felt with anyone else. Rey made her feel as if she could do anything. He made her feel strong and confident and safe.

She glanced up at him while they shared a hymnal and he forgot what he was singing. They searched each other's eyes slowly, until they realized that everybody else had stopped singing and were sitting down. Smiling sheepishly, Rey sat down and tugged her down beside him.

After the service, they got amused, affectionate looks from bystanders who knew Rey and had heard about his new cook.

But he didn't seem to be the least bit embarrassed by the attention. In fact, he made a point of introducing Meredith to several people, adding the little known information that she was a licensed nurse practitioner as well as a great biscuit chef.

Meredith flushed, because it sounded as if he were very proud of her, especially when he related how her quick thinking had probably saved Billy Joe's life at the target range. Billy Joe was well-known and liked locally, so that brought even more smiles. She clung to his hand with un-ashamed delight when they left.

"See, you're already a local celebrity," he teased. "And I didn't even get around to mentioning the snake."

"We should forget the snake," she said quickly.

He chuckled. "No, we shouldn't. It wins me points if I have a…cook who isn't even afraid of poisonous snakes."

She heard that hesitation before "cook," as if he wanted to say something else instead. It made her tingle all over. She couldn't stop smiling, all the way to the Jaguar convertible he drove when he wasn't working.

"This is a very flashy car," she commented as he put her in on the passenger side.

"I like sports cars," he said with a grin.

"So do I," she confessed. She didn't even put on a scarf. In fact, she pulled the pins out of her hair and let it fall around her shoulders.

"Won't it tangle in the wind?" he asked when they were seat-belted in place.

"I don't care." She looked at him and smiled warmly. "I like to feel the wind."

"Me, too."

He started the car, put it in gear, and pulled out onto the highway. When they were on the interstate, heading toward Houston, he let the powerful car do its best.

"Now this is a HORSE!" he called over the roar of the wind.

She laughed with pure delight. It was the most wonderful day of her life. She even forgot where they were going in the excitement of being with him in the elegant vehicle.

But all too soon, they were pulling up at an impressive brick building with its function discreetly labeled on a

metal plate near the door. It was a substance abuse reha-
bilitation center, three stories tall, and staffed impressively
with psychologists, psychiatrists, and health professionals,
including physicians.

Rey held her hand to the information desk and then up
to the second floor waiting room, where her father would
be brought to visit with them.

"They don't like visitors the first week," Rey explained
to her. "You probably knew that," he added, remembering
her profession.

"I've never had anybody in here," she said quietly. She
was nervous and she looked it.

He caught her fingers in his again and held them tight.
"It's going to be all right," he said firmly.

She met his eyes and took a deep breath. "Okay," she
said after a minute, and her body lost some of its rigidity.

There were footsteps and muffled voices. A minute later,
her father came in the door, wearing slacks and a knit shirt,
and behind him was a uniformed woman with a clipboard.

"Miss Johns? I'm Gladys Bartlett," the woman introduced herself with a firm handshake. "I'm the staff psychologist on your father's case."

"Hello, Merry," her father said hesitantly. He winced
when he noticed the faded bruises on her face. "I'm sorry,
my dear," he choked.

Meredith let go of Rey's hand and went forward to hug
her father warmly. Mr. Johns closed his eyes and hugged
her back, hard. His lips trembled as he forced them together, but tears ran down his lean, pale cheeks. "I'm so
sorry," he sobbed.

She patted him on the back and tears fell hotly from her
own eyes. "It's okay, Daddy," she whispered brokenly,
comforting him the way he'd once comforted her and Mike
when they were little, and something had hurt them. He'd

been a wonderful father. "It's okay," she said again. "You're going to be fine. We both are."

"My son. My boy!" He shook all over. "I said I was too busy to take her to the bank. I asked him...I *asked* Mike...to go instead. He'd be alive, but for me!"

"Now, Mr. Johns," the counselor said gently, "we've been over this several times already. You can't assume blame for the lawless acts of other people. Ninety-nine times out of a hundred, nothing would have happened if you'd asked your son to go to the bank on your behalf."

"But this was the one out of a hundred," he husked. "And I can't live with the guilt!"

"I've had my own problems with it," Meredith confessed. "I could have refused to go in to work that day and taken her instead."

"And you'd be lying dead instead of Mike," her father replied curtly. "And I'd be just as eaten up with guilt!"

"You're both missing the point," Rey said, standing up. "You can't control life. Nobody can."

They all looked at him. He stood quietly, his hands deep in his slacks pockets, and stared back. "Einstein said that God didn't play dice with the universe, and he was right. Even in seeming chaos, there's an order to things, a chain of events that leads inevitably to conclusions. People are links in the chain, but people don't control the events. Life has a pattern, even if we don't see it."

"You've studied philosophy," Mr. Johns said quietly.

Rey nodded. "Yes, I have."

The older man, with thinning hair and glasses and a faintly stooped posture, moved away from Meredith and smiled. "I took several courses in it, myself. You have a degree, haven't you?"

"I do, in business. A master's, from Harvard," Rey volunteered, something that Meredith hadn't even known.

"Mine is in medicine. Veterinary medicine. I'm..."

"I know. You're Dr. Alan Johns," Rey said, shaking

hands. "Your daughter is staying with us on the ranch in Jacobsville, baking biscuits, while she recovers."

Dr. Johns winced and flushed. "They told me what I did to you," he said, glancing shamefaced at his daughter. "I swear before God, I'll never take another drink as long as I live!"

"You won't get the chance," Rey said. "I intend to watch you like a red-tailed hawk."

"Excuse me?" Dr. Johns stammered.

Rey studied his boots. "We don't have a vet on staff. We have to call one down from Victoria, because our vets are overworked to death. It would be nice to have our own vet. We pay competitive salaries and you'd have your own house."

Dr. Johns sat down quickly. "Young man, I...!"

Rey lifted his head and stared him in the eyes. "You made a mistake. People do. That's why they put erasers on pencils. You can work for us. We'll keep you straight, and you won't have to take some sort of menial job in Houston just to make ends meet. You'll like the ranch," he added. "We have a good crew."

"Someone might know what I did," Dr. Johns stammered.

"Everybody knows already," Rey said, and shrugged. "It's no big deal to us. We've got one man who came back from cocaine addiction—let me tell you, that was a story and a half—and another one who was a habitual DWI for six years until we hired him and helped him get straight." He smiled. "We don't hold a man's past against him, as long as he's willing to stay straight and work hard."

Dr. Johns was having a hard time keeping control of himself, and it was obvious. "Young man, I'll work without a salary, if that's what it takes. And I promise, you'll never have cause to regret giving me a job."

"Not unless you keep calling me 'young man,'" Rey

said with a grin. "I'm Reynard Hart, but everybody calls me Rey."

"Glad to meet you," the older man said. "Rey."

Rey nodded. "How much longer will they keep you?" he asked, and glanced at the woman with the clipboard.

"Another week should do it," she said with a big smile. "And how nice, to see him with a settled environment to look forward to the day he leaves! I believe in minor miracles, but I don't see many. This is certainly one."

Rey gave her a complacent smile. "Miracles only happen for people who believe in them," he said, chuckling.

"Thanks, Rey," Meredith said huskily.

He only shrugged. "How could I ignore the father of the only woman who ever proposed to me?" he said, matter-of-factly, and with a smile that made her blush.

"You proposed to him?" her father asked with raised eyebrows.

"Several times," she said with mock disgust. "But he has to wash his dogs, so he can't marry me."

Dr. Johns laughed heartily.

The counselor relaxed. This was going to work out. Dr. Johns was never going to end up in rehab again, she was certain of it. She only wished she could say the same for more of her poor patients.

On the drive back to Jacobsville, Meredith was on top of the world. "Not only does he get a new job, but one doing what he always loved best, working around large animals."

"He likes cattle, does he?" Rey asked absently, enjoying Meredith's animated company.

"He grew up on a cattle ranch in Montana," she explained. "He was even in rodeo for six or seven years before he went to college."

Rey expelled a breath. This was going to work out even better than he'd dreamed. Amazing, he thought, how a single act of kindness could expand like ripples around a rock dropped into a pond.

"He's not much good on a horse anymore," she continued chattily, "but he really knows veterinary medicine."

"He might go back to teaching one day. Not in Houston," he added gently. "But Texas is a big state, and when he's been away from alcohol a couple of years, who knows?"

"The ranch will be good for him. You did mean it, didn't you?" she added quickly. "It wasn't something you said to help him want to get better?"

"I very rarely say things I don't mean, Meredith," he replied. "Well," he added with a frown, "I wasn't exactly telling the truth about washing the dogs."

"Excuses, excuses." She toyed with her purse. "Rey, thank you for giving him a second chance."

He laughed gently. "I've got an ulterior motive," he murmured dryly. "When you come to the ranch to visit him, you can make me a pan of biscuits."

"Just you? Not one to share with Leo?"

He shifted behind the wheel. "He can go find someone to make him biscuits," he said. "Surely, somewhere in Texas, there's a woman who'd do it just for him."

"Your other brothers, do their wives bake?"

"Dorie and Tess do," he said. "But Tira hasn't got a clue how to," he added on a sigh. "Simon doesn't mind. They have a cook who can. Although he's really not much on biscuits, so it doesn't matter." He grinned. "You should see him with his sons. Two of them now. They're still toddlers, and he's a whiz at fatherhood. Dorie and Corrigan have a boy and a girl and Cag and Tess have a son. That makes me an uncle five times over! Christmas is going to be a real treat this year."

She thought about Christmas. It was going to be a lonely one for her, with her father down here on the ranch.

He saw the look on her face and reached out to catch

her hand in his. "Hey," he said softly, "you're invited for Christmas, you know. We'll pack up the kids and go over to the annual Christmas party at the Doctors Coltrain. They have huge layouts of Lionel trains that they run every year, especially with a little boy of their own who'll be big enough to play with them in a couple of years. Draws a big crowd. Do you like train sets?"

She smiled. "I do." It lifted her heart to know that she was going to be included in the family get-together. She loved children. It would make the season less traumatic for her and her father, because they were missing two members of their immediate family.

"We'll make it a happy Christmas," he said softly.

She tangled her fingers into his. "I'll have that to look forward to, when I go back."

"It's premature right now, but if you decide to move down here, too, I'd bet good money that Micah Steele would offer you work."

She looked at his big, warm hand holding hers. "I like Jacobsville."

His fingers grew possessive. "I like *you*."

"Thanks. I like you, too, and if you'll loan me your cell phone, I'll call the minister right now and we can set a date," she added with wicked haste.

He chuckled. "Hold on, tiger, I may have been lying about washing the dogs, but marriage is a big step. You have to look out for me. I know you can tame snakes and handle heart attacks, and you bake good biscuits. But how do you look in a suit, and can you dance?"

"I look great in a suit," she said firmly, "and I can do Latin dances."

He grimaced. "I can't. How about a nice, slow two-step?"

"I can do that, too!"

He glanced at her. "What do you like to read?" he asked.

The next few minutes were spent in gleeful harmony, going over things they had in common. They liked the same basic forms of relaxation, and they even thought alike on politics and child-raising. It was a very good start. Meredith had seen far too many relationships start out with nothing more than sex for a foundation, and they didn't last. It took common interests, common beliefs, friendship, to make a lasting marriage.

Marriage. That word, once so warily approached, now seemed as natural as letting Rey hold her hand all the way back to Jacobsville. She wondered where they were going together in the future, and hoped it was someplace nice.

She had to go back to work the following week. Friday morning she had her suitcase packed. She was wearing her tailored beige suit with her blond hair in a neat ponytail when she followed Rey out the front door. He carried her suitcase to his car and put it in the trunk.

"I'll be back late this afternoon," he told Leo. "If you need me, I'll be on my cell phone." He patted the cell phone carrier on his belt.

"Oh, I think I can cope," Leo drawled with a wink at Meredith. "Don't be a stranger, Meredith," he added. "We'll miss you. But thanks for making us all those pans of frozen biscuits!"

"It's a good thing you have a walk-in freezer, is all I can say," she mused, chuckling. "But don't forget the directions on how to cook them," she added. "They're only dough until then."

"I'll have it all down pat in no time," Leo promised. "Meanwhile," he added, rubbing his big hands together with visible delight, "there are still six biscuits left over from breakfast!"

"No use asking you to save me a couple, is there?" Rey asked on a sigh.

"Blood is thicker than water, except where biscuits are involved," Leo shot back. "Sorry."

Rey got in the car and started the engine without another word.

Meredith was quiet most of the way to Houston. She was oddly reluctant to go back to work, although she loved her job. She was going to miss Rey and Leo and Mrs. Lewis. She was even going to miss the chickens.

"You can come down anytime you want to," Rey reminded her, when he noticed that she was brooding. It had been hard, but he'd kept his hands to himself for the duration of her stay at the ranch. He was planning a frontal assault in the near future. This wasn't the time, though.

"I know." She stared out the window at the bare trees and chilly flat landscape. "Thanksgiving comes along pretty soon."

"Your father will be working for us by then. You can come and spend a few days while you're off."

"I might still be on call," she worried.

He was grim and silent himself, after she said that. The rest of the way to Houston, he had the radio on, letting it fill the cool silence.

He dropped her off at her father's house. It looked cold and unwelcoming as she unlocked the front door so that he could sit her suitcase inside.

She turned back to him, her grey eyes wide and sad as they met his dark ones. He hadn't removed his hat, and it was hard to see his face in the shadow of it.

"Well, thanks for everything," she began.

He stared down at her with a sense of loss. After their ride up to Houston to visit her father, there seemed to be a curtain between them. They'd been very close that Sunday. But he'd gotten cold feet, he admitted to himself, and he'd drawn back. He felt the threat of her in his heart and he was trying to run from it. Suddenly it was like trying to run from himself.

"You'll be here alone," he said quietly. "Make sure you keep your door locked. We haven't had any reports that they caught the guys who rolled Leo. Just in case, don't let your guard down."

"I'll be fine," she promised him.

She looked so small and vulnerable standing there. He hated leaving her.

"You wear your jacket when it's cold like this," she told him firmly, noticing that he was standing in the cold wind in just the shirtsleeves of his chambray shirt.

"And my raincoat when it's raining," he said with a mocking smile. "You wear yours, too."

She hesitated. "Well, goodbye," she said after a minute.

"You and I won't ever say goodbye, Meredith," he replied. "It's 'so long.'"

She forced a smile to her lips. "So long, then."

He was still hesitating. His face was absolutely grim.

"I know where a jeweler's is open this early," she said suddenly, with mischievous enthusiasm.

It warmed him to hear her tease, to see that wonderful smile. "Do you, really?"

She nodded. "You can even have a diamond. But it would have to be a small one."

His dark eyes twinkled. "You just hold that thought," he said gently. "One of these days we might talk about this marriage hang-up of yours. Meanwhile, I've got to…"

"If you say 'wash the dogs,'" she interrupted, "I'll slug you!"

He chuckled. "I wasn't going to say that. I've got to get back and finish my marketing strategy for the next year before we have our year-end board meeting."

"I guess that's pretty complicated."

"No more than treating diseases and plotting nutrition,"

he replied. He studied her quietly. "I'll miss you. Don't stay away too long."

"Why?" she prodded.

"You have to save me from attacks on my virtue from hordes of amorous, sex-crazed women," he said without cracking a smile. "Who knows when I might weaken and give in to one of them, and then where would we be?"

"I've got my heart set on a virgin," she informed him.

He laughed helplessly. "Sorry, honey, you missed the boat by a decade or so."

She snapped her fingers. "Damn!"

"On the other hand, I didn't," he said in a deep, soft voice, and moved closer. He framed her face in his lean hands and studied it hungrily for several seconds. "You make me ache every time I touch you," he whispered, bending. "I'll starve to death before you get back."

"Starve…?" She wasn't thinking. She was watching his long, hard mouth come closer. She held her breath until it settled, ever so softly, on her parted lips. And then she didn't think at all for several long, tempestuous seconds.

Too soon, he caught her by the arms and pushed her away. "You stop that," he muttered breathlessly. "I refuse to be seduced on the front lawn."

She was trying to catch her own breath. "No problem. There's a nice soft carpet just five steps this way," she indicated the hall.

"I'm not that kind of man," he said haughtily.

She made a face at him.

He chuckled and kissed her one last time, teasingly, before he pulled back and started toward his car. "I'll call you."

"That's what they all say!" she cried after him.

"Then you call me, honey," he said in that deep, sexy voice that made her melt. "You've got my number, even if you don't know it yet." He winked and went on to the car. He didn't look back, even as he drove away. Meredith's eyes followed the car until it was out of sight. She didn't cry until she was inside, behind the closed door.

She was back at work and going crazy in no time, overrun by people with everything from stomach viruses to the flu. She had a good immune system, and she didn't catch any of the ailments, but she missed Rey terribly.

Three days before Thanksgiving, her father telephoned her from the ranch, full of excitement about his new job. He seemed like a different person. He told her he was still going to therapy sessions, but in Jacobsville with a psychologist. He was doing much better, and he was going to make everything up to his daughter, he swore it. And wasn't she coming for Thanksgiving?

It took real nerve to tell him the truth, that she hadn't been able to get off because of the time she'd already missed. There was simply nobody available to replace her. She'd have Thanksgiving Day, but nothing more.

She'd tried to beg the time off to have a long weekend, but her boss hadn't been pleased and he refused. He wanted her on call that weekend, and she couldn't be and go to Jacobsville. The office held a huge clinic for the local immigrant population on Saturdays, as well as Sunday afternoons, and Meredith was competently bilingual in medical terms. It made her indispensable. Not that she minded. These people were desperately in need of even the most basic health care, and Meredith was a whiz at preventive medicine. She counseled them, advised them on nutrition and wellness, and tried not to let her heart break at the sight of little children with rotting teeth and poor vision and a dozen other ailments that money could have corrected easily. The disparity between the rich and the poor was never more evident than in minority communities.

But the fact was, she had one day off for Thanksgiving and no real time for herself. It was a reminder of just how pressured her job really was, and how demanding. She loved what she did, but she hated being made to feel guilty when she asked for time off—something she hadn't done since her brother's and mother's untimely deaths. Actually it had been a battle royal to get time off for bereavement leave, and the funerals, and she'd had to go right back to work the day after the burials. It had been too soon, but she'd thought work would be good medicine.

Perhaps it had been, but she was living on nerves. The weeks at the Hart ranch had given her a taste of a whole other life. It was one she recalled with joy and missed every day. Most of all, she missed Rey. Now she wouldn't even see him. Her father said that he'd ask someone to loan him a vehicle, and he'd come to have Thanksgiving with her. That cheered her up a little, but it would mean she wouldn't see Rey. It was a bad blow. She told her father that she'd make dinner, which cheered him up as well.

Thanksgiving Day came, and Meredith got up before daylight to start cooking. She was determined that she and her father were going to have the best Thanksgiving dinner she could manage. She'd bought a turkey and a small ham, and raw ingredients to make dressing and sweet potato soufflé, green beans, ambrosia, homemade rolls and cherry and pumpkin pies.

She'd just taken the last pie out of the oven when she heard a car pull up in front of the house. She didn't stop to take off her apron or run a brush through her disheveled hair. She ran to the front door and opened it, just in time to see her father and Rey come up on the porch.

"Happy Thanksgiving, Merry," her father said, and hugged her warmly.

Rey grinned. "We thought you might like company to help you eat all that food," he told her.

"I didn't make any biscuits," she said worriedly. "Just homemade rolls."

"I love rolls." He held out his arms. "Well, come on,"

he chided when she hesitated. "You can't treat a red-hot matrimonial prospect like me to the cold shoulder! You'll never get me to say 'yes' from arm's length!"

Her father coughed. "I'll just, uh, check on the turkey," he said with an impish smile and went into the kitchen.

Rey nudged Meredith back inside the house, closed the door, and kissed her to within an inch of her life. He barely stopped to breathe before he was kissing her again, enfolding her in a bearish embrace while he made up for what seemed like years of abstinence.

"You'll smother me," she complained weakly.

"Stop complaining and kiss me," he murmured against her swollen lips. He kissed her ever harder.

"I'm not...complaining!" she gasped when he finally stopped.

He bit her lower lip ardently. "I am," he groaned. "Come on, woman, ravish me!"

"Here?" she exclaimed, wide-eyed.

"Well, give your father a quarter and send him to the store for cigarettes!" he asked with comical desperation between kisses.

"Nobody here smokes," she pointed out.

"Excuses, excuses," he murmured against her lips, using her own favorite complaint. His arms tightened and he only stopped when he had to breathe. "What a long, dry spell it's been, Merry," he whispered huskily. "Come back here..."

She kissed him and kissed him with no thought of the future. It was wonderful to be held and cuddled and wanted. She thought she'd never felt so much joy in her whole life as she did here, in Rey's hard arms.

"There's that carpet you mentioned when I left here last time," he said breathlessly, indicating the floor. He wiggled both eyebrows. "We can lock your father in the kitchen and you can ravish me, right here!"

"Not on your life." She linked her arms around his neck.

"I won't ravish you until you agree to marry me," she managed unsteadily.

"Is that a proposal?" he murmured huskily.

"Sure. You can have a ring. I think there's a ten-year-old cigar around here somewhere with a band on it…"

He was still kissing her between words. "I'll phone the minister first thing tomorrow. You can have a blood test at work. I already had Micah Steele do one on me. He said he'd love to have a nurse practitioner of his very own, by the way, if you're interested. We can have a Christmas wedding in Jacobsville."

Her mind was spinning. She couldn't quite understand what he was saying. Of course, he was kissing her and she could hardly think at all. "Blood test…work for Micah…Christmas wedding?" she murmured.

"Mmm-hmm," he whispered, kissing her again. "You can get me a ring whenever you like, but I got you one already." He fumbled in his jacket pocket and pulled out a velvet-covered jeweler's box. He opened it and showed it to her. Inside was a glorious emerald solitaire, and a diamond and emerald wedding band. "If you don't like it, we can throw it in the fishpond and go buy you something else…"

"I love it!" she exclaimed, flustered by the sudden turn of events.

"Good. Here." He took out the engagement ring, pocketed the box and slid it gently onto her ring finger. "Now it's official. We're engaged. Remember what you just promised," he added with a wicked grin. "The minute your father leaves, I'll let you ravish me on the carpet!"

Eleven

"But, Rey, Daddy won't leave," she whispered. "There's a turkey in the kitchen!"

"He can take it with him," he said generously.

She laughed and hugged him very hard. "I can't believe this."

"Neither can I," he said, nuzzling his cheek against hers. His arms tightened. "Even when I was suspicious of you, I couldn't bear you out of my sight. I still can't. This past week has been endless. I thought we could cool it for a few weeks, while I got things into perspective. But the only thing I got into perspective was how lonely I was without you." He lifted his head and looked down into her wide, rapt eyes. "I love my freedom. But not as much as I love you."

"And I love you, Rey," she said huskily. "I was lonely, too. I feel as if I've known you for centuries."

"Same here," he replied. "We're going to make a good marriage."

"A very good marriage," she agreed, and lifted her face so that he could kiss her again. He did, at length and very nicely, until her father came out of the kitchen with a turkey leg in one hand and asked if there were plans to take the dressing out of the oven before it got any blacker. Rey told him their news while Meredith took off at a dead run to rescue dinner.

Meredith worked out a two-week notice and gave up her job, to the dismay and regret of her boss, who hadn't wanted to lose her. He did see that she couldn't have a husband in Jacobsville and a job in Houston, however, and he made them a wedding present of a beautiful faceted crystal bowl.

Micah Steele offered her a job at his office, which she accepted with pleasure, on the understanding that she could work three days a week instead of six. Micah understood being a newlywed, since he and his Callie were still newlyweds as well, even with a baby on the way.

The only hitch was that all Rey's brothers got together and took over the wedding plans, to his dismay and Meredith's horror.

"It's going to be a humdinger of a wedding," Leo promised with relish, rubbing his hands together. "Cag had this great idea for entertainment."

"I don't want to hear it," Rey said firmly.

"You'll love this," Leo continued, unabashed. "He's got this great hard-rock band from Montana coming down to play their new hit record. They just had a hit single about getting married," he added with a rakish grin. "And they're having a caterer from San Antonio bring down the buffet lunch. The wedding gown is coming from one of the couture houses in Paris…"

"But you don't even know my size!" Meredith protested breathlessly.

"We looked in your dresses," he said imperturbably.

"Got your shoe size, too, and we also looked in your drawers and got the, ahem, other sizes." He grinned sheepishly. "Everything is couture, and silk. Only the best for our new sister-in-law," he added sweepingly.

Meredith didn't know whether to laugh or scream.

"We booked you a room at a five-star hotel for your honeymoon," he continued, glancing at Rey. "You still speak French, don't you?"

"French?" Meredith gasped.

"Well, your rooms are in Nice," he said. "The French Riviera. You've got a suite, overlooking the beach. Monaco is just on down the beach from there."

Rey whistled. "Not bad, for a rush job."

"We try to be efficient," Leo said, and his eyes twinkled. "We even ordered her a trousseau with formal gowns and casual clothes. Lots of pinks and blues and soft beige colors. We thought pastels would suit her."

Her mouth was open. She was trying to take it all in without fainting. She was only beginning to realize that the horror stories she'd heard from Tess about weddings and the brothers were true.

"You did kidnap Dorie and tie her in a sack with ribbon and carry her home to Corrigan!" she gasped.

"He didn't have a Christmas present," Leo explained patiently. "We gave him one. Look how well it worked out!"

"You hooligans!"

"Our hearts are all in the right place," Leo protested. "Besides, Dorie could bake. Which brings us to Tess, who could also bake…"

"You blackmailed Callaghan into marrying her, I heard!" Meredith was getting her second wind now.

"He's very happy. So is Tess."

"And poor Tira," she continued, unabashed. "You arranged her wedding and she didn't even get to choose her own gown, either!"

"She was pregnant. We had to hurry, there was no time," Leo explained matter-of-factly.

"I am not pregnant!" she exclaimed, red-faced.

Leo gave Rey a quick, speculative glance. "Yet," he replied. He grinned.

"If you would just give me a little time to organize my own wedding," she began, exasperated, and thought, I'm being nibbled to death by ducks...!

Leo checked his watch. "Sorry, I'm running late. The printer is waiting for me to check the proofs."

"Of what?" she burst out.

"Oh, just the wedding invitations. We're overnighting them to the people we invited. The governor's coming, so is the lieutenant governor. The vice president wanted to come, but he has to be in Singapore..." He frowned and checked his back pocket. "There they are! I almost forgot the interview questions. Here." He handed Rey two folded sheets of paper. "You'll have time to look them over before the camera crews move in."

Meredith and Rey exchanged wide glances. "What camera crews?" she asked.

"Just a few reporters," Leo waved them away with a lean hand. "You know, CNN, Fox, the international press...got to run!"

"International press!" Meredith choked.

"We've just signed an important export deal with Japan, didn't I mention it?" Leo called back. "They love organic beef, and we've got some. I mentioned it to our public relations people and they called the news people for us. Your father's writing the statement we're giving them. He's sure got a way with words, hasn't he?"

He waved again, climbed into his truck, and sped off.

"Invitations," Meredith said haltingly. "Clothes. Honeymoons. Reporters."

"Now, now," he said, pulling her into his arms. "Just think of all the work they've saved you. You'll have nothing to do but dress and say yes, and fly off to the Riviera with your brand-new husband!''

"But, but," she blurted.

"I want to marry you right away," he added. "You're a qualified health professional, and I have a terrible pain that you can cure in only one night."

She got the idea, belatedly, and hit him.

He chuckled, bending to kiss her gently. "It's no use trying to stop them," he said. "Besides, they're very good at it. I used to be, too." He scowled. "Somehow, it's not as much fun being on the receiving end, though."

She just shook her head.

The wedding was beautiful, despite her misgivings. Meredith wore the most gorgeous gown she'd ever seen, with yards and yards of exquisite lace over satin, with a long veil made of the same lace and a bouquet of pure white roses. Her father gave her away, and all four of Rey's brothers were best men. Tess, Cag's wife, stood with Meredith as her matron of honor. In a very short time, the two women had become close friends.

Most of Jacobsville turned out for the affair, but Meredith had eyes only for her handsome husband, who was dressed to the hilt as well. They exchanged rings and Rey lifted the veil very slowly. He'd been romantic and gentle and teasing over the days before the wedding. But when he looked at her now, his eyes were quiet and loving and very solemn. He bent and kissed her with such tenderness that she knew she'd remember the moment for the rest of her life.

They clasped hands and ran down the aisle and out of the church together, laughing gaily as they were pelted with rice and rose petals. At the waiting limousine, Meredith turned and tossed her bouquet. Surprisingly it was caught by Janie Brewster, notorious locally for her rubber chicken dinners and trying to catch Leo Hart's eye. She blushed vividly and clutched the bouquet, her eyes on it and not on anyone nearby. Which was as well, because Leo looked suddenly homicidal as the ranch foreman elbowed him and grinned.

The newlyweds waved and dived into the limousine, already packed and ready to take them to the airport. They'd already announced that the reception would have to go on without them, to the brothers' shock and dismay.

"I hated for us to miss it," Rey told her on the way to the airport, "but I know my brothers. They'd have found some way to embarrass us."

She chuckled, snuggling close to him. "Well, we're safe now."

The flight to France was long and boring. They held hands and couldn't sleep as the little computers above the seats marked the long trail on a map, showing the progress of the flight. When the jumbo jet finally landed, they walked like zombies into the airport to go through passport control and then on to wait for their luggage so that they could get through customs and to the waiting car that would take them to their hotel. The driver, holding a sign that read Hart Newlyweds had met them at the gate and arranged to meet them at customs. Meredith was yawning visibly when they found the driver and followed him and the wheeled luggage out the door. He and Rey exchanged comments that went right over Meredith's head.

"I don't speak French," she said worriedly when they were in the car. "I took a double minor in German and Spanish."

"No Latin?" he teased.

"There's a special course of it for nursing students," she replied with a smile. "Fortunately you don't have to learn the whole language anymore, although I wouldn't have minded. I'm so tired!"

"We'll have a nice long rest when we get to the hotel." He pulled her close. "I could use a little sleep myself!"

The car pulled up under the covered entrance and a bellboy came out to get the luggage. Rey paid the driver and made arrangements to contact him when they were ready to go sightseeing in a day or two.

Meredith followed Rey and the luggage to the desk clerk and waited while he got the key to their suite.

It didn't take long. Rey unlocked the door and opened it. And the bellhop burst into helpless laughter.

There, on the bed, very obviously courtesy of the Hart boys, were two life-size blow-up dolls, a blond female and a dark-haired male, in the midst of a garden of thornless roses of every color known to man. They were obviously engaged in a notorious newlywed ritual.

Rey tipped the bellhop and opened the door himself, waving the man out while he tried not to bend over double laughing.

When he closed the door again, Meredith was removing the dolls and roses with tears of mirth running down her cheeks.

"Just wait until they break something, anything," she threatened. "We can have them put in body casts for a sprained ankle…!"

He came up behind her and caught her around the waist. "And I'll help you. But, later, sweetheart," he added in a soft, hungry tone as he turned her into his arms. "Much, much…later!"

She was a professional health care worker. She knew all the mechanics of marriage. In fact, she counseled young wives in them. This was totally out of her experience.

Rey undressed her with slow precision, while he kissed every soft inch of skin as he uncovered it. He never rushed. He seemed to have committed the whole night to her arousal, and he went about it like a soldier with a battle plan.

She was teased, caressed, kissed until she felt as if there wasn't a bed under her at all. The roses were scattered over the carpet by now, along with half the bed linen. She was under him and then over him as he increased the insistence of his hands and mouth on her body. She heard high-pitched little cries of pleasure and barely realized that they were coming from her own throat.

One particularly enthusiastic embrace landed them on the carpet, cushioned by the sheet and blanket and, under them, the thick comforter.

"The bed," she whispered, trembling with unsatisfied hunger.

"It will still be there when we're finished," he replied breathlessly as his mouth bent again to her taut, arching breasts. "Yes, do that again, sweetheart!" he added when she pulled his head down to her.

He guided her hands along his lean, fit body to his hips and pressed them there as he suddenly shifted between her soft legs and his mouth ground into hers with intent.

The abrupt shift in intensity took her by surprise and lessened the sharp pain of his possession of her. His hard mouth absorbed the tiny cry that pulsed out of her tight throat, and his hands moved under her hips to caress her.

After a few seconds, she began to relax. He shifted again and found the place, and the pressure, that made her lift toward him instead of trying to escape the downward rhythm of his hips.

She clung to his damp shoulders as the little bites of pleasure became great, shivering waves. She could feel him in every cell of her body, and she wanted to look at him, to see his face, but she was intent on some distant goal of pleasure that grew by the second. Her mouth opened against the hollow of his shoulder and she moaned, her eyes closed, her body following the lead of his own as the heated minutes lengthened.

Her nails suddenly stabbed into his back and she gasped.

"Yes," he groaned at her ear. "Now, baby, now, now...!"

As if her body had given him some secret signal, his hips became insistent and the rhythm increased to madness. She reached, reached...reached...until the pleasure exploded inside her and began to spread in racking hot waves from her head to her toes. She rippled with him, sobbed against his skin, as the ecstasy she'd never known flamed through her with hurricane force.

"Rey!" She cried out pitifully as the wave peaked, and she felt her body go incandescent with joy.

His hands gripped her hips as he riveted her to his insistent hips. She heard his breathing become raspy and hoarse and then stop as he groaned endlessly against her throat and his entire body convulsed over her.

She felt him shake as the madness began to drift away.

"Are you all right?" she whispered urgently.

"I'm...dying," he choked.

"Rey!"

She held him close until the harsh contractions of his body slowed and then stopped. He collapsed on her with his whole weight, his breathing as labored as his heartbeat. His mouth burrowed into her throat hungrily.

"Never like that, Mrs. Hart," he whispered huskily. "You just made me a whole man!"

"Did I, really?" she whispered with a silly giggle.

He laughed, too. "That's what it felt like." He sighed heavily and lifted his head to look at her. His hair was as damp as hers, and he looked exhausted. He brushed loose blond strands away from her cheeks. "I'm glad we waited. I hope you are."

"Yes." Filled with wonder, she touched his hard mouth, which was swollen from its long contact with hers. "I think

I swallowed the sun," she whispered. "It was…glorious!" She hid her face in his throat, still shy of him, especially now.

He laughed again, lazily brushing his mouth over her closed eyes. "Glorious," he agreed with a long sigh. He rolled away from her gently, onto his back, and pulled her against him. "We fell off the bed," he remarked after a minute.

"I thought we were thrown off it," she murmured sleepily. "You know, by the hurricane."

"Hurricane." He kissed her forehead gently. "That's what it felt like."

"I'm sleepy. Is it normal?"

"Yes, it is, and it does worlds for my masculinity," he drawled. "Feel free to tell anyone you like that you ravished me to such an extent that I fell out of bed in my excitement, and you went to sleep from the tidal wave of pleasure!"

She managed one tired little chuckle. "I'll take out an ad in a magazine," she promised. She wrapped her arms and one leg around him, completely uninhibited now. "I love you, but I have to go to sleep now."

"Suit yourself, but I hope you're not throwing in the towel. I'm a brand-new bridegroom, remember, you can't just roll over and go to sleep once you've had your way with me…Meredith? Meredith!"

It was no use. She was sound asleep, worn-out by the pace of the wedding and her first passion. He lay watching her sleep, his eyes quiet and tender and loving. It had already been, he mused, one hell of a wedding night, even if they hadn't waited for it to get dark.

When she woke up, she was wearing a nightgown and lying on the bed, under the covers. Rey was sipping coffee and sniffing freshly cooked food under silver lids. He glanced up as Meredith sat up in bed and blinked her eyes sleepily.

"Supper?" she asked.

He grinned. "Supper. Come and eat something."

She pulled herself out of bed, feeling a little uncomfortable and grinning as she realized why. She sat down beside Rey, who was wearing a pair of blue silk pajama bottoms and nothing else, and looked under lids.

"Seafood," she sighed, smiling. "My favorite."

"Mine, too. Dig in, honey." He reached over and kissed her softly and gave her a wicked grin. "It's going to be a long, lovely night!"

And it was.

They came back to the ranch after several magical, wonderful days together to find the house deserted. There was a note propped up on the kitchen table, obviously left by Leo, because his name was signed to it.

"Goodbye, cruel world," it read. "Have run out of biscuits. No relief in sight. Can't go on. Have gone into Jacobsville to kidnap a cook or beg door-to-door for biscuits. If I fail, drag the river. P.S. Congratulations Meredith and Rey. Hope you liked the wedding present. Love, Leo."

"He wouldn't really kidnap a cook," Meredith said.

"Of course not," Rey agreed. But he had a very odd look on his face.

"Or beg door-to-door for a biscuit."

"Of course not," Rey repeated.

Meredith went to the telephone. "I'll call Dad."

He waited while she dialed the cottage her father occupied and tapped his foot while it rang and rang.

"Dad?" she asked suddenly. "Have you seen Leo?"

There was a pause, while Rey gestured with his hands for her to tell him something. She flapped a hand at him while she listened and nodded.

"Okay, Dad, thanks! Yes, we had a lovely honeymoon! We'll have you up for supper tomorrow. Love you, too!"

She hung up and sighed. "Well, Leo's gone to San Antonio."

"What the hell for?" he exclaimed.

"Apparently he walked out of Barbara's café with a cook in his arms and put him in the ranch truck…"

"*Him?*" Rey exclaimed.

"Him." She sighed. "The cook escaped out the other door and ran to get Chet Blake."

"The chief of police?" Rey looked horrified.

"Chet was laughing so hard that he didn't get to the café before Leo took off in a cloud of dust, barely escaping public disgrace. He tried to hire the little man to bake him some biscuits, but the cook refused, so Leo took harsh measures." She chuckled. "Dad said he phoned halfway to San Antonio and said he'd be back in a few days. He thinks he'll go to that genetics workshop until the heat dies down here."

"We'll never live that story down," Rey sighed, shaking his head.

"There is a solution," she remarked. "We can find him a nice wife."

He laughed even harder. "Leo's the one of us who'll have to be dragged to the altar behind a big horse," he told her. "For all that Janie Brewster is desperate to marry him, he's as elusive as smoke."

"Janie's pretty," she recalled, because the girl caught her bridal bouquet at the wedding.

"She's a doll, but she can't boil water," Rey told her. "He'd never get a biscuit if he married Janie. Besides, she's not mature enough for him."

"She could change."

"So could he, sweetheart," he drawled, pulling her close to kiss her. "But I wouldn't hold my breath in either case. Now here we are, at home, and all alone, and I'll give you one guess what I'd like you to do next," he whispered suggestively.

She smiled under his lips. "Would it have something to do with flour and olive oil and skim milk and a hot oven?" she whispered back.

He actually gasped. "Darling!" he exclaimed, and kissed her even harder.

She linked her arms around his neck. "So," she whispered, moving closer, "Just how badly do you want that pan of biscuits, sweetheart?" she teased.

Chuckling, he bent and lifted her clear of the floor and turned down the hall. "Let me show you!"

Eventually he got a pan of fresh biscuits and a whole jar of fresh apple butter to go on them—along with a nice pat of low-fat margarine. And he didn't even complain!

* * * * *

*Watch out for Cord Romero's scintillating
story to unfold in December 2003 from
Silhouette Books—*

Desperado

*by international bestselling author
Diana Palmer.*

Turn the page for a sneak preview…

Desperado

by

Diana Palmer

The ranch outside Houston was big and sprawling. It was surrounded by neat white fences that concealed electrical ones, to keep in the purebred Santa Gertrudis cattle that Cord Romero owned. There was also a bull, a special bull, that had been spared from a corrida in Spain by Cord's father, Mejias Romero—one of the most famous bullfighters in Spain—just before his untimely death in America. Once Cord grew up and had money of his own, he had traveled to his elderly cousin's ranch in Andalusia to get the bull and have it shipped to Texas. Cord called the old bull Hijito, little boy. The creature was still all muscle, although most of it was in his huge chest. He followed Cord around the ranch like a pet dog.

As Maggie Barton exited the cab with her suitcase, the big bull snorted and tossed his head on the other side of the fence. Maggie barely spared him a glance after she paid the driver. She'd come rushing home from Morocco in a tangle of missed planes, delays, cancellations and other obstacles that had caused her to be three days in transit. Cord, a professional mercenary and her foster brother, had been blinded. Most surprising, he'd asked for her through his friend Eb Scott. Maggie hadn't been able to get home fast enough. The delays had been agony. Perhaps, finally, Cord had realized that he cared for her…!

With her heart pounding, she pressed the doorbell on the spacious front porch with its green swing and glider and rocking chairs. There were pots of ferns and flowers everywhere.

Sharp, quick footsteps sounded on the bare wooden floors in the house and Maggie frowned as she pushed her long, wavy black hair out of her worried green eyes. Those steps didn't sound like Cord's. He had an elegance of movement in his stride that was long and effortless, masculine but gliding. This was a short, staccato step, more like a woman's. Her heart stopped. Did he have a girlfriend she didn't know about? Had she misinterpreted Eb Scott's phone call? Her confidence nosedived.

The door opened and a slight blond woman with dark eyes looked up at her. "Yes?" she asked politely.

"I came to see Cord," Maggie blurted out. Jet lag was already setting in on her. She didn't even think to give her name.

"I'm sorry, he isn't seeing people just yet. He's been in an accident."

"I know that," Maggie said impatiently. She softened the words with a smile. "Tell him it's Maggie. Please."

The other woman, who must have been all of nineteen, grimaced. "He'll kill me if I let you in! He said he didn't want to see anybody. I'm really sorry...."

Jet lag and irritability combined to break the bonds of Maggie's temper. "Listen, I've just come over a thousand miles.... Oh, the hell with it! Cord?" she yelled past the girl, who grimaced again. "Cord!"

There was a pause, then a cold, short "Let her in, June!"

June stepped aside at once. Maggie was made uneasy by the harsh note in Cord's deep voice. She left her suitcase on the porch. June gave it a curious glance before she closed the door.

Cord was standing at the fireplace in the spacious living room. Just the sight of him fed Maggie's heart. He was tall and lean, powerfully built for all his slimness, a tiger of a man who feared nothing in this world. He made his living as a professional soldier, and he had few peers. He was handsome, with light olive skin and jet-black hair with a slight wave. His eyes were large, deep set, dark brown. His eyebrows were drawn into a scowl as Maggie walked in, and except for the red wounds around his eyes and cheeks, he actually looked normal. He looked as if he could see her. Ridiculous, of course. A bomb he'd tried to defuse had gone off right in his face. Eb said he was blind.

She stared at him. This man was the love of her life. There had never been anyone but him in her heart. She was amazed that he'd never noticed, in the eighteen years their lives had been connected. Even his brief tragic marriage hadn't altered those feelings. Like him, she was widowed—but she didn't grieve for her husband the way he'd grieved for Patricia.

Her eyes fell helplessly to his wide, chiseled mouth. She remembered, oh, so well, the feel of it on hers in the darkness. It had been heaven to be held by him, kissed by him, after years of anguished longing. But very quickly the pleasure had become pain. Cord hadn't known she was innocent....

"How are you?" Maggie blurted out, hesitating just beyond the doorway, suddenly tongue-tied.

His square jaw seemed to tighten, but he smiled

coldly. "A bomb exploded in my face four days ago. How the hell do you think I am?" he drawled sarcastically.

He was anything but welcoming. So much for fantasies. He didn't need her. He didn't want her around. It was just like old times. And she'd come running. What a joke.

"It amazes me that even a bomb could faze you," she remarked with her old self-possession. She even smiled. "Mr. Cold Steel repels bullets, bombs and, especially, me!"

He didn't react. "Nice of you to stop by. And so promptly," he added.

She didn't understand the remark. He seemed to feel she'd procrastinated about visiting. "Eb Scott phoned and said you'd been hurt. He said..." She hesitated, uncertain whether or not to tell him everything Eb had said to her. She went for broke, but she laughed to camouflage her raw emotions. "He said you wanted me to come nurse you. Funny, huh?"

He didn't laugh. "Hilarious."

She felt the familiar whip of his sarcasm with pain she didn't try to hide. After all, he couldn't see it. "That's our Eb," she agreed. "A real kidder. I guess you have—what was her name?—June to take care of you," she added with forced lightness.

"That's right. I have June. She's been here since I got home." He emphasized the pronoun, for reasons of his own. He smiled deliberately. "June is all I need. She's sweet and kindhearted, and she really cares about me."

She forced a smile. "She's pretty, too."

He nodded. "Isn't she, though? Pretty, smart and

a good cook. And she's blond,'' he added in a cold, soft voice that made chills run down her spine.

She didn't have to puzzle out the remark. He was partial to blondes. His late wife, Patricia, had been a blonde. He'd loved Patricia....

She rubbed her fingers over the strap of her shoulder bag and realized with a start how tired she was. Airport after airport, dragging her suitcase, agonizing over Cord's true state of health for three long days, just trying to get home to him—and he acted as if she'd muscled her way in. Perhaps she had. Eb should have told her the truth, that Cord still didn't want her in his life, even when he was injured.

She gave him a long, anguished look and moved one shoulder restlessly. ''Well, that puts me in my place,'' she said pleasantly. ''I'm sure not blond. Nice to see you're still on your feet. But I'm sorry about your eyes,'' she added.

''What about my eyes?'' he asked curtly, scowling fiercely.

''Eb said you were blinded,'' she replied.

''Temporarily blinded,'' he corrected. ''It's not a permanent condition. I can see fairly well now, and the ophthalmologist expects a complete recovery.''

Her heart jumped. He could see? She realized then that he was watching her, not just staring into a void. It came as a shock. She hadn't been guarding her expressions. She felt uncomfortable, knowing he'd been able to glimpse the misery and worry on her face.

''No kidding? That's great news!'' she said, and forced a convincing smile. She was getting the hang of this. Her face would be permanently gleeful, like a piece of fired sculpture. She could hire it out for celebrations. This wasn't one.

"Isn't it?" he agreed, but his returned smile wasn't pleasant at all.

She shifted the strap of her bag again, feeling weak at the knees and embarrassed by her headlong rush to his side. She'd given up her new job and come running home to take care of Cord. But he didn't need her, or want her here. Now she had no job, no place to live and only her savings to get her through the time until she could find employment. She never learned.

He was barely courteous, and his expression was hostile. "Thanks for coming. I'm sorry you have to leave so soon," he added. "I'll be glad to walk you to the door."

She lifted an eyebrow, and gave him a sardonic look. "No need to give me the bum's rush," she said, falling back into her old habit of meeting sarcasm with sarcasm. "I got the message, loud and clear. I'm not welcome. Fine. I'll leave skid marks going out the door. You can have June scrub them off later."

"Everything's a joke with you," he accused coldly.

"It beats crying," she replied pleasantly. "I need my head read for coming out here in the first place. I don't know why I bothered!"

"Neither do I," he agreed with soft venom. "A day late and a dollar short, at that."

This was enigmatic, but she was too angry to question his phrasing. "You don't have to belabor the point. I'm going," she assured him. "In fact, it's just a matter of another few interviews and I can arrange things so that you'll never have to see me again."

"That would be a real pleasure," he said with a bite in his deep voice. He was still glaring at her. "I'll give a party."

He was laying it on thick. It was as if he were furious with her for some reason. Perhaps just her presence was enough to set him off. That was nothing new.

She only laughed. She'd had years to perfect her emotional camouflage. It was dangerous to give Cord an opening. He had no compunction about sticking the knife in. They were old adversaries.

"I won't expect an invitation," she told him complacently. "Ever thought of taking early retirement, while you still have a head that can be blown off?" she added.

He didn't answer. He just glared.

She shrugged and sighed. "I must be in demand somewhere," she told the room at large. "I'll have myself paged at the airport and find out."

She gave him one long, last look, certain that it would be the last time her eyes would see that handsome face. There was some old saying about divine punishment in the form of showing paradise to a victim and then tossing him back into reality. It was like that with Maggie, having known the utter delight of Cord's lovemaking only once. Despite the pain and embarrassment, and his fury afterward, she'd never been able to forget the wonder of his mouth on her body for the first time. The rejection she felt now was almost palpable, and she had to hide it.

It wasn't easy....

* * *

On sale in December 2003.

THE MILLIONAIRE'S PREGNANT BRIDE

by
Dixie Browning

DIXIE BROWNING

is an award-winning painter and writer, mother and grandmother. Her father was a big-league baseball player, her grandfather a sea captain. In addition to her nearly 80 contemporary romances, Dixie and her sister, Mary Williams, have written more than a dozen historical romances under the name Bronwyn Williams. Contact Dixie at www.dixiebrowning.com or at PO Box 1389, Buxton, NC 27920, USA.

One

Will Bradford switched off the lights in his tenth-floor office in the Wescott Building and debated whether or not to stop off at the Royal Diner for a bowl of chili on the way home. Too much trouble, he decided. After spending one more in a long string of eighteen-hour days trying to unravel the mess left behind by the unexpected death of his partner and one-time friend, Jack Wescott, he wasn't up to dealing with anything as complicated as a grease-stained menu. His three-day-a-week housekeeper would have left something in the freezer he could zap in the microwave.

That is, if he could stay awake long enough to eat.

You'd think the man had deliberately tried to scramble the books, Will mused tiredly as he reached for the coat of his rumpled, Western-cut suit, slung it over his left shoulder and headed for the elevator.

God knows, Jack Wescott had shaved a few corners over the years, but things were in worse shape than anyone had expected. A fanatic regarding privacy, Jack had essentially distrusted anything with a hard drive. Like most successful enterprises, Wescott Oil had a large computer division, yet Jack had insisted on keeping a hands-on set of paper files under lock and key.

Probably, Will mused, because he'd engaged in more than a few questionable business practices along the way to building his oil empire. Jack had been equally reckless in his personal life. Will had known about some of it and suspected more, even though the friendship that had begun more than fifteen years ago had cooled over the past few years.

Jack had been a womanizer, both before and after his marriage had ended. That sort of thing wasn't easy to keep hidden in a town like Royal, where gossip was a stock in trade. What had taken everyone by surprise, however, had been the sudden appearance of an illegitimate son shortly after Jack's death; Dorian Brady had turned up last month in Royal.

The resemblance between Dorian and Sebastian Wescott, Jack's legitimate son and heir, was striking enough that no one had doubted the relationship, even before it had been checked out. It seemed that when any of Jack's old flames got pregnant, he bought them a one-way ticket out of town. Evidently one of them had read about Jack's death and told her son, who figured it was time to call in a long-overdue debt.

As much as he hated the scandal for Sebastian's sake, Will couldn't blame the guy. If Dorian resented Jack's shabby treatment of him and his mother, he

hid it well. Sebastian had accepted him to the extent
of taking his half brother into his home and giving
him a job in the computer division of Wescott Oil.
Now Seb was pushing for Dorian's membership in
the Texas Cattlemen's Club.

Will decided to reserve judgment.

Jack's secretary was another matter. The first time
he'd seen her, she'd been backing out of the Royal
Diner, talking to someone still inside. He'd held the
door and waited patiently—tired, but not too tired to
appreciate the view.

Not that she'd been advertising the view. Just the
opposite, in fact. There'd been nothing at all outstanding in the tan-gray gabardine dress she'd been
wearing. The color had a name: one of those colors
with "au" in the middle. Mauve, taupe. He could
never remember what it was. With her glossy, brown
hair and delicate build, it had looked coolly elegant
on a day when the temperature could frazzle the
calmest nerves.

Two shapely young women passed by the diner
licking ice cream cones. They were wearing tight
jeans and skimpy, skin-tight tops. He'd barely spared
them a glance.

"It's over next to the library, I think," the lady
standing in the doorway was saying. "I've got several boxes to go, once I sort through them."

Nice hips. Slender build, rounded in just the right
places. Gabardine was a surprisingly sexy fabric
when it hung—as this did—over a shapely pair of
hips, merely hinting at the surface beneath.

He must have sighed. Will knew he hadn't said
anything, because what could he have said other
than, "Would you please either come in or go out,

lady? It's nearly three in the afternoon and I haven't had lunch.''

She turned—gasped—and wiped a three-scoop ice cream cone across his chest. ''Oh, my— Oh, dear— I'm so sorry!''

Will backed up, staring blankly down at the mess she'd made of one of his favorite ties. ''It's all right,'' he assured her. Then, when she began mopping the mess up with a handkerchief in one hand, the rapidly melting cone in the other, he said, ''Look, it's really all right, okay? No harm done.''

No harm a dry cleaner couldn't take care of. Trouble was, he had that three-thirty meeting. He could either go home and change clothes or go inside and have a quick lunch.

''Oh, Lord, I can't believe—and I think I know you, too. That's even worse.''

He was edging away, wanting to escape before his shoes caught the rest of her melting chocolate ice cream. ''No problem. It's all right.'' She looked as if she might burst into tears, which would be the last straw. He didn't know her. Might have seen her around town somewhere—she was the kind of woman a man wouldn't notice right off, but when he did, she'd be worth a second look.

Only not today. Not under these circumstances.

''Excuse me, I think I'll go drown myself.''

Sticky, hot, irritated, he managed a smile. ''Swimming pools frown on that sort of thing.''

''Is there still a French Foreign Legion? Do they take women? Look, I'm really, really—''

''Don't say it. Better go back inside and wash your hands before you get into more trouble.''

She opened her mouth, closed it again and sighed.

Looking disgustedly at the melting mess in her left hand, she tossed it in the trash receptacle, sighed again and walked away.

For several minutes Will stared after her. She was worth watching. Again, nothing particularly outstanding—no twitchy little behind, no slinky movements, she simply walked. Where the devil, he wondered, had he seen her before? There was something about her...

The second time he saw her was several days after the ice-cream episode. She was just coming out of the secretarial pool. On his way to meet someone in the lobby, he'd stopped and stared, tempted to go and ask her name and if she worked there and whether or not she'd be interested in exploring a brief, nonbinding relationship with him. Fortunately, she hadn't noticed. Fortunately, no one else had, either.

Equally fortunately, common sense had kicked in before he could be accused of workplace harassment. The trouble was, his social life had been moderated along with just about everything else as he'd neared the four-oh mark. He was out of practice.

He had seen her several times after that, and the less she did to call attention to her sexuality, the more intrigued he became. There was something challenging about a woman who went out of her way to downplay her feminine attractions. Made a man wonder what was under all the muted colors and understated styles. The lady was a challenge, and if there was one thing Will thrived on, it was challenge.

But not this kind of challenge.

He told himself it was probably something simple—maybe a minor midlife crisis. He'd made a policy of never mixing business with pleasure. In today's litigious society, it simply wasn't worth the risk of future embarrassment, awkwardness or worse. Even so, he'd been almost at the point of breaking his own rule and asking her out when Jack had moved in and staked a claim by whisking her up to the executive floor as his personal secretary.

Jack's tastes had invariably run to leggy blondes in thigh-high skirts, with big boobs and big blond hair. The Foster woman was a marked improvement. Quelling his own disappointment, Will had gone out three nights in a row with three different women and—always the gentleman—had managed to conceal his boredom.

As for what Diana Foster had seen in Jack Wescott, that was easy. At fifty-eight, the wealthy oilman had been in peak physical condition until he'd dropped dead of a massive heart attack. It was widely known that wealth was among the world's greatest aphrodisiacs, and Jack had been a practiced philanderer who enjoyed bragging about the notches on his bedpost.

At least he hadn't bragged about his latest conquest. If he had, Will might have decked the man. After which, Will would have been forced to sell his stock, turn in his resignation and move out to his ranch a few years earlier than he'd planned to retire.

What he couldn't understand now, after Jack's death, was what the quietly elegant Ms. Foster had gained from the affair. She still drove the same elderly sedan, still wore the same inexpensive classic styles and—so far as he could tell—owned no jewelry other than pearl studs and the type of wristwatch that could be purchased at most drugstores.

Not that he'd paid any particular attention to her, once he'd realized she was having an affair with his business partner. For all he knew, Jack might've been planning to marry the woman, even though Jack had sworn he would never let himself be trapped into marriage again.

But, if that had been the case, surely he'd have had his lawyers drawing up a prenuptial agreement, and there'd been nothing like that in the works when he'd died. As a rule, Jack had even his mistresses sign a settlement agreement so that they couldn't come back to haunt him. Dorian's mother had signed one, but obviously Dorian didn't consider the terms of the agreement to apply to him.

Waiting for the elevator, Will stroked the back of his neck, massaging away the tension that always seemed to settle there. Jack's will, which had been read four days ago, had been simple and direct. Other than a few token gifts to his household staff, Sebastian had inherited everything the IRS didn't claim.

As executor of Jack's estate, Will was still trying to reconcile a few discrepancies in his personal accounts. Jack had been notoriously delinquent when it came to balancing his own checkbooks.

Nodding to the night security guard who let him out of the building, Will set off to walk the eleven blocks to his own apartment. Maybe fresh air would work a miracle. Maybe his headache would ease and the incomprehensible entries on Jack's personal check stubs would miraculously begin to make sense.

And maybe he would quit obsessing on the quiet, elegant beauty who had begun to crop up in more than a few of his dreams.

On the long walk home, Will mulled over a few

minor discrepancies he'd come across just today. While the business's financial records were in excellent condition, thanks largely to his own hand on the controls, Jack's personal affairs weren't quite so tidy. In building the empire that bore his name, he had stepped on more than a few toes, cut more than a few corners and no doubt had paid off his share of politicians and predatory women. Which might account for the unexplained drafts for tens of thousands of dollars in the past few months.

Poor guy. He'd been warned more than once to tone down his lifestyle. Will had often heard him joke about having a few wild chickens come home to roost. One of them, Dorian Brady, already had.

How many more would there be?

Urged by the board to take over as president, Will had declined the honor. With Jack gone, he was now the senior partner, but getting himself mired any deeper in corporate crap wasn't among his long-term plans for the future. Once he turned over his tenth-floor offices to the mandatory outside auditors, he would have to clear out Jack's tower office to prepare for the new regime. Which meant he was probably going to need the help of Jack's secretary. He didn't know whether to dread it or look forward to it. All he knew was that the woman affected him in a way no woman had in nearly twenty years.

Midlife crisis?

Yeah…probably. And dammit, he didn't have time for it now.

Shoulders hunched, the tall, lean Texan strode along the empty sidewalk. This time of night, traffic was light. The weather was unusually mild for February despite the wind and the threat of rain. If he finished up by Friday, maybe he could spend a couple of days out at the ranch.

Or maybe not. There was still a lot of sludge to wade through before the company could move ahead at full speed. For a business the size of Wescott Oil to be run like a mom and pop market was not only criminal, it was damn near impossible in this age of government regulations and demanding stockholders. But by bribing and threatening the right people, Jack had managed to do things his way right up to the end.

The end...

God, what a waste. At fifty-eight, he'd looked no older than Will himself did at forty-one, thanks to great tailor, a good barber, a personal trainer and a top-notch plastic surgeon. For a man who routinely managed to tick off half of the Texas legislature and buy off the rest, he'd been one hell of a guy. He was going to be missed.

While a scratchy recording of Fleetwood Mac flowed from a battered portable phonograph, Diana propped a bare foot up on her lap and carefully painted her big toenail a deep shade of coral. Tears ran a crooked trail down her face, not because she missed Jack, exactly, but because...

Well, because it was such a waste. Underneath his crazy suspicions and his domineering ways, he'd been a good man. In some ways. At least he'd been good to her when it mattered most. Her mother had had the very best care right up to the end, and if it meant giving herself—Diana refused to call it selling herself—to a man like Jack Wescott, then it was well worth the shame.

Or the guilt. Whatever she was feeling, it probably wasn't grief, which was even more of a reason to feel guilty.

She screwed the cap on the bottle of nail polish, which she used only on her toes where it wouldn't show, and grabbed a tissue to blow her nose. "Get over it, Foster," she muttered. People said that all the time. Get over it. Deal with it.

And she would, she really would. She was nothing if not a realist. The thing was, she had never really wanted to be anyone's lover, especially having grown up in a household where love was never a factor.

Her parents had been what she'd once heard referred to as "tie-dyed rebels for peace." When the rebellion had lost its luster, her father had left his wife and daughter to "find himself." Lila, her mother, had gone to work in the cosmetics department of a local discount store for minimum wages and no benefits other than a minuscule discount.

Her father had eventually come back—still lost—and taken a job selling paper products. Less than a month later he had gotten drunk, blacked both his wife's eyes so she couldn't go to work, and then left town again.

They'd been "flower children." Their mottos: Make Love, Not War; If It Feels Good, Do It.

Growing up, Diana had rebelled against her parents' entire generation. Eventually she might have ended up marrying some nice, dull man, the antithesis of her own father. Someone who would have been good with children and kind to pets. Someone who would, at least, be there for his family.

Jack hadn't been a dull man, nor had he always

been nice. And while she'd let herself believe at first that he wanted to marry her, that had never been in the cards. He had set out on a deliberate campaign to seduce her, and once he'd discovered her weakness, he'd succeeded.

And now Jack was dead and she would soon be back in the secretarial pool. Jack's son Sebastian would be the new chairman, and Sebastian already had his own executive secretary, one who was more qualified for the position.

Diana's mother had never reconciled herself to the fact that her only child—her little princess—had settled for a secretarial course instead of trying for a college scholarship. "But, honey, you're so creative," she'd exclaimed so often in her fade-away voice.

"You mean because I used to write those awful poems for your birthday and Mother's Day? Mama, grow up. It's about time somebody in this family did."

That had been several years ago, before her mother had been diagnosed with cancer. Since then Diana had come a long way. She had found a job to help pay the bills and had ended up working for a man who had insisted on doing things in a way that would have probably driven most secretaries up the nearest wall. The system they'd worked out together had been somewhat unorthodox, but it had suited them both.

Well, she thought, sniffing and sighing heavily, that, too, was over. Done with. *Fini.* Period.

Period? Which reminded her of another possible problem....

But that was stress. Of course it was stress. They'd

always been careful—almost always. Although Jack, for all his polished charm, could occasionally be demanding, impatient and insensitive.

But it was over now, and she could get on with her life. Diana stretched her leg and wiggled her newly polished toes. Nail polish had been her favorite treat as a little girl. Her mother would polish her toenails and tell her it was because she was a princess, only she couldn't tell anyone. And they would look at each other and smile, and when her father came home, Diana would huddle in bed and listen to the awful fights and think, *I'm a secret princess. As soon as I'm big enough, Mama and I will go find our real home, and Daddy can't ever go there.*

Daddy had been killed when she was fourteen. By then she'd known she was no princess but only the daughter of a disillusioned flower child who lacked the courage to break away from her abusive marriage to an ex-hippy. Diana remembered her father chiefly for his long absences and his vicious temper.

"Girl, you are a mess! Get it together!" she growled softly to herself.

And she was going to, she really was. It would be awkward returning to the secretarial pool after months of working on the executive floor. For one thing it was a world-class rumor mill, and she herself would be the focus of an uncomfortable amount of gossip.

But before she made any decision she was going to have to help Mr. William K. Bradford, the senior partner and chief financial officer, sort out the mess Jack had left behind. And wouldn't you know, he'd turned out to be the man she'd plastered with melted chocolate ice cream.

Since then she'd tried to avoid him, hoping he would forget the incident, or at least forget who ruined what had to be a custom-tailored suit and a designer tie. Not to mention the white shirt. Chocolate stains were impossible to remove.

She could only hope he wouldn't remember her. He'd been wearing sunglasses. Maybe some of the ice cream had spattered those, too, and he hadn't seen her clearly.

The trouble was, she'd seen him. Had a good look at him, from his broad shoulders to his thick, dark hair and his wonderfully irregular features. What was there about certain men that made them so heartbreakingly attractive? There were probably thousands of men who were more handsome. Hundreds.

Dozens, at least. She didn't lose any sleep over any of them, while the very thought of having to work in close contact with Will Bradford was enough to make her break out in a heat rash. She hadn't exactly led a sheltered existence. She did know the facts of life. She simply didn't know how to deal with a man who made her think wicked thoughts so soon after her mother had died and she'd broken off with Jack.

So much for disapproving of her parents' early lifestyle. If It Feels Good, Do It.

She'd done it, and it hadn't even felt particularly good.

Huddling in the lopsided recliner her mother had bought at a going-out-of-business sale, she thought some more about William Bradford. He struck her as the kind of man who lived his life by a set of ironclad rules. She liked that in a man. Purpose. Discipline. Order.

From now on, Diana vowed, she would make rules of her own, rule number one being that she was in sole control of Diana Foster. From this day forward she would take complete responsibility for her own life.

Will was the last to arrive for the weekly dinner meeting in one of the smaller private rooms at the Texas Cattleman's Club, an exclusive establishment formed originally so that a few wealthy cattle barons and some of the early oilmen could escape from their wives for a night out. As years passed it had served as a convenient cover for a number of covert operations. Of the small group of close friends, all were ex-military and had been involved in any number of operations that never hit the news. Thank God things had been quiet on that front lately. With Jack's unexpected death, Will had had enough on his mind without having to fly off at a moment's notice to rescue some poor unfortunate who'd blundered into trouble.

Between missions, the club served as a fund-raising organization for various charities that had arisen as the small town of Royal doubled and tripled its size. Will was, unfortunately, a member of the club's committee whose duty it was to sift through the dozens of applications and choose a worthy recipient for the funds raised by the annual charity ball. He'd just as soon divide the take equally among the charities, but tradition precluded such a simple solution.

After nodding to a few of the older members doz-

ing over their *Wall Street Journal*s in the cigar,
brandy and wax-scented great room, Will opened the
massive oak door and closed it quietly behind him.
"Evening, gentleman," he greeted.

"Man, you look like hell." It was Jason, foreign
advisor and CIA agent, the youngest of the group,
who passed judgment on him.

Sebastian, Jack's son and newly appointed CEO
of Wescott Oil, looked as though he hadn't slept in
weeks. It was obvious his father's death and the new
responsibilities had taken their toll. Gamely he
grinned. "Things are that bad in your neck of the
woods, huh?"

"Not bad. Shall we say...disorganized? If your
father had suspected an OPEC spy of trying to infil-
trate the company to gather information, he might
have devised a similar plan for throwing him off
track. Anyone ordered yet? What are we having?"

Their tastes were as varied as the men themselves.
Keith Owens, owner of a computer software company, was still studying the bill of fare. Robert Cole,
private detective with an old-money background,
usually ordered seafood.

Will chose steak, medium rare, with a baked potato, no sour cream and a salad, which he didn't particularly want but which he ordered anyway because
at his age a smart man started thinking about health
and his own mortality.

Pity poor Jack hadn't started earlier.

Will hadn't had time to stop by the club in more
than a week. Since every man present was the son,
if not the grandson, of a former member, this group
was the closest thing to family he was ever apt to
have. He asked after each man individually, then

took a sip of the single drink he allowed himself each evening and said, "Want to tell me what all the snickers were about when I walked in?"

"What snickers? Oh, you must mean the bet. Seb has the dubious honor of heading up this year's gala, and he suggested that since we're all aging bachelors, we place a bet on which one will still be standing alone by the end of the year. Whoever wins can have the consolation prize of choosing the beneficiary," Rob explained.

Will looked from one man to the other. "You're not serious. Hell, I outgrew that kind of thing in prep school."

Jason, the youngest member of the group, enjoyed his playboy reputation enough to pick up the challenge. "Not that I'm particularly interested in game playing—" he was widely known for his games with the fairer sex "—but I'll win this one in a walk-away."

"Pretty sure of yourself, aren't you, old boy?"

Jason, his eyes alight with amusement, said, "Yeah, that about covers it." It was widely known, as well, that Jason was allergic to marriage.

And while Will didn't particularly want to win the consolation prize, marriage was definitely not in his future. Once had been enough.

"So, that's settled," Sebastian said, sounding vastly relieved. "Lets me off the hook."

It occurred to Will that, under the circumstances, maybe one of the others should have taken over the task of heading up this year's shindig. It was a daunting task at the best of times, and the man had just lost his father, after all.

"Next item on the agenda," Keith Owens said

around a mouthful of stuffed quail. "What about Dorian? Do we invite him to join the club?"

Sebastian abstained from commenting. Caution urged Will to suggest they not make any hasty decisions, but before he could voice the thought, Jason spoke up. "I vote we sit on it for a few weeks. All due respect, Seb, but we don't really know this guy."

After a brief discussion, it was decided to postpone making a decision. Will was relieved. Jason had razor-sharp instincts. Will trusted his instinct on most matters. By the time his dessert of fresh fruit compote was served, he was too tired to enjoy it. Shoving it across the table, he said, "Sorry, fellows, but if I don't make it to bed in the next half hour, you'll have to scrape me up off the street. Been a hell of a week."

After handing the accounting books to the outside auditors, Will turned his full attention to Jack's messy personal records. Will had already learned two disturbing things. First, that Diana Foster lacked the required qualifications for the position she'd been given. Second, that aside from a nice raise, she'd been the recipient of several large sums of money deposited to a checking account soon after she'd been promoted to the position of Jack's executive secretary. Putting that together with a remark Jack had once made about Diana's mother being ill, Will came to a conclusion that had set his blood to boiling.

It wasn't the kind of thing he could come right out and ask: Did you sleep with Jack so that he would pay your mother's medical expenses? Hell, he didn't know her well enough to ask anything that personal. He wasn't sure he really wanted to know the answer.

Oh, yeah, and there was a third thing, too. He learned that Diana, in a pair of black slacks, bending over an open carton on the floor, had a sweetly rounded bottom that could make a marble statue salivate.

On the way up to the tower office, Will reminded himself that only a few months ago Jack's old secretary, Miss Lucy, had been put out to pasture, if not with a golden parachute, at least with a gold-plated umbrella. Shortly after that, Miss Foster had been yanked out of the secretarial pool and propelled upstairs to the executive suite.

Knowing the lady had sold herself to the highest bidder, Will felt slightly sick. She might not look the part, but she'd evidently become just one more in a long line of Jack's women.

What was she, vamp or virgin?

Obviously not the latter.

Which didn't change the fact that for the past few months, whenever they'd found themselves in the same elevator together he'd had to stare at the indicator buttons and think about something else. The ranch. His favorite horse. The chances of being trapped overnight in an elevator with Diana Foster.

None of which had helped. He had a feeling that in the pitch-dark depths of a West Virginia coal mine, he would be aware of her nearness. Aware that she had hair like a dark silk waterfall, eyes like melted chocolate and skin that looked cool as snow but hinted at banked fires underneath. If she wore perfume, it was not easily discernible. Instead there was an aura about her that reminded him of dark roses, satiny wood and fine wine.

Probably because he'd seen her on more than a few occasions in Jack's walnut-paneled offices.

It was Saturday morning. Will and Diana had both come in to clear out the last of the personal items in Jack's office so that the cleaning crew could do their job and Seb could call in the decorators. He managed to keep his mind on business for almost an hour until she turned, tape roller in hand, her dark hair brushing her shoulder. "Shall I label this box personal and put it with those others for Sebastian?"

"What's in it? Oh, yeah—trophies, certificates, pictures..." Jack with several politicians. Jack with a couple of Hollywood types. Jack with his foot on the neck of a dead lion, and another eight-by-ten glossy of Jack with a dead blue marlin. "Yeah, go ahead. Here, I'll move it for you."

"Use your knees, not your back," she warned in the voice that had come as something of a surprise the first time he'd ever heard it. Quiet, a little bit husky. The type of voice advertisers paid a fortune for, but without the fake seductiveness that was used to sell everything from potency pills to plumbing supplies.

"Huh?" Real intelligent, Bradford.

"To lift the box. Squat, don't just bend over. Better yet, drag it like I did all the others."

Will had a feeling Sebastian was going to want to change quite a few things now that he had the power. Father and son were nothing at all alike. They hadn't gotten along particularly well, although each was brilliant in his own way.

"Yes, ma'am," Will muttered, amused at Diana's

bossiness. Nevertheless, he bent his knees slightly, leaned over and lifted the box, which was filled with books, trophies and framed photographs. "Where?" he said with a grunt.

"There." She pointed.

He set it up on top of the stack by the door and managed to resist grabbing his back. Masking his grimace with a smile, he said, "I could do with some lunch, how about you?"

Turning slowly, Diana surveyed the spacious tower office with its paneled walls, the walnut louvered shutters and the heavy, lined linen draperies. Not for Jack Wescott the usual preference for glass, leather and steel.

"How much more do we have to do? I cleaned out the records room and the bathroom." A length of hair fell forward, and she brushed it back. That morning her heavy, straight brown hair had been confined in one of those twisted arrangements on the back of her head. He could have told her about hair like hers and the laws of gravity.

"Then that about does it," he said. "Cleaning staff will be in tonight. They can take down the curtains and either toss 'em or send 'em out to be cleaned. They've been here for as long as I can remember."

She touched the soft, sun-faded fabric the way a woman would. "I don't think Jack ever even noticed them. I guess most men wouldn't, but they're sort of nice, aren't they? In a subtle, understated kind of way."

"Yeah, I suppose so." So are you, lady. In a subtle, understated kind of way.

Will made up his mind to give her the draperies

once they came back from the cleaners. Unless her living quarters were a hell of a lot larger than his, he had no idea what she would do with all those yards of heavy, lined fabric. Slipcover her house, maybe.

Still, it eased his conscience, because as soon as they wound things up here, he'd already made up his mind to offer her a bonus and encourage her to leave town. The last thing poor Seb needed after dealing with the sudden death of his father and the appearance of an illegitimate half brother was to have to deal with any possible demands from his father's ex-mistress.

After washing up in the luxurious washroom, they locked the door and crossed the hall to the elevators. Dorian Brady and two clerks from the computer department got on at the floor below. Will nodded to Dorian. He was still withholding judgment when it came to Jack's by-blow. There was something about him—almost a watchfulness—that raised a few red flags.

But then, that was probably because Seb was Will's friend, and this guy, whatever his credentials, was an interloper.

As the elevator sped silently down to the lobby, Diana said, "What about the boxes of files I took home with me? Is there any hurry about going through them?"

The doors opened soundlessly, and the small group filed out but lingered nearby. Will, noticing the way Dorian was eyeing his late-father's secretary, moved to block his view as they crossed the plush lobby. If any man was going to ogle the woman, it wasn't going to be some shifty-eyed kid in a flashy two-toned suit and a bolo tie.

Not until they were outside did he answer her question. "It's all personal stuff, isn't it? Nothing to do with the estate?"

"The boxes? As far as I know."

"Then let's let it ride, okay? What do say we stop by the Royal for some chili and coconut pie?" He made the offer only because he'd kept her long past lunch time. All he really wanted to do was go home, watch headline news and sleep for the next twenty-four hours.

Well, maybe not all... "Or if you'd rather, we could drive over to Claire's."

And then, damned if she didn't start crying, right there in broad daylight.

Thank God the Saturday-morning traffic was light.

Well, hell...

Two

They ate at the Royal Diner. Diana ordered the chili and a glass of milk to douse the fire. She didn't talk much, but then, Will wasn't used to having conversation with his meals unless he ate at the club. He was still trying to figure out why she'd started crying, but when he'd asked her, she'd just shaken her head.

Women.

At least she'd stopped crying as suddenly as she'd started. Claimed dust had blown in her eye.

Sure it had.

"World-class coconut pie," he said, forking up the last bite from his plate. "Want to take a slice home with you—or maybe a whole pie?"

Another thing about her that got to him was her smile. It started with a crinkling of the eyes, tweaked the corners of her lips and then it was gone, almost making a man wonder if he'd only imagined it.

"No, but thank you. I'd better get home before the rain starts again. It doesn't rain often around here, but once it starts, it can make up for lost time."

"Weather's been crazy everywhere these past few years."

So Will drove her back to the office building and left her at her car. Earlier that morning he'd carried down a box of her personal belongings. A small box. Evidently, she traveled light. He'd found himself wondering what was in it. Her own personal photographs? Family? A boyfriend? He doubted that, under the circumstances.

He hardly knew her, but if he had to guess, he'd say she wasn't the type of woman to spread her personal relics around for public view.

But then, if he'd had to guess, he would never have pegged her for one of Jack's conquests, either.

When she started to close her car door, he held it open and leaned down. "You're sure you're all right, Diana? You look a little washed out."

"Thanks," she said, and shot him another one of her quirky smiles. "Nothing a little blusher won't take care of, I hope."

Will watched her as she drove away in an eighties model sedan that was just one of the mysteries about Diana Foster that plagued him. She had a face that could easily be called patrician. A body that was tall, almost too lean, yet definitely, temptingly feminine. She wore outfits that could be bought at any discount store, yet he could easily imagine her striding down a runway wearing one of those slinky, transparent, cut-down-to-here-and-up-to-there outfits designed to raise a man's blood pressure into the danger zone.

She could do that wearing black polyester slacks,

a cotton pullover sweater and a battered twill raincoat.

Watching her drive off, swerving to avoid the deepest puddles, he visualized her mouth. She hadn't bothered to replace the lipstick she'd eaten off with her chili.

Because she'd forgotten?

Or because he wasn't worth the bother?

If she had any idea how vulnerable her naked lips looked, she'd have layered it on with a roller.

Vulnerable?

Where the hell had that come from? Tack, his ranch manager would have told him he'd been smoking too much locoweed.

One thing for sure—once the transition at work was completed, he was going to hightail it out to the ranch, spend a couple of weeks working with his stock, and then maybe go fishing. Maybe Baja. Maybe even the Outer Banks. Somewhere where nobody had ever heard of Wescott Oil.

It was still fairly early. Things were moving along faster than she'd expected at the office, thanks to Will Bradford's efficiency. The rest could probably be accomplished in a few days. Mostly they had worked on weekends, to avoid interference by curious staff members eager to see what changes would be made, not only to the decor but to the operations. Sebastian and his father had never seen eye-to-eye on many things.

Pulling out of the employees' parking lot, Diana imagined the big mug of cocoa she would have as soon as she got home. Since earliest childhood it had been her favorite comfort food, and, for no reason at all, she felt in sudden need of comfort. Probably this crazy weather. The temperature had dropped since they'd left the diner. A gust of wind sent a plastic bag and a large paper cup, complete with lid and straw, scurrying across the street in front of her car, distracting her from her thoughts momentarily.

This was the kind of weather when she would like nothing better than to curl up with a good book and alternately read and doze for the next twelve hours.

She yawned. Stress again. Too many decisions to be made.

What she *should* do was go through those boxes Jack had sent home with her, as if he'd had some sort of premonition. For all she knew, they contained Sebastian's baby pictures and report cards. Or maybe love letters from all the women who had gone before her. She'd heard the whispers before she'd ever met the man.

But she was simply too tired tonight. Ever since Jack had died, two months ago, she'd been trying to make plans for the future. The trouble was she couldn't seem to stay awake long enough to eat, much less to decide whether or not to move back to the secretarial pool at Wescott or pack up, leave town and look for another job in a new town where she didn't know a soul.

Lately, all she seemed able to do was weep and sleep. Maybe she needed vitamins.

Without thinking, she pulled into the parking lot outside the small walk-in clinic she had passed every day on her way to work. There was probably nothing wrong with her that a handful of vitamins and a good night's sleep wouldn't cure, but why take chances? She needed to recover her energy if she was going to get through these next few days and decide on her future. Preventive medicine couldn't prevent everything, but she was still a firm believer in taking control. Of her health, her life—everything. It wouldn't hurt to have a professional check her out while she still had her company insurance, in case she decided to move on.

Little more than an hour later Diana walked out in a daze, oblivious to the rain that pounded down on her bare head. Oblivious to the wind that whipped her tan trench coat around her legs.

Pregnant?

Impossible!

Impossible but true. Three months, as far as Dr. Woodbury could determine without further tests. "Does it have to go on my record?" Diana had asked the nurse, thinking of all the embarrassing questions that could, and probably would, be asked. She didn't know how many people had guessed about her and Jack—they'd both gone out of their way to be discreet, but in a town like Royal, secrets had a way of leaking out.

"Not if you don't intend to use your insurance."

"Oh. Well, could I just pay cash today and think about it?" With any luck, she could be in another town, settled in another job before she needed further medical attention.

Was pregnancy considered a preexisting condition?

Diana had a feeling the nurse was good at reading between the lines. "We can work it out any way that suits you, hon. Stop by the window and you can either pay today or we'll bill you. Here, you'll want to read these pamphlets. They tell you what to expect at which stage. Right now it's one thing, tomorrow it might be something else. We'll make you an appointment for six weeks, shall we?''

Diana nodded, knowing she wouldn't be in Royal in another six weeks. This changed everything. Leaving was no longer an option, it was imperative. Once the pregnancy began to show and people put two and two together and realized whose baby she was carrying, things would be awkward, to say the least.

A baby.

To think she'd vowed to take control of her own life from here on out. Evidently, she hadn't made the decision soon enough. She had always tried to be careful, but there had been that one time…. Jack had never been known for his patience. One time was all it took.

Out on the sidewalk she took a deep breath and tried to quell the rising panic by reminding herself that she'd always been the most levelheaded member of her family. The *only* levelheaded member.

After her father had died, her mother had fallen apart. Blamed herself and wept endlessly, claiming she hadn't been a good enough wife. As much as she hated to admit it now, Diana had lost patience with her mother more than once. She had honestly thought, though, that if they moved to a new locale, her mother might perk up and take an interest in life again.

So they'd moved to Royal, Texas, a place she'd heard mentioned on the news one night, and she'd got a job as a secretary at Wescott Oil.

Instead of perking up, Lila Foster's depression had grown worse, until Diana had insisted she undergo a

complete examination to rule out any physical cause
for her lethargy. It was only then that her mother had
been diagnosed with advanced ovarian cancer.

Frantic, Diana had been arguing with the insurance
department at Wescott the day she'd met Jack Wescott, founder and chief shareholder of Wescott Oil.

"Whoa, little lady," he'd said, clasping her by the
arms as she'd backed out the door, still yelling, just
as he was entering the building. He had held her a
moment too long, staring at her angry tears, then he'd
asked her name.

A week later she'd been moved up to the executive
floors, where Jack, who was old enough to be her
father, had begun a determined assault on her heart.

At least, she'd thought at the time it was her heart.
Frantic with worry, she'd made mistake after mistake. It was a wonder she hadn't been fired, but instead Jack had given her a raise and stepped up his
courtship, offering her jewelry, a car, even a house.

It was when she'd burst into tears and poured out
her story that he'd offered the one thing she hadn't
been able to refuse. The finest care available for her
mother.

By the time her mother had died, Diana had been
spending her days at the hospital and at least three
nights a week with Jack at his lake cabin. Numbly,
she'd gone through the motions of sex, often crying
before it was over.

If he'd been brutal, she could almost have borne
it better, but instead he'd been tender. They hadn't
been in love, but the relationship they'd shared had
had value to him. She had an idea she was the only
one who had realized it, but in his own way, Jack

had been as lonely as she was. She had broken it off after her mother's death. He'd seemed to understand.

And now she was going to have his baby. Thank goodness no one knew about it. The sooner she left town, the better.

The next morning Diana lay in bed, trying to find the energy to get up. She hadn't accomplished a single thing when she'd gotten home from the clinic the day before. Instead she'd crashed on the miserable sofa with a sprung spring stabbing her in the ribs. She had slept, woken up and eaten half a box of vanilla wafers and then slept some more. That night she had lain awake for hours, trying to organize her life into some workable pattern.

A baby. Dear Lord, she couldn't even manage to make decisions for herself. How could she ever take care of a baby?

By morning the rain had ended, but the temperature had plummeted still further. She crawled out of bed shivering, thought about breakfast and decided against it—too many vanilla wafers in the middle of the night could do that to a woman. Instead she dressed in her warmest slacks and a turtleneck sweater and headed for the office. There was a certain security in habit. Time to start breaking old habits and forming new ones, Diana reminded herself, only not quite yet. Not today.

Now, eleven stories up in the tower office where she'd worked for the past few months, Diana gazed out the undraped windows, watching as men in overcoats and wool-lined denim jackets moved briskly along the sidewalks below. Limousines and pickup trucks moved sedately along Royal's Main Street.

Women wearing fur coats and custom-made boots dashed from heated cars to heated churches.

Winter came in several varieties in Texas. Wet and cold was the worst. Silently she vowed that the next time she relocated, it would be to a place where the seasons were more temperate. She'd had enough of extremes.

Will, too, was leaning against a windowsill. He'd been there when she'd come in, and she'd apologized for no logical reason for being late. Neither of them had been obligated to come in today. There wasn't that much more to do.

"I don't know what's wrong with me." Well, she did, of course.... "I've always been a morning person."

"Not a problem. I wasn't expecting you, anyway. There's nothing much more to be done here."

The cleaning crew had already started. The curtains were gone, the carpet people would be in next. Diana was surprised that Will was there at all, but then, his own office was probably overrun with auditors.

"You're right." She sighed, marveling at how drastically life had changed for a little girl who had once depended on toenail polish for her identity.

Feeling his eyes on her, she glanced up, wondering at the fleeting expression of...what? Interest? She'd known for days that he was curious about her. The trouble was, she'd been just as curious—just as interested in him, even before that. What woman wouldn't be?

But anything more than the business relationship they had cautiously established was out of the question. If she'd learned one lesson it was the value of separating business from personal life. By now everyone must have guessed why the newest hired secretary in the pool had been yanked upstairs to work for the boss.

Will must certainly have guessed. Avoiding his look, she scuffed the toe of her loafers over an ink stain on the carpet under the edge of Jack's desk. "I hope the cleaners can get it out. But then, Sebastian..." She didn't know him personally, but for now there was only one Mr. Wescott at Wescott Oil, and that was still Jack. "He'll probably want to have the whole place recarpeted."

Ignoring her remark, Will said, "What would you say to transferring to the Houston offices?"

She felt behind her for a chair. As much as she'd been thinking about relocating—especially now that she knew about the baby—the one thing she hadn't considered was a transfer. "You mean go on working for Wescott Oil?"

He nodded. The way he was studying her made her wonder if she'd remembered to floss her teeth before she'd dashed out that morning. Lately she'd been feeling so awful it was all she could do to get out of bed. She still felt queasy, probably from skipping breakfast.

Or maybe not.

"You don't have any family here, as I understand it. No...close relationships?"

He *had* to have suspected what had been going on. The two men had been friends for years, according to Jack. Besides, as CFO, he must have known about the money Jack had given her to pay her mother's bills, even though she was almost certain it had come out of Jack's personal account.

Had Sebastian known?

How utterly embarrassing. Houston might not be far enough away if everyone in town knew about her relationship with the Wescott of Wescott Oil.

Sebastian and her baby would be half brothers. And half brother to the new man in the computer division, Dorian Brady. According to the grapevine, he'd been another of Jack's mistakes.

Diana took three deep, slow breaths. It didn't help. She swallowed a sudden surge of nausea. Things were getting entirely too complicated. If Sebastian had any idea she was pregnant with Jack's baby, would he try to take it away from her? *Could* he?

He was certainly in a better position to take care of a child than she was. Hadn't he taken in his illegitimate half brother, Dorian?

If she'd had to have an affair, why couldn't it have been with an ordinary man instead of a man who could reach out from the grave and steal her baby from her?

But, of course, an ordinary man would never have been able to do what Jack had done for her mother.

Will moved away from the window, flexing his broad shoulders. Even looking as if she'd swallowed a fly, the lady was a major distraction. "We've got everything under control here. Why don't you take off for a few days. Think over what I said about transferring to Houston and give me your answer next week, all right?"

He watched the last dregs of color fade from her face and wondered what the devil he'd said to cause her to look as if she'd lost her last friend in the world.

Suddenly she turned and rushed into the private bathroom Jack had recently had fitted out with a hot tub and a large screen TV. Sounds of retching came clearly through the door, which had bounced open when she'd slammed it behind her.

"Miss Foster? Diana? Are you okay?"

Come to think of it, she'd looked sort of shaky every morning they'd worked together. No matter what she'd said about being a morning person, some women simply weren't at their best early in the day.

She was on her knees, struggling to get to her feet when he let himself in. "Diana? Look, if you need to go home, I'll drive you, all right? You're obviously in no shape to drive yourself."

She turned to him then. Big brown eyes, looking like chestnuts in the snow. "Yes, I am," she said, swallowing hard. "I'm just fine."

Will dampened a towel and handed it to her, and she held it to her face for a moment. A long moment. He was still standing there, feeling acutely uncomfortable, when she looked up at him again.

"If I transfer to Houston, I'd still have my company insurance, wouldn't I?"

"Insurance? Yeah, sure. Want to tell me why that's so important?"

She stared at him, abject misery in every line of her slender body, and the answer suddenly blindsided him. "Oh, hell. You're pregnant, aren't you?"

To her credit, she didn't try to lie. "Just barely."

"Just barely? Just a *little bit* pregnant?"

"Look, it's not a problem. I mean, I can go on working for months once my hormones settle down, according to—well, the experts."

"And which experts would that be?"

She shook her head, reached behind her to put down the lid, then sat on the commode. Will sat on the edge of the monstrous hot tub with the gold-plated faucets and the mini refrigerator within easy reach. He wondered if Diana and Jack had ever used it together.

"It doesn't matter. It doesn't concern you or Wescott Oil or anyone else but me. I paid cash at the clinic. And Houston's fine. How soon can I transfer?"

"Whoa, hang on a minute. This changes things."

"No, it doesn't."

She was making an effort to conceal it, but the lady was scared out of her penny loafers. She was shivering, and the temperature was somewhere in the low seventies.

"Hot tea? Isn't that the usual prescription? I'll make some tea and see if I can find some crackers."

"No, that's…" Her voice trailed off, and she nodded weakly. "A cola? Something carbonated?"

So he led her back into the office and settled her in the most comfortable chair. She looked lost. Vulnerable. He didn't think she'd appreciate being told as much, so he poured a freshly opened soda over ice and waited for it to fizz down while he thought of the best course of action.

Under the circumstances there was no best course of action. All the same, he knew what he had to do.

"Is it Jack's?" He was pretty sure it was, but he was a firm believer in covering all the bases.

"That doesn't concern you." She met his eyes with a miserable but unwavering look that was sheer bravado.

The baby was Jack's. Otherwise, she would have denied it. He'd come to recognize a basic honesty about the woman in the brief time they'd been working together. It was just one of too many things about her that drove him a little crazy. One minute he'd be thinking of her as just another in a long line of Jack's women. The next, he'd be looking at her as the innocent victim of a lecherous jerk who knew exactly which button to push when he wanted something.

Or someone.

For years Will had been dealing with the untidy loose ends left by his hardheaded, heedless friend. Ladies who claimed Jack had promised to marry them, when Will knew damned well the man had never promised any such thing. Jack had been married once, to Sebastian's mother. That had been before Will's time. Will hadn't asked about it, and Jack had never volunteered any information. Neither had Sebastian.

As for his long string of alliances, most lasting no more than a few months, Jack usually made the women sign releases before he even took them to bed. He hadn't gotten where he was by being careless about minor details.

One woman claimed he'd given her a house in Midland but had forgotten to give over the deed. Jack had been dead only three days when she'd come barreling up to the top floor to demand that deed.

Will, still in shock himself, had taken the time to look into the matter and discovered that his reckless friend had given her a one-year lease on a tract house. As the lease still had seven months to run, he'd let it stand.

No woman, to his knowledge, had ever come forth claiming to be pregnant with a little Wescott heir, though it was possible that more than one had found herself in that condition. As a rule Jack paid his women off and hustled them out of town if there was the slightest possibility of that happening.

Matter of fact, this woman hadn't made the claim, either. Which was only one of the reasons why Will decided to clean up one last mess his untidy friend had left behind. He wasn't sure Diana could handle it financially—knew damned well she couldn't handle it emotionally if today was an example.

"Feeling better now? Look, don't worry about the insurance. If I set the wheels in motion right away, we can be married within the week."

Her jaw fell. It was a delicate jaw, one he'd like to cup with his hand, but this was hardly the time. "I'm talking a business arrangement, Diana. I have a pretty good idea of your resources—" At her look of indignation, he said, "Yeah, I know, I had no right, but you see, one of the trails I had to follow to unravel Jack's financial affairs led directly to your bank account. I finally figured it out with a little research." Not to mention recalling a few of Jack's insensitive remarks that Will had only recently put into context.

She was breathing too fast. There was an angry spark in her eyes that he'd as soon not have to deal with. But determined to settle things before she split, he plowed ahead.

"Look, it makes sense as a purely business arrangement. I'm unattached. You're unattached. You need something that I can offer."

"Fine." She crossed her arms over her chest— breasts. Uh-uh, he preferred to think of the area as a chest. "What do you need, Mr. Bradford? That is, what would you get out of it?"

His smile held little warmth. "Call me Will...Danny."

"My name is Diana," she snapped icily.

"Right. Diana. As for what I need, how about that warm feeling you get when you write a check to your favorite charity?"

Oops. Another misstep. Switching gears, he leaned his hips against the windowsill and tried to reason with her from another direction. "I take it Jack didn't ask you to sign an agreement?" At her look of confusion, he nodded. "I thought not. By paying your mother's hospital bills he had you right where he wanted you. But you see, Jack's gone now. You're going to need some help and I don't want Sebastian to be—"

"As if I would go to Sebastian! This is none of his business—nor yours, either!"

"Are you going to keep it?"

"My baby? Of course I'm going to keep it, it's mine!" Her hands went to her stomach, still flat and almost too lean.

Will read her thoughts as clearly as if she'd spoken them. In a few months—maybe even a few weeks— it wouldn't be quite so flat. There was bound to be talk, even if she transferred to Houston. Hell, half the folks in Texas knew Jack's reputation. All it would take was a few words, and poor Seb would find himself saddled with another of his father's by-blows. Whether or not she agreed, Seb's conscience would make him step in.

"Look, if we get married, there are several ways we can handle this. We can settle on a lump sum— enough to support you and the baby until you can get back on your feet, or we can—"

"Absolutely not!" Her eyes sparkled angrily.

"Or I could lease you a place to live and arrange for a monthly stipend to be paid into an account. Of course, you'd have to sign a release, but we can work that out later."

He wondered if she was going to take a swing at him. In all honesty he couldn't much blame her if she did. It was a hell of a position to be in, having to insult a woman to make sure she was taken care of. "You don't have to decide right this minute."

"Fine. I'll let you know in a few years what you can do with your generous offer."

Ouch. How the hell did a man handle a pregnant female porcupine? It wasn't as if he was interested in her personally.

At least, not seriously. That wouldn't even make sense.

"I'm talking about a business arrangement. Think about it and I'll call you in the morning."

Five minutes after Will left, Diana was sitting where he had left her, staring at a tiny dark spot on the cream carpet where one of Jack's cigar ashes had fallen. Jack had been rough on carpets.

On women, too, she thought sadly.

As for Will, he was out of his mind. Did he really think she was that desperate? If there was one thing she had learned early in life it was that a bad marriage was not the answer to anyone's problems. No child of hers was going to grow up the way she had, hiding her head under the covers, telling herself that any day now a kindly king would see the polish on her toenails and recognize her as his long-lost daughter.

A business arrangement. Ha!

First thing in the morning she would call personnel and see if she could set the transfer into motion herself.

One floor below, Will sat in his own quiet office, both feet propped on his desk, and stared at the single painting on his wall. It was one he'd commissioned of the modest ranch he'd bought soon after he'd gone to work for Jack Wescott. He'd had nothing particular in mind when he'd bought the place—a few thousand acres of woods and grassland, with a farmhouse and a few outbuildings. Since then he had built himself a house and hired a couple to stay in the old house and look after things. He'd simply needed something more than his job. A bolt hole, in case Jack ever went too far over the line and things blew up.

It hadn't happened. Jack had managed to stay just this side of the law, including the countless miles of red tape that all but hamstrung the oil industry. Will had become a full partner, and the ranch had become a place to unwind when he could spare the time. He had a small herd of quarter horses, good breeding stock. Tack Gilbert, his manager, had hired a few hands to look after the place. Diana could stay there until the baby was born, and then they could renegotiate.

At least he'd do better by her than Jack had done by Dorian's mother. Whoever the poor woman had been, she'd probably deserved better than being handed a one-way ticket out of town.

Will had no interest in marrying again, in spite of that damn fool bet the guys had made the other night at the club. He'd never forgiven himself for not being there when Shelly, his wife, had been killed.

But in this case, marriage was the simplest solution. He could marry Diana, claim the baby as his own and spare poor Seb from any more unpleasant revelations. Whether or not anyone believed him, they'd have better sense than to question his claim. He and Diana could spend the occasional weekend together for the sake of appearances, then, after a year or so, they could renegotiate.

Hell, even that much was better than a lot of the marriages he knew about. Half the men his age had been married and divorced at least once.

He happened to know Diana's age. She was twenty-eight to his forty-one. An uncomfortable stretch if this were to be a normal marriage, but it wasn't. She was carrying another man's baby and as for him, lust notwithstanding, he was long past the age for romance.

"Ah, Jack, you sorry son of a gun," he muttered. "You're not worth the salt it would take to cure your hide. I'm doing this for your kid's sake, not yours."

Maybe he was, and maybe he was doing it for another reason, one he'd as soon not examine too closely.

Hell, it was the right thing to do, and so he'd do it.

Three

Diana dressed carefully in a black three-piece suit with a gray silk blouse, examined her image in the mirror, then quickly removed the outfit and tossed it on the pile on her bed.

Smile, for heaven's sake, you're getting married today!

The softest, most romantic thing she owned was a muumuu or her peach-colored sweatsuit. Hardly wedding wear, she thought ruefully.

It was a business arrangement, strictly, and only that, she reminded herself. She had called Will on the private number he'd given her and had said, "Yes. All right, I will." Just that, no more. Then she'd congratulated herself on taking control of her life and doing what was best for her baby.

Will had set the time and place with no more interest in his voice than if he'd been scheduling a routine visit to the dentist. He would probably wear the same thing he wore to work every day—one of those stunning suits that whispered "Texas" without all the fancy piping and waist-hugging style so many men seemed to go for.

By all rights, she should wear the same kind of thing she'd worn every day to the office. Something that wouldn't demand attention, that wouldn't have to be dry-cleaned after each wearing and something that could in no way be described as seductive. Something suitably secretarial.

One look at her apartment reminded her of why she dressed the way she did—in tailored suits, shirt-waist dresses in conservative colors and sensible shoes.

"Oh, Mama, you really did a number on me, didn't you?" she whispered, picking up one of Lila's beloved candles, the scented wax embedded with seashells. Her mother's touch was everywhere, from the lava lamps and beaded macramé wall hangings to the lavender walls and orange shag rug. Hoping to pull her out of her depression when they'd moved to Royal, Diana had encouraged Lila to decorate their small apartment, claiming she was too busy settling into her new job.

The result had turned out to be a colorful cross between early thrift shop and late Woodstock, but Diana hadn't complained—she'd hardly noticed. With settling into a new job in a new town and worrying about her mother's increasing listlessness, a tacky apartment had been the least of her concerns. She had lived in far worse places.

Then her mother's condition had been diagnosed. After that, the apartment had served only as a place where she kept her clothes so that she could rush in and change between work and the hospital.

And Jack's cabin….

Now, without ever having come to terms with the past, she was about to take on the role of Mrs. William Bradford. A *temporary* role, she told herself. Just until the baby came and she was settled in a new job, a new town. It might seem as if she was relinquishing control over her life, but she wasn't. Not really. She was only being sensible. The best insurance she could have was that her baby would be born a Bradford. Without DNA testing, which she would refuse to permit, no one could prove otherwise. At the very least it should settle any perceived risk of her cashing in on Jack's name.

"I'll make sure to lay in a good supply of nail polish, honey pie," she murmured, touching the place where only inches away, her daughter or son lay sleeping.

What if it was a boy? She could hardly polish his toenails and offer him hope by telling him he was a secret prince. Maybe she could afford to buy him a pony. What little boy wouldn't love to grow up to be a cowboy?

The wedding was to take place in Judge Shirley Mattock's offices on Friday afternoon at four. The guests consisted of Will's closest friends, Sebastian Wescott, Jason Windover, Keith Owens and Robert Cole. She had met Sebastian, of course, at work. The others were strangers.

Why hadn't she thought to invite someone of her own?

Not that she had any close friends in Royal. There hadn't really been time to make friends before she'd been plucked out of the secretarial pool and sent up to the tower office. After that, the other women she'd worked with had seemed rather cool.

Don't you dare get sick, she warned herself silently, quelling a familiar uneasy feeling. Will had insisted on picking her up, but she'd insisted right back. "It's unlucky for the groom to see the bride on her wedding day," she'd told him. "I'll drive."

She pulled in to the parking lot behind the courthouse only five minutes later. Will was there to meet her. "I was afraid you'd changed your mind and skipped town."

"I can still do that," she told him. "It's not too late to withdraw your offer." So much for that old superstition about the bride and groom not seeing each other before the ceremony on the day of the wedding. Maybe it didn't count, since it wasn't that kind of a wedding.

"We had an agreement. I don't go back on my word." He leveled a piercing stare at her and asked, "Do you?"

By then they were at the door. She thought fleetingly of what she had sacrificed for her mother. Her self-respect, for one thing. There was no real sacrifice involved in entering into a business arrangement, as long as both parties agreed in advance on the rules. For no real reason other than her woman's intuition, she trusted Will Bradford. He was the kind of man who looked you directly in the eye and spoke his mind, like it or not.

One who looked entirely too masculine, entirely too sexy, entirely too attractive...

But that was neither here nor there.

By that time they had reached the judge's office.

Several men were already there. "Sebastian," she greeted, marveling all over again that he would be her baby's half brother. By looking at him now, she might even have a glimpse of the future—of what her own son would look like years from now. Unless he turned out to be a daughter.

Introductions were made, and Diana managed to hang on to her composure by a thread. Having Will's steadying hand under her elbow helped. These were Will's friends. Under other circumstances, if this marriage had been more than a business arrangement, they might have become her friends.

"How do you do?" she murmured calmly, trying to fix each man's face and name in her mind.

Someone made a joke about Will's going to great lengths to keep from picking out a charity. She hadn't the least idea what that was all about and was far too nervous even to wonder. Standing there in her tea-colored silk suit and her only decent pair of heels, she clutched the bouquet Will had handed her when she'd arrived. It had struck her as odd, but a sweet gesture. Fighting panic, she clutched her purse in one hand and the flowers in the other and thought, Business arrangement. Happens every day. Mergers—takeovers.

It wasn't going to be a takeover, not in any sense of the word. She had made that clear from the first. She was doing it to give her baby a name, and Will was doing it because...well, probably because Jack had been his friend, and for all she knew, they could have had an agreement. If anything happened to either of them, the other would look after the survivor's interests.

"Watch it, Danny, you're hyperventilating," Will

whispered as Judge Shirley entered in a swirl of black robes and Georgio perfume.

"No'm not," she whispered back and even managed a stiff-lipped smile. "Don't call me Danny."

For some reason, she recalled stories her mother used to tell her about the early days when a young Lila Smothers had first met the man she had later married. Liam Foster, long-haired, bearded and ponytailed, had played guitar with a group that never quite made it. He'd written poetry that no one who wasn't stoned, drunk or high could appreciate. According to Lila, he had once gone without eating meat products for an entire year protesting cruelty to animals and had been jailed more than once for protesting against the capitalistic establishment.

Funny, the way things had turned out, Diana thought, gripping the stems of her flowers with damp, trembling hands. It was the so-called establishment that had given her mother a job after Liam had wrapped his delivery van around a telephone pole one icy night back in Pennsylvania. It was the establishment that had fought to save her mother's life against insurmountable odds.

And it was the establishment his daughter was marrying into at this very moment.

"Miss Foster?"

"Diana?"

"What?" she snapped, whipping her head around to glare at the man she was about to tie herself to.

"The judge wants to know if you do."

"If I do what?"

Snickering sounded behind her. Someone touched her on the arm. It was Sebastian, who was grinning from ear to ear.

Blinking herself back to the present, Diana said, "Of course I do. That's why we're here, isn't it?"

One of the men—Jason, she thought—chuckled softly. The others tried and failed to control their smiles. Even Will's lips were twitching.

"Well, I do—I said I would, but I still can't imagine why *you* do," she whispered fiercely.

"Matter of fact, neither can I," Will said dryly.

It was all over then but the signing. When documents were placed in front of her, she signed her name, adding Bradford only when Will reminded her. They gathered at the door a few minutes later and Sebastian said, "We've set up a big spread at the club. Judge, you're invited."

"Sorry—traffic court in half an hour. One speeder, two jaywalkers. We're making a killing on crime around these parts."

Evidently, Diana told herself, justice in Royal, Texas, had a sense of humor. Once outside, she braced herself to go celebrate her marriage to a man she hardly knew, in the company of four other men she knew not at all. She might have been involved in more ludicrous situations at some point in her life, but at the moment she couldn't think of a single one.

"Seb, how about driving Diana's car to the club? We'll be right behind you," Will said, taking Diana's keys from her hand and tossing them to Sebastian.

Before Diana could open her mouth to protest, Will took her bouquet and ushered her into a metallic gunmetal-gray luxury sedan. She tried to think of something to say, and decided her silence would probably be more appreciated than any inane remark she could make. Something told her that Will had a low tolerance for small talk.

A low tolerance for women, as well, according to secretarial pool gossip. She remembered the sighs and groans he drew whenever he strode past on his way to purchasing. Her own, included.

"What I wouldn't give to see that man without his shirt on."

"Honey, don't stop there. He can park those boots under my bed any old time."

"Hush, y'all, it's *him!* He just got off the elevator!"

Amazingly enough, she was now Mrs. *Him!*

Did everyone at Wescott Oil know? What did they think—that she'd slept her way to the top?

Well, in a way, she had, only that had never been her intention.

"How do you think Sebastian will do as CEO?" Calmly discussing business on the way to her wedding reception should let him know she wasn't expecting anything more than what he'd offered. His name. Protection for her baby in case anyone should put two and two together and come up with the truth.

He glanced at her as he turned onto Main Street. "He'll do fine."

So much for talking business.

So much for talking anything. If she had her car right now, she'd go home, put on her sweats, jog a fast couple of miles and then get busy going through her mother's things and packing them away. And then she'd tackle Jack's boxes. It was time to sweep out the past in order to make room for the future.

Hugging herself, Diana inhaled a provocative mixture of leather upholstery, wilted wedding bouquet and some subtle masculine cologne that reminded her of tall evergreen trees. Cool, dark and lofty.

Just like the man, she thought, and shivered.

"Did you eat breakfast?"

"Of course." A small portion of whole-grain cereal with two dried apricot halves and a cup of tea. She was eating for two now. No more skipped meals, even if she was feeling queasy—which she had been for the last three mornings in a row.

"I don't know what the menu is, but there'll be champagne and wedding cake."

Great. Just what she needed. "I don't drink much."

"Neither do I, but we can sip a few toasts."

She would sip, but having seen what alcohol—as well as a whole pharmacopoeia of drugs, could do to a body, she would settle for sipping a seltzer with a twist.

Silence prevailed. Will thought, this is a hell of a note. Newlyweds who can't think of a damned thing to say. Maybe he should have paid her off, transferred her to Houston and let it go at that, only his conscience wouldn't have allowed it. The woman was pregnant and Jack probably wouldn't have married her even if he'd still been alive. He'd proved that much by his treatment of Dorian's mother.

Besides, dammit, something about her intrigued him. He might have forgotten how to love, but he hadn't forgotten how to lust. This arrangement would benefit them both. She would have care and protection for her baby, while he would have...

Nothing. Frustration, he thought, reminding himself of the specs he had laid out for their merger.

Gripping the wheel of his late-model luxury sedan, he willed his body into submission. No use in inviting a lot of pointed looks and lewd remarks. The guys were curious enough as it was.

Her car was already parked in the visitor's section when they reached the club. He'd have to see to having it driven to his apartment. Slanting a quick look at her still face as he shut off ignition, Will felt himself growing aroused all over again.

Deep breath. Think of an icy long-neck—think of an icy shower. This is strictly a business arrangement. No more, no less.

She unclipped her seatbelt and shifted a pair of nylon-clad legs, and he added world-class ankles to a growing list of attributes he'd been trying hard to ignore. Things like large, slumberous eyes, a soft, vulnerable mouth, a straight, elegant nose and a long, graceful neck that invited exploration.

She started to let herself out, and he hurried to open her door. It wasn't a militant feminist thing— he'd never seen any signs of that. The best he could figure was that she wasn't used to small courtesies. Jack might have been big on magnanimous gestures, but he'd seldom bothered with gentlemanly manners.

She shivered. The rain that had pounded down for days had ended, bringing down a blast of Alaskan air. The jet stream was really doing a number on them.

Will placed his hand on her back as they walked toward the side entrance. "I'll show you where you can freshen up. Sure you're feeling all right?"

Be a hell of a note if she got sick and everyone guessed she was pregnant. He didn't know how many, if any, of the guys knew about her affair with Jack. If they'd suspected, they'd have kept quiet about it out of consideration for Seb, who had probably guessed, even though he and Jack hadn't been close in years.

The celebration was held in one of the smallest rooms as if to make up for the lack of celebrants. Will had considered asking several other secretaries, but as he wouldn't have known where to draw the line, he'd decided against it. It hadn't occurred to him that she wouldn't have invited a few friends of her own.

He held the door and waited for her to enter. "I'm afraid it turned out to be a stag party. Sorry about that."

"I don't know many people here. We've—that is, I've only been here for a few months, and I've been…busy."

Her mother, he thought. She'd lost her mother shortly after moving to Royal. Hell, she was still grieving for her mother, and he'd pushed her into a marriage she didn't want. Talk about timing!

Her lips were trembling. Acting purely on impulse, he leaned over and kissed her. "Bear up, Mrs. Bradford. Half an hour or so and we can go home, kick off our shoes and turn on T.V. You like old movies?"

Blinking back tears after the fleeting kiss, Diana collected her wits enough to say, "Actually, I do. Is that your idea of a proper celebration?" And then she turned beet red. "I didn't— What I meant was—"

"Hush, honey, I know what you meant. Look, we'll just play it by ear, shall we? We got along just fine clearing out Jack's office. No reason why we can't go on the same way."

Dammit, he hadn't meant to drag Jack's name into

it. She needed to put the past behind her so that they could forge some kind of a workable relationship.

A champagne cork popped. Someone had brought in a few balloons, strung a few streamers. Will thought it looked absurd in the masculine realm of the Texas Cattleman's Club, but he supposed he appreciated the gesture.

"I think they're waiting on you to cut the cake." He indicated the five-tier confection gracing the center of the round table. "You want to try a few of the nibbles first?"

She nodded, looking warily at the dark paneled walls festooned with white ribbons and foil-covered bells draped over the heavy frames of paintings of several famous and obviously well-endowed bulls.

Will glared at Sebastian, wondering if he'd done it deliberately. It was more in line with Jason's puckish sense of humor, but it might have been a joint effort.

Or purely unintentional.

Dammit, he didn't need any reminders. This was his wedding day, only there wasn't going to be a wedding night. At least, not in the traditional sense. But, of course, the guys couldn't have known that.

"Are they all waiting for me to go first?" she whispered.

"I think so. Otherwise, they'd be pigging out. These guys aren't known for their reserve." Wasn't *that* the truth!

He took a thin, gold-banded plate and loaded it with finger food. Diana eyed it warily. Her queasiness wasn't restricted to mornings. The buffalo wings she'd pass on. The cheese and salsa on rye crackers was a possibility. The black bean dip looked good, so she helped herself to a spoonful and took half a dozen more crackers.

"So, tell me, Di, what did you see in this guy? Did he tell you he was a hotshot cowboy? Bet he forgot to tell you his own horse threw him once and he was laid up for three weeks." That was from Jason. She was getting to know them a bit better.

"The horse was spooked by a rattlesnake while I was trying to talk on my cell phone, or it never would have happened," Will grumbled.

"Somehow, being an Easterner, I never pictured cowboys riding the range while they talked on cell phones." Diana found herself relaxing enough to share the joke. "Some states have a law about using the phone while you're driving."

And so it went—teasing, tall tales. At first the laughter was stiff, but soon it became more relaxed. They were all obviously trying to make her feel welcome, but she suspected they were curious as to why their friend would marry with no warning at all. Especially a woman he'd never even dated. What did they think the two of them had been doing up on the eleventh floor all those days when they'd worked together to clear out Jack's things?

"Cake time!" Sebastian announced. Diana was still a bit hazy on the others, but everyone at Wescott Oil knew Sebastian, the heir to his father's empire.

It was Keith—she thought—who said, "Let me move it closer so you can reach it."

White frosting, pure sugar. White cake, pure refined carbohydrate. In just the short time since she'd learned she was pregnant she'd become far more health conscious, but this was no time to be picky.

"Hold your plates," she said, and grimly attacked the fancy confection.

There was some teasing after that about whose cake they'd be cutting next. Something about a bet, which she'd heard referred to before. Will edged closer. "You're not eating. Nerves?"

"Oh, no...it's...it looks delicious!"

"Diana? You want to level with me?" asked Will. "If you're dieting, then don't. You could carry ten more pounds, easy, and still look like a million bucks."

So she nibbled a cracker dipped in black beans and salsa, praying she wouldn't get sick. He was standing close enough so that she could see the gold shards in his hazel eyes. Warily she said, "It's not that—I mean, thank you. I think. But I don't eat sweets very much."

"Not even your own wedding cake?" With his own fork he cut a bite of her cake and held it to her lips. "Come on, sweetheart—open up."

She let the endearment pass. He was obviously doing it for his friends' benefit, and she appreciated it, she really did. Leaning forward, she bit off what he was offering. This was her wedding day, after all. She could afford to make a few allowances.

Two of the men were discussing inducting someone or other into the club. Did grown men do that kind of thing? she wondered.

Later she asked Will about it, and without telling her who the honoree was to be, he admitted that, yeah, they did. "Frankly it strikes me as pretty juvenile, but tradition rules in an outfit like this. He'll be asked to address the membership committee at a black-tie dinner on the ten most embarrassing moments of his life and the ten things of which he's the proudest. That pretty well sizes a man up, don't you think?''

Come to think about it, she agreed it did. She wished she dared to ask those same questions of her new husband.

The others had champagne. Will arranged for her to be served a sparkling cider. She wrinkled her nose, half expecting the bubbles to tickle. She'd read that in so many books—the bubbles always tickled the heroine's nose. In her case they didn't, but since she was pretending to be the heroine of this farce—not a princess, but close enough—she might as well play the part properly.

''Ready to go home and kick back with a good video?''

''You read my mind. Actually, I wouldn't mind getting out of these shoes,'' she whispered.

He grinned, and she told herself that if he had truly read her mind, he'd know just how terrified she was of losing control of her life again. After growing up as she had in an abusive situation, she had vowed never to hand over control of her life to anyone. It had been her choice not to try for a college scholarship, but to take the secretarial course instead. Secretaries were always in demand, as she'd told her mother. It was a highly portable skill.

It had been her choice to move all the way across the country when her mother had apparently lost all interest in everything, including her job. That was when Diana had learned that no one has complete control over their life. Shortly after they'd settled in, she'd had another choice to make. Whether or not to trade an affair with a man nearly twice her age for her mother's health care. She hadn't been at Wescott Oil long enough for her company insurance to kick in, and even then, preexisting conditions would have been excluded.

She had made the decision.

And now she had made another decision. To marry a stranger in order to legalize and protect her baby. That meant she was still in control…didn't it?

"You can drop me off at my apartment," she said a few minutes after they left in a flurry of best wishes and ribald remarks. She told him the address. "I can always walk to work and pick up my car on the way home tomorrow. One of the things I like about living in a small town—almost everything's within walking distance."

In some of the neighborhoods where she'd lived with her mother over the past few years, she had quickly learned that walking was not an option. Shortly after that they would pull up stakes and move again, hoping for something better. Always hoping…

"Depends on what you call a 'walking distance.'" Idling at the stoplight, Will turned to study her averted face.

"Three miles a day, at least five days a week?"

He shot her an admiring look. "Nice going. But another thing about small towns—it's hard to keep secrets."

Her stricken look made him wish he'd kept his mouth shut.

"What I meant was that there was some speculation about you and Jack. A gated community like Pine Valley is hardly the best place to carry on a clandestine affair."

"I hate that word."

"Affair?"

"Clandestine. As if we'd been sneaking around like a couple of underage kids. Anyway, mostly we stayed at his cabin."

He drove past her turnoff, and she sat up, alarmed. "I live on Macauley Street. The Lennox Apartments." It was an old building, hanging on to respectability by a thread, but it was all she'd been able to afford at the time they'd moved to Royal.

"Like I said, small towns are big on gossip," he said. "We both know the reason for this marriage. It's hardly a love match." Damn. Why not rub it in? Will mocked himself silently.

Not by so much as a flicker of an eyelash did her expression change, but her mouth—too large, too naked, too vulnerable—seemed to tighten just a bit. "Don't you ever wear makeup?" he asked, irritated for no good reason.

"I always wear makeup." It was a lie and they both knew it. Her kind of skin didn't require any enhancement. "I must have chewed off my lipstick. Sometimes I do that when I'm nervous. There's no room in this purse to carry much makeup." She held up something that was roughly the size and shape of a business envelope. "My other one's a black leather tote—hardly suitable for wedding wear."

He pulled into the parking area behind his own apartment complex. It wasn't up to Pine Valley standards, but it served his purpose. He'd never been big on status symbols. Switching off the engine, he stared through a row of carefully nurtured Leyland cypresses at the sunset—like an abstract painting done in shades of gray, gold and copper.

Now what? He asked himself. Some genius had

once said, "Begin as you mean to go on," or words to that effect. In their case it meant giving her a key, not carrying her over the threshold.

His palms were damp. Any kind of marriage, no matter what the reasons behind it, was a big step for a guy who'd avoided entanglements as long as he had. Even with all the safeguards, no man with half a grain of sense went into something like this without a few reservations.

She didn't wear perfume—at least, not the kind that announced her presence the minute she entered a room. Yet, oddly enough, he was more aware of her than he'd been of any woman in a long, long time. The subtle scent of her skin—her soap and shampoo…

"I think we pretty well understand each other," he said with a calmness that hid an increasing number of doubts. He would like to attribute the edginess he was feeling to filling up with junk food in the middle of the afternoon. "I should have scheduled things so that we could at least have a decent meal afterward. I didn't plan the party, that was Seb's idea."

"It was a lovely idea. I like your friends. They don't seem to—I mean, well—the fact that I was Sebastian's father's secretary…"

As well as his mistress. The words hung in the cool air, unspoken.

Diana unclipped her seat belt but made no move to get out. "Don't they think it's odd that we got married the way we did?"

"You mean in the courthouse instead of the church?"

"I mean you being who you are and me being who I am. We hardly even know each other."

"Who we are is irrelevant. As for the rest—why we married, that's nobody's business but ours."

What could he say? That they'd taken one look at each other and fallen madly in love? The guys would never buy it, not in a million years. After his first brief marriage, Will had made a point of avoiding long-term relationships.

Besides which, Seb probably knew about her relationship with Jack. As for the others, he couldn't say. For a bunch of guys who had shared more than a few high-risk escapades, they respected each other's privacy. Maybe he could remind them of an article he'd read recently about the increased life span of married men.

He went around to open her door. She sat there, making no move to get out. "Uh, Mrs. Bradford, we're home."

"*You're* home. I told you where I live."

"Look, Diana, one of the reasons we both agreed to this deal was to obscure the fact that in a few months you're going to be having Jack's baby. Another little Wescott contender. Or have you changed your mind about keeping it?"

"No," she whispered.

"Right. Then we stick together for the duration. As a cover, I'll admit it's pretty thin, but it won't even stand a chance if we live apart." She sat there while he held the door open. The insulation on a few more overworked nerves began to unravel. "You don't want to move in with me? Fine, we'll stay at your place. Just let me run in and grab a few things for tonight. I can move the rest later."

Diana looked up in horror at the thought of having him see where she lived. The thrift-shop specials, the things her mother had dragged all the way across the country. Tacky remnants of an idealistic age that had largely ended before she'd even been born.

"No—that is, we might as well stay here, but I'll need something to sleep in. Some personal items."

"I can lend you something to sleep in tonight, and I probably have a spare toothbrush, but if you'd rather, we can go back now and pack whatever you'll need for the next few days. It's early yet."

She was tempted.

Actually she was tempted to crawl into bed, pull the covers over her head and pretend none of this had ever happened. Pretend her mother was still alive, listening to Joan Baez on the stereo while she wove her beaded macramé wall hangings. Or playing along on her old Gibson guitar that wouldn't stay tuned because the tuning gears were shot.

Pretend she herself wasn't pregnant, much less married to a man who both attracted and repelled her because he was too large, too reserved and too domineering, if only in the nicest possible way.

"Well...tomorrow, I guess. I can go by after breakfast. Do you have a kitchen in your apartment?"

He grinned, his lean cheeks that were already showing signs of what used to be called five-o'clock shadow before it became fashionable, creasing in a pair of unlikely dimples. "I thought you'd never ask."

Four

This had to be the strangest wedding night in recorded history, Diana told herself a few hours later as she sat cross-legged on a large leather covered couch, eating curried garbanzos and watching a video of an old World War II submarine movie.

She slanted a look at her bridegroom, sprawled in a massive lounger, his eyes half-closed. His five-o'clock shadow was now a fledgling beard. He was barefoot, wearing jeans and what must once have been a black T-shirt. Thanks to improper laundering, it was now a mottled shade of purple. Quite a change from the well-dressed executive whose department took up the entire tenth floor of the eleven-story Wescott Building.

Absently, Will held out a bowl of popcorn, and she helped herself to a handful. He'd offered to grill steaks, but she'd been feeling queasy again. So much for morning sickness. In her case, it was an equal-opportunity affliction.

"I've been wondering—where am I supposed to report for work on Monday?" She waited for a lull in the dialogue to ask, but the question had been bothering her. She no longer had an office.

Did she even have a job?

"I wouldn't be in any great rush to go back to work. Take a few days off. It's expected of honeymooners."

She sent him a mocking look. "Oh? And how long are you going to take off?"

"About a week should do it. I thought we might drive out to the ranch for a few days. You like horses?"

Horses? He expected her to go horseback riding? In her condition? Was it safe, even if she knew how? "Well, I don't exactly dislike them. Actually, I've never met one."

"I'll introduce you. We'll start out nice and easy and let nature take its course."

Was he talking about her and his horse or her and their business-arrangement marriage?

On the TV screen, terror stalked in the form of a pair of swift, silent torpedoes. In black-and-white, on a small screen, the horror was no less potent. While Will sat seemingly relaxed and watched, Diana studied him. Studied his hands, which lay relaxed on his thighs. Studied the length—not to mention the strength—of his long legs.

Oh, she'd noticed him, all right, on the few occasions their paths had crossed at work. What woman wouldn't? Even if his looks had been ordinary, the way he carried himself—assured without being noticeably arrogant, would have earned him more than a few admiring glances. At close range he radiated a tightly leashed sexuality that Jack, for all his polish, all his wealth and efforts, had never managed to achieve.

Jack had mentioned once that Will never used the private gym he had set up for senior employees. Could horseback riding have developed those long, smooth muscles?

He caught her studying his rugged profile, and she hurriedly lowered her eyes. "It's nice. Your apartment. Have you lived here long?"

Oh, for Pete's sake! *Hello, cowboy, where're you from?*

Her mother would have asked him his sign by now, and told him more than he ever wanted to know about his traits, his future and his love life. Astrology had rated right up there with folk music and beaded macramé among her mother's early passions.

"About ten years. It's comfortable," he said in answer to the questions she'd forgotten she'd asked.

For a man rumored to be extremely wealthy, it had come as something of a surprise, Will's apartment. It was spacious, but hardly luxurious. The floors were carpeted in a muted neutral, the walls a slightly deeper shade of the same color. Fawn, perhaps. There were no pictures on the wall, not even any family photographs. The furniture, oak and leather, for the most part, was probably hideously expensive, but it had been chosen for comfort rather than style. Books overflowed the bookshelves and were stacked on the floor, along with videos.

The guest bedroom was small, but more than adequate.

"You mentioned a spare toothbrush?" She forced a yawn and followed it with a genuine one. And then another. "Mercy, it's been a long day."

"You feeling all right? You're not, uh—feeling upset or anything, are you?"

"No, I'm fine." And she would be, once her hormones settled down and she got back on a regular schedule. "As long as I remember to eat and don't get stressed out, I'm in great health. The morning sickness is only temporary. It shouldn't last much longer."

He eyed her intently, making her wonder why hazel eyes were so underrated. *Piercing* was the word that came to mind.

Smoldering was the word that followed. Like banked coals.

"Wake me anytime if you need anything, promise? Anything at all. I'm a light sleeper."

Suddenly she was fighting tears. When had *anyone* ever made that offer? Her mother hadn't, not in a long, long time. It would never have occurred to Jack. He'd paid her mother's hospitalization, which had been more than generous of him, but he had never wanted to hear about Diana's personal needs, her fears, her hopes.

It had never occurred to her to share them with him.

"Thanks," she said gruffly. "I'm an early riser, but I'll try to be quiet."

"No problem." He stood, unfolding his six-foot-plus length from the dark-brown recliner. "Coffee, tea or decaf?"

"For breakfast? Coffee if you have it. The real

thing. I'll have to taper off caffeine soon, but I'd rather do it gradually.''

Will lay awake, his mind taking off down a few strange pathways. He was married again. Something he could have sworn he would never be. The first time had hurt too damned much, for too damned long.

Somewhere along the line, his brief marriage nearly twenty years earlier to Shelly of the infectious laughter, the flashing blue eyes, the sexy sulks that always ended in bed, had faded like an old photograph exposed to the light too long. When had that happened? He'd been too busy to notice, but obviously today's events had stirred a few ashes.

They were nothing at all alike, his two wives.

But then, he was nothing like the eager young gyrene he'd been when he'd married, fresh out of boot camp. He'd owned the world then—a gorgeous bride and a promising career as a marine.

It had all come crashing down the day some drugged-up, two-bit hood had broken into their duplex. He'd headed straight for the bedroom and Shelly's jewelry case. Hearing something, she'd come up from the basement where she'd been doing the laundry, and he had shoved her back down the stairs.

At least she hadn't suffered. According to the authorities, she had died instantly of a broken neck. Someone in the neighborhood had seen the punk running across the backyard to the woods beyond and reported it. He'd been picked up, tried for manslaughter and sentenced to ten years, which in Will's estimation was a joke. An insult. A slap on the wrist.

Will had been sent back to the States. Vowing to be waiting for the murdering son of a gun the day he got out of prison, he had grimly served out the rest of his hitch. By the time he left the service, his lust for revenge had faded just enough for common sense to take over.

Instead of setting himself up for a murder charge, he'd moved across the country. Still driven by anger and grief, he had earned a degree in accounting. Numbers were emotionless, exact—both qualities that had appealed to him back then.

Eventually the raw wound had healed over, but the scars were a permanent part of him. Over the years he had managed to fill a few of the hollow places inside him with challenging work, new friends and a few sub rosa missions with other members of the Cattleman's Club. Not to mention half a dozen charities he funded anonymously. What more could a man expect out of life?

Sex, came the instant answer.

But *not* with his wife.

It was going to be a long, dry spell. He had taken certain vows. Not in a church, but nonetheless binding. For the next year or two, until Diana and the child were ready to move on with their own lives, he would abide by those promises.

It was still dark the next morning when Will rolled over, groaned and sat up in his rumpled bed. Too many champagne toasts hadn't done his head any good. While it was still dark, he might run a few miles to clear away the static. This time of morning the sidewalks would be empty.

In honor of having a woman under his roof, he'd

slept in sweats instead of his usual nothing. They would do to run in, as he was no more inclined to wear suitable running gear than he was to drive out to the park and jog along a designated track. His method of waking up his body was more efficient. Get up, get it done, get to work.

On the ranch, unloading a truckload of hay, checking a few miles of fence and maybe going after the big cat that had been spooking his mares would have done it.

In town he was forced to improvise.

She was in his kitchen. "Hi," she said, her soft voice husky with sleep. "Hope you don't mind, but I warned you, I'm an early riser."

"No. I mean, that's great—uh, I don't suppose you'd like to go for a short run with me?"

Glancing down at the oversize gray sweats he'd lent her to sleep in and her bare feet, she said, "Hardly. I'd better go home and pack a few things."

"Yeah, sure." Her skin had a pink glow that he knew damned well didn't come from cosmetics. She'd braided her hair, but it was half-unraveled. There was something different about her—a certain softness instead of her usual patrician aloofness.

Yeah, softness—that was it. He'd lay odds that softness was hardly a quality the cool, conservatively dressed Miss Foster aspired to.

Amused for no real reason, he said, "Good morning, Mrs. Bradford," and damned if she didn't blush. Hell, he was only teasing—he hadn't meant anything by it. At least, nothing personal.

"My car—you said you were going to have it driven to my apartment?"

"Right. Look, I don't feel like running, anyway.

My head would probably fall off and roll down a storm drain before I reached the end of the block. How about we have some coffee, think about breakfast, then I'll drive you to your place and you can take your time packing and drive your car back here when you're finished.''

While she was considering the offer, the coffeemaker gurgled its last gasp. Reaching past her for a mug, Will was conscious of the heat of her body and the scent of soap and toothpaste and woman.

How personal could you get? Good thing his sweats were baggy.

"Okay, coffee. I've already nibbled some saltines—I think things are settling down by now.''

He offered to cook bacon and eggs, and she said politely, "Thank you. One slice, one egg, both well done, please.''

"Hey, you're eating for two now, don't forget.''

"I'm also about to outgrow everything I own, so let's not rush the process.''

She smiled. He chuckled. Some of the tension faded, but as his kitchen was small, physical contact was a given. Her arm brushed his shoulder when she reached for plates. He backed into her as he opened the massive stainless-steel refrigerator, muttered an apology and then stepped on her toe.

"Well, hell,'' he said plaintively. "It's not like I ever won any waltzing contests, but normally I'm slightly less clumsy than a three-legged ox.''

It wasn't as if they hadn't worked in close confines before, either. While Jack's office was certainly spacious, there was only so much room in front of a filing cabinet. He must have managed to bump into her a dozen times—looking back, it might even have been deliberate. But that had been different.

Yeah, she wasn't your wife then.

"Crazy weather we're having, huh?" Go ahead, Bradford, impress her with your brilliant conversation.

"Did you mean what you said last night?"

He rifled through his brain, searching for any indiscretion he might have committed. "Uh, you mean about…?"

"Going to your ranch?"

He let out his breath in a sigh of relief, poured two mugs of coffee and flipped the bacon. One slice for her, two for him, when he could easily have put away half a dozen. Jack's death had been a warning. "Sure, if you'd like to go. Matter of fact, I've been thinking about taking a month off, maybe spending a couple of weeks at the ranch and then heading for salt water to do some serious fishing. You like fishing?"

She was beating up the eggs while he cooked the bacon. She added a dash of salt, a dash of black pepper, and he started to suggest a whopping dollop of *salsa con queso*—the hot variety—but decided the baby might not care for it.

"Fishing? I don't know, I've never tried it." She handed him the bowl and he poured the eggs in the pan and stirred while she made toast. Nothing like teamwork.

"You like seafood?" he asked. Breakfast with a woman was a new experience. He hadn't had time to get used to it when he was married the first time, and since then, his dalliances had rarely included breakfast.

"Hmm," she said, and bit her lip. He watched, wondering what it felt like. Soft. Moist. Naked...vulnerable. Maybe there was a reason why women wore lipstick. In men, war paint was used to lend a feeling of invincibility.

Not until they had sampled the fare did she speak again. "If by seafood you mean frozen breaded fish sticks, then not particularly. Canned tuna is okay—I've never tried clams, but I looked at a raw oyster once, and it was horribly icky. I could never eat one."

Will tilted back his chair and laughed until his headache reminded him that he needed to take a couple of aspirin tablets. "We'll break you in easy, shall we? I'll take you to Claire's for some mountain trout. Did Jack take you there?"

The question lay between them like a dead horse.

"Actually, Jack never took me anywhere. We were—that is, we tried..."

"I know, I know. Look, I'm sorry. Like I said, I never won any waltzing contests, and waltzing around the obvious comes under that heading." Might as well lay it all out on the table, between the apple jelly and the Texas Pete. "For what it's worth, Diana, I doubt if too many people knew about you and Jack, so why don't we start today with us. You and me. Not you and Jack and me."

"How about you and me and Jack's baby?" She blotted her lips on a paper napkin, which was the only kind he had.

"How about you and me and *your* baby? By the time it's born it'll be our baby."

Suddenly her eyes were flooded with tears. She laughed, a soft, broken sound that twisted his gut.

"Sorry—I'm not crying, honestly I'm not. It's these hormones of mine. At least it's better than having to rush to the bathroom to be sick every morning."

"I never knew about any of this stuff. About pregnancy, I mean. And listen, Diana, before you go getting the wind up about what I said—I mean, about it being our baby—no way would I ever try to take him away from you. For any reason. I just want to do what I think Jack would have done—that is, to look after you until you're on your feet again."

Liar, he thought. Jack would've bought her a one-way ticket out of town.

She yawned, and he said, "Why don't we leave the dishes and go for a walk. Not a run—you probably shouldn't be running, anyway, in case you—uh, jar something loose."

"Honestly, I'm not always like this," she said, laughing, then yawning again.

"Hey, I understand. Besides, even Sleeping Beauty eventually woke up, didn't she?"

Rising, Will set his dishes on the counter, then impulsively leaned down and kissed her. There was nothing at all sexual about it, and she told herself that what she was feeling—the simmering warmth, the neediness—was only hormones.

Well, of course it is, you ninny! she thought. What do you think drives a woman's libido?

That afternoon she called the clinic and asked to speak to Dr. Woodbury.

"He's out, but if I can help you? I'm Kelly Cartwright, the nurse practitioner."

"Oh. Well, my name is Diana Foster, uh, Bradford. I was in a few weeks ago, and…well, I'm pregnant, and—"

"Just let me pull your chart, Ms. Foster-Bradford."

"It would be under Foster, but call me Diana...please."

"Okay, Diana, you were suffering the usual symptoms, morning sickness, sleepiness, right?"

"The morning sickness seems to have stopped, but now I can't seem to stay awake. Besides that, I cry at nothing at all. Last night I started crying in the middle of an old Smothers Brothers video. Is this normal? I mean, I don't even show yet. What's going to happen once I get really going on this thing?"

The nurse practitioner, who invited Diana to call her Kelly, laughed. "The only thing you have to watch is your nibbling. Stick to pickles and low-fat ice cream, and you'll be just fine. Luckily, you can afford to gain at least twenty pounds, but let's not do it all at once, shall we? As for other symptoms, you might even skip the heartburn, but chances are, you'll be sticking pretty close to a bathroom as more pressure is put on your bladder. Oh, and sex is just fine until you get close to term. We'll talk about it when you come in."

Sex was just fine? Well, great. Now that she was married to a man who could curl her toes with a single sweep of his eyelashes, sex was not an option.

Talk about life's little ironies.

After making an appointment, she settled back in Will's marvelously comfortable chair. She had a feeling it wasn't one of those that could be had in any furniture store. It was brown cowhide, with creases and natural scars showing. Her mother would have hated it. She'd have wanted to cover it with a zebra-print throw.

Oh, Mama, I wish you could be here. I need to talk to you. We always had each other, but now I don't have anyone at all.

For a long time she sat and thought about the crazy route her life had taken. From Shinglehouse, Pennsylvania, to Royal, Texas, with half a dozen stops along the way. There was no knowing how long her mother had been ill, as the symptoms didn't manifest until nearly the end. The daughter of a New England clergyman who had disowned her after she'd run away to something called a love-in, Lila Smithers Foster had made her share of mistakes, but in her own way she'd been a good mother. She would have made a wonderful grandmother, Diana thought tearfully.

She dried her eyes, then thought about the way Will had accepted her mother's idea of decorating as graciously as if Martha Stewart had done the job. She'd tried her best to keep him from helping her move, but he was too much the gentleman.

"Honey, we can't have you straining yourself," he'd said. "You do the packing, I'll do the donkey work."

So she'd unlocked the door, painfully conscious of the posters, the lumpy, uneven, hemp wall hangings, the tacky lava lamp and the leopard-print throw on the back of the thrift-shop sofa. For someone who hated the use of animal products, her mother had dearly loved animal prints. Then there were the dried flowers in lumpy, unglazed pots thrown by long-forgotten potters. And her mother's old Gibson propped in a corner in the battered hardshell case decorated with peace symbols and painted daisies.

Will had carried it out to the car as carefully as if it had been a Stradivarius.

Diana had stared at the stack of tattered music that neither she nor her mother could read, and teared up again. Her mother had taught her the words and they'd sung together, old songs from the days of protests and idealism. Songs filled with hope, which—at least in her mother's case—had died a long and painful death.

"It's going to take a while," she'd warned her new husband, looking at all the boxes she'd packed and left stacked in her mother's bedroom.

"No hurry. Pack what you'll need and I'll have someone come in and do the rest."

"I'd rather do it myself. I know it's not much, but my mother was— That is, she was—"

"Your mother," he'd said quietly.

She'd had to swallow hard several times to keep from bawling her eyes out all over again. The man was almost *too* kind.

She'd left the furnishings—after all, the lease still had almost a month to go—but she'd taken a few things, such as the guitar and a matted watercolor some long-ago unknown artist had done that she particularly liked.

Somewhat to her surprise, Will had liked it, too. He'd insisted on having it framed for her. He brought it back from the framers on the way home the next day, and now he wanted to hang it in the living room.

Predictably Diana burst into tears. "You shouldn't," she sobbed.

"We can hang it in the guest room if you don't want it in here. It needs to be kept under glass for protection against air pollution, though. The framer said it probably wouldn't have lasted much longer unframed.''

When had his arms closed around her? When had she wrapped her own arms around his neck?

She cried some more, then hiccuped a few times, and then she laughed. ''Is there a medal for men who take on the care and feeding of newly pregnant women? I think I must have saved up a lifetime of tears just waiting for a handy shoulder to drench.''

He laughed, and then he kissed her, salty tears and all. She thought, if only she hadn't messed up her life so thoroughly. If only she could have had waited....

''Yeah, I know, it's the hormones,'' he murmured. ''I should have guessed right off when you tackled me with that triple cone of chocolate.'' She had told him what the nurse practitioner had said about the quirky symptoms of early pregnancy. ''Besides which,'' he added gently, ''I suspect you're hauling around a lot of baggage you need to get out of your system.''

If only he knew. ''You're never going to let me live that down, are you?'' She pulled away, her lips still tingling from a kiss that had been over almost as quickly as it had begun. Soft, almost tentative, there'd been nothing at all sexual about it.

Correction. Everything about this man was sexual, only he hadn't intended it that way, and she had no business interpreting it that way.

Hugging herself, Diana watched as he hammered a nail into his pristine wall and hung the newly framed watercolor. She pictured his long, lean, muscular body wearing nothing at all instead of the body-hugging chambray shirt and blue jeans he wore to relax in.

Among the symptoms the nurse had mentioned was a heightened libido. Which had to explain, Diana rationalized, why she found herself picturing him in her bed, in her arms, sharing her afternoon naps and making slow, sweet love to her. Whispering words that no man had ever said to her—words about love and together and forever....

Five

___

Will poured himself a cup of coffee, the morning paper tucked under his arm, and then settled down to read the business section. He needed to go by the office this morning. He would leave a note for Diana, suggesting that when she felt like it, she might drive over to her old place, pack a few more things, and he would pick them up this afternoon. The more of her belongings she surrounded herself with, the sooner she would adapt.

Or so he told himself. Pregnant women were a breed apart, he was discovering.

The market was taking another nosedive. Tech stocks down heavily—utilities holding. Thank God. Will scanned the section, then went back and glanced at headlines—no surprises there. He was on the sports section when he heard the bathroom door close.

By the time he'd finished his coffee and dressed in modified business attire—casual suit, no tie—he heard the shower cut off. Might as well wait instead of leaving a note. They were honeymooning, after all. It wouldn't do to rush downtown too early.

A few minutes later she emerged, flush-faced, in a cloud of talcum-scented steam, wearing a yellow flannel bathrobe, her hair covered by a towel.

"Oh! You startled me. You're already dressed. Are we going somewhere?"

"I've been thinking—why don't we close out the lease on the Lennox place and move all your things here. We can rent a storage unit for whatever we can't fit in."

"You're kidding…right?"

"Why would I do that?"

"Will, look at this place." She waved her arms expressively, so he looked. It was your typical upper-end apartment. Nothing outstanding. Certainly not as…distinctive, he thought for want of a better term, as her own apartment. Having noticed her when she'd first come to work at Wescott Oil, he could vouch for Diana's taste. While not expensive, it was impeccable—which meant someone else was responsible for the decor of her old apartment. Chances were, it had been her mother.

"Thanks for letting me bring as much as I did, but most of what's left came from the local thrift shop. It can go back there once I'm finished with it."

"You're finished with it." Will knew the moment the words left his tongue it was the wrong thing to say. "That is, you can take your time. Naturally, you'll stay here, though."

She grabbed the towel with both hands, gave her

hair a thorough rubbing, then looked him squarely in the eye. "Don't tell me what to do. Please. I make my own decisions."

He swore softly. "Don't yank my chain, lady. I've got troubles enough at work without adding any domestic games."

She took a deep breath that caused her robe to gape open, revealing the soft swell of her breasts. "Let me put it another way. There's nothing domestic involved here. Ours is strictly a business arrangement. We both agreed to that, else I'd never have gone through with it. And I certainly I don't remember anything in our agreement that says you get to take control of my life now."

"You're ready to give up on this so soon? Come on, Danny, girl—give me another chance." His tone was openly mocking, his deep-set eyes glinting with something that might—or might not—be amusement.

Wariness came over her like a dark shadow. She wrapped her robe more closely around her body. "Yes, well…I just wanted to be sure we understood each other."

He said nothing, his very silence an invitation to babble on, to try desperately to explain something she didn't understand herself. "I mean, it's not as if we were— Well, you know…"

"No I don't. We aren't what, Danny?"

"We aren't really married!"

"We're not? Funny—I distinctly remember paying for a license. The judge said all the right words. At least I don't think she left out anything important. We both signed certain documents. In my book, that makes us legally wed." He knew what she was trying to say, but he wasn't ready to let her off the hook.

If there was one thing he insisted on in both his business and his personal dealings—and marriage was the most personal of all—it was honesty. Square dealing.

She flung out her arms again. Funny, he'd never noticed the way she used gestures to emphasize her words. "Haven't you ever heard of a marriage of convenience, for mercy's sake? Read a romance! Half of them are based on marriages of convenience!"

"Why?"

"Why what?" She blinked. Freshly scrubbed, free of any possible enhancement, lashes like hers should be registered as lethal weapons.

"Why are marriages of convenience considered romantic?"

She took a deep breath, crossed her arms over her modest bosom, and he thought, Aha! Gotcha!

"How do I know? I'm no expert on romance. Look, can we please change the subject? You're all dressed to go out somewhere, and I've got loads of things I need to do today."

Name one, he wanted to say, but didn't. His gaze moved over her, this woman he had married because it had seemed like the honorable thing to do and he was in a position to do it. And, yeah, because she intrigued him. "I'm going in to work for a few hours. I'm not telling you where to go or what to do, but I'd appreciate not having to track you down. Might spoil the illusion we're trying to create." He didn't bother to hide the sarcasm.

Funny thing—he seldom resorted to sarcasm. The lady had a talent for bringing out hidden facets of his personality.

"All right," she said grudgingly. "But anytime you change your mind and want to get out of this marriage, it's just fine with me. I didn't suggest it in the first place, if you'll remember. If you're afraid Sebastian might be embarrassed about the baby, then I can leave town. In fact, I'd planned to relocate." Her rich-brown eyes took on a militant sparkle. "But just so you know, I don't need you or anyone else to take care of me. I've been taking care of myself all my adult life—even before that."

Will wasn't in the habit of badgering anyone, especially not a woman. Especially not a woman he was married to—and especially not about matters such as the one they were discussing now.

Taking a deep, steadying breath, he scratched his jaw and apologized. "I guess I came on too strong." He wasn't about to admit that, convenient or not, she and her baby were now his responsibility. He was learning what set her off and what he could get away with.

"I guess you did. But you need to understand that being in control of my own life is important to me. I, um, I might have overreacted, too." If her quick, tremulous smile was meant to disarm, it did the trick. "And we haven't really known each other very long."

"Or very well. I think it's about time to change that, don't you?"

She came away from the wall as if she'd backed into a live wire. "Oh, well, as to that, I think we're doing just fine. I mean, look at the way we work together in the kitchen. And I'm even learning to like old submarine movies."

Slowly he shook his head. "Diana, Diana. What

am I going to do with you?'' He knew what he'd like to do, but it wasn't going to happen. That hadn't been a part of the bargain. ''What do you say we head out of town and take it easy for a few days after I get done at the office? You might want to check with your friend at the clinic about riding. Horses, that is.''

His grin had been purely wicked, Diana thought a few hours later as she dressed for her first visit to a real working ranch. She thought they might have clarified their relationship, but she couldn't be sure. Just when she thought she understood where he was coming from, he moved.

Her mother used to say, ''Just when I think I know where it's at, it moves.''

Evidently knowing ''where it was at'' was big back in the seventies.

Diana didn't even know what *it* was, much less where.

She must have yawned a dozen times between looking over the old apartment to see if there was anything she needed to bring back with her and dragging out her suitcase to pack for a weekend on a real ranch.

A ranch! Imagine that. After all her childish fantasies, she was going to get to play cowgirl.

With a real live cowboy, too. Better watch it, princess.

She yawned some more over sandwiches eaten at the bar in the kitchen after Will returned from the office. ''Honestly, it's not the company, it's one of the early symptoms of pregnancy,'' she said after apologizing. "I wonder if anyone ever slept through the entire nine months."

Will was watching the noon business report and only murmured, "Hmm."

Greenspan said something about creeping inflation, and Diana reminded herself to go easy on the mayo from now on. Her waistbands were already getting a bit snug. On the other hand, it had been almost two days since she'd felt the slightest queasiness.

"What were you saying?" he asked when a commercial came on.

"I was saying that I can stay awake now for hours without yawning."

"The question is, can you stay on a horse without falling off?"

"Was Roy Rogers's horse named Trigger?"

"That good, huh?"

"You're not the only one who likes old movies. I used to watch cowboy movies every Saturday morning. Why do you think I moved to Texas?"

"Let me guess. The lush jungles? The ice-capped mountains?"

The gentle teasing was still new enough to cause flutters in her modest bosom. The bosom that would probably grow a full cup size, if the pamphlets she'd read could be believed.

Would he notice?

Do you want him to notice?

As unlikely as it was that she could ever have become the mistress of a wealthy oil tycoon, Diana marveled even more at finding herself married to a man like William K. Bradford, who'd been referred to by several women in the secretarial pool as a hunky stud.

Or maybe it was a studly hunk. Either description applied, although, according to rumor he never mixed business with pleasure.

She was beginning to wonder about that. He was still wearing his business suit, and they were both taking pleasure in the sandwiches she'd created from practically nothing. Cheese, salsa and bacon on pumpernickel.

"What does the *K* stand for?" she asked a couple of hours later as they left the outskirts of Royal behind and headed southwest. She had packed her black slacks, two pairs of jeans, two pullover sweaters and her warmest fleece jacket.

Will downshifted for a patch of sand that had blown across the highway. "King," he said grimly. "No cracks, please."

"I wouldn't think of it," she murmured with mock solemnity. And then, in the same solemn tone, "Does that make me Diana Queen Bradford?"

He shook his head, swerved to avoid a pothole, then glanced at her with a wicked grin. "You wish," he teased. "You do realize, don't you, that now that you know my secret, I'm going to have to find a way to silence you?"

Her mind zapped instantly to one of the more pleasurable methods he might use to silence her and Diana found herself struggling to catch her breath. She hadn't forgotten the way his kiss had felt, not for a moment. Its very gentleness had set it apart from every kiss she had ever received from any other man.

Not that there'd been all that many. An impatient

man, Jack had seldom bothered to kiss her. When he had, it had been an obvious part of his lovemaking routine. As foreplay, it had all the passion of a paint-by-numbers masterpiece.

Taking charge of her thoughts, she closed the door on the past. "King, hmm? You said the place doesn't have a name—have you ever considered calling your ranch the King Ranch?"

He chuckled. "I'm afraid somebody beat me to it. Have you ever considered calling yourself Lady Diana?"

"No, but when I was about five or six, I used to pretend I was a princess. It was a game my mother and I made up."

They fell silent again, but it was a surprisingly comfortable silence. When they passed a truck stop, Will turned off the highway and pulled up to the gas pumps. "Rest rooms are inside. I'll meet you there in five, and we'll stock up on junk food."

Feeling suddenly carefree and optimistic for no real reason, Diana stepped out and found herself unexpectedly surrounded by her husband's arms. Flushed, she said, "Careful with those promises, dude—I'm eating for two, remember?"

"I remember," he said, his voice a shade deeper, huskier than usual. She was still surrounded by his loose embrace, and just before he stepped away, he leaned down and placed his firm lips over hers.

And, just as it had before, the world tilted on its axis and trembled for an instant before righting itself again.

"Well," she said breathlessly, sidestepping his arms. "I'd better—that is, I really do have to, um, wash up."

Will didn't say a word, but he stood and watched as she scurried across the paved apron and let herself inside Taylor's Trux Top, Gas and Great Eats. First thing he needed to do was go online and check out the care and feeding of a pregnant female. An elusive, funny, increasingly fascinating pregnant female.

Less than an hour later, having made little conversation but great inroads in the popcorn, the fat-free corn chips and the bottled iced tea, Will turned off at a mailbox onto an unmarked road that was obviously well maintained. "Look, I'd better warn you, Miss Emma's going to want to fatten you up. In fact, once she finds out about the baby, she might not even allow you out of bed. Her husband, Tack Gilbert, manages the ranch, but Miss Emma runs the house with an iron hand."

"So what if we don't tell her?" Diana suggested. "About the baby, I mean?"

"Does it show yet?" He glanced at her flat stomach. "I didn't mean that, exactly, but is there some clue—something women pick up on that men don't?"

"Later there might be. Dark patches on my face." He looked so horrified that she burst out laughing. "What, you're going to divorce me if I get a few brown patches? What about stretch marks?"

Her smile faded as the implications struck them both. If she had stretch marks—and she probably would before it was over—he would never see them. They didn't have that kind of relationship.

And crazy or not, Diana found herself almost wishing they did.

Then she was staring at the house. From what he'd

said, about the ranch not having a name, she had expected a small frame house and a few unpainted outbuildings.

Rancho Anonymous was far more than that. The main house was built of log and cedar siding, with lots of stone and glass. There was a wraparound deck, part of it open, the rest roofed over. Perfect, she thought, for watching the sun go down over that pasture full of horses.

"Oh, my," she breathed. "I didn't know there was that much green grass out in the country."

Will pointed out the windmill and explained about the irrigation system. "Those hedgerows you see out there are all that keep the sand from covering it when we get a hard blow." Taking her arm, he led her toward the house. "Ranching's a hell of a lot more interesting than spreadsheets."

"I can imagine," she said, and she could. Funny thing—seeing him at work, she could never have imagined him on a ranch, looking as though he belonged. Yet, now that she'd seen him here, she had trouble picturing him back at work, soberly suited, addressing a meeting of the board.

"Is that an airport?" She pointed to a flat metal building in the distance with a wind sock on the roof.

"Just a hangar. I keep a couple of small planes here in case I need to get back to town in a hurry."

A couple of small planes. Uh-huh. It was just beginning to sink in that her husband was an extremely wealthy man. With Jack, it had showed. The house he'd lived in—the expensive toys with which he surrounded himself. He'd collected old cars. Bentleys. He'd once joked that while a Bentley wasn't quite as ostentatious as a Rolls, it was common knowledge that anyone who could afford a Bentley could easily afford a Rolls.

It hadn't been common knowledge to her. She'd never even heard of a Bentley. Will drove a luxury sedan, but she didn't think it was a Bentley, much less a Rolls. But at least it didn't have a gigantic pair of horns mounted on the hood. He owned two planes and probably one of those pickup trucks she saw over by one of the barns.

Her father had driven a battered old VW bug covered with faded hand-painted slogans. Flower Power. Make Love, Not War.

Feeling suddenly out of her depth, Diana glanced uncertainly at the man beside her. He dropped a casual arm across her shoulder and led her toward the house. "Come on inside and meet Emma. Tack can bring in our bags later."

She was no horsewoman. That much quickly became evident. Even though Will had put her up on the fattest, oldest, slowest mare in his stable, she clung to the reins and the saddle horn with both hands and tried to hook her legs around the creature's broad belly.

"You dig your toes in any deeper and she's going to take off with you," he warned. The manager, Tack, was grinning through his tobacco-stained handlebar moustache.

"Fat chance. Look, you wanted me to ride, I'm riding, okay? Can I help it if he doesn't feel like moving?"

"He's a she. Her name's Mairsy."

"You're kidding."

"No'm not. Some kid named her Mairsy Doats

before I ever got her. Actually, she sort of came with the ranch. Want to try something a bit more challenging?''

Diana looked at him as if he'd lost his mind. And then she tried to remember how Dale Evans had looked in all those old Saturday-morning movies. Petite and relaxed, for one thing—not gawky and scared half to death. A white hat and a fringed skirt probably wouldn't change anything where she was concerned. ''You know what? I sort of feel like lying down for a while.'' She wasn't above playing the pregnant female card. Might as well take advantage of it while she could.

''Sore butt, huh? Come on, then. We'll give it another shot tomorrow.''

She scowled at him. Sure they would. And the sun would rise in the west.

Miss Emma took everything in her stride. When Will had first introduced her as his wife, she'd looked startled, but quickly rallied. ''Well, now, I'd better put another pillow on the bed. Mr. Will uses both of 'em. You want one or two?''

Diana's mouth must have fallen open. Will had closed it for her with a thumb under her chin and said, ''Give us any extras you can round up, Emma. We'll work it out, all right?''

They had worked it out. The first night she had slept in the master bedroom while Will slept in the room across the hall. He'd been willing to share a room, but as he was pretty sure she wasn't ready for anything like that, he hadn't suggested it. If Emma had any question, he'd blame it on his snoring.

Which he didn't. Or at least, no one had ever complained.

Diana thought Will looked incredibly masculine in
his ranch wear, which consisted of scuffed boots, a
flannel shirt worn with a leather vest, and a pair of
jeans that were worn thin and faded in all the stra-
tegic places. All he needed, she decided, was a white
hat, and he could easily play the good guy in any
Western.

It had been her decision to tell the housekeeper
about her pregnancy. Will readily agreed. So they
told both Gilberts over breakfast, allowing them to
believe the baby was Will's.

"Lord bless you, honey, I know how that is. My
oldest sister's been pregnant half her life. Raised
seven young'uns, then helped raise two grandkids.
Still looks young as ever, too, even with white hair.
Claims it's all on account of the way she eats. Stuff
I can't even pronounce. If beans and greens and good
beefsteak aren't healthy, I don't know what is."

"That was easy," Diana remarked afterward.

And it had been, but after that, Emma insisted on
coddling her, making her come in and rest when
she'd rather be outside watching the horses or exploring the various outbuildings. Making her eat all
her greens, which she truly didn't care for, and seeing
that she had an afternoon nap.

"You take that girl up to bed, Mr. Will," she said
as soon as Diana had washed up from her second
horse-riding experience, which had gone only
slightly better than the first.

Diana felt herself blushing. She rather thought
Will might be blushing, too, but then, it could be just

a result of coming into a warm kitchen after being out in a cold, blustery wind for hours.

"Come on, little mama, let's settle you down for a nap," he said, and she had no choice but to accompany him up the stairs.

"I might not know much about horses, but I do know how to take a nap," she grumbled. "I certainly don't need you to show me how."

"You sure of that?" Those incongruous dimples flashed in his cheeks. "You were pretty cocky when you climbed up on that mare today, too, weren't you?"

"It twitched. How did I know it was going to twitch before I could get settled?" Okay, so she'd made a tiny little noise. At least she hadn't fallen off.

"And besides," she said moments later when he opened the bedroom door and ushered her inside, "I'm hungry. I need something to tide me over until supper."

"I'll bring you up a snack."

"Oh, don't bother," she grumbled. "I hate crumbs in my bed."

"Seriously, as thin as you are now—"

"I'm slender, not thin!"

"Right. Well, as slender as you are now, you're still going to need to watch your weight. I went online last night after you turned in, and one of the things I learned was that—"

"I've never had a weight problem. As long as I exercise regularly and watch what I eat, I never will."

"Never?" he drawled, staring directly at the part of her body just below the braided leather belt. Making her entire body tingle with awareness. "Honey, pretty soon folks are going to start thinking you swallowed a watermelon seed.''

She sighed, then grinned. "Look, what if we tell Emma that my restlessness keeps you awake and that's why we sleep in separate rooms? She was giving me a funny look this morning."

"What if we don't?" His voice was too quiet, his intent too clear. She could easily have avoided him, but instead, she stood there and let nature take its course.

The kiss started out as gently as the others had. Then Will tilted his head, bringing his hands up to clasp her face, and something changed. That tilting axis effect again. Feeling the tip of his tongue tracing the seam of her lips, she moaned softly in surrender.

Hot, wet satin. How could anything so soft feel so firm? He tasted of coffee and smelled of horses and leather and grain. Those long, hard muscles she had admired so much on their wedding night hardened still more as his hand dropped below her waist, cupped her bottom and pressed her even closer. Feeling his arousal stirring against her, she caught fire.

It's not the man, it's you, you fool! It's those crazy hormones of yours acting up again!

Whatever it was, she was suddenly more aroused than she had ever been in her life. The embarrassing dampness between her thighs, this fierce, mindless urgency....

Stop it before it's too late, a voice whispered.

Too late, too late, came the echo as Will eased her toward the bed. He was breathing as if he'd just chased down a herd of wild horses. On foot.

"I probably ought to sleep," she panted.

"You'll be sore. Let me at least give you a back rub."

She choked off a laugh. "It's not my back that aches."

His warm hand slid under her hips. "Here?" he suggested. "Or here?" he murmured when both hands came under her and he cupped her cheeks. "Or here?" His palms slid down her thighs and moved inside, where she was feeling the slightest bit of irritation from miles of walking and trying to ride that damned old plug.

Trouble was, she couldn't catch her breath to tell him to stop—to tell him that all she needed was a nap and a dusting of talc.

It wasn't true. What she needed was far more complicated and far more dangerous.

What she needed was him. This stranger she'd married. Needed him around her, beneath her, on top of her—inside her.

Later she never knew if it was her own frantic uncertainty or Will's common sense that came to the rescue. She only knew he drew away, leaving her feeling bereft. Deserted.

In a voice that sounded like a rusty hinge, he said, "Sorry. Why don't you sleep awhile? Maybe later I'll drive you down to my favorite watering hole."

She wanted to grab him by the shirttail and cry, Come back here, dammit, and finish what you started!

Which was a clear indication that pregnancy also affected the brain. So she rolled over onto her stomach and pretended to sleep.

Six

Will leaned against the door, eyes closed, and waited until his breathing returned to normal before going back downstairs. He didn't trust Emma not to see something that might not be obvious to someone else.

At least, he hoped to hell it wasn't obvious.

Nothing that pulling his shirttail out wouldn't take care of.

A simple case of lust, that's all it was. Lust shouldn't even be a problem when the woman he lusted after was his own wife…. What he needed was a long, cold shower followed by a long, hard ride.

He'd never thought of himself as a predator. They had a business agreement, that was all. He would look after her the way any decent man would under the circumstances. In this case marriage had seemed advisable just to prevent any awkward occurrences down the line. He was protecting the company name and coffers—not to mention one of his closest friends.

In Diana's case, her baby would have a father on the record, and she wouldn't have to worry about supporting them until she was on her feet again. No, not even then. He'd already made up his mind to ensure her future security. He had more money than he would ever need and no one to benefit from his years of hard work other than the few private charities he supported.

The one thing he hadn't bargained on was this "personal interest," for want of a better term. If he had to analyze it, he'd say it was comprised of equal parts of liking, respect and lust.

Lust alone would be bad enough, but combined with the rest, it was about as safe as nitroglycerine.

He was headed down the stairs when Tuck whispered loudly from below. "Hey, boss, are you awake? If you're done up there, how about riding some fence. Just got a call from Wiggins—he says some of our stock's broke into his west pasture."

Saved by the bell, he thought ruefully, collecting his hat and cell phone on the way out.

Supper that evening turned out to be a surprisingly enjoyable social event. Evidently, word had spread that Will Bradford had brought home a bride. Neighbors from miles away came bringing gifts of food, potted plants, whisky and two kittens that needed a home.

Diana leaned back in her chair at the supper table in the large, log-walled dining room with its massive rock fireplace, and thought, how remarkable—how truly astounding it was that even on a temporary basis, she was a part of all this. Her marriage might not be a real one, but there was nothing at all awkward later when the men migrated into the parlor while the women sat around the kitchen table, munching on leftovers and gossiping as they put away the food and dealt with the dishes.

Emma presided, after trying unsuccessfully to ease Diana into the position of hostess. There was no real hostessing to be done. All the women knew one another, and of the five, including Diana, three were pregnant. With the exception of Emma, it was a young group. Charlie and Wilma Wiggins were the nearest neighbors. Wilma, eight months along, with the broadest, warmest smile despite a serious overbite, leaned closer and patted Diana on the hand.

"Listen, honey, you might think you're sleepy now, but wait till you spend a few nights walking the floor with a colicky baby. Believe me, I've got two more at home, and not a one of 'em but what didn't wear me plumb out! See this patch of gray hair?" She grabbed a streak of white among the faded red curls. "This was Zac. And this?" She touched its counterpart at her left temple. "This was Zeb. Would you believe I'm only seventeen?" She rolled her eyes, and everyone laughed.

Talk turned to tomorrow's Valentine's Day play at the elementary school and moved swiftly through local politics and various ailments, pregnancy-related and otherwise. Everyone chimed in with a story of having to lose weight, cook for a husband with cholesterol problems or manage the inevitable heartburn of late pregnancy.

"Oh, honey, you haven't seen anything yet," said

Wilma as she scooped up one of the kittens and settled it on her lap. "You gonna keep 'em both, aren't you?"

"I'm not even sure if Will's apartment has a no-pets clause."

"Then move. No time like the honeymoon to get a man used to following orders."

There was a general outburst of laughter and scoffing remarks. Diana said, "Evidently, you don't know Will Bradford. He's the original immovable object." It was the sort of thing wives said about their men. Everyone knew they were only joking, still Diana felt as if she had just betrayed her marriage.

It was Emma who got her off the hook. "That man. I declare, him and Tack is a pair, all right." She handed Diana a yellow kitten and rose to turn off the sputtering coffeemaker. "Stubborn as a pair of rocks."

"Yes, but even rocks can be moved with the right equipment," one of the women—Gail, she thought—quipped. "Obviously, Diana's got the right equipment."

Everyone laughed. Diana blushed, and Emma glanced at her thoughtfully and said, "Why not leave them kittens here? We need a couple of good mousers."

And so it went until one of them men stuck his head inside the kitchen and said, "Honey, anytime you're ready." After that, there was a general shuffling as people collected coats and Emma and Diana cut several slices of cake and wrapped them to go.

"Go ahead, you better take it with you," Emma insisted. "We're headed into town tonight, too, me and Tack, and there's no point in leaving too much temptation in Diana's way.''

"Ask me, she's got more than enough tempta- tion," said Debbie Truett, with a sly glance at Will, who had just stepped away to answer the phone.

Emma Gilbert put on a red wool coat and collected a shiny black purse. "Tack's shut up the barn and I've started the dishwasher and locked the back door. We'll be back by the middle of the morning.''

This, as the housekeeper had informed her earlier, was their night on the town. Bingo, square dancing and a motel in honor of St. Valentine's Day.

Before the last of the taillights disappeared, Will joined her at the glass-topped front door. Slipping an arm around her waist, he said, "Reminds me—I didn't get you a valentine.''

"Good, because I didn't get you one, either.'' She'd have been embarrassed to give him anything involving a mushy sentiment that didn't apply in their case.

"Had a good time, did you?" he asked after a few moments passed in surprisingly comfortable silence. Both kittens had finally grown tired of chasing an empty spool and were curled up in a box, asleep.

As if she'd been doing it all her life, Diana leaned her head against his shoulder. "I did. And you know what? It's the strangest thing, but I feel like I've known them all my life. They're all so nice.''

"Hmm. Did you have a good nap today?"

She could feel the heat rising to her face. At the advanced age of twenty-eight, with two or three boy- friends and one full-fledged affair behind her, she had no more control over such things than she'd had at fourteen. "I slept like a log," she lied.

"Good. Because I'm afraid I'll need to head back to town first thing tomorrow. You might as well stay here—I'll be back as soon as I check out a few things at the office."

Lifting her head, she stared up at him. "Has something happened?"

"I'm not sure. Something's cropped up with the audit."

"Who called?"

"Jason Windover. He said Seb's kind of spooked, but he hated to interrupt our honeymoon. You remember Jason from our reception, don't you?"

"Dark curly hair, blue-green eyes and a terrific smile?"

Will's eyebrows climbed several degrees. "You noticed all that, hmm?"

"I noticed everyone there. Want me to describe them all to you?"

He grinned, and his arm tightened momentarily, then fell away. "Not particularly. Maybe I'd better warn you, they're all confirmed bachelors."

"So were you," she reminded him, and then wished she hadn't.

"Well, yeah…" He caught the tip of her nose between thumb and forefinger and tweaked it ever so gently. "In my case it was a TKO."

"A *what?*"

"A technical knockout. Don't you watch boxing?"

"The daughter of a couple of peaceniks watch boxing? Perish the thought."

But the irony of it had struck her long ago. Her father, a card-carrying member of the love generation, protesting for peace and eventually turning into an abusive husband and father.

She shuddered, and Will's arm tightened around her. "You're bushed. You need a glass of milk or something before we go up? Maybe another piece of that coconut cake? You've only had three slices."

What she needed was to delay the moment until she could align her defenses again. Tonight had been too pleasant, too relaxing. Too disarming. And with Emma and Tack gone, they were alone in the house.

"You go on upstairs. I want to make a couple of phone calls."

Forty-five minutes later Will replaced the phone and stared unseeingly at a photograph of Windrunner, an eight-year-old stallion, father of more than half the new crop of foals.

What the hell was going on? He'd left Eric to oversee the outside audit. Eric Chambers was young, but as vice president of accounting, he was more than up to the job. Odds were that he'd be taking over as CFO one of these days when Will himself decided to retire.

It hadn't been Eric who'd called, it had been Jason Windover. According to Jason, Eric—trying to convince himself nothing was wrong—had mentioned the discrepancy to Seb. Seb had put it down to inept auditors, but had confided his own growing unease to Jason, who, as a retired CIA agent had some experience with such matters.

"Look, Will, this doesn't involve me, but if you want my advice, you'll get back to town and check it out for yourself. We both know Seb has a few problems of his own to deal with at the moment. He might not be the most objective man when it comes to any mess Wescott left behind.''

It was common knowledge that Sebastian had never seen eye-to-eye with his father about much of anything, yet that hadn't stopped him from joining the family business. Now, along with trying to reconcile a mixture of grief, guilt and unresolved anger, he had his father's illegitimate son to deal with.

Will himself had taken measures to see that Diana's baby would never become that sort of problem. Seb might suspect, but he could never be sure, which was the best they could hope for, under the circumstance.

Whatever was going on at Wescott Oil, Seb didn't need anything else on his plate right now. After promising to fly in first thing in the morning, Will replaced the phone and spent the next half hour thinking over the possibilities. He knew damned well the books were in good shape. As chief financial officer, he ran a tight ship, everything documented and accounted for. If there was a blip on the radar screen, the only thing he could come up with was a mathematically challenged auditor.

While he was in town, he'd give Seb a call about another matter—maybe get his mind off the dark stuff and onto something lighter. Both he and Jason had a few reservations about Dorian Brady—hell, half brother or not, he was still a stranger. But they'd agreed tonight that if Seb wanted the guy inducted into the club, neither of them would stand in the way. No one else was apt to blackball him.

Standing, he flexed the stiff muscles of his back— it always took him a few days to switch from city mode to ranch mode. The two lifestyles used different sets of muscles.

By now Diana would be asleep, otherwise he might be tempted to talk it over with her. In which case one thing might lead to another…and then another…

He wasn't ready to broaden their relationship. His brain knew it. Hell, he had self-imposed rules about those things. Trouble was, his body was a slow learner. Good thing, he told himself, that underneath that elegant, understated beauty of hers lurked an iron will and a stubborn refusal to be taken over. He admired that in a woman.

However, whether or not she liked it, he was going to be looking after her for the next several months. Once the baby came they could renegotiate.

Earlier he'd gone online and found any number of interesting sites for pregnant women. One of the things he'd learned was that in the early months, and often right up to term, most women experienced an increased sexual interest. Again, something to do with hormones.

It had hit him like a ton of bricks. One minute he was studiously clicking away, reading about folic acid and calcium, physical and emotional changes, and the next, he was fully aroused. Libido fully engaged, and hell—he wasn't even pregnant.

His personal noninvolvement policy notwithstanding, he wanted her. Worse still, he was fast coming to suspect he might want more than just a sex partner. Which might be a problem, because once she no longer needed him it would be a case of, Thank you so much, sir, but now that Junior's six weeks old, I'm moving back to Pennsylvania and taking a position that offers day care, so toodle-oo. Been nice knowing you.

"When hell freezes over, lady," he muttered now. They'd both said a bunch of words in the Judge's office, and Will didn't recall any escape clauses.

Not that one couldn't be found. Hell, half the people he knew were divorced at least once. But that wasn't his idea of what marriage was all about. He'd had no control over what had happened to his first marriage, but this time he was here, on the scene. In control.

In the kitchen he poured himself a glass of milk, downed it in three gulps, then headed upstairs. Opening the master bedroom door, he waited for his eyes to adjust to the pale sliver of moonlight before approaching the bed.

She slept on her side with one fist curled under her chin. In the silence, he could hear the soft, puffy sound of each breath.

You don't know it yet, lady—hell, I just figured it out, myself. But this is it. You and me. Me and you and whoever that is taking up space inside your body. That makes a solid *us*.

A few minutes later, after a quick detour to the bathroom, he carefully lifted the covers and slid in behind her, easing up to her warmth. The puffing sound stopped, and he held his own breath.

Then it came again and he edged closer, fitting his body around hers and placing his arm carefully around her waist. Not a smart move, he thought, making no move to leave.

There was no need to set an alarm. He'd be awake at six, at which time he would ease out of bed without disturbing her—Diana. His wife. After leaving her a note, he'd grab a bowl of cereal and a pint of coffee and jog on out to the hangar. By eight-thirty he'd be in Royal, ready to tackle whatever the auditors thought they'd uncovered.

Diana opened her eyes. Something—a sound?—had disturbed her. She'd been a light sleeper ever since her mother's illness had been diagnosed, often lying awake for hours in the night, worrying, listening for sounds of distress—searching for answers.

Pregnancy didn't help. All those daytime naps…

Heat. Hot flashes were one thing, but the weight around her waist was no hot flash. Neither was the warm current of air that stirred the hair on top of her head.

Realization came instantly, and with it, a rush of arousal that was shocking in its intensity.

She knew the very moment he came awake. Felt his chest grow still, felt another part of his body come awake.

"Diana?" The sound barely registered on the black velvet silence.

"What are you doing here?" Her own whisper sounded harsh in the darkness.

"I didn't mean to wake you."

"Then why are you in my bed instead of your own?" She could hear her own heart. The more she listened, the harder it pounded—and the faster.

"Actually, I, uh—I needed to tell you something, but you were asleep."

"So tell me."

"I'm leaving early, but I should be back before dark."

"I already knew that. Not when you were coming

back, but we talked it over, remember?'' She tried to be angry with him, but how could she possibly do that when his arm was holding her cupped to his hard body—when his breath was stirring against her hair.

When his arousal was moving against her with alarming eagerness.

''If you're leaving, it's probably time for you to get up,'' she said, shifting in an effort to escape his seductive warmth. ''I'll just go back to sleep.''

His hand brushed the lower edges of her breast. ''Too early. Can't fly out until daylight.''

''Well, but can't you—''

''Nights are longer now. Longest night of the year, in fact.'' They were both whispering, not that there was anyone to overhear them.

''That's next week. I think. Will, this is going to complicate our—our arrangement.''

''Our arrangement?'' His thumb and fingers captured her nipple and tweaked it gently. ''Don't you mean our marriage?''

She flopped over onto her back and glared up at the darkness. His warm palm, dislodged from her breast, settled on her stomach. ''Our so-called marriage is a business arrangement,'' she whispered fiercely. ''You know that—we both agreed to it, so how could you possibly think I would...that I'd want to—''

''Make love?'' He nuzzled her ear, sending chills down her side. ''Don't you want to?''

How could she deny it when there was nothing on earth she wanted more? Tomorrow would be time enough for regrets.

Turning in his arms, she lifted her face to argue, and that was all it took. A few hours ago he had kissed her so thoroughly her toes had curled. Now he was going to kiss her again, and she was suddenly starved for the taste of his mouth. Some kisses were like Chinese food. It was impossible to get enough.

This time there were no gentle preliminaries. This time his mouth devoured hers until both of them were gasping for breath. Hot, sweet fire streaked through her loins, and her hands slipped over his sleek, hard shoulders, then moved down his chest to encounter his small, hard nipples. She could actually feel the shock waves echoing down his body, like a high-voltage current that affected everything within range.

She could have sworn he couldn't get any harder.

She was wrong. In the pale-gray light just beginning to filter through the window, she watched the planes of his face flatten out, watched his eyes darken as a grimace that almost resembled pain spread over his features. When his fingers trailed a lingering path up the inside of her thigh, she closed her eyes and whimpered with need.

Never in her entire life had she whimpered. With need, or anything else. Fragments of warning flickered in her mind like snowflakes, only to melt in the blinding, white-hot fire that threatened to consume her.

Please—oh, please…

Had she said it aloud?

Daring to take the lead, she shifted her position so that she could kiss his eyelids, each in turn, then his nose, that crooked, aggressive masculine blade of a nose. She kissed his chin, drawing her tongue lovingly along the angle of his jaw, then she buried her face in his neck, nibbling her way down the most sensitive trail to the hollow at the base of his throat.

He was groaning as if he were in great pain. "God, Diana, what are you doing to me? I'm only human," he whispered hoarsely.

"I'd noticed that," she murmured, heady with the unaccustomed feeling of power.

With one hand he threw off the covers. "You're not cold, are you?"

She laughed, a shaky sound that sounded different. Almost daring. "Do I feel cold?"

"Ah, Diana, Diana…what am I going to do with you?"

"I thought you knew. One of us probably ought to know what we're doing." She laughed softly again, trying to sound as if the earth wasn't shifting under her feet. She had never felt more unsure of herself, yet she couldn't have turned back now if her life depended on it.

His hands began a slow, incendiary journey of exploration. Fondling the sensitive slopes of her breast, he lowered his head to scour one nipple with a hot tongue.

A stifled sound escaped her, and her thighs quivered with the need to cradle his narrow hips.

"Not yet," he murmured at her small, instinctive movements. "You drove me quietly out of my head—now it's your turn." Matching actions to words, he proceeded to salute each needy part of her body, leaving kisses in each small hollow, tracing the crest of each separate curve with his lips, his tongue.

Her eyes widened, then closed tightly as molten lava flowed through her body, filling the valley of her desire. She pleaded with him incoherently. Bits of phrases—mostly sighs and whimpers.

Instead of mounting her, he took her hand and, one by one, kissed each finger. Then he nibbled the pad at the base of her thumb. His tongue traced a path across the hollow of her palm. Not until she was gasping for breath did he roll onto his back and lift her over him. Settling her astride his hips, he brought her down on him with exquisite slowness until her long, satiny legs were curled at his sides.

Somewhere along the way he had sensed that she had a thing about being in control. This much he could do for her, he thought—his last rational thought as the pressure built to unbearable levels.

Desperately he tried to hold back—to prolong the mind-shattering ecstasy, but it was too late. Far too late. Easier to hold back the sea, the rising sun....

In his last lucid moment he heard a cascade of sound. A soft, disbelieving *Oh, oh, oh!*

Seven

He left her sleeping—left with the feeling that something more was needed. That words that should have been spoken had gone unsaid. But even if he'd known the words, he wouldn't have spoken them.

Not this soon—not after mind-boggling sex. No lawyer in the world would accept words spoken under such circumstances. He was no lawyer, but even he knew the meaning of undue influence. Business was business, pleasure was pleasure, and trying to mix the two—trying to change the rules in the middle of the game—was asking for trouble.

Will made coffee, folded a slab of cheese into a slice of bread and let himself out, locking the door behind him. There was no crime in the area, unless a few straying horses and a broken fence could be considered crime. More a case of the grass-is-always-greener, he thought wryly as he went over his pre-flight checkup.

One of the skills he had cultivated over the years was an ability to prioritize. Making a deliberate effort to disconnect his emotions, he focused on the problem at hand.

The immediate problem, he amended. Unless he misjudged the woman he'd left in his bed, that particular problem was going to require time, the patience of a saint and the tact of a diplomat.

A little while later, while circling over the Royal Municipal Airport, he completed the disconnect, knowing that the sooner he could find out what the hell was going on at Wescott Oil, the sooner he could get back to the ranch.

To Diana.

Hunger drove her downstairs. Diana showered and dressed in record time, hoping Will hadn't yet left so that she could settle things between them.

Praying he had, because she hadn't the slightest idea what she was going to say. Thank you, I had a lovely time, didn't quite seem to cover it.

He was gone, of course. It was half past ten. So she made herself a hasty breakfast of half a cup of whole-grain cereal with skim milk and three dried apricots and a pint of coffee, to take out onto the deck. Sooner or later she would have to cut back on the caffeine, but not yet. Not when her whole life had unexpectedly taken a dangerous new turn. A woman needed a few vices to get her over the rough patches.

She let the kittens outside, then she bundled up in Will's flannel-lined denim jacket, sat out on the deck and watched the steam rise from her coffee mug. It was going to take more than caffeine, she mused, to get her through this particular patch.

Of all the crazy things to do! It wasn't as if she was in love with the man.

Of course, she hadn't been in love with Jack, either, but at least she'd had a good excuse. Her mother's needs had come before all else.

How could she have allowed herself to think pregnancy was a good enough excuse? This was the twenty-first century. Wescott Oil paid well, the benefits were great—they even had child care. And single mothers were almost the norm these days. While it was far from an ideal situation, not every marriage was made in heaven. Her parents' marriage certainly hadn't been.

Nor was her own. Strictly speaking, it was a temporary legal arrangement between two consenting adults to provide for the security of a third party. Her baby. If Will hadn't rushed her—if he had allowed her more time to consider her options, she would never have taken such a drastic step.

And now, after last night, what should have been a straightforward business arrangement had become complicated beyond belief.

He probably considered it a quid pro quo. Damn all men.

Taking a sip of coffee, she burned her tongue and swore, more than the slight injury called for. She was still sitting on the deck, soaking up sun now that the morning chill had dissipated, when Tack and Emma drove up.

Diana rose to greet them. Tack headed for the barn while Emma came up onto the porch, her plump face oddly flushed. There was something about her smile that made Diana suspect that bingo wasn't all they'd played last night.

"Where's Mr. Will? Did you two make out all right for breakfast? I should have thought to make a sausage and cheese casserole and leave it in the refrigerator."

"We did fine." Diana collected her empty cereal bowl and coffee mug and followed the older woman inside. "Will had to leave first thing this morning. Something came up at work."

Emma shook her head and made a sound with her tongue and teeth. "That man. I declare, I don't know what it is with men and their work," she said as she took off her coat and reached for her apron. "Tack's just like him. Can't stand to be away from those horses of his more'n a few hours. You'd think they were his children, the way he frets about the least little sniffle."

"Yes, well. If you don't need me for anything, I think I'll take a walk. This is a lovely place to walk, much nicer than Royalty Park."

Emma took a roast large enough to feed a small army from the freezer and glanced at the kitchen clock, as if wondering if she had time to thaw and cook it for dinner.

"Uh…count me out," Diana said. "If Will's not back by noon, I think I'll drive back to town. I've still got some unpacking to do." And if Emma thought she was still in the process of moving in with Will, so be it. It was the literal truth—she did have some unpacking to do, including those old files of Jack's, which were probably of no use to anyone at this point.

Before Emma could argue, she hurried back to the bedroom and changed into her most comfortable sneakers, taking time while she was there to stuff her belongings back into her suitcase. She looked around at the room—at the bed—and sighed. She could have loved this place, but it was Will's home, not hers.

Striding out briskly for her walk, she followed the fence lines, pausing now and then to admire the horses. Quarter horses, Will had said, not that she would know one variety from another. She could tell a mule from a horse, and a cow from a mule. She knew from her brief experience that horses smelled like dried grass and manure, which, surprisingly enough, wasn't quiet as unpleasant as it sounded.

Maybe pregnancy affected her olfactory senses, as well as everything else.

One of the brown ones, more curious than the others, trotted over to the fence and blew its nose. Sort of a whuffling sound. It looked friendly, but Diana wasn't about to risk her fingers. "Nice horsey," she said.

The horse shook her head and backed away, and Diana continued down the dusty road. Walking always helped clear her mind. Exercise was more important now than ever. But even before she set out to walk her daily two miles, she knew what she had to do. If Will came back and she was still here, things would be awkward to say the least.

Dear heavens, they had made love and it had been the most splendid, mind-shattering thing she'd ever experienced! How could she go on living in the same apartment, working in the same office building with Will and not want to do it again? It would be like trying to walk lightly across a lake of quicksand.

It hadn't mattered with Jack—working with him days, sleeping with him nights. Every speck of feelings she'd had had been focused on her mother. With Jack she'd merely gone through the motions, and apparently that had been enough. He hadn't wanted more from her—although he'd told her once that her aloofness intrigued him.

With Will, aloofness wasn't even a remote possibility. She could just imagine going upstairs with him after the late news. What would they say, "Good night"? "See you in the morning"?

Or, "Shall we try for an encore…my bed or yours?"

The question was bound to arise, even if the words weren't actually spoken, and at the moment she wasn't prepared to deal with it. Her life was complicated enough as it was. Sleeping with a temporary husband—worse yet, falling in love with him— would only make matters worse. As long as she could hold on to her common sense and not get carried away by any romantic ideas, she stood a good chance of remaining in control.

"So that's what I'm going to do," she told Emma half an hour later, drinking a glass of tomato juice with a slice of lemon on the side. "I'll have to drive Will's car."

"I'll keep both kittens until you find out if you can keep them in town. When Will brings the plane back, he'll need some way to get back to town. Had you thought about that?" Clearly the woman was puzzled by more than their modes of transportation.

"What about the trucks? Couldn't he drive one of those back to Royal?" A week ago Diana couldn't have pictured him driving a dusty pickup truck. Now she could.

Now she could picture him in far too many ways for her own peace of mind.

"I reckon he could. Lord knows, we got enough of 'em around here. Next time you two come home, you can drive the car and he can bring the truck back, then everything'll be back in its rightful place."

Everything but her. Diana sighed. This was just one more indication of how inconvenient her life had become since she'd entered into a marriage of convenience.

She finished packing her suitcase, stripped the bed and offered to do a load of laundry, hoping Emma wouldn't take her up on it. She needed to be gone by the time Will got back. The next time she saw him she intended to have her armor in place and her arguments all lined up.

"We've done the honeymoon," she would say, "and it was lovely, it really was. But now I intend to go back to my own apartment. You see, if we stay together, I might want to make love again because it was the most...the most..."

She didn't know how to describe it, she only knew that if it happened again, some part of her that had remained untouched for twenty-eight years would be seriously threatened. And she simply couldn't afford to have that happen.

What was the slogan she'd seen once on a T-shirt? Life Is What Happens When You're Busy Making Plans.

Too true, she told herself as she braked at the end of the long drive, then turned off onto the highway. And, speaking of making plans, she would have to go by the personnel office first thing in the morning to find out where to report. The sooner she got her life back on a nice, stress-free track, the better.

Something was wrong. Something was definitely going on here, but for the life of him, Will couldn't put his finger on who was involved and whether or not it was deliberate.

Yeah...it was deliberate. Frowning at one of several computers in his private office, he wondered what he had missed. He'd gone over every entry on every single account until he'd practically memorized the damned things. In a company the size of Wescott Oil, that was a considerable feat.

Conclusion? Whoever had fiddled with the books was either incredibly smart or incredibly lucky. Will worked alone. For the time being he had to be suspicious of everyone with access. It had taken him all day and half the night to home in on the trouble area. Now he knew the accounts involved. All he had to find out was how many of his employees had access, narrow it down and go from there. He had a feeling the trail might lead eventually to an offshore account. Grand Cayman, perhaps—even Guam.

Eric was in the clear; it was Eric who had discovered the problem. On the other hand, knowing that the discrepancy would soon be discovered by the outside audit anyway, a smart crook might play innocent by pointing out the problem.

"Damn, damn, damn," Will swore tiredly. His collar was open, his shirtsleeves rolled up. He looked, as Tack was fond of saying, as if he'd been rode hard and put away wet. Diana wasn't the only one who was fond of old cowboy movies.

Diana…

He couldn't afford to be distracted until this mess was settled, but it was hard to keep the firewalls in place when he was so damned tired. God, he'd hated to leave her this morning. Every instinct he possessed had urged him to hold on to her—not to let her get her second wind and start thinking about what had happened. He had a feeling she'd been as stunned as he was at the intensity. Over the years he had slept with a number of women. Among them had been a few screamers, a yelper, even one or two groaners. Nothing had ever affected him like the startled symphony of notes that had cascaded over him when Diana had climaxed.

Even thinking about it now, he felt his body stir to life.

"Lady, you and I have some unfinished business once I get back to the ranch," he muttered. Reaching over his shoulder, he worked on a few of the knots at the back of his neck, wishing those in his head were as easy to reach.

He'd done about all he could do until he caught a few hours of sleep. Maybe tomorrow, with a fresh perspective, he could lay it all out so that it made sense.

Reaching for the phone on his desk, he let his hand fall back. Too late to call now. Emma would know that if he wasn't back by dark, he wouldn't be coming until tomorrow. He was too tired to fly, anyhow. What he wouldn't give, though, to stand under a shower until he ran out of hot water, then crawl into bed with Diana and hold her—just hold her in his arms. Absorb her warmth, her sweetness, the calm stoicism she'd shown in the face of what had to have been some pretty heavy stuff.

He still had a lot to learn about the woman he'd married, but one of the more endearing qualities he'd discovered was her ability to stand there with tears running down her face and calmly make the decisions that had to be made.

Unflappable. Yeah, that described her. Or maybe flappable on the surface, but deep inside, where it counted, she had her own north star.

Will's car stood out like a sore thumb in the parking lot behind Diana's apartment, but there was nothing she could do about it now. It was too late, and she was too tired to play car tag. Half her clothes were at his place, but she had enough to get by with.

First thing in the morning she would drive his car to his apartment and walk to work. Before she settled on her next move, she had to know where she would be working.

Awkward didn't begin to describe the situation she found herself in. Will wasn't going to like it, either. Him and his rule about mixing business with personal matters. Jack had had no such rules.

But she couldn't afford to think about Jack now. She refused to think about what Will would say when he found her working nine floors below, in a tiny cubicle.

She got out the iron and pressed a beige wraparound skirt and a darker tunic top, both of which would serve nicely as early maternity wear. Her hair, which she'd worn in a single braid at the ranch because Will liked it that way, would be twisted up on top of her head and anchored with a small clip and a few hairpins. If she was very careful, no one would guess how many butterflies were fluttering around in her stomach.

And if worse came to worst and there was no place for her at Wescott, she would look elsewhere for a job. It would have to be here in Royal, because she still had almost a month left on her lease. At the moment she'd be hard-pressed to come up with a security deposit on another place, much less a month's rent in advance.

After putting away the ironing board, she yawned, but was too keyed up to sleep. She was hungry, but too tense to risk eating. When Will got back to the ranch and discovered she'd left....

Well. She would think about that tomorrow.

Will sat in the rental he'd driven from the airport and studied the gunmetal-gray sedan occupying his parking space. He scratched his head and wondered, not for the first time, if he was headed for a premature mid-life crisis.

Headed for? Hell—he was in over his head. That car was supposed to be back at the ranch. If Tack had come to town, he'd have driven one of the trucks. Emma didn't drive at all. Which meant...

A few minutes later he unlocked the door of his spacious apartment. Adrenaline coursed though his body like water from a fire hose. "Diana?"

Silence.

"Dammit, Diana!"

She wasn't there. He knew it without even looking. The place felt empty in a way it never had before she'd come into his life.

He'd driven directly from the airport to the office.

This was the first time he'd been back since they'd left for the ranch three days ago. Still swearing, he tossed his coat onto the bed and headed for the bathroom. Leaning over, he splashed cold water over his face. He could have used a shower—felt as if he'd been living in the same clothes for a week, but it would have to wait.

He didn't take time to call the ranch to see if by chance she was still there, and someone who happened to drive the same model car he did had confiscated his parking place.

The lights were on in the third-floor apartment on the corner of Macauley and Spring Streets. Not bothering with the elevator, which was evidently one of Mr. Otis's early experimental models, he took the stairs two at a time, building a head of steam as he went.

He hadn't intended to pound on her door, but by the time he reached the third floor, he'd had it. Flat-out had all he could take.

The door opened. "I thought you might show up," she said quietly. "You could have called first."

Fist raised for another attack on the door, he was caught off guard. Couldn't think of a single thing to say.

"Do you want to come in for a few minutes? I can make coffee."

So he uttered the first dumb words that popped into his mind. "You drink too much coffee."

Well, hell, she was standing there in that awful place of hers, wearing what looked like a Polynesian circus tent, with her hair all wet and her eyes all pink-rimmed. Dignity, though. Oh, yeah—more dignity than a bucket of starch.

"Coffee would be nice." Even as he entered her lair, the weight of the past fourteen hours settled in on him, like a ton of bricks. After a quick glance around the room, he headed for the rump-sprung sofa with the fake fur throw.

"I'll just be a minute," she said.

He was asleep by the time Diana came back with a hand-painted tray bearing two mugs of coffee and a cream pitcher in the shape of a Holstein cow.

For a long time she stood gazing down at him—at the unshaven face with the incongruous creases that deepened into dimples when he laughed. At the shadows under his eyes and the touches of gray at his temples. How could any man look so exhausted, so distinguished and so sexy at the same time?

That was when it struck her that she loved this man.

Not just that she was in love with him. To her way of thinking, being *in* love was too often a temporary condition. Occasionally it might deepen into the real thing, but as often as not it faded once two people got to know each other and both stopped being on their best courting behavior.

Loving was different. It was a for-better-or-worse thing. Something that lasted even when both parties had aged beyond recognition. Something that encompassed all that had gone before as well as all that lay ahead.

She didn't know how she knew this—she simply did.

Being careful not to make a sound, she set the tray down on the painted footlocker that served as a coffee table, then lowered herself into a chair and waited to see if he would wake up. They had things to talk about—things to settle between them. He probably wasn't going to like her decision to move back to her own apartment.

Then again, he might like it just fine. After all, he'd been a bachelor most of his life. If he'd wanted to be a husband, he could have easily found a far more suitable wife. According to one of the women she'd met when she'd first gone to work at Wescott, he'd once been listed in some magazine as one of Texas's ten most eligible bachelors.

She could kiss him now and he would never know it. Did the sleeping beauty thing work in reverse? Would he wake up and fall instantly, irrevocably in love?

Or would she turn into a frog?

Eight

Without opening his eyes, Will came instantly awake. Sensing her presence, he tried to assemble his thoughts—his arguments. The spring that was stabbing him in the rump didn't help.

Neither did the smell of her soap and shampoo. The subtle scent of her skin. He knew her too well.

He didn't know her at all.

"Are you in there?" she whispered.

He slitted his eyes. "Am I in where?"

Diana shrugged and looked away. "It's just something my mother used to say when I'd close my eyes and try to shut out the—that is, try to pretend I was sleeping."

Interesting… "Is that coffee I smell?"

"It's probably cooled off by now. You were sleeping so hard I hated to wake you up, but I was afraid the rogue spring would get you."

He slid a hand beneath him, trying to hang on to the anger he'd brought with him. He had fully intended to remind her of a few pertinent facts, then haul her back and install her at his apartment until they could settle on some rules.

"Look, I thought we had a deal," he said. Tact and diplomacy was called for here. Not his long suit at the best of times, and this was hardly that.

"We sort of did, I guess."

"We *sort of did? You guess?* Try again, Diana." His wristwatch quietly signaled the hour. It had to be at least ten—maybe eleven. It felt like it had been a week since he'd left her in his bed back at the ranch.

"All right, we did. We agreed that your name will be on my baby's birth certificate, and by now everyone in Royal probably knows we're married. By the time my baby comes, people will have forgotten, if they ever knew about…well, about Jack and me."

"Uh-huh. Sure they will." Sitting up now, he gave her a curious look. "You really believe that, don't you? I don't know how things work where you came from, but I can guarantee that half the citizens of Royal will start counting on their fingers the day we deliver. The other half won't have to—they'll remember."

"Well, shoot!" she exclaimed indignantly. "Why bother to get married, then? And besides, I'm the one who's going to deliver. You don't have anything to do with it."

He studied her for several moments, trying to get a handle on her belligerence. He could have sworn it hadn't been there a moment ago. Wariness, maybe, but not belligerence. In fact, when he'd first opened his eyes, he'd seen something that looked almost like—

He must've been wrong. As tired as he was, mistakes were inevitable. "Correction," he said patiently. "We're both involved. That baby you call yours is going to be wearing my name when he comes into the world. That means I have a responsibility. And as long as you're carrying him, my responsibility extends to you, too. Are we clear on that much?"

She snatched up a mug of lukewarm black coffee, took a large swallow and grimaced. "All right, all right. Maybe I'm just not used to people who insist on taking responsibility. So here's what we'll do."

He figured he might as well listen. She had this thing about being in control. It wouldn't hurt to cut her some slack, just until he got to the bottom of this other matter. After that, well…they would see.

"I'll stay here at my place, you can stay in yours, that way things won't get, um, complicated."

"You mean you won't end up in my bed again."

He could practically hear the heat sizzle as it flooded her face. "That, too. It was just a—that is, we sort of—"

He took pity on her. They both knew what it was—a hell of a lot more than simple, no-strings-attached, mind-blowing sex. At the moment, though, she was spooked and he had too much on his mind to explore it in depth. "Sure, that's it. Propinquity."

"Pro…what?"

"Stuff happens when you're unexpectedly thrown into close contact. In our case, sex happened. We'll deal with it later."

"Or not. I've got plans all worked out. Long-term

and short-term. You've obviously got something on your mind, or you wouldn't have hurried back to town. So…'' She smiled, and it was almost convincing. ''Why don't we each go our own way, accomplish whatever needs accomplishing, and maybe have lunch together from time to time so that people will know we're still friends?''

It was put in the form of a question, and he didn't have the heart to tell her it ranked right up there among the top-ten lousy ideas. ''Still friends. Yeah. Okay, we'll give it a shot for a few days, then maybe we can have lunch and renegotiate.''

It was a weak shot across the bow to let her know that they weren't finished yet, not by any means. But for now he would have to set aside his personal problems and deal with something that involved several hundred employees directly, and peripherally, several thousand more.

The change of regime in the life of any big outfit was a critical period, even when the new CEO was a known factor. There were bound to be a few hold-your-breath situations right at first. Seb lacked his father's ruthlessness, but he was a damn good businessman. Besides, the board of directors would smooth over any rough patches.

On the other hand, the way the energy market had been fluctuating lately, if word leaked out of any past irregularities, things could spiral out of control before they could get a handle on it. The last thing they needed was a herd of stampeding stockholders.

Diana stood, looking oddly dignified in her colorful muumuu. ''Go home, Will. You look worn out. Get a good night's sleep. If there's anything I can do, just call.''

He stood, bracing himself against swaying; he was that tired. "Thanks, Danny." She usually objected when he called her that. This time she looked as if she might cry. So he leaned over and placed a lop-sided kiss on the side of her nose and escaped before she could throw him out.

What the devil, he wondered, had happened to his so-called people skills? He was no diplomat at the best of times, but normally he didn't go out of his way to make waves.

Left alone, Diana sat on the sofa, avoiding the middle cushion, and congratulated herself on taking control of her life. Just because she had wanted nothing so much as to throw herself into his arms and beg him to love her, that didn't mean she'd done it. No way had she surrendered a single speck of dignity. Just the opposite, in fact.

So why did she feel as if the world had just come to an end?

Sniffling, she felt for a tissue. She didn't have a tissue. In fact, the damned muumuu didn't even have a pocket. So she mopped her face with the hem of the short, full sleeve and thought with tear-stained amusement that her mother had been messy, too. It was evidently in her genes.

But as dearly as she'd loved her mother, Diana had never—at least not since she was ten years old—mistaken Lila Foster for a mature, responsible adult capable of directing her own life, much less her daughter's.

Even when he'd been there, her father had been worse than useless. He'd been vicious when he was drinking. When he was on drugs he tried to stay away rather than risk exposing them to that particular set of dangers. Which, she thought grudgingly, had been responsibility of a sort. The best Liam Foster could offer.

But it hadn't been enough. Not nearly enough. While he had never done more than threaten his daughter and slap her around, he had beaten his wife more times than Diana could recall while a terrified child had hidden under a quilt or in a closet and tried to find the courage to go for help.

It was a lose-lose situation. She hadn't even felt guilty at the relief she'd felt when he had piled up his van and had to be pried out with the Jaws of Life. Or in his case, the jaws of death.

By then she'd been fourteen, old enough to take control of her life. She had deliberately chosen the courses at high school that would pay off the quickest. Once her mother had got back on her feet emotionally, Diana had helped her go over the help-wanted ads. Fortunately, the economy had been in an upswing at the time. Diana had picked out a sedate new outfit for her mother and insisted she wear it to be interviewed.

Things had been good for the next few years, but gradually the past had begin to take its toll. Or so Diana had thought at the time. When Lila had lost interest in her job, as well as everything else, Diana had decided that it was their apartment, the same one they'd lived in for years, that was a constant reminder of the past.

That was when the moves had begun. Packing up all the posters and wall hangings, the linens and dishes and candles and pots and handwoven throws and whatever furniture they could cram into the rental trailer—most of it wasn't worth the cost of moving—they would find a new town and new jobs and start all over again. The pattern had repeated itself three times before they had reached the end of the line. Royal, Texas.

And now Diana was responsible for someone else.

Will stretched out his legs, tilted his chair and closed his eyes. For one brief moment Diana's face hovered on the fringes of his consciousness. Quickly he slammed the door shut before he could be tempted to linger there. All in all, it had been one hell of a day. He didn't need any distractions.

He thought about the way his ranch manager, Tack Gilbert, had been led kicking and screaming into the world of technology. Farm records, breeding records, sales records had all been kept in a series of dog-eared ledgers. "Who the devil needs one o' them machines when he's got pencil and paper?"

Who the devil, indeed. One of the reasons Jack's business affairs had taken so long to sort out was his insistence on his own paranoid brand of bookkeeping, backed up with scribbled records which he stashed away in places that had taken weeks to discover. A few transactions, Will suspected, had never been recorded at all.

All of which probably had nothing to do with the problem they were facing at the moment. Whoever he was, the modern-day pirate who had been smart enough to set up a string of phony accounts had excellent computer skills. He'd been savvy enough to wipe out his tracks so thoroughly that it had taken an outside expert to even get close to the truth.

Eric Chambers had given him the name of an ex-employee of the Department of Defense who could, in Eric's words, bleed a turnip bone dry.

"First the good news," the DOD expert had said after a marathon session that had left Will's office littered with chili-dog wrappers and cigar ashes. He was going to have to have the whole tenth floor fumigated. "I managed to follow the trail through four offshore banks and narrow it down to two separate accounts. The bad news is that I don't have a name for you. Whoever pulled it off was smart enough to wipe out most of the hard drive by overwriting it with zeros. That's a DOD method, if that gives you a clue. You might want to check your personnel files for a connection there. Maybe he got in a hurry, I don't know, but he didn't do a thorough enough job, which is the only reason I found out as much as I did."

"So that's where matters stand," Will had told Robert Cole a short time later. The two men had met at the gazebo in Royalty Park. It was about the most unlikely place Will could think of. He didn't trust whoever had milked Wescott Oil for an indecent amount of money not to have bugged his office, his apartment and for all he knew, the meeting rooms at the Cattleman's Club.

"I'll need to see the personnel files."

"My computer expert said you might want to look for DOD connections. Then again, geekdom prevails in some pretty strange places." Ordinarily, the first place he'd have looked was in his own department, but aside from Eric, he was no longer certain who he could trust.

"It could be a new hire or an older employee with a grudge. Lot of that going around lately."

"You show me a roughneck who's spent his life in the oil field who can make a computer sing soprano and I'll hand him the money, tax-free."

"Don't make any hasty promises. You'd be surprised the kind of people who take to computers like a bear to honey."

Will's temper, already on a short rein, tightened dangerously. He needed a shave, he needed a shower, he needed some food and about twenty-four hours of sleep. Even a couple hours would help.

He wasn't likely to get any of the above in the near future.

The shower, maybe...

"Don't make any rash promises," Robert had warned. "How many people know about the losses?"

"Eric, of course. He managed to stall the outside auditors until we can get a handle on it. Don't ask me how, because these guys are supposed to be hell on wheels."

"One of 'em's Eric's cousin on his mama's side."

Will stared at him, dumbfounded. "How the devil did you know that?"

Robert shrugged. "Hey, I'm a P.I. It's what we do. Impress the clients by coming up with irrelevant information."

"Which may be relevant in this case."

"I don't think so." Robert shook his head.

"Why not?"

Instead of answering, the young private investigator had shoved his hands in his pockets. Blue eyes twinkling, he'd changed the subject. "How's married life?"

"Keep your prying eyes off my marriage, okay?"

"So where's the bride? How does she like having her honeymoon interrupted by a little financial hanky-panky?"

"I left her at the ranch," Will said, but hell—this was Robert. The two men had been friends for years. "She drove herself back to town. At the moment we've agreed to put our relationship on hold until I can get a handle on this business at the company."

"Smart man. The way I hear it—not that I have any firsthand experience with wedded bliss, you understand—these things are tricky. Takes a man's full concentration."

"Which things, marriage or embezzlement?"

"Both," Robert had replied, grinning broadly.

"You got that right," Will muttered.

It was a few minutes past nine when Diana arrived at the Wescott Building the next morning. Not too early, not too late. Just right, in fact. Only the thing was, she didn't know where to report. She could just show up in the pool room, as the secretaries who worked there called it, or she could ask at personnel if she should report upstairs, and if so, to which particular office in which department. Maybe someone was going out on maternity leave and she could fill in until something else opened up.

After due consideration, she decided against just showing up in the pool room, where her cubicle was already occupied by someone else. It would be awkward at the very least. She had no idea how many people there knew she'd had an affair with Jack, but they probably all knew by now that she was married to the CFO. It would make a difference. She was hardly naive enough to believe it wouldn't.

Which was why she had a backup plan all ready in place. Not an ideal one, but any plan was better than none at all.

Twenty-five minutes later she sat in her car in the employees' parking lot and stared at the bug smears on her windshield. "I don't believe it," she said softly. She could not believe that Will would do such a thing. Had he deliberately set out to humiliate her? Presenting herself at the personnel office, she'd been offered smirking congratulations along with her severance pay. Severance pay!

"Well, we'll just see about that, boy-o," she muttered. Backing recklessly out of her slot, she came within inches of plowing down a fire hydrant.

The Royal Diner might look like a typical greasy spoon, but she hadn't lived in Royal long before she realized that everyone in town ate there at one time or another. At the moment, however, there was only one patron inside. It was too late for breakfast, too early for lunch.

Diana recognized the woman only in the way you would someone you'd seen several times but never spoken to. Passing the long Formica counter with the empty vinyl-covered bar stools and the row of booths, she headed for the door at the back with a sign that said, Office. No Smoking. And rapped sharply. She was still seething.

"Come in, come in, whatcha want, for Pete's sake, cantcha see I'm busy?" someone yelled from inside.

Anger was replaced by an impulse to flee, but before she could move, the door was opened and she was trapped. "Yeah?" said the woman with the neon-red hair and the cigarette dangling from the corner of her mouth.

Diana glanced quickly at the sign over the door, and the woman said, "Yeah, yeah, I know. Days like this don't count. You selling or collecting?"

"No—that is, I saw your sign on the window. The one that said Waitress Wanted?"

Six hours later she staggered into her apartment and collapsed on the sofa. Cursing the damned sprung spring, she shifted her position slightly, then leaned back and closed her eyes. Whoever thought being a waitress was easy work needed their head examined.

Slipping off her shoes, which had never been designed for waitressing, she rubbed her feet and thought longingly of easing them into a tub of hot salt water. Unfortunately, she didn't have a tub, only a shower.

Too much trouble. Just sitting would have to do for now.

The diner had indeed been in need of help. One waitress had left three days before to be married, another had called in sick that morning, and the one who had showed up for work had left with a severe case of cramps mere moments before Diana arrived.

Which was probably why the manager had handed Diana a clean apron, stuck a pad and pencil in her hand, and said, "You're hired. We'll do the paperwork later. Her over there." She'd nodded toward the sole patron. "See if she's ready yet to order. Been sitting there moping long enough to take root."

That's when Diana had learned that a waitress's duties included more than merely transporting food from kitchen to table and dirty dishes from table to kitchen.

The woman in the third booth was relatively new in town. She'd admitted as much when she'd placed an order for a Mexican omelet, a croissant and cappuccino. "I'm celebrating," she confided. "I just bought the flower shop—just now signed the final papers, in fact. Now I'm starting to have second thoughts." Her voice wavered, and her blue eyes looked suspiciously bright.

"You'll love it here," Diana said encouragingly. "I've been here less than a year, myself, but the people are so nice. What are you going to call your flower shop?" If the manager complained that she was wasting too much time listening to the customers, Diana might even rethink her impulsive decision to work here. She wasn't about to be rude to a woman who obviously needed reassurance.

"I haven't decided yet," said the woman, who had introduced herself as Rebecca Todman. And then she burst into tears. "Sorry. Don't mind me, I'm just— it's sort of an…an anniversary."

"Oh." Tears of joy? The poor woman didn't exactly look overcome with happiness. "Should I offer my congratulations?"

Rebecca had laughed through her tears. "Yes…maybe you should." And then she had told in starkest terms a story that made Diana feel incredibly fortunate by comparison.

"Hey, you! Bradford! This ain't no sorority party. If you're done over there, slice them pies, put 'em on plates and reload the pie case."

Several more customers had come in soon after that, and between keeping the dessert cases filled, taking and serving orders and clearing off tables, she hadn't had a single moment to sit, much less to think about her very first customer.

Did aspirin work on sore feet? she wondered just as someone began pounding on her door.

"Well...shoot," she muttered. In her stocking feet, she hobbled across the room and yanked the door open without bothering to ask who was there. The Lennox Apartments didn't run to security peep holes.

Will's fist was lifted to knock again, making Diana quip, "Déjà vu. We've got to stop meeting like this."

Nine

"You want to explain what you think you're doing?" Will told himself it probably wasn't the most tactful approach, but she was his wife, dammit.

"At the moment, I think I'm wondering which would suffer the most if I slammed the door—your nose or your fancy boots."

He frowned down at his boots. They weren't fancy. They were plain custom-made boots, the kind any Texan who preferred comfort over flashiness might wear. Just to be on the safe side, he blocked the door open by placing a hand on it. "We need to talk."

"Like I said before, déjà vu. We've already talked, Will. I think we settled everything we need to settle. Unless you'd care to explain why you saw fit to blackball me at the office?"

"Blackball! What the hell are you talking about?"

She turned away, and he followed her inside, noticing several things about her. Her hair, which always started out the day pinned up in a neat bundle on her head, was, as usual, responding to the laws of gravity. She was limping. "What happened to your feet?"

"I walked on them." She plopped down on the only decent chair in the room, leaving him the couch with the feral spring. "Why did you tell personnel I wouldn't be back?" she demanded.

"Because you won't. You know the rules."

"I know *your* rules. It's certainly not a company policy that employers and employees can't—that is they aren't allowed to—"

"Cohabit?"

"Yes, well we're not, are we? I live here. You live at your address."

"We're married, Danny." She looked so damned bushed he'd almost gotten over being furious with her.

"Don't call me that."

"Why not? You like it."

"When did I say that?" She was rubbing her left foot. Her ankles were swollen.

"You didn't have to say it, I saw the way you looked the first time I called you Danny. Like a little girl who'd been given a kitten and was hoping she'd get to keep it." He glanced around. "That reminds me, did you bring your cats home with you?"

"They're kittens, not cats, and they're more yours than mine. And no, I left them at *your* ranch."

"Did it ever occur to you that in your condition, you shouldn't be on your feet all day?" He'd come here mad enough to wring her dainty little neck, but one look at those sagging shoulders, the shadows under her eyes, and he'd lost his priming. How could he tell her that people were already talking about their hasty wedding? That there'd been whispers about the way she'd been whisked out of the secretarial pool to go upstairs and work for Jack? And now the rumor was, with Jack gone, she had set her sights on Jack's CFO.

Then, as if that weren't enough to set tongues wagging, she'd had to go and move out of his apartment and take a job at Royal's primary rumor mill—the diner. How the devil was he supposed to protect a woman who was so determined to self-destruct?

Summoning all the diplomacy at his command— which, at the moment, wasn't much—he said, "Honey, if you did it just to make a point, then you succeeded. Maybe I should have discussed it with you first, but—"

"Maybe? Just *maybe* you should have told me you intended to take control of my life? I don't remember anything in the wedding ceremony that gave you the right to tell me where I could or couldn't work."

She was on a roll now. Will leaned back and admired the glittering eyes, the pink cheeks, the thrust of her delicate jaw. He could have told her she didn't have what it took to threaten a man of his size, his age and his experience, but hell—he was a generous man. So he let her take the bit in her mouth and run with it for a little while. She obviously needed to vent.

When she'd gone on some more about being an adult, and about not needing anyone to tell her how to live her life, and that if she wanted to work at the

Royal Diner, there was nothing he could do about it, he figured it was time to reenter the conversation.

"Did the doctor say anything about stress being bad for a woman in your condition?" he asked in his mildest, most reasonable tone.

"Stress?"

"Yeah, you know—declarations of independence, shouting, threatening to break noses and toeses, issuing ultimatums?"

"I did not—" She clapped her hands to her cheeks. "I didn't...did I?"

"You did. What's the matter, didn't you get enough sleep last night?"

She glared at him. They both knew neither of them had gotten much sleep the night before.

"What did you eat today? You need to keep up your strength."

She paused. Knowing she could simmer down as quickly as she could come to a boil, he waited with every semblance of patience. It paid off.

With that quirky little half smile he'd come to look for, she admitted, "At least I got my exercise."

"At least? That means you didn't take time to eat. According to my sources, you worked your pretty little buns off on account of none of the other waitresses showed up for work today." Will levered himself carefully up from the sofa and stood, trying to look more benign than threatening. Threats didn't work. He'd learned that much. She just dug in her heels and defied him to do anything about it.

So he tried another approach. "Why don't I make you a fried egg sandwich while you change into something more comfortable?"

Oh, she was tempted, but Diana knew better than

to give an inch. "I'm perfectly comfortable," she lied. She'd worn tan, midheel pumps, her tan skirt and brown tunic top to the office that morning, then worked all day at the diner wearing the same clothes. The shoes were going to Goodwill first thing tomorrow. The rest smelled of fried food and onions, nothing a good dry cleaning couldn't take care of. But she knew better than to change into anything now that might signal capitulation. She needed every possible advantage she could muster.

"Fine. You, uh…do have eggs, don't you?"

"Nope." She smiled, loving the way he suddenly looked less sure of himself. As much as she hated to admit it, he looked almost as tired as she felt.

It occurred to her that he might be in some kind of trouble. Could the company be in trouble? It was being audited, but that was standard procedure under the circumstances…wasn't it?

If she were any sort of wife at all, she would sit him down, bring him a drink and say, "Now tell me all about your day, dear."

But she wasn't, and so she didn't. Not that she wasn't tempted, but she knew better than to yield control, even to that extent. "Look, I really, really would like to get a hot soak and go to bed. I'll eat something later, okay? I'll open a can of soup and eat the whole thing. I really don't need a babysitter."

"It's not the baby I'm concerned about, Danny— at least, not entirely."

"Will, I'm fine, just bone tired. I'm going to work tomorrow at seven for the breakfast shift. Carla will be back by then, so it won't be like it was today.

They're still hiring—maybe someone else will show up.''

"And you'll quit." It was a statement, not a question.

"No I won't. They're shorthanded, and I need the work."

"The hell you do. No wife of mine—"

Knowing she had the upper hand, she smiled. The trick, she was learning, was to stand firm, not to give him any wiggle room. Whatever else he was, Will Bradford was a gentleman in the old-fashioned sense. He might rant and bluster, but he would never resort to violence the way a weaker man might.

"I hate you working there," he grumbled, looking tired and rumpled and entirely too lovable. Really, she was going to have to start building up her resistance against this man she'd married, or he'd be able to wrap her around his little finger.

"I know. And I'm sorry...your reputation and all—"

"Screw my reputation, it's you I'm worried about!"

"You know what they say—a woman's got to do what a woman's got to do."

"Okay. All right...for now." He was still frowning, and she wanted nothing so much as to walk right into his arms and kiss away his frown, but they both knew where that would lead.

No way, José, she thought, echoing a Texasism her new boss at the diner was fond of using. But, oh, how she wished things could be different....

The next morning, dressed in a gray knit skirt, a navy sweater and her most comfortable walking shoes, she left for work at twenty minutes to seven. The Royal Diner was only five blocks from her apartment, which meant she could save gas, save wear and tear on her car and get a head start on her daily quota of exercise. The stop-and-go kind of walking she did at the diner hardly qualified, but after a day of it, she probably wouldn't be in the mood for anything more than a shower and bed.

The shoes helped. Or maybe the job just got easier with practice. Since Carla was back at work, Diana took time for a bowl of chili and a salad at eleven, before the lunch rush began. The morning sickness was gone, but she found that a small meal or a snack every four hours made her feel better.

By the time her shift was over, she didn't particularly feel like walking home. Her feet ached all the way up to her hips. Obviously secretaries and waitresses used different sets of muscles. So when she let herself out and came face-to-face with a scowling husband—her own—she was tempted to take him up on his offer of a ride home.

"Whose home, mine or yours?" she asked warily.

"Mine would be better. Big bathtub full of hot water instead of a cramped little shower?"

He knew exactly which buttons to push. Which was one more reason to resist. She'd gone down that route before. "At least in a shower I won't be in danger of falling asleep and drowning."

"I have a shower, too. I'll even throw in a lifeguard." His smile was guaranteed to wear down a marble statue.

They finally compromised. He would take her to her own apartment to shower and change, then pick her up at seven for dinner, with a promise to return her before his car turned into a pumpkin. "You drive a hard bargain, Cinderella."

"I do, don't I?" she murmured proudly. As tired as she was, she was learning to handle him. The promise of dinner was not without risk, especially if he took her to Claire's, known for its romantic atmosphere. But it was important that they maintain some semblance of friendship, even she realized that. What was it they called arrangements like theirs? Open marriages? Or was that when both parties were free to roam?

The thought of Will with another woman made her feel slightly ill, but no more than the thought of herself with another man.

"Seven," she said when he dropped her off at her apartment. "Shall I dress?" If he was taking her to Claire's, jeans and a sweatshirt would hardly do.

"Strictly casual," he said, and she yawned and let herself out. He didn't get out and open her door. He didn't hint that he'd like to come in for a cup of coffee. Instead, he smiled, waved and left her standing on the sidewalk.

"Well, shoot," she whispered. She waited until he'd turned the corner and then she limped to the front door and let herself inside the shabby lobby.

Not until she had showered and shampooed the smell of fried onions from her skin and hair and slipped on her favorite muumuu did it occur to her that something was different. Everything, so far as she could see, was just the same—same sofa with the tacky throw. Same slightly tilted platform rocker, a ten-dollar steal at the thrift shop. Same books on the shelf.

But not in the same order. The Dummy books had

been on the middle shelf, the romantic suspense on the top...hadn't they? She could have sworn she'd left the book she'd been reading on the sofa instead of the coffee table.

And those boxes...

Had they been stacked on the left or the right inside her mother's room?

It had to be one of the more bizarre symptoms of pregnancy, but suddenly she was almost certain someone had been inside her apartment. A quick search revealed nothing missing. Not that she'd had anything of value to steal. Even her mother's guitar was at Will's place, along with the watercolor, which was nice but hardly worth breaking in for.

She put it down to an attack of prenatal paranoia. That and the fact that with all the recent changes, her life seemed to be coming apart at the seams.

Will had said seven. She didn't know where he was taking her. Claire's was hardly casual, and she seriously doubted he would take her to the Royal Diner for dinner. The greasy-spoon special of the day had been country-fried steaks and hash browns. The very thought made her sick.

She wore her black slacks and a beige turtleneck sweater that came down far enough to cover the slight thickening of her waistline. She'd had to loop a rubber band through the buttonhole at her waistband and slip it over the button.

Will arrived at three minutes before seven. She opened the door and thought, This is a mistake. This is like giving a candy addict a big box of chocolates and saying, Look but don't taste. Sniff all you want to—admire the little swirls on top, but don't you dare sink a tooth into all that luscious, delectable sweetness!

He was wearing khakis that hugged his lean hips like a glove, with a black flannel shirt. Evidently he'd left his jacket in the car. His cuffs were turned back to reveal several inches of tanned, muscular forearm, lightly dusted with dark hair.

It's not fair, she told herself. He had married her out of some misguided sense of obligation, and they might even have been able to work out a reasonable arrangement, but then he'd had to go and make love to her. Dammit, it just wasn't fair!

She smiled, and he said, "Ready to ride?"

"Do I need a coat?"

"It's not cold. The sweater should be enough for the amount of time we'll be outside."

Not until they'd driven several blocks did she begin to wonder. She knew where most of the restaurants were, and they were not in this direction. "Will?"

"Salmon. You like grilled salmon?"

"Of course I like grilled salmon—who wouldn't?" She'd never had it, only the canned variety. "But where are we?" And then she knew, of course. He pulled into the parking lot and parked in his usual spot, under the security light, nosed up against the row of lush Leyland cypresses.

She could have argued, and he would probably have argued right back that this was a civilized arrangement for a couple who were married but lived apart. And then what? Tell him she was didn't trust herself alone with him?

He would want to know why, and the answer was just too humiliating:

I know you married me out of some misguided sense of honor and duty. Maybe it's a marine thing— you were both marines, you and my baby's father. But you see, the trouble is, I'm dangerously close to loving you. If I get any closer, I might not survive.

Sure. She could just tell him all that and wait for him to howl with laughter. And just before she died of humiliation, she might even manage to laugh, too.

"I need to be home by nine," she declared firmly. "I'm working first shift again."

His lips tightened, and she knew a brief moment of satisfaction at having scored a hit.

The salads were made, the table set for two. With candles. There was brown rice in a special cooker, and salmon fillets ready to go into something that looked more like an autoclave than a grill.

Fancy-schmancy. When she caught him sneaking a look at the instructions, she had to smile. If he wanted to impress her with his culinary skills, she could afford to let herself be impressed.

She wandered into the other room, avoiding the bedroom wing. An open door led to what appeared to be a home office. There was a mixture of fiction and dull-looking accounting books on the shelf, interspersed with several photographs. The kind of pictures Jack had displayed in his office, but without the same ostentation.

Will standing between two horses, a battered black Stetson on his head, a cast on his left leg and a huge grin on his face. Roy Rogers, he was not. There was another picture of Will and Tack leading a knobby-kneed foal from a barn. Slightly out of focus, but easily recognizable. The foal was obviously the center of interest.

She almost missed the third photo, as it was half-hidden behind a cigar box filled with loose change. Carefully lifting it out, she studied the face and the inscription.

"All my love forever, Shelly."

His first wife. She'd never heard her name—or maybe she had. Jack might have mentioned it, and she'd forgotten, but she knew as well as she knew her own name that this was the woman Will had loved enough to marry. A beautiful, starry-eyed face, a mop of blond curly hair.

No two women could be more different, she thought with a sinking feeling, than the first Mrs. Bradford and the second.

"Soup's on," Will called out from the kitchen.

Replacing the picture, she hurried into the dining room, a fixed smile on her face. "Smells great," she said. Suddenly, her appetite was gone.

"Actually, I was lying. There's no soup. What you see is what you get. I, uh, bought a cake from the bakery, but it looks pretty dry."

The conversation was stilted at first. She complimented him on the salmon, and he told her the grill came with a guarantee.

He told her he'd noticed her car was due for inspection, and she started to fire off at him but relented. He was a responsible man. It was his nature. At this point he probably wasn't going to change.

Besides, it was one of his more admirable qualities. He had a long list of those, a few of which could be threatening to a woman who was teetering on the edge of love and trying hard not to fall in and drown.

After the meal was over he served dessert. The

cake was indeed dry, but she ate every bite to postpone whatever came next.

She knew what she wanted to come next.

She also knew it wasn't going to happen. Once was enough.

Once was too much.

"I was looking at your bookshelf," she said. "The pictures—" They had never talked about his first wife, but there were rumors about her among the secretaries. The fact that no one had met her only added fuel to the fire.

Instead, she found herself telling him about the latest among her symptoms. Thinking things were in the wrong place, when they couldn't possibly be.

"You know how it is," she said, laughing at her own silliness. "You take things off a shelf to dust and put them back out of order but don't notice it until later."

"When's the last time you dusted your bookshelves?"

She sobered at that. "I don't remember. Mama used to…"

"Anything else you don't remember?"

"Well, how would I know if I don't remember? How often do you dust your shelves?"

"I have a housekeeper three days a week. I'm serious, Danny. That place of yours could be broken into with a paper clip."

"Who'd want to? It's not like I was hiding anything of value. You've seen the place—what would anyone want to steal? My new toaster?" She tried to laugh it off, but he was making her uneasy by taking it so seriously.

"You asked about my wife—"

She hadn't. She'd intended to but lost her nerve. "Shelly was killed when some kid broke into our place. God knows, we didn't have much to steal, but she ended up dead, anyway."

Dear Lord, she thought, appalled. "Will, I never knew—that is, I'm so sorry."

"Yeah, well…it was a long time ago. But Shelly wasn't thinking about break-ins, either, she was going about her business. And it happened. It…*happened.*"

What could she say? What could she do? "I'll get a stronger chain," she promised. The one she had wasn't even real brass. Even the screws were loose. She hardly ever remembered to use it.

"Stay here."

"Will, I can't do that."

"Dammit, things are going on at work, and I can't afford to be distracted by worrying about you staying alone in that dump."

"Thanks," she said dryly. "You can take me off your worry list."

"That's just it," he exclaimed, scraping his chair back so that it struck the fawn-colored wall. He raked a hand through his hair and stared out the window at the lights of the business district, only a mile or so away.

Diana stood, torn between offering comfort and escaping before things got out of hand. A quiet, civilized dinner conversation she could manage. Comforting a man who was tired, distraught and utterly irresistible was out of bounds.

Everything about him affected her. She knew how his skin felt—the resilient muscles, the silken hair on his chest that grew wiry below the belt. Her hands reached out before she could stop herself, and she must have made a sound because he turned.

"Danny…"

"No. I can't—don't ask that of me, Will. Please?"

"I'd better take you home," he said after a hollow moment of silence.

Neither of them spoke on the way. "Don't get out," she told him, knowing it would do no good to protest.

"I'll see you upstairs and look around, then I'll leave."

The truth was she wanted him to. Maybe not leave, but that was another matter. She had never felt threatened before, even though they had lived in some rough neighborhoods.

At least, not threatened by strangers.

"All clear," he said after a quick walk-through of her four rooms and bath. "See anything that doesn't look right?"

She shook her head. "It's all the way I left it. Empty milk glass on the table, shoes under the sofa." She tried to make a joke of it, but they both knew that not all the tension was due to the possibility of an intruder.

"Then I'll see you tomorrow."

"I'm working."

"I'll come for lunch," he said with a wintery smile.

She rolled her eyes. "Oh, God, as if there wasn't enough speculation."

And then, just as she thought she was safe, he turned and took her in his arms, kissing her so thoroughly her knees threatened to buckle.

''What was that for?'' she gasped when she could catch her breath.

''Luck? A down payment?'' He shrugged and opened the door. ''Hook the chain behind me, will you? You might want to shove a chair under the knob.''

''Now you're making me nervous,'' she said with a shaky laugh.

''Good. It'll do...for now.''

Ten

Diana paused outside the corner drugstore on the way to work the next morning after another largely sleepless night. Between her coffee habit and Will, she couldn't seem to fall asleep. What she needed was to start tapering off caffeine.

Better yet, start tapering off Will, she thought ruefully. Will might be good for her baby, but he certainly wasn't helping her peace of mind.

While she waited for the light to change, she considered going inside to buy liniment and a new set of shoe inserts. She was still contemplating when the light turned green. Maybe thick socks would help pad her insoles....

Deciding to give it another day, then pick up whatever she needed on the way home, she stepped off the curb. Instantly a car that had been idling at the curb picked up speed and raced toward her. Startled, she jumped back, but not soon enough. Something slammed into her hip, spinning her around as she fell.

"Oh, my God, did you see that?"

"He ran her down! He ran a damned red light!"

"Lady, are you all right?"

Of course she was all right, Diana thought calmly. She was simply lying there on the gritty sidewalk watching the fireworks display. But the dazzling lights quickly faded, and she realized in some corner of her brain that wasn't about to explode that they weren't real.

It actually happens, just like in books, she marveled with a disoriented sort of pride. She'd seen stars.

Slowly she became aware of the noise. The shouts, the cursing, screeching brakes and blowing horns. At least she could hear, which meant she probably wasn't dead yet. She seemed to be lying on her back with her head against the curb. She was still breathing. Dazed and terrified, but still alive.

Hands were reaching for her, touching her. Someone urged her to sit up and someone else said lie still until the ambulance crew could check her over. She tried to speak, to tell them that she was fine, just fine, but couldn't seem to coordinate her tongue and her brain, so she simply closed her eyes. Her head felt like a cantaloupe that had tumbled off a truck, but at least it seemed to be working. After a fashion.

"Did you see that idiot?"

"I called the ambulance! Lie still, lady."

"Call the cops— Ma'am, don't try to move, y'hear?"

She heard the voices. It was like dozing through an old movie—something that didn't really affect her personally. Breathing through her mouth, Diana opened her eyes, then closed them again. Looking up at the ring of concerned faces, she felt a sudden surge of nausea. *Not now! I don't want to be sick in public!*

"Shh, don't you worry, honey, you're going to be just fine," said a heavy woman with the face of an angel.

You're going to be just fine. Hold that thought, Princess Danny.

She was in a hospital bed. Her head hurt. Her arm hurt. Her everything hurt! "My husband—did anybody call…?"

"Yes, ma'am, he's on his way right now. He was in Houston when they got ahold of him, but I 'spect he'll be walking though that door most any minute now." The nurse adjusted her pillow.

"My baby?"

"Still doing just fine. You've got a goose egg— more like an ostrich egg—on back of your head, but other than that and a few scrapes and bruises, you checked out just fine. Doc Woodbury happened to be here when they brought you in. He called the clinic and had your chart sent over. He'll be by directly to talk to you."

She felt sick. Not morning sickness, but sort of the same. And her head really, really hurt, but pain medication wouldn't be good for the baby. Besides, she probably couldn't keep anything down, the way she felt now.

"Water?" she whispered.

"A sip." The nurse held the straw to her lips. She sipped and would have grabbed it for more, but her hands were shaking too hard.

And then Will was there, looking thunderous—looking so concerned she wanted to cry, but for once in her life the tears wouldn't come.

"Don't say anything," he said. "Don't try to talk," he said, and when the nurse left the room, he leaned over and kissed her on the mouth. Which was probably the only part of her that didn't actually hurt.

"Now you can talk." His smile was beautiful, but it didn't reach his eyes. Those were dark with concern.

Or anger?

No, it was concern. For her, she thought, and felt the tears clog her throat all over again. She swallowed hard, determined not to show weakness, and when the absurdity of that thought struck her, she had to choke back a giggle. "Emotions all over the place. Hormones strike again," she murmured drowsily.

Will hitched a chair closer and straddled it. "It was a clear case of hit and run. Several witnesses said you looked both ways and—"

"I always do."

"—and just as you stepped off, a car that had been idling at the curb pulled out, revved up and kept going, after it had knocked you down. If it had had time to pick up any speed, you'd have been—"

She reached blindly for his hand, managed to find it and gripped tightly. "Don't say it. I don't want to hear it. I obviously wasn't as careful as I thought I was being."

"Something on your mind?" He arched his brows, and she was tempted to pull her hand away, but she needed his strength. Just for now. Just until she got over this awful shakiness.

"I was considering whether to buy liniment and shoe liners before or after work. Did anybody think to call the diner and tell them I'd be late?"

He hooted with laughter. "Honey, I suspect they've already guessed as much. News like that takes about ten nanoseconds to make the rounds. Right now they're probably placing bets down at the diner as to how long it'll take before the damn fool will be hauled up on a charge of assault with a lethal weapon."

She sighed, aware of aches she hadn't felt a few minutes earlier. "I guess I wasn't paying attention. Could I have some more water? I hurt all over, but the nurse said nothing's broken and the baby's still doing fine."

Will lifted her bandaged head carefully and let her take a few sips of ice water from the straw. Every instinct he possessed urged him to sweep her up, blanket and all, and carry her off somewhere where nothing could ever hurt her again. If he'd needed a clue that he was edging over into no-man's land, this was it.

He'd talked to the doctor. He'd talked to the cops. The vehicle had been found abandoned about eight miles out of town. The guy it was registered to had reported it stolen a few hours earlier.

"They're going to keep you overnight for observation." He broke the news, hoping she wouldn't kick up a fuss. Holding up two fingers, he said, "How many?"

"Seventeen."

"Smart mouth."

She smiled, then winced, and he wondered how he was going to break the rest of the news—that he was taking her home with him and keeping her there for the next sixty or seventy years.

Correction—until he could sort out this mess at work, get things running on an even keel again—and then he just might retire. He considered asking her how she would like to live at the ranch permanently, but this wasn't the time.

He had already lined up a nurse to stay with her while he was at the office, but that, too, could wait until she was back in fighting trim. "Go to sleep, honey. I'm going to stay here awhile and read the paper. I'm supposed to wake you every three minutes—"

"Three days," she whispered.

"Whatever. Anyway, don't count on getting much rest."

She was already asleep. For a long time, he sat there and studied her, wondering abstractedly just what it was about this one woman that made him act so out of character.

He hadn't been obligated to marry her. There'd been a time when he and Jack had been as close as any brothers. They'd both been marines, although they'd served at different times. They'd both married young. Neither marriage had lasted long, for quite different reasons. Needing someone to head up the financial end of the business, Jack had brought him in when he'd first set out to build his empire. They'd built the empire—Will liked to think he'd had a large hand in it, but Jack had been the driving force. Gradually, though, the friendship had cooled, due in large part to Jack's increasing recklessness and corner cutting. Of an entirely different temperament, Will had nevertheless stayed on, doing his best to keep them out of trouble with the stockholders and various government agencies. It had been a challenge, and he'd always thrived on challenge.

The woman beside him, looking so heartbreakingly fragile, was the biggest challenge of all. One he had accepted without realizing what it was going to involve.

How the devil did a man make a woman fall in love with him?

She protested, just as he'd known she would, when, instead of turning off at her corner the next morning, he continued toward his own address. "I've hired a nurse to stay for as long as you need help. She's Emma's niece. You'll like her."

"I don't need any help. I'm stiff and sore, but I'm perfectly capable of looking after myself."

He went on as if she hadn't spoken. "Her name's Annie. If you don't like her, I'll get someone else."

"I told you, I don't need—"

"Shh, think of the baby. She got pretty shook up yesterday—you don't want her stress levels shooting into the red, do you?"

"Her what?"

He grinned as proudly as if he'd just won the calf-roping event. "I've been reading up on the care and feeding of mamas and unborn babies. Care to ask me a question?"

Instead of answering, she yawned. Which was better than taking a swing at him.

Inhaling a deep breath, he thought smugly, Round One to the Texas Tiger. Little Miss Muffet has finally met her match.

By the time he had her settled in his bedroom—

they'd argued about that, too, but he'd stood his ground—she was too exhausted to go another round. "Let her sleep for a while." He handed Annie a slip of paper with his cell phone number written on it. "Call me at this number the minute she wakes up."

"Will do, Will. Don't worry about a thing. If she's half as nice as Aunt Emma said she was, you're a real lucky man."

"Thanks, Annie. She is, and I am."

The first day Diana was too miserable to argue. Annie was quiet, Will was absent, so mostly she slept, waking only when Annie brought her something to eat, or helped her hobble to the bathroom.

She had a lot of time to think, and mostly she thought about Will and her baby. Thinking about the man she was dangerously close to loving only made her more miserable, so she tried not to think about him and thought instead about the baby she was carrying.

What if it turned out to be a girl and she looked like Sebastian? How would chestnut hair with red highlights and silver-gray eyes translate in a tiny baby girl?

She thought about how startled she'd been the first time she'd seen Dorian Brady and mistaken him for his half brother. Sebastian had been out of town, so when she'd seen a man she took to be Sebastian coming out of his office on a Sunday morning when no one was there, except for a few people who were working to clear out Jack's suite of offices, naturally she'd been surprised.

She'd said, "Sebastian? Mr. Wescott?"

And the man had turned and she'd seen that it

wasn't Sebastian, so she'd apologized and hurried on to records, where she'd been returning a stack of files.

He had watched her all the way down the hall—she could see his reflection in the plate glass window at the end. Probably thought she was flirting...or just a little bit nuts.

Her baby would be Dorian's half sibling, too. Which somehow wasn't as welcome a thought.

She hoped it was a little girl, but as long as she was healthy, who cared what she looked like? Toenail polish did wonders for self-esteem.

Two days later, when Diana could manage to hobble around without feeling as if her left hip was going to shatter, she took matters into her own hands. "Look, I need to be in my own place, and whatever Will told you, this is not my home, it's his. We had this agreement—" She broke off, too uncomfortable to explain their complex relationship.

"He's going to kick up a fuss," Annie warned. For all her loyalty to Will, she was inclined to side with the woman when it came to a battle between the sexes, having just gone through a bitter divorce herself.

"We both know what kind of man he is." The kind any woman would be lucky to have, but not as an object of charity. "He thinks it's his job to look after any woman he considers too weak to look after herself. And I'm not. I might be a little banged up—"

"A little! You're lucky to be able to get out of bed, much less pack up and go home."

The smile Diana gave her was strictly woman-to-woman. ''Does that mean you'll help me?''

No such luck. ''Uh-uh. I'll drive you out to the ranch and let Aunt Emma look after you, but Will would skin me alive if I took you anyplace else here in town. Wanna know what I think?''

Diana didn't, but she had an idea she was going to hear it, anyway.

''I think you're the luckiest woman alive for being married to a man like Will Bradford. Believe me, there aren't very many good guys left.''

''I know,'' she said, and sighed. ''Is there any more ice cream?''

It wasn't going to be easy. Will knew that much. But for the moment he had to take a chance she'd stay put. The doctor had said her soreness would probably get worse before it got better. He recommended water therapy—hot, but not too hot, which Will could provide.

In fact, he might just join her in the hot tub. The thing had come with the apartment, but it had gone largely unused. When it came to socializing—or even unwinding—a hot tub, even with the jets turned on full blast, wasn't his first choice. He'd tried it a couple of times and could hardly drag himself to bed afterward.

However, it might be just the thing for what ailed Diana. Maybe he'd have one installed at the ranch, he mused, smiling at the memory of Diana perched up on top of old Mairsy, hanging on for dear life.

With that thought in mind, Will had removed his tie by the time he reached the door of his apartment. First thing he'd do would be to give Annie the night

off. He didn't need a nurse to supervise what he had
in mind. But before he could open the door, his cell
phone rang. He muttered a soft oath. Not now—I've
got plans, he thought.

Jason had reported in, less than an hour ago. Seb
was up to his ears, getting ready to take over. Eric
was out of town—at least, so far as anyone knew.
He hadn't come in to work today, which was odd,
come to think of it. His secretary said he'd been complaining of hay fever.

"Bradford," he snapped, holding the phone in one
hand, unbuttoning his shirt with the other. He
glanced around for a glimpse of either Annie or Diana. Yesterday he had brought over some boxes from
her old place and put them in the spare room. If she
was up to going through them, that was a good sign
she was up for something a bit more strenuous. If
not, he'd just have to soak the resistance out of her,
because one way or another, they were going to settle
things between them.

"Jason?" A moment later his face turned ash gray.
He lowered his voice and said, "You're sure. There's
no chance of, uh, mistaken identity?"

Moments later he signed off. Eric wasn't suffering
from hay fever. He wasn't suffering at all. Eric was
dead, strangled in his own home.

"Will? Is that you?" The husky voice drifted
down the hallway.

Schooling his face not to reveal his thoughts, Will
headed for the spare room, where Diana was kneel-
ing over a battered cardboard carton. Surrounding her
were stacks of what appeared to be sheet music, note-
books—the kind kids used in school—and posters,
unrolled and weighted down with books and several

old records. The vinyl kind. Santana. Jimi Hendrix. Janis Joplin.

''Hi, honey,'' he said gently, setting aside for the moment the murder of a man he had worked with for the past four years. ''Feeling better, are we?''

''I am. I'm not sure about you. You look like you have a headache.''

He had a headache, a heartache—aches in a few other places that weren't about to find relief anytime soon. ''What did you eat today?'' he asked, hoping to divert her attention. She didn't need to hear what had happened—not yet. Not until they knew more.

''My, aren't we nosy? For breakfast I had choco-late-covered peanuts. Baby had whole-grain cereal and low-fat milk. For lunch I had a giant serving of tin roof sundae ice cream—baby had mozzarella and salsa on whole grain bread.''

Still on her knees beside the sagging double bed, she was grinning up at him. Teasing him. As if she sensed something was wrong and was doing her best to distract him.

He could have told her that verbal distraction wouldn't cut it. God, what he wouldn't give to hold her until the world settled back on its axis. To lose himself in her warm, sweet depths. To keep her—to keep his precious new family together from now on.

Instead he lowered himself to the floor beside her, shoving aside a framed black-and-white photograph. She reached for it, studying it with a wistful look on her face. ''My family portrait…or at least, the closest I'll ever have to one.'' She pointed out a small blond woman wearing the uniform of the day—bell-bottom jeans with what appeared to be embroidery trailing up the legs. At least she was wearing a blouse. A few of the women weren't. Most of the men weren't.

"That was Mama. This was my father." Another out-of-focus face, this one with a scraggly beard. He was holding what was obviously a pot pipe as if it were a trophy he was waving. They were in a muddy field that was crowded with tents and open-sided vans. Guitars, drums and bass fiddles abounded.

She stood, stretched and rubbed her hip, then sat down on the edge of the bed. "I think there might be a cousin there somewhere, but I never met him. By now he's probably a stodgy old businessman with a wife and family, living somewhere like Dubuque."

It hit him then, the loneliness behind her wistful words. Struck an echoing chord he'd kept buried for so long it had scarred over. "Want me to track him down for you?"

She shook her head, but he settled down beside her. Protectively, he told himself. She had no business crawling around on the floor after what had just recently happened to her.

Somehow her hand had found its way to his thigh and rested there, as easily as a tame bird. "Don't bother. I might not like him, and then where would I be?"

"Better the devil you know than the one you don't, huh?"

"At least you're not going to run me down in the street."

Frowning, he touched the knot on her head, which was smaller today, but still very much in evidence under the glossy mane of hair. Probably because her scalp was still sore, she had let it hang loose. It was tempting beyond his ability to resist.

So he stroked her hair, and from there it took only a small amount of pressure to ease her head over onto his shoulder. "Haven't you done enough work for one day?" he asked. "There's always tomorrow."

But was there? Will knew he owed it to her to tell her what had happened at the office. The embezzlement that had suddenly taken a drastic turn for the worst. But that could wait.

This couldn't. This had waited long enough.

If he'd needed a reminder of just how fleeting life was, the phone call from Jason had done it.

"Diana, Diana..." he whispered. He needed her. The need was there in his voice, and she turned to him and lifted her face.

It started with a kiss. They had kissed before, but there was something different about this kiss. Not the effect—that was inevitable. All he had to do was touch her, think about her, and every part of his body was on standby alert.

She was with him all the way, her eyes told him that much. As did the shuddering little breaths she took, long moments later, when they were lying side by side and his hands moved up to cup her breasts. Carefully, reverently, he lifted her shirt, unfastened the bra underneath and paid homage to her newly full breasts, with the proudly swollen nipples.

Dear heaven, she was beautiful to his eyes. If she'd protested he would have stopped. It might have killed him, but not for the world would he try to lead her into anything she wasn't ready for. This hadn't been a part of the bargain.

But she didn't protest, and Will didn't stop, despite his concern about her injuries and the baby. "I'll be careful,'' he promised, adding silently, Darling. Sweetheart. Love…

And carefully he led her to a place all true lovers knew. A place where there was no yesterday, no tomorrow, only now. Two pairs of eyes began to glow. Two pairs of lips parted, sighed and then gasped with pleasure as tentative touches grew bolder. Caresses more creative. Her hands were timid at first, then bolder. Will forced himself to hold back his own impatience.

"Does this…? May I…?" she queried softly.

"Yesss!" he rasped as her hands continued to explore his naked body. Please, please don't let me disgrace myself!

She delighted him with her earnest attentions. It was almost as if she'd never done such a thing before. Never taken the time to discover all the places on a man's body where a single touch could be explosive, incendiary.

Where a kiss could cause an instant conflagration.

"Wait…give me a minute." Gasping, he covered her roving hands with his own, stilling them until he could regain control. He had promised himself to go slow in deference to her delicate condition. If she didn't choose to play by the same rules, that might be a promise he'd have trouble keeping.

She was more than ready, and not afraid to let him know. Lying artlessly on her back, her full breasts gloriously flushed from his attentions, she smiled at him. "Well, are we going to do it, or are we going to take it up with the board of directors first and form a study commission?"

He burst out laughing and swiftly moved over her, carefully spreading her thighs to accommodate his hips. It was another first for him. The laughter. Humor had never been a part of sex before. "Did anyone ever tell you you're impertinent?"

"No...ahh!" She closed her eyes and bit her lower lip as he moved inside with the ease of someone coming home. Almost before he started to move, the pulsating bands of pleasure began gathering tighter, closing in on them like a vibrant rainbow.

"Your hip—"

"Oh, yes...more, more! Yes, like that." Breathing in tiny gasps, she clutched his shoulders and began to rock to his rhythm.

Moments later, when the world exploded, Will collapsed on top of her, then rolled over onto his side, carrying her with him. Holding her tightly, he breathed in the essence of slightly musky linens, sex and some herbal shampoo.

And love, he thought, amazed at this thing that had taken him so completely off guard.

Dare he hope she felt the same way? Was it possible?

Only one way to find out. "Diana—Danny—I've got something to confess, and I want you to have patience. I'm not very good at this kind of thing. Not smooth. But that doesn't mean I'm not sincere." Lying naked against her nakedness, their damp bodies still entwined, he searched for the right way to tell her how he felt about her, and about their so-called marriage of convenience. If she was afraid of commitment...

"Oh, hell, I love you, okay?" he blurted.

He'd expected most any reaction but the one he got.

She laughed. Again. One of her arms flopped out,

knocking a tattered copy of *Mad Magazine* off the bedside table onto the floor. She howled.

Disgruntled, he said, "Well, it wasn't all that funny. At least, it wasn't meant to be funny."

Rolling back into his arms, Diana gazed up at him, eyes brimming with laughter. "Want to know what I think?" she asked, her husky voice teasing.

He was afraid to ask, but she told him anyway, whispering, "Oh, hell, I love you, too."

It was long after midnight when someone pounded on his door. He'd unplugged the house phones and left his cellular in the other room. They were lying in bed, damp from exertions, not the hot tub. That would come later, when they'd got their second wind.

"Wait right here. Don't move," he said, and she smiled drowsily.

"I couldn't if I tried."

It was Jason. The low-voiced conference was brief. "Seb and Rob Cole are looking into the murder. I've got my sources working on the money drain. The two things are connected."

"God, not now," he muttered, squelching a stab of guilt. But if things were going to break loose— and it had been inevitable—he'd as soon it waited until he'd had time to ease into this new phase of marriage. Like maybe the next fifty-odd years.

Will's shoulders sagged. "Evidence?"

Jason, looking older than his twenty-eight years, shook his head. "Give me a few days. A week, at most. Meanwhile, keep a close eye on your lady. I think maybe her accident might be connected to what's been going on."

The trouble was, Will did, too. The thought of anything happening to Diana made his blood run cold. "I know how to protect my own," he said grimly.

"You've got all the help you'll need. Once we get this wrapped up…"

"The sooner the better. Meanwhile, there are things I can do to make sure she's fully protected."

"She's worth it, man. You're the luckiest loser I ever met."

He was referring to the bet they had made concerning their bachelor status. "You got that right," Will said with a grim smile.

He saw Jason out, placed a call to a top notch security firm with twenty-four-hour service, then went back to the bedroom.

She was sleeping, smiling at her dreams.

Easing into bed beside her, Will gathered her into his arms and made a promise. You and me, love. You and me and our baby. Everything else will just have to wait till tomorrow.

*   *   *   *   *

Watch for the next two instalments of

THE MILLIONAIRE'S CLUB

with

Her Lone Star Protector
by Peggy Moreland

and

Tall, Dark and…Framed?
by Cathleen Galitz

*Coming to you from Silhouette Desire
in June 2003.*

And now for a sneak preview of

Her Lone Star Protector,

please turn the page.

Her Lone Star Protector

by

Peggy Moreland

Mornings were usually quiet at the Texas Cattleman's Club. But on this particular morning, there was a different quality to the silence. A heaviness. A somberness. Yet, the air seemed to hold an electrical charge, as well. A sense of expectancy crackled through the club. One of impatience. A need for action.

A murder had been committed in Royal, the victim an employee of a member of the Texas Cattleman's Club, and what affected one club member affected them all.

Though usually empty at that time of day, the club's cigar lounge was almost filled to capacity, with members having dragged the heavy leather chairs into huddled groups of four and eight. The members' conversations were low, hushed, as they reviewed the facts of the case and speculated on the identity of the murderer.

In a far corner of the room, Sebastian Wescott sat with a group of his closest and most trusted friends. William Bradford, CFO and partner in Wescott Oil Enterprises. Keith Owens, owner of a computer software firm. Dorian Brady, Seb's half brother and an employee of Wescott Oil. CIA agent Jason Windover. And Rob Cole, private investigator.

Though all of the men were included in on the conversation, it was Rob and Jason whose expertise Seb sought in finding Eric Chambers's murderer.

Seb glanced at Jason. "I know that your participation on this case will have to remain unofficial, due to your status as a CIA agent, but I'd appreciate any assistance or advice you have to offer."

Jason tightened his lips and nodded. "You know I'll do everything I can."

Seb turned to Rob Cole. "The police, of course, are conducting their own investigation, but I want you on the case. I've already informed the police that they are to coordinate their efforts with yours."

Rob nodded, his mind moving automatically into investigative mode. "Brief me on what you know about the murder."

Seb dragged a weary hand down his face, but didn't come close to smoothing away the deep lines of tension that creased it. "Not much."

"Who found the body?"

"Rebecca Todman. New in town. A neighbor of Eric's. She owns a floral shop and, according to her, was hired by him to tend his plants."

Rob frowned as he studied Seb. "You don't believe her story?"

Seb shot to his feet, tossing up a hand. "Hell, I don't know who or what to believe!" He paced away a few steps, then stopped and rammed his hands in his pockets. He heaved a breath, then glanced back at Rob. "Sorry," he muttered. "I haven't had more than three straight hours of sleep in the past week, and when I arrived back at the office this morning, I had *this* dumped on me. The only thing I know for sure is that Eric is dead. And I want his murderer found."

"Okay," Rob agreed carefully, aware of the responsibility Seb assumed for all his employees. "Let's start at the beginning and review the facts."

Seb sat back down, more in control now, but a far cry from calm. "According to the police reports, the Todman woman found Eric this morning around eight when she went to water his plants. He'd been strangled with his own necktie."

Rob leaned forward, bracing his elbows on his knees. "Any sign of a break-in?"

"No."

"Robbery?"

"Not that the police have been able to determine."

"Any known enemies?"

"None that I'm aware of."

"How about women? Any disgruntled girlfriends in his past? A jealous husband maybe looking to get even?"

Seb lifted a brow. "Eric?" At Rob's nod, he snorted. "Hardly. I don't think Eric's ever had a girlfriend. Lived with his mother until she died a couple of years ago. The only woman in Eric's life is— was," he clarified, frowning, "a cat. Sadie. Treated her like she was human. Rushed home from work at lunch every day, just to check on her." He shook his head. "No. Eric didn't have any jealous husbands gunning for him, and he didn't have any girlfriends, either. Just old Sadie."

"What about this Todman woman?" Rob pressed. "Do you think she and Eric have been involved?"

Seb lifted a shoulder. "Maybe. Though I doubt it. Eric was…well, he was a bit on the strange side. A loner who kept to himself. Very protective of his personal life. No," he said, his frown deepening, as he considered, "More like secretive. Forget it," he said, waving away Rob's suggestion of a possible relationship. "There was nothing between them. He was a lot older than her. And he was fussy, if you get what I mean. About the way he dressed. The way he kept his house and car. Lived his whole life on a time schedule, never deviating a minute or two one way or the other. Hell, a woman would have messed up his life too much for him to ever want one around. The guy was a confirmed bachelor."

"Sounds like about 90 percent of the members of the Texas Cattleman's Club."

Seb cut Rob a curious glance, then leaned back in his chair, chuckling. "Yeah, it does. Though that number's dwindling fast. I'm beginning to wonder how we're going to decide how to fund the profits from the Texas Cattleman's Ball."

"I thought the terms of the bet were that the last bachelor standing prior to the Ball got to choose which charity would receive the money?" Jason interjected.

"True," Seb conceded. "But since Will here is married now and out of the running, that only leaves four of us. Just makes me wonder how many more will fall before it's time for the Ball.''

Rob rose, preparing to leave. "You can quit your worrying, because there'll be at least one." At Seb's questioning look, he tapped a finger against his chest. "Me."

* * * * *

Don't forget Her Lone Star Protector
by Peggy Moreland and
Tall, Dark...and Framed? *by Cathleen Galitz*
will continue the exciting
MILLIONAIRE'S CLUB story in June 2003.

0503/51a

♥ SILHOUETTE®
DESIRE™ 2-IN-1
AVAILABLE FROM 16TH MAY 2003

PLAIN JANE & DOCTOR DAD Kate Little

Dynasties: The Connellys

Handsome doctor Doug Connelly suggested a marriage of convenience to help Maura Chambers with her unborn baby—but the hungry look in his amber eyes had her hoping for more. Until she discovered his little secret…

AND THE WINNER GETS…MARRIED! Metsy Hingle

Dynasties: The Connellys

Buying her boss, gorgeous Justin Connelly, in a bachelor auction allowed Kimberly Lindgren to have one fantasy night. But how could she give her virgin heart in the dark of night and take it back in the light of day?

HER LONE STAR PROTECTOR Peggy Moreland

Millionaire's Club

Gruff private investigator Robert Cole was smitten by lovely florist Rebecca Todman, but secrets in her past made her wary. Could he convince her of the depth of his feelings and win her trust…and her heart?

TALL, DARK…AND FRAMED? Cathleen Galitz

Millionaire's Club

Tycoon Sebastian Wescott was innocent—he certainly didn't need alluring attorney Susan Wysocki to defend him! But while she tried to prove his innocence, he found himself increasingly guilty—of falling in love…

A PRINCESS IN WAITING Carol Grace

Royally Wed: The Missing Heir

Dashing Charles Rodin *seems* to be marrying pregnant beauty Lise to right the wrongs of her ex-husband, his brother. But Charles has always loved Lise…

A PRINCE AT LAST! Cathie Linz

Royally Wed: The Missing Heir

Luc Dumont, head of palace security, is the new king—and Juliet Beaudreau is to teach him royal protocol. He's determined to sweep her into his arms, but can he convince her to be his queen?

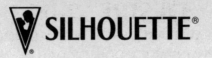

world's most
Eligible Bachelors

RICH, GORGEOUS, SEXY AND SINGLE!

An exciting new series featuring the sexiest, most successful, dynamic men in the world!

Millionaire to Marry *by Rachel Lee*	18th April 2003
Detective Dad *by Marie Ferrarella*	16th May 2003
His Business, Her Baby *by Dixie Browning*	16th May 2003
That Mysterious Man *by Maggie Shayne*	20th June 2003

Coming Soon!

SILHOUETTE®
SPECIAL EDITION™

proudly presents seven more fantastic stories
from

Lindsay McKenna's

exciting series

MORGAN'S
MERCENARIES

Meet Morgan's newest team:
courageous men and women destined for
greatness — fated to fall in love!

SILHOUETTE® SENSATION™

presents

ROMANCING THE CROWN

The Royal family of Montebello is determined to find their missing heir. But the search for the prince is not without danger—or passion!

0103/SH/LC50

SILHOUETTE® SUPERROMANCE™

is proud to present

THREE GOOD COPS

by

Janice Kay Johnson

The McLean brothers are all good,
strong, honest, men. Men a woman
can trust…with her heart!

HIS PARTNER'S WIFE
May 2003

THE WORD OF A CHILD
July 2003

MATERNAL INSTINCT
September 2003

0503/SH/LC64

FREE!
1 Book
and a surprise gift!

We would like to take this opportunity to thank you for reading this Silhouette® book by offering you the chance to take another specially selected title from the Desire™ series absolutely FREE! We're also making this offer to introduce you to the benefits of the Reader Service™—

- ★ FREE home delivery
- ★ FREE gifts and competitions
- ★ FREE monthly Newsletter
- ★ Books available before they're in the shops
- ★ Exclusive Reader Service discount offer

Accepting this FREE book and gift places you under no obligation to buy; you may cancel at any time, even after receiving your free shipment. Simply complete your details below and return the entire page to the address below. **You don't even need a stamp!**

YES! Please send me 1 free Desire book and a surprise gift. I understand that unless you hear from me, I will receive 2 superb new titles every month for just £4.99 each, postage and packing free. I am under no obligation to purchase any books and may cancel my subscription at any time. The free books and gift will be mine to keep in any case.

D3ZEB

Ms/Mrs/Miss/Mr ....Initials ....
BLOCK CAPITALS PLEASE

Surname ....

Address ....

....

....Postcode ....

Send this whole page to:
UK: The Reader Service, FREEPOST CN81, Croydon, CR9 3WZ
EIRE: The Reader Service, PO Box 4546, Kilcock, County Kildare (stamp required)